the sordid selection

Pretty Little Robots
Book One

jerri chisholm

WISE WOLF
BOOKS

WISE WOLF BOOKS
An Imprint of Wolfpack Publishing
wisewolfbooks.com
9850 S. Maryland Parkway, Suite A-5 #323, Las Vegas, Nevada 89183

This is a work of fiction. All of the characters, organizations, publications, and events portrayed in this novel are either products of the author's imagination or are used fictitiously.

Cover design by Wise Wolf Books

Paperback ISBN 978-1-957548-66-1
eBook ISBN 978-1-957548-65-4
LCCN 2023939008

the sordid selection

preamble

. . .

We, the unified people of Airo-Aurora, proud of a resplendent dawn, solemnly declare to self-govern our state without interference from our forefathers of the United States of America or surrounding nations borne of the new spring, to destroy all social vices and injustice and to elevate the quality of life for all citizens with the aid of Artificial Intelligence and an undying dynasty that forever works to uphold this Constitution.

preamble

one

THIS IS IT. The moment I've been readying for. Years of preparation, all for a single point in time that'll decide *everything*.

My fingers shake as they begin sectioning pieces of my hair, idly forming a braid. I chew on my bottom lip. *Pianist, pilot, or librarian.*

I say it again and again, and again. I do it so the microchips inside my brain take notice.

Not that I really need to.

Years spent practicing the piano, flying a helicopter, and reading any book I could get my hands on should be more than enough. Sure, the Mainframe can't be *tricked*. We can't simply *choose* whichever career we'd like. That's ridiculous. But who could be more suited to those positions than me? I smile to myself because I know the answer.

Nobody.

With a deep breath, I see my future flash in front of me —easy and secure, tucked comfortably inside my district of Quire—and it sparkles. Suddenly I'm not nervous...I'm *excited*.

The technician sitting on the other side of the desk looks

expectantly at me, and I give her a nod. I let my hair fall through my fingers. Then I grab the arms of the chair. I sit up straight. When she starts tapping the keyboard, I close my eyes. I imagine what's happening: the Mainframe scanning the data that's been transmitted wirelessly from my brain over the years, from the chips that record all I see, all I hear, all I feel. And then I imagine the next step.

The next step's legendary. All citizens of Airo-Aurora, in our eighteenth year, undergo this very moment. Our *Selection*. Where the Mainframe uses all those years of data to find for us our most fitting career. The one we're most suited to—the best possible choice for each of us.

It's described as the eternal gift of the Mainframe because it ensures contentedness for all—that and productivity. Happy citizens, happy Airo-Aurora. And now...it's my turn.

Normally I'm not so confident about things, but I *am* confident about this. I *know* that I'm most suited to being a pianist, or a pilot, or a librarian. I know that after years of practice, I'd perform any of those jobs well and with ease. And I know the data-crunching, all-knowing Mainframe will determine that too.

Finally, over the rattling of the space heater under the desk and the hammering of my heart, I hear the technician clear her throat. I try to bite away my smile, but I can't. My Selection result is ready.

———

"ALEX?"

I hear the voice from far away. I feel like I'm waking from a dream. That or standing on the edge of a cliff. And the little bit of confidence I'd managed a few minutes earlier? Crashed to the ground below, blown into bits.

"Alex, miss? Did you hear?" The technician reaches across the desk and prods my arm.

I shake my head. No, I didn't hear...I couldn't possibly have heard...

"A handmaid, miss," she says, repeating those dreadful words. "That's what I said. That's your result for the Careers categ—"

"No."

"No?"

I shake my head again, this time trying not to laugh. Me—a *handmaid*? I couldn't imagine a job I'd be *worse* at, not to mention the fact that it's not one of the careers I've been preparing for.

How could the Mainframe be so wrong? Why—in all its infinite wisdom—haven't I been given a position of pianist? Or pilot? Or librarian?

No, it doesn't make sense. I must...I must be dreaming.

The technician peers at me through her round eyeglasses. "Shall I continue with the second phase of the Selection, miss?"

The urge to laugh evaporates, and my eyes swell with tears—I was just so *sure* it'd be pianist, or pilot, or librarian. I was *sure* I knew what my future looked like. I *wanted* that future!

"No...please don't," I whisper.

She lifts an eyebrow.

"That—that result. It's a mistake. It has to be."

"Mistakes don't happen."

"A misreading, then, of the data. Please. The scan...it has to be run again."

"Alex," she says, sighing. "Second scans are simply not offered—"

"*Please*, ma'am!"

She must hear the desperation in my voice—that or she

can see it—because she makes a face, then taps at her keyboard.

Thank god.

A second scan for the Careers category, and my stomach leaps. Because it'll be different this time. It *will* be different.

I try to distract myself from the agonizing wait by staring out the window at the snow that falls over the city like a tapestry. From the other side of the building, the side that faces south, come the distant sounds of a bustling city. The roar of snowplows, the honking of horns. But here on the northern side, there's just stillness.

No more city—only a hill, and at the top of the hill a palace known as Strath Glen. Its residents, aside from the occasional announcement sent over the state broadcasting system by the King, are never seen or heard, at least not in my district of Quire. I wonder if *they* ever partook in the Selection.

"It will be just a minute more, miss."

"Thank you," I say. "Really." Because it's not often they run another scan, I know that. I've actually never heard of it happening, now that I think about it. Of course, I've never heard of a mistake happening either, and yet here we are.

Pianist, pilot, or librarian. I say it again and again under my breath. I make a wish on each flake of snow that passes by the window.

And then the technician's eyes narrow in on the computer screen, and my spine goes rigid; I grip the edge of the desk so tightly that my knuckles turn white.

She makes a face. Too slowly, she shifts her bespectacled gaze to me, and I can feel the result before it's even spoken. I drop my head to my knees.

"Handmaid," she confirms.

I feel dizzy and dazed. *Handmaid.*

"How can that be? I don't have the slightest—"

"You must have faith in the Mainframe. In the Selection

system. In the *King*! Certainly, we wouldn't have such a beautiful nation if it made fools of us. Now, from time to time over my years of employment, I've had the misfortune of delivering to folks the news of careers that didn't much excite them, and can you guess what transpired?"

She stares at me expectantly but receives no response, not even a shift of the features. A face carved from wax, now most likely tinted green.

"What transpired is that they came to adore their positions," she continues, as though prompted. "They realized that this is the very reason we have these chips in the first place." She taps a finger to her head. "The machines know us better than we know ourselves!"

"But—"

"Something in your past, in your temperament, must make you perfectly suited to such a career. Something that you aren't seeing."

I can't even bring myself to speak.

"Give it time. That's all I ask."

"Give it—give it *time*," I finally sputter. "And then?"

The technician considers her fingernails. And then nothing. Because there's no second option, no appeal. I have to fulfill my position or spend my days imprisoned, as per the laws of Airo-Aurora.

I pinch my temples, trying to soothe a now-throbbing head, then ask in a defeated voice, "A handmaid where, ma'am?"

"Well," she begins, waiting for the engine of a nearby snowplow to quiet before continuing. When only the hum of the heater can be heard, she says in a hoarse whisper, "It says here...Strath Glen."

Strath Glen.

That cold palace with windows that look only out. The one exposed to the elements way up there on the hill. The one that runs and rules our nation...

I guess I should've known. Because even among the well-to-do a *handmaid* must be a rarity.

The technician clears her throat. "I feel I should warn you," she says, and there's something in her voice that makes my stomach squeeze. She clears her throat a second time. "Servants at Strath Glen, well. It's expected—see. It goes without saying..."

"Yes?"

"Do you have someone in the lobby I can call in? You're looking a little sick. Your parents, perhaps?"

I shake my head. There's nothing I'd like more than to have my parents waiting for me in the lobby, but seeing as how they've been dead for three years, well...trying to ignore the fresh wave of sadness brought on by the reminder, I prompt the technician: "As you were saying..."

"As I'm sure you've observed, miss, Strath Glen is a very private residence indeed. Servants simply aren't permitted to come and go. Besides, who knows when Master might ring! So be sure to pack some overnight bags before the morning," she continues. "As a handmaid, I daresay you'll be expected to reside there."

I stare at her.

The silence in the small room reserved for the yearly Selection feels heavy, oppressive. Not a person in all the Mainframe seems to make a noise, no matter that countless other Selections take place at the same moment. And there's no sound in the glittering city of Airo-Aurora, or in the forests that make up our nation-state, or in the cluster of surrounding countries that voted for independence from America alongside ours half a century earlier. Not even in my own mind is there any noise. No humming of thought or whirring of computer chips.

No, there's nothing but hollow blackness, a void in which information of my future falls, one word after another, down and away into emptiness.

Slowly I blink. I try to wrap my brain around my new reality. I must live...there. In that towering palace. Starting *tomorrow*. And despite all that training, all that preparation, all that anticipation for a career I'd find familiar...not a pianist. Not a pilot. Not a librarian.

And, worse yet, I'll have to say goodbye to my neighborhood of Quire, my aunt's house with all its appetizing aromas, my small yet hard-earned patchwork of friends.

"Shall I run the second part of your Selection now, miss?"

My breath hitches. The second part of my Selection...I'd completely forgotten.

Because the Selection doesn't just determine a person's most ideal career—it determines their most ideal spouse, too.

"Typically, live-in servants are matched with other servants, for obvious reasons. I'm just saying it now to prepare you. There's a good possibility that you don't yet know your groom-to-be."

I lean back in my chair and close my eyes. The first phase of the test gave results that were shocking enough. And the second phase, I'm now realizing, might even top that.

Ten minutes ago, when I sat down across from the bespectacled technician, I was certain I'd wind up with Patrick Nash—an old friend, one I know would make a good husband. He's so warm, so generous...and it wasn't just the man, Patrick, I'd been excited for. It was the life I'd pictured for the two of us, a comfortable one. An *easy* one, doing something I enjoyed, sharing the fruits of my labor with someone I knew well, maybe even starting a family together one day.

Now those dreams crumble around me. The likelihood of marrying Patrick is practically nil since I'll be residing for the rest of my life at my place of employment. And the thought of wedding a stranger makes a weight sink to the bottom of my stomach. It makes me feel cold, and unwell. It makes me feel like I could erupt with nerves.

"Ah—well, that *is* unusual," I hear. "My, oh my," continues the technician, and I frown at the undercurrent of energy in her voice, one that sounds close to excitement. "Alex, miss—it looks as though I was quite wrong about your husband!"

I open my eyes. A wave of relief draws me to the edge of my seat. "So it *is* Patrick, then?"

"What? No."

"*Who*, then?"

"Says here you'll be serving as handmaid to your future husband, Viscount Wolfe Rocksavage of Airo-Aurora, nephew to the King himself!"

two

. . .

A GUARD DRESSED in olive green guides me toward the lobby of the Mainframe, and with every step the lights grow brighter, more glaring. There's a sharp, pulsating pain behind my right eye, and I feel like I could be sick.

A handmaid to the *viscount* of all people—my future *husband*.

What about Quire? What about those jobs I actually wanted? What about *Patrick*?

"Is there anyone here to see you home?" the greencoat asks as he pulls open the door to the lobby and ushers me through.

I shake my head. Nobody waits for me—I told Aunt Jo I didn't need an escort, and just as well. The thought of seeing anyone familiar is too much to bear. Because seeing them would involve talking with them, and talking with them would involve talk of the Selection. Talk of *results*. And that would make the results seem just too real when of course they're not.

No, something's gone wrong. What I need to do is fix the mistake, and with that thought in mind, I turn to the greencoat before he can go: "Sir, can I speak with the manager, please?"

He shakes his head. "All the staff's tied up with today's Selection, and since yours is finished with, out you go. See that? Snow's even slowing down for you as we speak." He gestures outside, then he's gone.

A strong gust of wind lifts my hair the moment I leave. Cold bites at my fingertips. Contrary to the greencoat's words, snow drives toward the earth as if weighted, each flake the size of my fist. I take a moment to search through my pockets for a pair of gloves, then take a deep breath. Okay. I may be barred from the Mainframe today, but he didn't say anything about tomorrow. I'll report for duty at Strath Glen, just like I have to, but as soon as I'm given a break I'll come back.

I'll get the matter sorted out. I'll get the mistake fixed if it's the last thing I do.

I start off for my aunt's house, but I only get a few feet before pausing mid-stride. I turn to stare at the nondescript white building that I came from, low-slung and stretching the length of several football fields. Funny that something so plain and ordinary could have such influence. And not just for my life but for all in our nation-state. An entire future determined in just a few spare minutes. I sigh, and eventually my gaze lifts from the almighty Mainframe to the building that looms behind it, one even more powerful.

Ever since I was a young child, the sight of Strath Glen made a chill run down my spine, today's no exception. It's just so devoid of life—without whimsy, without cheer. An opulent bore at best, a sinister recluse at worst...

I chew my lip. My mother's refrain—*look on the bright side*—echoes through my mind.

Is there a chance that chill was nothing more than the fanciful thinking of a little girl? Maybe it *isn't* so bad—maybe a future there'd be better than I'm imagining.

I start tentatively toward it, to an apple orchard that lies just north of the Mainframe parking lot, at the foot of the hill. Carefully I slip between trees, around branches so gnarled and twisted they look nothing like the tidy saplings throughout the rest of the city. The smell of rotting apples lifts from beneath my boots.

I walk through to the other side so that even though I'm still nestled between the branches, the palace spreads above me.

It's beautiful, and breathtaking, but—all I want to do is run in the opposite direction.

I sigh, then pull from the nearest branch an apple, one as perfect as the future I was denied, then polish it on my coat. I bring the shiny red globe to my mouth—and scream.

The apple slips between my fingers, and I stare down at the gaping wound in its backside—one full of twisting worms. At that moment a breeze lifts my hair and I glance skyward, my sightline landing on the palace's top row of windows.

There stands an unmistakable figure of a man, mostly hidden by shadows, and even though I'm too far removed to know for sure, I'd bet my life that he stares straight at me, grinning.

———

THE HOBBY HANGAR, where I learned to fly a helicopter with my father, sits at the southeast edge of Airo-Aurora, near the segment of the Bavarian Alps imported years ago, abutting the dense woods that encircle the city. It's there that I sometimes hear the spray of bullets when hunting season's open. That familiar sound of popping is what I hear now, wrapped in a flannel-backed quilt in my aunt's guest room.

This time, though, it's fireworks to blame.

Celebration's in full swing, as it is every year on this day, to cap off the resounding success of yet another Selection. I thought me and my friend Agnes would be pacing the streets tonight, celebrating careers we were sure to love, dancing with fiancés we were sure to love even more. I thought my future would be everything I could ever want— quiet, predictable, *easy*.

Instead, I lie in bed, refusing all attempts from my aunt to move.

"Alex," she repeats, then she sits on the bed next to me.

I stare up at her. It isn't just that I don't want to go to Strath Glen, it's that I don't want to leave *her*. Because the mere sight of the woman is a comfort, right down to her apron. The house that smells of cinnamon and garlic, her two most-beloved ingredients, is a comfort. The room that I've called my own for the past three years that's still decorated with floral pillows and prints of meadows, just like it was when I was a child and would visit with my parents, is a comfort. And tomorrow in the early morning I'm expected to pack up my belongings and bid it all goodbye.

I want to scream just thinking about it.

"Go on, now," she says gently. "Agnes is waiting at the front door. The whole town's celebrating. Seems a shame to miss out just because you don't like your results, doesn't it?"

"Don't *like* them? *That's* an understatement." I roll onto my side and exhale.

"Let's try to focus on the positive, shall we? You get to marry a prince—"

"A viscount."

"You marry a prince, and you live in a palace, and you live well!"

"He's a stranger."

"Not for long."

"He's not Patrick."

"Maybe he's better. Maybe he's just lovely!"

I give her a look over my shoulder. "Maybe he's worse. Maybe he's *awful*. Besides, nobody else has to move out right now—not until the engagement's over with."

"Yes, you'll have to move out a bit earlier than we thought, but is that really the end of the world?"

I nod.

She runs a hand through my hair. "I know you had your heart set on being a pianist, or a pilot, but—"

"Or a librarian," I remind her. "All of which I'm perfectly qualified for. So *why* didn't the Mainframe put me in one of those positions? None of it makes sense. *None* of it."

"It must know you'll be an excellent handmaid."

I roll my eyes. We both know that isn't true.

"Maybe you'll end up doing administrative work for his professional duties, isn't that possible?"

I groan.

"Or perhaps it's just a title, *handmaid*, but once the children arrive—"

I cover my head with a pillow and groan even louder.

"A night out will help," she says, laughing. "Go on, Agnes is waiting, don't make me say it again."

"Tell her to go without me, please?"

"Sorry," she says cheerily. The bed creaks as she stands. "I'm not a messenger."

"Funny, seeing as how you deliver post for a living!" I yell after her. But not wanting to hold up Agnes any longer, I push the quilt down, muttering. I shield my eyes from the angry glare of the hallway light. I ignore the cherry grandfather clock that pulls itself taller as I pass, ticking louder, taunting me with the passage of time.

Not long now until morning, not that I need any reminding. No, I can feel each passing second in my bones—

"Aggggghhh!"

I blink, dazed.

Agnes dances a jig. "Your aunt told me the news!"

"News?"

"Royalty," she whispers theatrically, then drops into a curtsy.

I'm not sure whether to laugh, or cry. "It isn't like that," I finally say. "And...there isn't any curtsying involved."

"How do you know?"

It's a fair point. The only times I've glimpsed the royals, after all, have been on a television screen, the King seated behind a large desk, delivering a speech peppered with cheery winks and beguiling grins. So, maybe they do curtsy.

"It doesn't matter, because—I won't be joining them in the first place."

Agnes laughs, displaying white, wide-spaced teeth. "Oh, you *won't*?"

I shake my head. "Honestly, I think there's been a mistake. I've been going over it all day, and that's the only explanation I can come up with."

"A mistake?" She pulls off her beanie and a shock of black curls stands upright. "What, by the Mainframe?"

"Exactly."

Outside, sounds of revelry fill the streets and fireworks bang overhead without break. In Aunt Jo's house, however, there's nothing but silence. Agnes, looking less than convinced, busies herself with her shoelace.

Finally, she stands and says tactfully, "Did you hear my results, at least?" She removes a glove to reveal a finger now decorated with a gold ring. A purple gem in the shape of a triangle sits inside it. "Miller," she states. "He had the ring ready and everything. Can you believe it, a proper engagement ring!"

I give her a hug. "Congratulations—Miller, just like you wanted!"

"And can you believe he had a ring ready?"

"A touching sentiment, indeed," I indulge. I'm happy for Agnes, without question. But there's something else there, too. Jealousy? Not over the ring, as kind a gesture as it was. Or the man, Miller. No, it's simply that my friend had gotten from the Selection what she'd predicted she would, and I'd gotten the exact opposite.

The burden of a mistake.

"Your royal dude might be awesome," Agnes says suddenly, knocking me on the shoulder.

"He's not Patrick," I remind her.

"True. Sorry, Alex. I kind of forgot about the two of you in all the craziness today. Are you crushed?"

"I think I'm in too much shock." I chew my lip for a moment, then ask, "Do you know who he was paired with?"

She shakes her head. "You know, if I were you, I'd give this palace guy a chance. You're such a doll—he'll love you. Who wouldn't? And think of the jewels!"

"Have you ever seen me wear a necklace? A bracelet?"

"Good point. You do have horrible fashion sense."

I grin. "So, what about you? Which career is yours?"

"Working at a nursery at the bottom of Quire."

"With children?"

"Yes, with *children*."

"But you don't know a thing about them."

"I've taken care of my kid brother before!"

"They'll be lucky to have you," says Aunt Jo, striding into the hall. Then, with a look of finality in her eye, she begins tossing items of outerwear in my direction. "This, this..." she mutters under her breath, then she points to a grease stain across the front of my double-breasted, camel-colored overcoat.

"Some well-oiled tools I used at the Hangar," I explain.

"You'll be a perfect fit at Strath Glen," says Agnes, laughing.

"Time you took off, the pair of you," says Aunt Jo. "Lots to talk about and much to celebrate—oh, don't give me that look."

"But—"

Without ceremony, we're pushed clear of the house and into the festivities, the door closing behind us before I can finish my sentence. A moment later I let Agnes drag me forward and into the throngs of people waiting on the street, their laughter and cheer only widening the chasm lying between my Selection results and theirs, underscoring my belief that a mistake was made, that a glitch was responsible for this unwanted future.

three

. . .

THE NEXT MORNING, I wake to rain that drives against the side of my aunt's house with fury, melting away all traces of the snow that blanketed Airo-Aurora the night before. Wind rattles the windowpanes and makes the house groan, and the sky churns with shades of ever deepening gray that I glimpse through gaps in my aunt's lace curtains. I rub my eyes and decide I can't be expected to cross the entire city with my luggage in tow in such dismal conditions. Instead, I curl deeper under the quilt, one worn soft with age, and breathe in the scent of cinnamon wafting under the guest room door from the kitchen.

After an evening spent walking the cold streets with Agnes, and a night spent tossing and turning, I'm exhausted. Even a strong cup of coffee, I suspect, won't help. No, the only remedy is to stay put, right where I am.

My eyelids grow heavy, and the swell of sleep carries me away...onto a sheet of ice suspended in midair, a bottomless gulf separating me from all that's warm and familiar. A dinghy bobs nearby, caressed by nonexistent waves, and I go to it at once, slipping and sliding until I drag myself aboard.

I pick up an oar but try as I might, progress alludes me. Paddling doesn't propel—

"Get. Moving."

I blink my eyes open and Aunt Jo's face crests through the fog.

"No family of mine shows up late to work, certainly not on the very first day."

The sound of the house being pummeled with rain drives away my strange dream, and I groan. But I do as my aunt says, drawing myself upright, one eye squeezed shut and the other glimpsing a steaming mug etched with the phrase "Girl Power" being pushed into my hand.

"Thank you."

She sighs. "I'm no monster. Breakfast's on in ten. Get yourself to the shower in the meantime."

The coffee's just as I like it, strong but with generous helpings of cream and sugar—a heart attack in a mug as my father used to say, though he enjoyed his just the same. I drink it quickly, and warmth spreads to my fingertips. From the kitchen comes the sound of a woman trying intentionally to be loud: the clanging of utensils, the rattling of stoneware, the banging of cupboard doors, and I smile. My aunt's anything but subtle. I place the empty mug on the bedside table and head to the bathroom.

The combination of caffeine and a piping-hot shower is effective. By the time I turn the water off, I feel ready to start the day—I even feel confident that I'll be able to convince the Mainframe manager to re-administer my Selection. But just as I'm thinking about what to say, I slip, falling headfirst into the vanity. A sharp pain rises across my forehead, and I swear.

"You okay in there?"

"Yes," I mumble.

"Make yourself decent, I'm coming in," and no sooner do I pull around a frayed towel does the door swing open. She tuts her tongue as she gazes down at me, then runs a finger over the injury. "You've got a bump the size of Quire coming to. No way to meet your prince like that, now is it."

"I think your priorities are somewhat misaligned," I tell her. "And he isn't a prince."

"Right. What is he, again?"

"Viscount."

"You'll still want to make a fine first impression on him and make Quire proud while you're at it. Breakfast will be ready in two," she adds as she heads out.

When I finally stand and gaze in the mirror, I sigh. Half my forehead is swallowed by an angry welt and judging by the chime of the grandfather clock outside the bathroom door, there won't be enough time to ice it. Not enough time to dry my hair, either, which will make for a cold walk all the way across town. The rest of my face, I note wearily, is not much better. The prospect of the day ahead has drained all the blood from it. Or maybe a concussion is to blame.

Whatever the cause, staring back at me is a face robbed of its usual healthy glow. My nose and mouth may be unblemished, but my large eyes, normally my favorite feature, now have black circles riding underneath. As I stare at them, I tilt my head back and forth, doing my best to imagine them belonging to a handmaid at Strath Glen. I force my mouth open and up, an attempt at a smile, and do my best to imagine flashing it at the viscount, my fiancé.

No. I don't look like a handmaid, and I don't look like the wife of a viscount. And I definitely don't look like a conflated version of the two, because no such thing exists. How can I be both royalty *and* a servant? Both the employer *and* the employee? It was a glitch in the system, of that, I'm sure.

A few minutes later I sit in my usual seat at the kitchen table, one closest to the woodstove, and therefore, the warmest spot in the house. My aunt had declared it much too hot for her liking, but I know it was her own before I moved in.

"You can't go looking like that!" she howls.

"You scared me! I thought there was something—"

"There is something wrong," she insists, waving her spatula in my direction and carefully tracing my profile head to toe. "All of this—wrong, wrong, wrong. Wet scraggly hair? Wrong. Sweatpants? Wrong. A sweatshirt with—what's this—a hole in it? *Wrong.*"

"It doesn't matter what *Wolfe* thinks of me—"

"That isn't the issue, although I suppose it should be. Like it or not, this is proper work you'll be doing, even if it's just for one day. Showing up looking untidy is unacceptable."

"But it's comfortable," I protest. "And I'm sure they'll have uniforms for me to wear. It's a *palace*, after all."

"Go on, put on something smart. And hurry up or there's no breakfast for you. Wait—here's some ice for that head." She throws a bag of frozen peas at me, which I fumble. I scoop it up and grumble all the way back to the guest room closet, finally settling on a pair of herringbone trousers with a well-starched pleat, a white button-up blouse, and a knit sweater the color of molasses. I pull my wet hair into a ponytail, tuck the loose bits behind my ears, and return to the kitchen.

"Not great," she says at once. "But better. Don't you own a dress?"

"No."

"Why's that, again?"

"I don't like them."

"Right. Well, at least that bump on your forehead is quieting down." She sets a plate in front of me stacked with French toast, and beside it, quiche and sausage pie. My aunt, a terrific cook, had done her best to pass on her talents to me over the past few years, and though I'd avoided such lessons with might, I had against my will mastered a few simple dishes, a savory meat pie and fruit cobbler among them. So. Will I be expected to prepare as much for the viscount today? I bite down hard on my lip at the thought.

Then I sigh. Because as delicious as my breakfast looks, the thought of putting food into my stomach right now has little appeal. There's too much dread, and too many nerves. But feeling my aunt's watchful gaze, I pick up my fork. Leaving the meal untouched would be like a slap in the face, and—no matter how nauseous I might feel—I wouldn't dare do that, not after all she's done for me over the years.

At the first bite, she beams. At the second bite she bursts, "Need to send you off with a full stomach, an aunt's duty, you know!" and on the third bite she squeezes me around the shoulders. "How is it?"

"Delicious," I reply, then I place a hand over hers. "Thank you."

Pleased, she throws another log into the wood stove. "Terrible, miserable old morning out there. You'll need to dress warm, that rain is ice-cold. Felt it myself when I fetched the morning paper—can't say I look forward to delivering post in these elements. Might be best to catch a bus and spare yourself a bit of trouble. Speaking of, are your bags packed?"

"Well, no," I admit, eyeing her. "I mean, I'm hoping that I won't be needing them."

She nods, then grabs a cloth and begins to scrub at the countertop. Next, she grabs the broom. I watch carefully as she moves from task to task, not altogether a foreign sight, but the way she attacks each job before abandoning it for another gives me pause.

When she starts and stops the washing up, I say, "Aunt Jo?"

She startles. "Alex?"

"Is everything okay?"

"What, with me? Nothing. Er—yes, everything. Every-thing's fine. Just going to miss you around here, that's all."

I'd been worried about that. Another reason, then, to sort out this mess. "I'll be back by nightfall," I say.

And then from the front door comes the sound of knock-ing. It pierces the sound of falling rain; it invades the small house with its pointedness.

"Sit," Aunt Jo instructs, as I push out my chair. "Finish your breakfast."

Slowly I chew a mouthful of sausage and pastry. Maybe it's Agnes. Yes, that'd make sense—stopping by on this wet morning to wish me luck with what promises to be an inter-esting day. Or, I realize with a tightening in my stomach, Patrick, to have that awkward talk that needs having since we've both been betrothed to others. It would've been a shock to him as well; all of Quire thought we were an obvious match.

But on hearing a voice not belonging to anyone recogniz-able, not even old Mary Beth from next door, I carefully lift my napkin and stand. I edge closer to the entryway. "...to pick up a Miss Alex of Quire residing with Madam Josephine of the same address," I overhear. "Do I have the correct house?"

Peering around the corner, I see a well-dressed and minute man standing in my aunt's foyer, wearing a black trench beaded with rain. His umbrella leaks water onto the tile but he doesn't seem to notice. He does, however, notice *me*.

"Ah, here's the ticket," he says, as though the fact is plainly obvious. "You look near the proper age, if not a bit young. Are you quite ready?"

"Quite ready," I repeat, as a sinking feeling comes over me. "Who...who *are* you?"

He bows deeply. "Monsieur Sawyer, official chauffeur to Strath Glen. I've been sent to fetch you by the viscount himself. I am to understand the palace will be both your place of employment and, ah-hem, your residence."

I step all the way into the foyer, ignoring the way he stares at my trousers. "You say it as though it's a novelty, sir. I was led to believe that all servants were required to reside at the palace."

"In the servants' quarters, of course," he says quickly, dashing my hopes in one breath. "You, too, shall reside there, for now. But, given the—ah-hem—special circumstances, I daresay you'll be sharing the viscount's private suite before long." He flashes me a mischievous grin. "*And* his bed."

For a minute I just gape at him. "I-I won't be sharing his bed...or his private suite...or even his palace," I finally manage to say, as my aunt's rich breakfast swirls in my stomach.

The man bends at the waist in disbelief. "Par-don me?"

"It's all a mistake."

"A mistake?"

"By the Mainframe," I add.

"Well, miss. I do hope my ears are playing tricks on me, for I must say, a girl of your stature having the opportunity to marry into the royal fam—"

"I don't want to."

The man no longer stares at my strange attire, but at me. His eyes bulge. "Excuse me, miss, but if the royal family could hear the way you speak of them at this very moment—"

"They wouldn't want me either. I know that, and I know you made the trip all the way across town to pick me up, but..." I pull at my lip. Avoiding Strath Glen feels more pressing than before. So pressing that reporting for duty at the palace isn't something I think I should do.

"But?"

"But...I'm going to go to the Mainframe instead," I

finally decide. "I'm going to get this mess sorted out. I don't expect we'll meet again," I add.

The chauffeur doesn't move; he simply taps his nose knowingly. "An innocent look, but what lies beneath?" He cackles, and my aunt and I glance at each other. Just as quickly, his laughter fades away and he says in a professional tone, "I'm afraid I'm under orders from the viscount himself, as said, and so there really is no choice in the matter. Once I have you safely delivered unto the palace you can do as you will, but between you and me, miss, I'm not about to lose my job over the likes of you." He winks.

I feel hot and cold all over. I feel like I could vomit.

"Madam?" continues the chauffeur, turning to my aunt. "Might you assist me in fetching young Alex's overnight bags?"

"I don't believe she packed any," she says carefully, watching me.

The chauffeur throws the door open. "Have it your way, then. Do say your goodbyes," he shouts over the pounding rain.

For a moment I just stand there, staring motionless at the far wall. But when my aunt crushes me into a hug, I can't help but hug in return the woman who's been nothing short of my savior.

"Thank you for breakfast," I say in a small voice. To say more would be to risk a complete unraveling.

Aunt Jo grasps me tightly on either side of the head and smacks her lips next to the welt. Then with an iron gaze and what sounds like a frog in her throat, she whispers, "You've been through so much in your life—this is nothing. *Nothing.* You're stronger than you know, Alex. Whatever happens at the Mainframe, keep that chin lifted and remember that, do you understand?"

I nod.

Over my shoulder, Monsieur announces, "Your official

departure, miss. May I?" He holds out his arm as I'm released by my aunt.

I don't move.

He bows his head. "Your own choosing. After you." With a flourish, he steps aside and gestures to the soggy dreariness awaiting on the front stoop.

I'm still as a statue. I just can't bring myself to leave—not when every cell in my body longs to stay.

The chauffeur dives into another deep bow, then says, "You've quite forced me." And with that he grabs my coat and pushes me roughly through the open door.

four

. . .

I GLARE AT THE CHAUFFEUR. Locked inside a behemoth of a car? Forced from my aunt's house against my will? My glare intensifies.

"You gave me no choice, Miss Alex," he says, when he notices. "And besides—my loyalty resides with Strath Glen, not with the likes of you. Now, put on that revolting thing you call a coat and bid farewell to dumpy old Quire." And with a roguish glance at me over his shoulder, he snaps closed the partition between us and slams his foot on the accelerator. Shivering, I pull on my coat, a piece I discovered in my aunt's attic once belonging to my late uncle and stare out the window at my fast-disappearing and much-beloved district.

To dismiss it as dumpy is not to know it, to not appreciate the generous people living behind those arched wooden doors, or even the beauty of the tiny circular homes themselves, dotted with windows and rambling vines that bloom wildly in the warmest months and offer berries for birds when the weather turns cold. Past the Quire florist we go, a woman who gives away flowers by the bundle when they near their peak rather than letting them spoil unseen, past the butcher whose neighborhood pig roast is so delicious it attracts kids from outside districts who're never denied a ham roll, past the corner store, past the park.

With Quire gone, I gaze around the limousine, at the gray leather seats and ceiling and floor, all of which match the sky overhead. Beads of rain tick against the glass, interrupted only by the occasional slap of wind that does nothing to impede the tank in which I'm trapped. I burrow my head into the upturned collar of my coat to hide my tears.

Finally, we turn onto the busiest and widest canal of Airo-Aurora, Central Boulevard. Here the streets are lined with giant digital screens that glitter like gemstones. Twinkling white lights criss cross overhead, and behind wide sidewalks are a collection of upmarket shops. Today, even the twinkling lights and flashing screens can't lift my spirits, and it's only when the limo roars past the Mainframe that I sit straighter in my seat. It looks different, I notice, as I wipe my eyes. Less sprawling, more imposing. Stark...and clinical. Uninviting.

Today's circumstances are imbuing it with more weight than normal.

Just past it lies the grove of twisted apple trees, and then...with a tightening in my stomach, I lift my gaze up, up, up to Strath Glen itself.

I try to look on the bright side, but I can't—it glowers at me. Rows of curtained windows grow smaller to keep out my curious gaze, elaborate cornices extend into bars that block my entrance, greencoats that flank an impressive entranceway place their palms over pistols as they watch the limousine roll closer.

I pull at my coat, cinching the belt around the waist as tightly as it'll go, then rub my hands together. It's senseless —nothing can stop that chill. I feel just like I did as a child, walking by it with my mother. Except now there's no hand to hold, and there's no alternate direction in which I can turn. With every second that passes, the behemoth inches closer and closer to our inevitable destination.

I expect the limousine to stop at the towering front steps that lead up to the entrance, but we inch past it, past the sprawling lawns running vertical, up a small mound of pavement and through a garage door that opens seamlessly into an underground parking garage lit with tightly spaced rows of yellow bulbs. A flock of black birds erupt from the rafters, veering narrowly around the limousine and out the garage door just before it seals itself shut.

I swallow.

The space is empty, aside from a fleet of vehicles similar to the one I ride in, but then at the far end of the garage I notice a group of people in the middle of some commotion.

An old man, by the looks of it, cursing loudly. Two blue-coats—Mainframe officers—attempt to penguin-march him to an awaiting black car, but he struggles with surprising ferociousness against their grip. I lean forward in my seat, watching intently as a man in a white coat slips from the automobile. Whatever happens next is blocked from view, given the turning of the limousine, and when I next catch sight, I notice that the old man no longer resists. In fact, he could be sleeping. A second later their group disappears into the car, which speeds in the direction of the exit.

Feeling even more unsettled than before, I knock on the partition separating me from Monsieur Sawyer. He opens it as narrowly as possible.

"Who was that man?" I ask. "What were they doing to him?"

"Ah. Poor Miss Alex. One must not ask questions; that's the first rule of life here at Strath Glen." With that he snaps shut the partition.

I knock again. "How am I expected to get any work done without the asking of questions?"

"What questions need asking, Miss Alex?"

"Well, am I supposed to guess at which shoes the viscount would like polished? What pants need pressing? Whether he prefers his eggs over-easy or sunny-side-up?"

My questions are mostly asked in earnest, but there's a hint of sarcasm there too, and Monsieur isn't fooled. "I mightily suggest you learn to control that attitude of yours, Miss Alex," he snaps, "or you'll end up like wretched Mr. Worthers there. Sacked. Good riddance to him, the son of a bitch."

"That man was *sacked*? He was a servant? So why were officers from the Mainframe taking him?" It's a fair question, that last one; bluecoats work to keep the peace, and mainly by making house calls.

Nonetheless, it's a question not appreciated by Monsieur. He jams on the brakes so hard that I squash my nose on the back of his seat. Then he leans around to glare at me. "Handmaids," he says harshly, "are not allowed to ask questions. Precisely how much clearer I must make myself, I do not know."

I rub my nose, my bad mood getting worse by the minute. "Well, then, it just so happens I'm not asking as a *handmaid*. I'm asking as the viscount's fiancée."

At this Monsieur snaps shut the partition and stops the limousine. A moment later the door swings open and he pushes his face close to mine. "Two lessons," he says in a high-pitched voice. "The first is that dissidence isn't taken lightly at Strath Glen, and now you can't say that you haven't been warned. The second," he continues, "is that your *engagement* to the great Sir Viscount means nothing to me or to anyone else within this fine institution. Those here with power have cultivated it from the ground up, no matter their station, and you, Miss Alex, will be starting from the bottom—generously betrothed or not."

He turns on his heel, leaving me to digest his words. A minute later I follow him through a gate, then a door, then up a narrow and winding flight of stone stairs. All the while his warnings echo in my mind.

Just as my legs begin to ache, he pushes open yet another door. Through it and for the very first time in my life, I glimpse the inside of the ominous Strath Glen.

five

A SPLASH of dried rice and colorful paper hits me in the face. Looking down, I see confetti clinging to my coat, and I hear a treble of laughter rising lightly from my side.

"Evie," a voice says sharply from across the room, a man's voice, particularly low. "Go to your studies."

"Come, now," says the girl. She has a similar manner of speaking. "I'm just trying to lighten the mood. And my studies can absolutely wait; we have a wedding to plan!"

There comes a clicking of the tongue, and when I finally clear my eyes of glitter I see the tongue-clicking comes from a navy-clad figure on the far side of what appears to be an oversized living room. *Devonshire Commons*, states the gold plaque hanging on the wall. Underfoot is smooth carpet, the color of fresh-drawn blood, and overhead the ceiling is criss-crossed with molding, as high as the rooftops of Quire. But once again my gaze returns to that man on the other side of the room.

He's tall, that figure, unnaturally so, with brown skin and black curly hair cut short. He also happens to have his back to me, busying himself with some papers and showing no interest whatsoever in the new addition to the room. A comely girl in a school tunic with waist-length hair the same color and texture as the man's moves into my vision.

"Might I make introductions?" suggests the chauffeur. He bounds deeper into the room.

"Oh, there's no need for any of that," says the girl, almost reproachfully. She dangles a well-manicured hand in my direction. "Such formalities are so boring, don't you find? Do you know who I am? I'm Evie and you, obviously, are the girl from Quire, isn't that so? Selected to marry my brother and serve as his handmaid. The palace has been in an uproar since news broke yesterday," she adds, with a touch of conspiracy. Then, as I accept her hand, and feeling incredibly out of place, she bursts into a fit of giggles. "You smell positively like the inside of a wood stove, no offense! And that coat! What caused such a ghastly stain?" Before I can respond the girl gasps. "Your forehead! My, you are a proper mess, aren't you?" She laughs again, then lifts her voice: "Come now, brother. Despite all that, she isn't frightful—not in the least! You're being rude!"

The man at the far side of the room appears to be completely consumed with the papers he holds. All he does by way of reply is grumble something indecipherable.

So. That's him, then, and my stomach sinks at the realization. That impossibly tall man who refuses to so much as look over his shoulder at me—that's *him*. I'd been prepared for the fact that the viscount wouldn't exactly be excited to be paired with a stranger from a modest neighborhood; it didn't occur to me that he'd loathe the idea as much as I do.

I really need to find a way out of this mess.

Evie, unbothered by her brother's lackluster response, grabs me around the shoulders and whirls me in the direction of Monsieur Sawyer. "Oh—do we have time to fix her up proper before they arrive?"

But just as I open my mouth to both refuse the suggestion and ask who "they" are, the man shakes his head. "Miss Alex here," he says pointedly, "lacks the very enthusiasm with her newfound position that was anticipated. I daresay a makeover will be met with resistance on her part, though, Viscountess, you are deadly right at the need for it."

Evie lifts perfectly plucked eyebrows. "Was there a problem in fetching her?"

The chauffeur throws an accusatory glance at me. "One could say that."

"There wasn't a *problem*," I say, embarrassed. "But this... this man refused to answer my questions, and—he dragged me from my aunt's house—"

"I thought I told you," shouts the chauffeur, as Evie stares between us with unabashed interest, "dissidence is not accepted at Strath Glen!"

"And I told you, I don't belong at Strath Glen! It was a—"

At that moment two things happen simultaneously. The first is that the viscount finally lifts his head from his papers and looks directly at me. The second, and the one that holds my own gaze, is that the double doors on the far side of the room burst open and a large group of people push inside, all of them chattering loudly and drowning out my remaining words. My eyes widen at the mass that descends on me, reminding me as they do of a group of elegantly dressed vultures.

"She's here!"

"Oh, she's hideous! Look at the state of her coat!"

"Did she injure herself on the way over, or are such bumps and bruises commonplace down there?"

"Why is the child's hair wet—how uncouth!"

"Have proper introductions been made?"

"Where is the viscount?"

They surround me, these vultures, circling me, picking at my clothing and hair. Over their spinning heads, I see the far door open, and the viscount disappear.

Suddenly they go still.

"Does she talk?" the young woman standing directly in front of me asks in a honey-sweet voice, seemingly the most important of the group given the way the others make room for her. She's also the most extraordinarily dressed, in bubble-gum-pink gauze from floor to chin, apart from a peekaboo cut-out across her chest that displays ample cleavage. Glossy yellow hair is twirled into a towering up-do, punctuated by diamond-studded pins made to look like sprinkles. Slowly she waves a jeweled hand in front of my face. "Pity me to the heavens. I suppose she doesn't!"

I look around at the others, trying to read their faces, but there's no shift in features. So quietly, I ask, "Who do you pose the question to?"

It's the wrong thing to say—the well-powdered face sours. Then she pulls a tube of lipstick from a fold in her dress and anoints each lip in fluorescent pink, her gaze set on me the entire time. It strikes me as I watch her that she could devour me whole.

Finally, lipstick complete, the woman says in that honeyed voice, "You poor little thing. Boy, I pity you. Really, I do. You're as unmemorable as the dinner I ate two moons prior!" She pulls from another fold in her dress a small vial that she uncaps as she laughs to herself. She inhales deeply the oil of frankincense, then disappears to a bay window where a servant holds a crystal decanter and refers to her as *Princess Aubrey*.

The King's daughter. Well, then, certainly *that'd* explain her importance.

Just then another of the vulture pack stirs, a man this time, dressed in canary yellow. He has the same butter-blonde hair as Aubrey, the same ample figure, and the same way of staring. "My dear cousin really has the most terrible luck," he laments lazily over his shoulder, to no one in particular, then his gaze drops down to my boots that deposit drops of water on the carpet. "You're wet."

"It's raining."

"A girl from Quire, talking to me! The prince!" He places both hands over his breastbone, as if it's really something remarkable. "My Morocco will be so disappointed," he adds to the others, before following in Aubrey's footsteps.

"Prince James," the servant mutters as James grabs his glass, spills half its contents to the carpet, then tosses the rest down his throat as a trio of servants tend to the mess.

Neither he or his sister bear any resemblance to Evie or Wolfe, fair as they are, yet if Wolfe is nephew to the King— he must be first cousin to these dreadful people. I can't stand to think that far off in the future, one of the two will rule my beautiful Airo-Aurora...

In time, when the rest of the vultures grow tired of star- ing, and a quartet of strings begin playing in the corner, they move to the window for a drink of their own. All, that is, except a mature couple standing at the back of the pack. The parents of my betrothed: the Duke and Duchess of Airo-Aurora.

The woman's the giveaway. She's lean, like him, though her skin's far darker. Box braids sit on top of her head in a towering bun, a look that's both elegant and intimidating. The father, tall and fair like the others, loses interest in me almost at once. His gaze moves to that crystal decanter. But the gaze of the mother lingers. She tilts her head ever so slightly as she scrutinizes the girl she expects her son to wed.

"He will worry over you," she comments, after a while.

I frown. Who will worry—Wolfe? Why would he worry over me when he clearly loathes the idea of our marriage as much as I do? And, more pressing, what exactly is there to worry over in the first place? What dangers could possibly lurk here among the old tapestries and taffeta dresses?

Before I can ask, the pair turn for the exit. They take a reluctant Evie with them, chiding her as they do for missing her lessons.

I stare around Devonshire Commons, startled to find a parrot sitting in a cage nearby. With one eye on me, it ruffles its feathers and says, "Killed by a curse? Killed by a curse."

In the corner, the cellist plays with his eyes closed, while near the window the young royals pay out bets placed on my head, tossing money to one another as if it's paper waste. From what I can hear of their conversation, expectations for the nobody from Quire had been exponentially low, and yet I'd still managed to disappoint.

Right now, I have two options. I can start my work as handmaid until I'm offered a break, then go to the Mainframe. Or I can find the nearest exit and go to the Mainframe at once, waiting there until it opens. I turn to question Monsieur Sawyer about my duties and to ask him where the closest exit is, but already he's disappeared.

"Killed by a curse? Killed by a curse."

Another round of drinks is poured, another decanter fetched, the vial of frankincense opened and closed, open and closed, until I almost gag at the stench. The decibel in the room inches up as inhibitions lower. Still, I don't move—it's like I'm rooted to the floor. Eventually a clown arrives, juggling daggers, and a magician follows behind with a bag of party tricks. A redheaded vulture drags another woman to the floor, sitting on her ribs and waving a brass locket over her head, chanting under her breath. Others laugh wildly. Aubrey lays a finger along the mouth of a man decades her senior, whispering something in his ear until his face glows pink. And James, who sports a dazzling wedding ring, slides his arm around a girl who immediately begins pecking his cheek as if obliged.

All the sounds and smells, even the colors, they begin to

bleed into one another, distorting reality until I feel like I'm hallucinating.

No.

No, this won't do. Strath Glen is a madhouse, there's no doubt about it. I'd been right to run in the opposite direction as a child. And my aunt and Agnes? They'd missed the mark: the viscount's no treat, not even close. Quire is where I belong. Surrounded by books and appetizing aromas from Aunt Jo's kitchen. A comfy old quilt, and a well-worn sofa.

Patrick, and the promise of an easy future.

As the minutes tick by, the situation deteriorates. The vultures dance sensuously to concertos, they pour liquor into one another's mouths, they touch each other in a manner that no respectable person should do. Their frequent bursts of laughter rise over the music like gunshots, echoing against the intricately molded ceiling as though it's crafted from tin. Not once do the revelers bother to glance in my direction. Finally, I look down to make sure the velvet cushions from the nearby sofa haven't swallowed me whole.

I've proven to be, just as Aubrey had said, completely unmemorable.

What terrific luck.

As Aubrey leaps onto the coffee table and tears away bubble-gum gauze to reveal a fur bodice, I start moving, darting forward and through the door on the far side of the room before anyone can spot me.

I let it close with a thud, and find myself in a wide hallway decorated with Ming vases taller than I am. The floor underfoot is a glittering black, like a well-lacquered piano, and the arched ceiling glows with golden frescoes. In another life I may've paused to admire its strange, almost sinister beauty, but the only thing on my mind right now is bidding it all goodbye. I fasten my stained coat, and then breathe a sigh of relief. Because at the end of the hall are two doors staggeringly tall—the official entrance of the palace. The official exit, too.

To make matters even better, I realize, as I start forward —the Mainframe should be open by now, so—

"Where are you going?" rings out a sharp voice from behind me.

My breath hitches, and slowly I turn. At the other end of the hall is a towering imperial staircase encased in gold. It arches gracefully in either direction, meeting at the top like a halo that lifts into a light-filled rotunda. And halfway up that staircase stands a sky-scraping Black man dressed in a navy suit, staring at me with more disdain than the rest of his vulture family combined.

Wolfe.

He has an immutable appearance, one that's difficult to describe. It's like he's been torn from an old painting by a great master. He looks completely out of place in the modern day.

"Well?"

Since my tongue feels like sandpaper, "Um" is the only sound I can make.

His brow pinches, right in the center. "Um?" He says it reproachfully, and mockingly, then marches down the steps. With more of his face in view, I faintly note a straight nose and eyes so dark brown they look like black holes. "Certainly you had no such difficulty holding your tongue earlier. *Alex.*" There's no glitter of warmth in his eye and no hint of it in his voice. The man exudes only coldness.

I push a loose coil of hair behind my ear, as my heart hammers. *No difficulty holding my tongue?* Vaguely I think of my argument with Monsieur, stating that I don't belong here.

"Where are you going?" he asks again.

I can't tell him the truth; I see that now. To insist the Mainframe had erred, to insist that deep within its rows of machinery it holds a better result for me, is to insult the dignity of a family that holds dignity above all else. It's all good and proper that Wolfe shouldn't want *me*—an unmemorable commoner from Quire—but the other way around?

And if this man, Wolfe—if this is his personality while civil, I can't bear to think of what he might be like angry.

"Viscount, sir!" hollers a man from another corridor. "Concerning payment for the roof repair—"

I use the distraction to my advantage, and a second later, breathing deeply, I push open heavy doors, relishing the slap of wind that feels like a new beginning—a welcome one at that.

From my vantage point up here, Airo-Aurora looks both staggeringly vast and so small that I could pick it up between my fingers. I stare with wonder over the shimmering city, beautiful even under churning gray skies and unwavering rain. The mountainscape to the east looks stately, proud, and though I might not know very much about the world that lies beyond all this, in the moment I don't care. Airo-Aurora is enough—it will always be enough.

The greencoats who flank the entrance stare curiously at me, and I nod to them before starting slowly down a staircase made slippery from the rain. By the time I reach street level, several minutes later, the bottoms of my trousers are soaked through and my hair—which had been almost dry—is plastered to my scalp. I traverse the wide road allowance that serves as a private drive for the palace, make a point of avoiding the apple grove where that rotted apple had been, push through several rows of spruce trees, and pick my way over a grassy boulevard until the low-slung white building known as the Mainframe lifts into view. Brushing rainwater from my face, my heart skips a beat. I have luck with me now, I can feel it.

Luck will wash away the grease stain that soils my coat. It will wash away the dull thudding in my forehead, and all memories of Strath Glen and its awful occupants. It'll see to it that I'm allotted a career I've prepared for, one I'll feel comfortable in. *Pianist, pilot, librarian.* I recite it again and again in my head.

Oh, yes. And a husband, a good one this time.

six

. . .

INSIDE THE MAINFRAME LOBBY, clear of the bitter winds and driving rain, I double-check my watch. Yes, I'm here well within opening hours. Strange, then, that the lights haven't been turned on. Strange too to find it empty. Not that there's much of a crowd on the three hundred sixty-four days of the year when the Selection *doesn't* take place. Still, there're usually a few sad souls here, waiting to visit the memories of their loved ones—another benefit to having one's brain recordings saved in perpetuity on machine.

It's a wait I'm familiar with. For over the past three years, at least once a week and usually much more than that, I've waited for my turn to sit inside a Visitation Room cubicle, to watch and listen to the data recorded by the chips in my parents' brains from before the accident. I've seen myself grow older through their eyes. I've relived each family Christmas. Each birthday party. Each celebration. And most of the quiet moments in between. It's maybe the best gift of the chip system—even more so than the calm and content society ensured by the Selection.

I ring the service bell, slip on the puddles I've brought

indoors, and take a seat in a plastic chair. I glance at the day's newspaper as I squeeze water from my coat.

SUSPECTED SELECTION AT STRATH GLEN! the headline roars, and immediately my wet coat's forgotten about. I take up the paper with both hands and begin to read:

> *According to a top-secret source at Strath Glen itself, the* Morning Herald *is excited to report that it wasn't just civilians engaging in yesterday's famed Selection! That is correct —supposedly a man ranking high within Airo-Aurora's secretive clan partook in the fun, meaning new blood is due to arrive on the palace's doorstep as early as today. In a titillating twist, it is said that this newly betrothed aristocrat underwent the confidential testing for only a spouse and not —as with the rest of the city—a career. Could this mean the debonair fellow had a career chosen for him at an earlier age? Could he be moving on to wife number two? Or is he simply work-shy? One can only speculate, as our top-secret source refused to say more for fear of exposure.*

"Can I help—? Oh."

I look up to see the same bespectacled technician who administered my Selection staring at me from behind the glass door. Since she seems to be considering backtracking, I rise quickly from my chair. "Yes, you can." Then, through a surge of adrenaline, I add: "I'd like to speak with your manager. Please."

"Miss, if it's about yesterday's result—"

Sensing it's my last chance to change everything, I speak boldly: "A mistake was made, that or there was a glitch in the system. There's nothing in my history that would support the result—not my career, not my betrothed. Besides, have you ever heard of a person being both royalty and servant? It's so ridiculous that the entire reputation of the Mainframe's at stake. Please, ma'am," I finish, "the manager."

The woman stares at me with exasperation. "The only manager there is, so to speak, is the King himself, and you certainly will not be able to schedule a sit-down with *him*."

"Then—then as a Mainframe technician, you're fit to re-administer—"

"I am fit to explain to you the reality of your situation, is what I am." The woman pauses to evaluate the small puddles that I've left on the floor. "A mistake made by the Mainframe," she continues, "is simply impossible. It runs the exact same algorithm for every Selection, yours included."

"A glitch, then."

The woman adjusts her glasses. "If there was a glitch, we technicians would surely know about it. I can assure you once and for all that mistakes and glitches do not happen. Free choice leads to errors; machines do not."

Wind whistles through cracks in the Mainframe's exterior. Thunder drums in the distance, and against the roof the pounding of rain is relentless. Above it all, however, is the whirring of my brain. That and the ticking of my pulse. "Then take mercy on me," I plead. "Run the scans again. Just one more time—"

"Miss," the technician interrupts, her voice doleful. "Not a soul within this building will allow you to go through the Selection process again. It simply isn't done. I'm sorry. But, if it's any consolation, I can assure you that even if you did undergo another Selection, your result would remain the same. Just as it did yesterday when I reran your Careers sca—"

"But—"

"Miss," she says, solemnly. "Your results will not change."

"Just—"

"Miss. Whomever it was I declared as your betrothed, that is your best match. Whichever job I said was yours, that is the most fitting. Accept that."

I stare at the woman. "You really don't remember?"

"The Selection results are confidential. It is my job to forget."

"And yet...my results were anything but forgettable."

The technician nudges her glasses up her nose. "I suppose the day's most unusual results take the longest to fade from memory."

"You admit my results were unusual?"

"Unusual? Yes. Erroneous? Most certainly not."

Probably I should accept what this woman says and try to come to terms with my new future. Probably I should thank her for her time and patience. And then I should return to Strath Glen, where I should make an effort to ingratiate myself with my new family and colleagues...and my future husband.

At that last thought, I push by the woman—into the heart of the Mainframe, more desperate than before. If that technician refuses to help, I'll find another who will.

Past the empty Selection rooms, through the unoccupied Visitation Room, along one dark corridor and then another, and not a soul to be seen. Undeterred, I push deeper into the Mainframe. I'll find someone who can help me. I *must*.

Then I stumble into a room so large that I go still. Rows of machinery fan out before me, stacked from floor to ceiling and made strangely alive by an orchestra of tiny flashing lights. Data storage, for all the people of Airo-Aurora, and for some reason the sight makes my hair stand on end.

After a few moments, I follow a narrow corridor of space between wall and machine, head swiveling down each row in search of life. But each one is empty, each one completely devoid of humans. Machinery, machinery, machinery, none of which can listen to reason, none that can show me mercy.

And just like that the wall gives way to a large pane of glass, and through the pane I see a series of desks, office chairs, and computer screens. More importantly, I see *people*.

They look to be in the middle of a party. Balloons cling to the ceiling, streamers too, and a large cake sits in front of the glass with a butcher's knife sticking through its center. Custodians hold party crackers instead of brooms, and instead of blocking my way olive-clad guards drink punch and trade jokes. Technicians wear pointy hats with polka dots and gather around a cheese plate.

Slowly they catch sight of me, and as the greencoats dash from the room, I focus on the only partygoer unfazed by my sudden appearance in the heart of the Mainframe. He's small, with a shock of black hair, thick-framed glasses, and, strangely, a smile—a sly one. I watch him closely as he taps a few buttons on his keyboard, as he rolls up the sleeves of the gray coat marking him a technician. Not once does he shift his gaze to mine.

It would mystify me more if it weren't for the sound of footsteps. I barely make it past the window when I'm grabbed from behind.

"There's a glitch—there's a glitch in the system!" I'm shouting, but it falls on deaf ears, and I'm pushed through poorly lit hallways all the way back to the lobby.

Trespassing, the guards say. Against the rules. Lucky they aren't calling the blackcoats to haul me to the prisons. The reprimands, for whatever they're worth, wash over me like the rainwater I'll soon be turned out into. Instead, I focus on my reality...

As much as I thought otherwise, as much as I hoped for it deep within the pit of my stomach, I won't be able to change my result. While certain as ever a glitch was responsible for a horrible future, it's been spoken for, and now all I can do is accept it.

I won't return to my aunt's home in comfortable Quire, I won't have a career of pianist or pilot or librarian like I wanted, I won't marry a familiar friend.

I'll spend my life serving as handmaid to my betrothed, the loathsome viscount of the frenetic madhouse known as Strath Glen.

seven

. . .

TIME PASSES. People come and go from the Mainframe; cars and buses push along the avenue sending sprays of wetness onto the sidewalk and into the faces of unlucky pedestrians. The giant screens lining Central Boulevard flicker in the distance, they cycle between ads and local news in an endless loop. Pigeons gather on the wet pavement, scouring the area for bits of food before taking their search elsewhere. It's only me who remains stationary.

I sit on the bench outside the Mainframe. Rain has soaked through my overcoat—now it works on my molasses-colored sweater. I shiver and shake, but I don't move.

Because there's nowhere to go, not really. To go back to Quire for a final goodbye would be too painful, for me and for my aunt, and if I were to barricade myself in the guest room and refuse to come out, I'd risk imprisonment. But to return to the palace requires more strength than I have. It requires a straight spine and a stiff upper lip, and all I can do right now is sit here, stunned.

Look on the bright side, comes a voice in my head.

What bright side?

I don't know how much time passes, but eventually I become aware of a new sound: the humming of a large automobile. That and shouting. I lift my head and wipe rainwater from my eyes.

Monsieur and the behemoth.

With a deep breath and no other options, I stand, then poke my way around puddles until only a foot of space remains between me and the chauffeur.

"Might I guess how your little visit to the Mainframe went?" he asks. "Have you been slotted into a position you find more desirable, with a mate more satisfactory to your needs than Lord Viscount?"

I mumble, "It didn't go well."

"No, I didn't expect as much. Listen, and carefully. I have other duties that need tending to, and rushing all over the city for the likes of you isn't high up on my list of priorities. I shall take you for a second time to Strath Glen, and I do not anticipate there will be a third."

The threat isn't lost on me. I nod.

"Daisies. Now, Miss Alex," he says as he swings open the rear door, "we're getting somewhere. Do hurry—the King would like a word, and don't tell me I didn't warn you."

I stare at him.

Revered by all of Airo-Aurora, the large man who's our ruler has been a fixture since I was little, showing up on my television a few times a year to address the nation with seasonal well-wishes, reassurances, and bragging points. Though I'd never said the words, I always found his wide smile a little too forced, a bit too sinister. It's not a shared feeling between me and the rest of the population.

And yet this vastly popular ruler wants a word...with me. A girl from Quire.

"The King wishes to speak to *me*?" I finally ask, finding that the point really does need clarification.

"Did I stutter?"

"But, why?"

A twisted smile turns his lip. "Why, Miss Alex—I thought the news would meet you happy. None of the technicians in this old place have the power to change your results, surely you realize that by now." He motions through the rain in the direction of the Mainframe. "But who provides oversight to the Mainframe? Who is its ruler?"

The King.

He would have the power to change my results. But how can I make the request without offending the dignity of the palace? It's impossible. And judging by the twinkle in Monsieur's eye, he knows the same to be true.

"Wait," I protest, as he pushes me inside the limousine. An icy feeling settles inside my stomach. "Does he know that I'm here? Does he know that I've attempted to change my results?"

"The King? Why, of course, Miss Alex! The whole palace knows by now. You will find at Strath Glen that word travels exceptionally fast."

I bite down hard on my lip. Already I can sense the position I've put myself in...I can feel the loathing of the indignant vultures from here.

"You should know," he continues, "that it wasn't I who spilled the beans on your little plan to visit the Mainframe and demand more fitting results." With a meaningful look he slams shut the door. A minute later, the behemoth inches away from the curb with the wipers on full tilt.

"If it wasn't you, how did word get around?"

The chauffeur glances over his shoulder at me as if I'm stupid. "Shortly after your getaway, a phone call was placed, as ordered by the viscount. Some nerve you have, I might add, turning your back on him like that."

"How—"

"One of the maids was dusting Counterdown and saw the whole thing." He chuckles to himself.

"A phone call," I repeat, rubbing my head. "To the Mainframe?"

"Of course to the Mainframe."

"But how did the viscount know that I was there in the first place?"

A city bus slams on the horn as Monsieur pulls the behemoth into a U-turn. He pays it no attention. "He didn't, naturally."

I shake my head. "I'm afraid I don't follow."

"All it takes from a place like Strath Glen is a request to pull up a person's feed. Pretty easy to guess their whereabouts when you can see and hear everything they can, don't you think? Not that they had to bother since you were running around the very place, and like a bozo to boot, from what I heard."

"You mean that my chips were going to be *hacked into*?"

"No need for theatrics, Miss Alex. Hardly a hack job. But yes, you get the gist. It just so happens the lady who picked up the telly had just been speaking to y—"

"So for the rest of my life—"

"They'll always be able to find you. Oh, don't look so dismayed. The rest of the population has much the same situation, do we not?"

As we start up the drive of the leering palace, I consider his question. It's true that adults are monitored closely, although I don't have any firsthand experience with it; my eighteenth birthday's still a few months away. But I'd witnessed it on occasion with my own parents—an unusual bout of emotions triggers an alert at the Mainframe; it gives the bluecoats a reason to place a phone call, to pay a visit.

Yet that always seemed like more of a state-sponsored wellness check than anything else. This? An invasion of privacy, a terrible one. *Surely* I'm not expected to be okay with my employer and my betrothed's family having the ability to track my every movement...

A few minutes later and my lips blue from cold, I step from the limousine into the underground parking garage, one that's now totally empty. The reality of my situation settles further into my brain. I'm *back*. Back at the madhouse.

Permanently, this time, or so it seems.

Up the narrow stone staircase we go, ascending much higher than earlier, each step adding another brick of weight to my shoulders. Candlesticks secured to the wall flicker as if swarmed by flies, and the muffled rain sounds like the thumping of a heart. Up and up, an unending climb. Finally, Monsieur Sawyer swings open a door and shoves me into a wide, dark corridor. Its arched ceiling is lined with black timbers. Its walls are lined with shelves set behind glass, and on the shelves are jars. In each jar floats a human head suspended in green-tinted liquid.

"Welcome to Bishop's Aisle, otherwise known as the top floor of Strath Glen."

"The top floor," I echo in a raspy voice. Just then a servant clutching a dartboard bursts by, startling me. Behind us, I notice next, at the far end of the corridor, several workers in overalls stand around a hole drilled into the wall, each taking turns peering inside. I'm distracted from them by a group of men in fedoras who storm purposefully past. "The top floor which houses what, exactly?" I ask.

"Offices, mainly. It's doubtful you'll be up here very often, so no need for a tour."

"Offices. For—"

"For keeping our nation-state humming along happily, of course." He winks darkly.

"And the...the heads?" I stare at the one closest to me, mouth gaping, eyes bulging, and with a shaved patch on the side of his head in the shape of a square. On closer inspection, I see the square is outlined by a bright red line, the remnants of an incision. I swallow.

"Well, Miss Alex. Surely you didn't expect those chips implanted in our brains to work on the very first try, hmm? These men and women were from the early days, the very first trials!" He gestures to what must amount to hundreds of heads lining the corridor with enthusiasm, then turns on his heel. "Do keep up," he mutters over his shoulder. "And remember to stifle your questions. I've already indulged you far too many."

Keeping my gaze away from the floating heads, I scan the placards hanging next to each door. Some are pegged as meeting rooms, while others—such as the Food Sciences office—serve a more specific purpose. Near the end of Bishop's Aisle, I notice the name of the viscount stamped in gold. His office, and the sight makes my boots slow. So, maybe he *isn't* work-shy.

"Come," Monsieur reminds me. He lifts his voice over the sound of drilling.

At the end of the corridor, he stops in front of oak doors eight feet tall. He knocks only once, and I know from the enormous placard that we've reached our destination. Despite feeling like I'm being marched to the principal's office for misbehaving, despite feeling a mix of dread and terror surrounding my future here at Strath Glen, a sense of curiosity gets the best of me. After all, this is the *King* of Airo-Aurora. The beloved ruler, one who has requested *my* presence.

A servant in black and white pulls the door open. Immediately he steps into the hall and lowers his voice to a whisper. "This is her, then? Comin' from the Mainframe like I heard, aye? Not no one here thought she'd be doin' the runnin'. Sue, Sue-Ellen, and Mitsy all think her head'll roll straight. Wanna cast your bet? I got eight booked already."

My eyes widen as Monsieur spurs the outstretched hand. "The door, Toddy."

With one last sidelong look, the man named Toddy steps aside and Monsieur shoves me across the threshold.

The first thing I notice is that even though the King's office is larger than Aunt Jo's entire house, it's inexplicably cramped for space. Several round coffee tables are assembled throughout the room, with a mishmash of leather chairs positioned around each. An armoire reaching to the ceiling hogs one wall, and bookshelves overflowing with bins and more of those hideous jars line another. In the middle of the room stand several large stage lights, as well as a video camera hanging in obvious disuse.

Servants, meanwhile, line the wall closest to the door, arms held politely behind their backs, sniggering to themselves. And on the far side, beyond the various seating options and other paraphernalia, is the desk. *The* desk. The one I've glimpsed over the years from my parents' couch. The one of mammoth proportions, so well-lacquered it resembles a mirror.

The man himself is blocked from view by the camera, but I can tell from the twist of smoke that rises to the ceiling that the most important seat in all of Airo-Aurora is occupied. I start to wonder whether it was the King himself that I noticed in the window right after my Selection, that shadowy figure way up high—but then I'm distracted by something.

The King isn't alone. Seated right across from him is the viscount.

No, not just the viscount. My fiancé. My *fiancé*. Because that's what I see this time around—the man I have to wed. Before he was simply a man I was temporarily bound to in a colossal mistake. Nothing more. Now I notice every detail with fresh eyes; I feel each nuance tight against my chest: how tall he is even when seated, how large his hands are, how strangely neat and intentional his stubble looks. I notice how impeccably dressed he is, right down to his upturned collar and shining cufflinks. I notice all these things, but mostly I notice his complete disinterest in me. It's impossible he hasn't noticed the new addition to the room, and yet he doesn't turn his head, doesn't shift his gaze. Instead, he continues to talk with the King about what sounds like a trade dispute, jotting down notes on a legal pad with total focus. If he's angry with me for fleeing to the Mainframe and demanding a new job and suitor, he has yet to show it.

Suddenly he snaps up his notepad and stands. The whispering of the servants and their muffled laughter ceases. "I'll have the export spat resolved by the end of the week," he announces. After a slight tilt of the head, he maneuvers expertly through the furniture, knowing by heart the most direct path to the door.

He doesn't glance my way, and I let out a sigh of relief.

"Your splendid Royal Majesty," announces Monsieur Sawyer, "I present to you—"

"Bring her near, bring her near," comes a wheezy and unrecognizable voice belonging to a very old man. Confused, I allow the chauffeur to propel me forward, around a sitting chair, past a coffee table, over an unplugged floor light, until I approach that shiny desk I know so well.

There, in front of me, sits the King of Airo-Aurora.

Smoke encircles his head like a wreath, and slowly he smiles as wide as a Cheshire cat. "Well, well, well..." he begins, the wheeziness gone. His voice is robust. "No need for introductions. This can be none other than the girl from Quire, destined to serve and wed my nephew." He beckons me closer.

Carefully I tiptoe forward, noting both the crown of jewels he wears on his head—blood-red rubies encased in gold and set against hair so white it's without a trace of pigment—and the fur cloak pulled over his shoulders skinned from a mink. Claws dangle around his elbows.

Then like a spring he stands, and I jump. His crown dispels the ring of smoke. He leans over the desk and before I can resist grabs hold of my chin. Tilting my face back and forth, as though studying every detail, he seems neither disappointed nor satisfied. "I heard from a birdie, dear girl," he begins, "that you aren't so happy about your new arrangement here at my homestead."

Something about his voice slithers like a snake, and I have the unmistakable urge to run. "Sir," I whisper, now fully understanding the reason I was summoned. "I—"

"Call me King," he interrupts.

I blink. "Okay. Okay, *King.*" I clear my throat. "As I was saying, I—I'm perfectly happy with the arrangement, of course I am. The problem is...well, I just found the whole thing peculiar, given—"

He silences me with a swish of his wrist. "Sit," he instructs.

I do, teetering on the edge of the chair that Wolfe had vacated. I smooth my herringbone trousers, still damp from the rain, and watch with bated breath as King walks slowly around his desk with the assistance of a silver walking stick, his steps painfully hobbled, his back rounded like an arch-way. And then in the blink of an eye he straightens, and his stride widens into a powerful gait.

The feeling of unease is almost too much to bear.

He positions himself on the edge of the desk, feet kicking noisily against it the way a child's might. He gazes down at me with that Cheshire smile returned to his face, and yet there isn't a hint of warmth in his eye, the smile's an illusion. "My dear," he begins quietly, "whether you find your results as peculiar as a fermented pig, when the Main-frame speaks, we listen." He tugs his ear.

"But," I insist, more determined than ever to find a way far from this man, and from Strath Glen, and from the viscount, "never—"

"Gaze out that window." He gestures to the one nearest to us with his walking stick. Beyond the triple pane of glass and black lattice sits all of Airo-Aurora, glittering under the gloom. "Nothing but happiness, dear Alex, no matter the corner. Our ancestors, oh, how they'd fight. They'd kill thy neighbor, they'd cut off the nose to spite the face! And all because they were gifted with the power of choice." He pauses to press his hands together as if in prayer. He squeezes his eyes shut. "Do you know what humans do?" he murmurs.

"No, sir. King."

"They choose incorrectly, dear girl. They choose a job that is wrong, wrong, wrong. They choose a mate who turns out to be piss. Oh, what a dark society that came to be. And then—" He slides off the desk and crouches beside me. He speaks quietly into my ear. "And then...a new dawn. Airo-Aurora, made so beautiful because of the miraculous chips implanted in our brains, feeding information to our trusty Mainframe, choices now made by science and guarded against error. We must put our trust in it, my dear girl. We must not be critical of a system that does nothing but give!"

With my chair suddenly knocked forward, I place a hand on the shiny desk to steady myself. Quick as a cat King shoots to his feet; he cuts his silver walking stick through the air in an arc until it crashes against my knuckles.

Blinding white-hot pain, and I scream.

"My dear, my dear," he says placidly. "My ears. My ears! Here at Strath Glen, we don't make a scene, no matter the circumstances. We don't make a fuss. We keep our heads down and we carry on, no matter the personal sacrifice. And we always—*always*—give respect where respect is due, whether that's to me, or your betrothed, or to the eternally precise Mainframe. To do otherwise would be to request punishment. Am I making myself clear? Are we thinking as one?"

My two largest knuckles bleed, and I'd be surprised, given the pain, if none of the bones had been broken. But still, I manage to nod. To do otherwise would be an act of disrespect, apparently; it would be to request punishment. And I definitely, *definitely* don't want that. Behind me and seemingly far off in the distance, the office door swings open, and I spot a woman with perfectly set curls enter as if on wheels. I recognize her as the Queen, not simply because of the tiara she wears on her head, but because I've seen her many times before, on the television standing behind her husband during his addresses.

"My dearest!" King shouts to her. "What perfect timing. This poor girl could use some bandages, would you be so kind?" He pulls from one of the bookcases a bin full of gauze, then stuffs a wad of it, along with some medical tape, into his wife's powdered hands. She glides toward me and, with some difficulty given her skirts, takes a knee.

For a moment I'm shocked at how empty the woman's eyes are, eyes that seem to stare straight through me. But then she blinks and smiles, and she busies herself lifting my crushed hand from the desk.

"This impish little creature," says King jovially, "is the newest addition to the family. Soon she will wed our nephew, the lucky duck. So. The most clumsy Alex of Quire, meet the dandiest Queen of Airo-Aurora."

"Madam," I mutter, through chattering teeth. Unsure of proper decorum, but unwilling to risk another punishment, I tip my head forward, the best I can manage from my seat with my shattered hand clasped between hers.

"A clumsy cat will get broken like that!" she trills happily. Nothing in her voice suggests she's heard of my slight against the royal family. Instead, she diligently loops layer after layer of gauze around my hand, finally taping it all in place with a crisscrossed application reminiscent of a child's art project. The padding's applied so thick I can barely move my fingertips.

"Thank you," I whisper. "It, er, feels better already."

She draws herself to her feet. After fluffing her skirts, she glances down at me. "Does it feel better, lovey-dovey?"

King stirs. "Her hearing isn't good," he mouths from over her shoulder, pulling at his ear.

I lift my voice. "It feels much better!" I shout. "Thank you!"

The Queen, with her serene smile, nods, causing her tiara to fall to the floor. Instead of scooping it up, she glides away, the heel of her shoe crushing the delicate metalwork as she goes.

I stare down at it, puzzled. I only straighten when I notice King watching me with one eyebrow lower than the other.

"Off to your room with you, little one. You must be frozen to the bone, sitting in wet clothes like that. Monsieur," he says to the chauffeur, "do show my favorite new addition to her room. I daresay she would benefit from a warm bath and a fresh change of clothes. I believe the guest quarters on the second floor are available?"

The chauffeur hesitates. He glances between King and me. "Your Majesty, I do believe a room has been prepared for Miss Alex in the basement, with the other support staff. You'll remember her role as handmaid?"

"Do as I say, Monsieur Sawyer."

Monsieur bows deeply, then ushers me from the room as the servants standing along the wall take turns glancing at one another.

"That ill-guided jaunt to the Mainframe might just be the nail in your coffin," Monsieur mutters.

I blink back tears, then lift my bandaged hand. "That's an understatement," I say in a hoarse voice.

"Not the hand, Miss Alex," says Monsieur, with a wink. "I'm talking about the guest room he's putting you up in."

I follow him wordlessly down the stone staircase, shivering from the cold, nauseated by my encounter with King, heartbroken by my failure at the Mainframe. Let the guest room be squalor—it won't make a difference, not at this point.

Squalor, however, isn't the word I'd use to describe the second floor of Strath Glen. Eccentric might better capture it. For though better lit than upstairs, no lush carpet rides underfoot; no handsome timbers line the ceiling. Instead, every inch is clad in either black or white, an unrelenting, dizzying checkerboard, one made even worse by the assortment of reflective materials hanging along the walls.

"Welcome, Miss Alex, to the House of Mirrors. Your new home."

Just then a draft hits me in the face, and I run a hand along the wall, looking absent-mindedly for its source. That's when I glimpse myself. My complexion matches the white of hall, my hair is flat from rain, my forehead is red and considerably swollen, my hand resembles a snowball, and the wetness of my camel coat seems to only accentuate the grease strain sprawled across it. I look every bit as sad, tired and frightened as I feel.

No wonder.

New home, new job, new fiancé—and not even time to say goodbye to my old life, or to mourn all that I'd lost. Because so many things *have* been lost, from my beloved hometown, to Patrick, to my aunt and, most of all...my dreams. I always knew the life I hoped for might not pan out. I'm at the mercy of the Mainframe, after all, just like everyone else. But it never occurred to me that it'd be *so* off the mark.

I want to sit on the checkerboard floor right now. I want to curl into a ball, and weep. But instead, I think of my aunt's words this morning as we were saying our goodbyes. I lift my chin ever so slightly. I force myself to be brave.

"Come," the chauffeur instructs.

"Assume it to be quite dilapidated?" he continues, a little farther along. "On the contrary," and he shoves open a well-varnished black door.

Through the threshold, I'm still.

The walls and ceiling are a sumptuous mottled gray, with three large windows framed in satin. Behind the four-poster bed is a mirror as large as the wall itself, and overhead is an extravagant chandelier fashioned from crystal. Directly in front of the bed sits a lush velvet couch, also gray, along with a cloth coffee table constructed from the same fabric. A small writing desk covered in mirrors and decorated with moth orchids sits along the wall, while the wall opposite leads to what looks like a closet and bath. Every detail, right down to the cushions, is a quality much finer than anyone in Quire could afford.

I stare at it, speechless. For a moment I even forget about the throbbing in my hand.

"Miss Alex. Do you approve?"

It's *beautiful*, there's no question about that. And yet all its elegance only makes me miss that guest room in Quire even more.

"I think I'd prefer a simple room," I finally answer. "Definitely with a quilt." Because at least there I'd feel at home. And what's a girl from Quire to do in a room fit for a princess?

He drums his fingers against his chin. "*Most* would be celebrating such generous accommodations."

"I guess I'm not *most* people."

"I suppose that you aren't. Too bad for you, I can't help you out of this fix. You are hereby relegated to luxury."

I smile, suddenly grateful for his company. "I guess there *are* worst fates. Tell me, where do the others sleep?"

"The others?"

"All those people, when we first arrived..."

"Most of them were visitors, and visitors tend to stay in the guest house located to the rear of Strath Glen where there are more beds. You'll find that the palace hosts friends and family on the regular. As for the others, the members of the senior aristocracy themselves, they reside here on this very floor, of course."

The viscount, and King, sleeping just down the hall...?

It isn't the answer I'd been hoping for. I chew on my lip as I move deeper into the room, finally perching on the oversized couch, feeling like a tiny child among the hulking furniture.

Then I cradle my injured hand and groan.

"Miss Alex?"

"I just remembered that I didn't pack a suitcase."

He stares at me with a furrowed brow. Finally, he sighs. "You have been nothing but a thorn in my side. Too much attitude and too many questions, and all from such a gentle little soul. Almost seems duplicitous. Nonetheless, I shall arrange to have the butler bring you some toiletries and clothing—proper palace garb, which you'll be needing anyhow. That is where my kindness ends. He'll also inform you of your handmaid responsibilities, meaning my usefulness has reached its natural conclusion. It's high time I bid you adieu."

"Monsieur, one last question, please," I say. "Why did King put me here, in all this?" Once again, I stare around the sumptuous room.

"I daresay you'll understand in due time," he replies, and with a roguish gleam in his eye walks out the door.

eight

. . .

I WAKE the next morning in a fog. Given the restlessness of my sleep, the plunging temperature of the palace at sundown, and the nonstop howling of creatures from the back stoop, another few hours of sleep are definitely called for, and I wonder what caused me to wake in the first place.

I settle back under the covers and close my eyes, but it's no use. As details from yesterday come back to me—like the fact that I failed at the Mainframe, that the viscount is so awful, that King administered such a horrible punishment— I wake the rest of the way and sigh.

Knock, knock.

Pushing down the sheets, I stare at the darkened outline of the door—the reason, I guess, for my early awakening. Then with my uninjured hand, I pull a pillow over my head and groan at the day in front of me.

Probably it's Gerard, the butler, with more clothes. He'd delivered a closet-worth the evening before—an assortment of dresses, evening gowns, riding gear, and cardigans with delicate buttons the shape of petals. None were so elaborate and off-putting as the get-ups I'd glimpsed yesterday on the others...but none were me. No matter how hard I scoured, there was no tweed among the collection, no elbow patches, no blazers, even no herringbone. I would've been disappointed had the butler not brought with him news that left the problem of the unappealing wardrobe look completely insignificant.

It isn't my handmaid responsibilities that are the issue—delivering to the viscount his breakfast and tidying his suite don't exactly sound difficult, although Gerard had mentioned that the viscount would hand out further work at his own discretion. No, a steady workload doesn't bother me. What bothers me is the expectation that I'm to dine with the royal family for dinner each evening, attending, no less, as Wolfe's fiancée.

I'm not sure which is worse: having to act as handmaid to him during the day, or as his future wife by night. The man is so terrible, so cold and unfriendly, so *rude*, that neither suits me. Neither will ever suit me, and yet my options for escape are virtually nonexistent thanks to the chips planted inside my brain. If once the Selection system sparkled as a testament to my beautiful city, with its lack of crime and abundant happiness, now it's turned to ashes. It has let me down, it has made me as discontented as a citizen can be made to be.

So, if it's Gerard out there with more gowns, I'd rather stay right here, under the covers.

Then I bite my lip. Am I being rude? Making enemies? And what if it isn't a gown delivery, after all?

Besides, since I missed lunch and dinner yesterday, I'm starving. Maybe I *should* get up, poke around the kitchen Gerard told me about in the basement for something for breakfa—

Breakfast. The viscount's breakfast.

I throw off the covers and, cradling my damaged hand, pull open the door expecting to see Gerard there not with dresses but with reprimands, or even Wolfe, hungry and unhappy. To my surprise, a young girl stands in front of me, red ringlets pulled back, a white apron tied around her waist. A servant.

"Miss Alex?"

I nod, and quickly she shoves a rolled-up scroll into my hand, then retrieves a silver tray from the floor. "Lord Viscount's breakfast. Wouldn't want to make you come all the way downstairs to fetch it proper. Besides," she adds with knitted brows, "the bacon was getting nippy. The viscount likes to rise early, aye."

"I'm sorry," I reply, horrified. "I overslept." Stifling a yawn, I take the tray, and am immediately staggered by its weight. It would have been nearly impossible to haul up three flights of stairs. I position it over the wrist of my injured hand so that the knuckles don't feel the brunt of its weight, then glance at the scroll. Though the first few letters are obscured by a pitcher of syrup, I can make out my name scrawled along it. And scrawled for sure—the handwriting is so messy, so askew, it looks as though a child had written it. "Who's this from?" I ask, staring at it.

"Don't know, right? Found it just now in the stables when I was freshenin' the horses' water trough. Was addressed to you, aye, so there you go." At that moment three servants bustle past the door carrying an assortment of empty suitcases. They nod to the girl, exchanging covert smiles.

"Thank you for bringing it to me," I add.

"Aye. One more thing." She stoops down and a moment later places over my shoulder a mound of clothing and starchy aprons in the same color palette as the hall. "Your handmaid uniform, aye. To be worn at all times."

"At all times?"

The girl stiffens. "You got a problem with that?"

"No—of course not, no." My arms begin to tremor from

the weight of the tray. "Definitely not," I reiterate, not wanting to cause her offense. "But—"

"But?"

"It's just that the butler had a number of items delivered to my suite yesterday—"

"Fancy yourself above a servant, is that so? Would rather wear posh ball gowns and tiaras!"

"It's not—"

"The posh stuff is for when the Lord Viscount asks you on a date, if he ever," she interrupts.

"For dates only. I completely understand. And so the evening meals, the ones I'm supposed to take with him and the others, I'm to wear my handmaid uniform even then, is that right?" The last thing I need, I'm beginning to realize, is to put another foot wrong with the royal family.

The girl seems to relax. "As I already said, miss—handmaids are expected to wear the uniform of a servant always, aye, unless invited otherwise."

"Understood perfectly. Thank you for all your helpfulness. Can I ask your name?"

She fidgets with her apron, then says, "Rebecca."

"Thanks again, Rebecca, for delivering all this," I say, hoping that I'm making my very first friend at Strath Glen. "As for the viscount's breakfast, I'll make sure to get it myself from now on so you don't have to trouble yourself."

"Aye," is all Rebecca says before turning for the stone staircase, one probably reserved for staff.

Using my sore hand to support the tray, I let the clothing drop inside my room. Next, I step into the House of Mirrors, determined not to waste another minute in delivering to the viscount his breakfast. I wonder what sort of punishment is in store for me if I'm late.

It would be useful, I realize, if I knew the location of the viscount's personal residence. I groan. Less than twenty-four hours in and already I'm horrible at my position. Why hadn't I thought to ask Gerard, or Rebecca, or Monsieur? To make matters worse, the tray's so heavy, so cumbersome, that at this pace it'll be lunch before I complete my first task.

A man in coattails swoops by just then, a high-ranking servant carrying several hot water bottles, and I call to him for help. He doesn't bother to slow. The next servant who carries an armload of white towels stained with what resembles blood is no better. Somewhere above me comes the sound of drilling, the same sound I heard yesterday in Bishop's Aisle, and it makes the silver creamer rattle against the china. Now, breathing heavily, I spot yet another servant who appears several paces down the corridor as if from thin air. This time I'm wiser. This time I block his path. "The viscount's quarters," I pant. "Can you point me in the right direction? Please?"

The man tucks an industrial-sized bottle of carpet cleaner under his arm and stares at me with interest. "Keep on," he says eventually. Before I can thank him, he disappears through one of the doors over my shoulder.

Black. White. Black. White. Sweat begins to curl my hairline. Black. White. Black. White. And then the hallway opens up and I find myself hovering over a ledge, dangling in space.

A staircase, the one I glimpsed Wolfe on yesterday. Catching myself from tumbling to a near-certain death and straining my back in the process, I stare up at the rotunda lined majestically with windows, then start around the stairway opening toward the remaining House of Mirrors. I don't get very far when a burst of laughter echoes from below. Aubrey and another woman stand at the foot of the stairs, howling so deeply they bend in half.

"And she wished to rid herself of *us*."

The words make me wince. What a fool I was, trying to get my results switched like that.

But just as I think I couldn't possibly be more mortified,

I remember I'm dressed in my nightgown, one brought by Gerard last evening, a green tartan flannel number several times too big. My feet are bare, my long hair still crumpled from the bit of sleep I'd managed.

Aubrey, on the other hand, is dressed to the nines in a floor-length chiffon dress the color of mint ice cream, a tiny black top hat the size of a teacup fixed to her hair. Black gloves cover her arms past the elbows, and through a deep slit in the dress I glimpse high-heeled boots that reach to her thighs. The other woman who has straight auburn hair bluntly cut wears a gown crafted entirely from gold chains. She displays ample curves and enough skin to make a grown man blush.

My stomach sinks, and this time it isn't just from embarrassment. It's because I *knew* I wouldn't fit in here. *How could the Mainframe have been so wrong?*

And then I'm distracted by a new sound—footsteps. I turn to see my soon-to-be in-laws, both dressed smartly in overcoats. A trio of servants trail behind them clutching heavy suitcases. Ignoring the way they stare at my tartan nightgown, I whisper to the mother, "Please, madam. I'm trying to find your son's room so that I can deliver his breakfast."

"Are you sure it isn't the Mainframe you are in search of?" she replies coldly. "You know precisely *its* location."

I wonder whether it's possible to die from embarrassment. Then I say, "*Please*, madam. I didn't mean to offend him—"

"My son has thicker skin than that," she interrupts. Her eyes are piercing. "He is, however, a busy man, and he doesn't have time for nonsense. I trust," she says pointedly, "that such an excursion won't happen again."

"No, madam. No more excursions and no more, er, nonsense."

"Very well. I take it that you weren't charmed by the welcoming party?"

"It was a little overwhelming."

The woman tilts her head back, but there's less steeliness in her gaze. "You'll find his quarters near to the very end of the corridor," and she motions in the direction that I came from.

"That way, madam? One of your servants told me to continue in this direction."

"Having a bit of fun at your expense. Indeed, that breakfast tray is larger than you are. A helpful hint, child? King's side of the family resides to the west of the staircase, while the rest of us reside to the east. You'll find the viscount's quarters labeled as such. Good luck to you, Alex of Quire," she adds, before placing her hand into her husband's. They descend the grand staircase to where Aubrey and the other woman now quietly wait.

As fast as possible I retrace my footsteps along the House of Mirrors, past my own quarters, past a number of unmarked doors I guess are linen closets given their proximity and the way servants flip between them with toiletries in hand, then finally past a lavish double door with a nameplate reading, "Viscountess Evie Rocksavage of Airo-Aurora."

Perfect. Her brother's residence must be close.

Just as my arms begin to shake from the effort of holding the tray, I spot his name adorned in gold. I shift the tray to my injured hand, lift a knee to help support it, and raise a fist.

A second later I gasp.

Instead of rapping against solid wood, my knuckles skid across shiny silver. It's the buckle of a narrow belt looped around the viscount's waist.

Sighing impatiently, he steps back, making way for me to enter into a small hall lined in walnut, two closed doors at either end. He relieves me of the tray with another loud sigh, and places it with roughness on a receiving table positioned under a mirror. Ignoring my throbbing back, I say, "I'm sorry I'm late—"

"What is that hideous thing you are wearing?" he interrupts, and his looks incredulous. "Did you just roll straight from bed?"

"I—I overslept, but I came as fast as I could once I realized. And then I couldn't find your room and—"

"What happened to your hand?" That shrewd gaze of his lingers on my bandages.

I draw it to my chest and say nothing.

"I take it my uncle felt punishment was in order."

"You take it correct."

Slowly, from his spot on high, the viscount arches his spine and pushes his chin forward until his face rests just inches from mine. His brow is drawn so tight that it forms a straight, unbending line. "Let that be a lesson for you." Each syllable is weighted with significance.

I swallow.

"My breakfast," he announces next, drawing himself back to full height and putting as much space as he can between us without actually leaving the room. "Place it here every morning. Knock once on this door but otherwise do not disturb me. Certainly don't wait for me to answer—I won't wish to see you. And never again leave your room in such a state." He frowns once more at my oversized flannel gown.

I pick a feather from the sleeve and nod.

"Why is it the chauffeur picked you up from your aunt's house yesterday? Your *aunt*, in particular."

The question catches me off guard, and I look up at him.

"Be quick with your answer," he says in a voice that's tight-lipped and abrupt. "I have things needing doing."

A servant appears in the threshold just then and tosses to

Wolfe a set of keys. He pockets them silently and dismisses the man with a flick of his chin, turning his attention back to me.

"I've lived with her for the past three years," I explain. "Since my parents passed."

The words must have an impact on him, because he turns away. But he says nothing of it; he offers no words of condolence. A moment later he gestures to the checkerboard floor. "What is that?"

I follow his gaze and spot the scroll, the one that bears my name. It must've fallen during the commotion with the breakfast tray. "Just some mail, I guess," I tell him as I retrieve it, pushing it into a pocket of the nightgown. "Do we normally receive correspondence delivered to our rooms?"

"*We?*" he hisses, rounding on me. "Do you think the two of us *equals*?"

There's no reason for the words to hurt. That's all they are: words. Not darts or arrows, not sticks or stones. And spoken by a high-ranking royal to a lowly girl from Quire. They're not surprising words, not unexpected in the least. But they sting like venom.

"As I don't think my answer will please you," I say in a low voice, lifting my chin. "I'll say nothing at all. Besides, I need my uninjured hand in good working order if I'm to vacuum up your crumbs. Tell me, are your trails of dirt also superior to mine?"

Surprise cuts across his features, but already I'm turning away, vowing silently to find a way to end this mutually unwanted engagement.

nine

. . .

WITH NO WORK given to me by the dreadful viscount, I spend the rest of the day exploring the palace under the guise of my handmaid uniform, that in a happy turn makes me completely invisible. Definitely the princess doesn't notice me poking around Devonshire Commons, even as she languishes on a daybed tossing her gloves through the air, or as she falls into a stupor while receiving a foot rub. In Counterdown Abbey, the library, Prince James doesn't notice me as he builds a house of cards that takes a quarter past an hour, even as I inspect Airo-Aurora's originating documents set out on display, ones signed by King's father fifty years earlier. And King doesn't glance my way as we cross paths in the rotunda, his attention focused instead on the aria he sings.

Nobody stops me from stealing a bun from the kitchen during lunch prep, and I'm sure that not even Wolfe, by far the most astute of the group, notices me perusing Bishop's Aisle as he moves from office to office in a bustle of paperwork.

I still don't have any idea how to get myself out of this situation—here, with *him*, but right now, there's no time to think about it. I stare at the clock nestled between moth orchids and groan. It's *time*. Time to go downstairs to the dining hall. Time to join the royal family for dinner while I should be joining my aunt for one of her mouthwatering meat pies. I think about our final breakfast together, I think about her sitting down for dinner alone right now, I think about all those meals with my parents from before the accident—

Quickly I smooth the well-starched apron of my uniform and go to the window. There I clear my throat, get a hold of myself, and stare at the outline of forest lying behind the palace. Already darkness has fallen, but under the light of the moon and with my nose pressed to the windowpane I can make out the white birch trees that bend with the never-ending wind up here on the hill. Same with the sturdy walls of the guest house, and the stables adorned with a wagon wheel and weather vane. A foreign world, all of it, one I'm expected to call home at the drop of a hat.

A burst of high-pitched laughter pushes my nose from the window. Hyenas, I realize slowly—a pack of them, from somewhere inside those bending trees.

Sighing, I shift my vision so that I stare at my own reflection. A pale face surrounded by a halo of hair stares back at me. Dread turns down the corners of my mouth, but at the very least yesterday's bump has disappeared. And then I notice the reflection of a white object, coming from the other side of the room—the scroll. In all the upset of the morning, I'd placed it on the nightstand and had completely forgotten about it.

I sit on the edge of my bed, curious, and smooth it open. Two names are scratched across it, written in the same scraggly cursive as on the outside:

Timothee Allen and Jill Nightingale.

At the bottom, as if signed, is the word, *Glitch*.

I turn it over. Nothing. I study the writing; I run my finger over the creamy paper. What significance do these names have? And what's *Glitch*? Who's it from? Why is it addressed to *me*?

Glitch.

Could it have something to do with my Selection results? I drum my fingers. Probably not. Probably it has nothing to do with it, *of course* it doesn't. I need to rein in my excitement.

Glancing again at the clock, I place the scroll inside the desk drawer. Whatever it is, whoever it's from, it'll have to wait until later. I slip noiselessly from my room and head for the servants' stairs.

With one curiosity suspended, I stumble immediately on another: at the far end of the House of Mirrors stands Wolfe, and he isn't alone.

No, in front of him stands a young woman with black hair, a solid build, and calculating eyes framed in mascara. She wears a fuchsia dress with a short hemline, and a silk coat is draped fashionably over one arm. But what really draws my attention is the way she and Wolfe hold themselves, almost stiffly, speaking in hushed tones, gesturing to one another with a hint of temper. Just as earlier, I find myself invisible in my handmaid uniform, and I watch from the shadows.

Who is she? A friend? A relation? Neither option seems quite right...

Could it be *romance* in the air?

"Liar!" the girl suddenly shrieks, making me jump. It's enough to attract their attention, and when Wolfe catches sight of me watching from down the hall, his eyes narrow into razors. I hurry the rest of the way to the stairwell and out of sight.

Well. If it wasn't going to be an uncomfortable evening before, it definitely promises to be now. *Good work, Alex.*

Finding the dining hall, or *Carnegie Reserve* as the nameplate reads, takes little time, located as it is almost directly beneath my room. I stare at the sealed doors and the way they tremble. It's the sound coming from the other side—a chorus of men, their melody punctuated by shrieks of laughter, high-pitched chatter, and high-heels clicking against the floor. What I had envisioned in my head was an intimate family meal, and yet what awaits on the other side of the doors sounds like a party in full swing.

Perfect. I'll be invisible from start to finish.

I push open the door and stare at elaborate chandeliers swinging from the ceiling at varying heights, at dim bulbs numbered in the thousands that create an effect echoing the night sky. Beneath the chandeliers are an assortment of tables, dressed in silk, surrounded by chairs draped in yards of white tulle. In the corner is the chorus, now singing what sounds like profanity-laced gospel, and around the perimeter of the room where it's darkest stand a small army of servants.

In its middle, in a riot of color, are the vultures.

Effervescent and lively, all of them have a drink on the go, and they chat loudly to one another as they drift from one group to the next, heads thrown back in fits of laughter, snatching hors d'oeuvres from silver trays like piranhas. Dancers in gold undergarments twist between them, while a group of mimes fashion balloon animals.

For a while my mouth hangs open. Then, resisting the urge to walk very quickly and with determination in the opposite direction, I step inside the room with a plan to lurk unseen in the shadows. But at that moment Aubrey turns and tosses a shrimp tail at a passing servant, and she notices the newest addition to the room. She drops her glass of wine.

The room quiets at the sound of shattering glass, servants burst forward to tend to the mess, and all eyes turn to the source of the disruption. A moment later the room explodes in laughter. Even the mimes silently shake.

I'm too mortified to run, too mortified to do anything. My ears feel like they're on fire—

Then a hand clamps over my shoulder; it drags me backward, through the doors and into the gold-crusted hall. Wolfe stares down at me with a fiery expression. "What are you wearing?" he demands.

"My handmaid uniform."

He closes his eyes, as though I really tire him. "*Why* are you wearing it?"

"I was told the handmaid uniform had to be worn at all—"

"Go change this instant. You are attending as my fiancée." He glances witheringly at me. "*Try* to look the part." With that he strides inside Carnegie, leaving me to retrace my way slowly upstairs, the self-loathing becoming more pronounced with every step.

I feel like such an *idiot*.

Once I reach the second floor, though, I pause. Because all day the corridors expanded and contracted with sound and movement: royals and servants bustling here and there, music emanating from all corners, drilling from the top floor filling the silences with its hum. Now the corridors are still. Empty, and I feel a tingling across my scalp, like someone is watching me.

When I whirl around, I see it's just my reflection. I laugh uneasily.

Vaguely I think of the girl I spotted with Wolfe, but there's no trace of her, and even though I find a window looking down on Airo-Aurora, I can't locate the fuchsia dress anywhere on the front grounds. Finally, I go to my room to find something to wear in keeping with a royal meal.

Plenty of options hang in the closet, but as I pull each dress from its hanger, I see they're all too big. A gauzy crimped silver one with long sleeves and a jewel sewn into the collar looks to be the smallest, and so carefully I set it on the bed, splash cold water on my face, then get changed. I stare at the reflection in the mirror and frown. I look like a child dressed up in her grandmother's finest. I feel like it too—I'm a fish out of water here at Strath Glen. The effect is only highlighted once I pull on my boots stained with salt, my only footwear.

I shake my head.

Back downstairs the revelers have been seated. A small tide of laughter rolls through the room as I look for a seat, but to my relief Evie waves me to a table she shares with her brother. I walk quickly in her direction without looking at the others.

There, and as though it requires great effort, Wolfe lifts his dark eyes to mine. Quickly they return to the drink he holds, amber liquid that tilts methodically back and forth between long fingers. He says nothing.

"Did you hear the hyenas out back? And the beasts last night—did they keep you up? Don't you have proper shoes? Those boots really don't match that dress at all, did you know? Did you hurt your hand?" All of this comes tumbling from Evie's mouth in quick succession.

After helping myself to a glass of wine, I turn to my soon-to-be sister-in-law. She wears the same school uniform as the day before. "To answer your questions, yes, yes, no, yes, and yes."

For a moment, Evie frowns as though tallying up my answers, then she laughs gaily. "Your efficiency will please my brother!" She draws her arms away from the table as servants with heavy plates appear, and I do the same.

"You look pretty, miss," Rebecca says into my ear. "Though I really do prefer the black and white, aye." She smiles smugly as she delivers our meals, then disappears before I can say a word.

I stare after her. So…it was a trick. A mean one—one that makes me feel even more isolated than before. So much for making a friend.

Chewing on my lip, I consider the pink slice of meat sitting in a watery pool of blood in front of me. Minced vegetables surround it, and I begin with those, wishing for one of my aunt's rosemary chicken pies instead.

Wishing for a lot of things instead.

"Girl from Quire!" booms a loud voice. "You rascal! That stunt with the servant costume was just the ticket to turn minds from your little jaunt to the Mainframe." King squeezes me tightly around the shoulders, and I go still. "You've endeared yourself, I think. Oops—off to the loo," he adds, before disappearing out the door.

I touch my shoulders where he had gripped them. The interaction hadn't felt all that ominous. In fact, the man—the *ruler*—seemed almost…jovial. And yet I can't dismiss what happened yesterday, in his office—can I?

And then there's his words—are they true? Had Rebecca unwittingly done me a favor?

"The hyenas have cross-bred with the wolverines, did you know that?" Evie asks, drawing herself up with importance. "Isn't that right, brother?" Wolfe doesn't lift his head from the paper. "They're one of the new super-beasts of Airo-Aurora," she continues. "Completely fearless, or so he says." Her eyes sparkle with excitement.

"Super-beasts?"

"You're not familiar with them? I wasn't either until brother told me. It's because of the fence."

"Which fence is that?" I ask, spearing a pea. The

exchange with King has lifted my spirits a little, and I'm hungrier than before.

"The one surrounding the entire nation, of *course*."

"I've never heard of it," I admit.

"You're kidding! It's an awfully important security feature. Could you even imagine a country without? An open border, my!"

"Do our neighboring countries have fences around their borders, too? Harbor, and Myopia, and Mastif—"

"But of course! Or at least I think as much. You know as well as I do that our curriculum focuses itself right here on our shining nation-state. Anyhow, that fence, it means fewer mates for the beasts to choose from, and so that's why they've started to breed across species. Sad, isn't it?"

I finish chewing a bite of meat, and say, "They have the ability to choose in the first place. It's more than what's offered to Airo-Aurora's citizenry."

Wolfe lifts his nose from the newspaper and stares openly at me. Evie, meanwhile, sticks her fork in my direction. "I suppose I never thought of it that way—"

Wolfe clicks his tongue. "That's enough, Evie."

Silently he returns to his paper and his sister returns to her meal. I use the lull in the conversation to study the room. The choir has been replaced by a small orchestra playing pieces from the Baroque era, and the entertainment has vanished, though several balloon animals still hover near the ceiling. King, the Queen, and their tablemates lift goblets into the air as King delivers what appears to be a toast. His children sit at the next table over with the woman wearing the gold-chained dress. Their three engage in a lively drinking game. Other tables feature similar spirited banter and bottomless consumption. It's only our table, I realize, that's quiet.

"So, sister," begins Evie, as she fluffs her hair, "may I call you that? It isn't terribly premature, is it? Forget I asked—I like how it sounds too much to have it any other way. Back to order. Have you decided on a theme for the big day?"

"The big day?" I drop my fork at the question.

"Of course, the big day. Your *wedding* day."

At that word—*wedding*—I take an interest in my lap. Because a wedding with the man seated across from me is the last thing I want to discuss. The thought alone is enough to make me lose my appetite. But saying so would be downright dangerous with Wolfe seated so close, so all I say is, "I'm afraid I haven't given it much thought."

Evie snorts. "I know you haven't thought about a wedding with my delightful big brother here—that was rather obvious when you tried to get your results switched —" And at this she covers her mouth as she chuckles. "I don't blame you, frankly," she adds as she throws a pea from her plate in his direction. To his credit, he ignores her completely. "But before the Selection, I mean. You must have had some ideas for your dream day?"

"I guess I've never been the type to think about such things," I say tactfully. "Sorry," I add, seeing the look of disappointment cut across her face.

"No need to apologize. My Selection isn't for a year, but I already have my entire wedding planned out, right down to the napkins. Cloth, white, trimmed in the most delicate pink stitching. They'll match the peonies with precision."

"I'm sure it'll be beautiful."

"Now all I have to get sorted is the groom." At this I notice Wolfe lift his dark eyes. "If I could just find the perfect fellow, I could trick the system into matching us u—"

"Focus on your studies, Evie," Wolfe interrupts, his voice brusque. "Not *fellows*. Besides, the Mainframe can't be *tricked*, and if it could, it would rather defeat the purpose, wouldn't it?"

She rolls her eyes. "You're such a bore, brother!" Then

she turns to me and rests her chin on her hands coquettishly. "He won't even let me have a *smidge* of fun. Now, tell me all about yourself, won't you? That might be enough to get me started."

"Get you started?"

"I should say so. It's customary for the sister-in-law to have a large role in the planning process and besides, there's nothing I adore more than throwing a party. You should have seen the garden party I prepared for Mother in the warm months—over a dozen varieties of tea and almost a thousand butterflies brought in for effect. It really was mesmerizing, wasn't it, brother?"

True to form, he doesn't reply.

"So, sister," she continues, "to the subject of you at once. What type of things do you enjoy?"

I tick off my interests without lifting my head: "Playing piano. Flying helicopters. Reading books."

Loudly Wolfe sighs. Evie, meanwhile, coughs into her hand, a poor attempt to muffle her sniggers.

"Did I say something funny?" I ask.

"Only everything! What a strange bird you are, Alex of Quire. Quite unlike anyone I've ever met, and certainly unlike Wolfe's previous—"

"*Evie.*" His voice cuts like the blade of a knife. It stops her in her tracks.

"Sorry, big brother."

I stare between them. *What exactly was she about to say?* Stopped with such force—surely it was something worth hiding. Certainly unlike Wolfe's previous *wife*, maybe? Was that the woman I'd seen upstairs? But if so, how? Divorce isn't an option in Airo-Aurora, although naturally the rules might be different for the Rocksavage clan...

My chest swells at the thought. Because if Wolfe managed to end a previous marriage, he can do it again—and no doubt he will considering his distaste for me. I just need to be patient. With any luck, he'll find a way to call off the whole thing before vows are exchanged in the first place.

I picture myself returning to Quire before spring, and smile.

Evie clears her throat. "Perhaps a theme—"

"That's enough talk of the wedding," Wolfe interrupts. He pulls the newspaper back under his nose and begins to read.

"I was almost done, anyhow," Evie pouts. "Tell me then, sister, has life here at Strath Glen been quite to your liking?"

I think of the vultures, and the heads lining Bishop's Aisle, and the punishment from King, and I want to laugh at the question. That or cry.

"I'll take that as a no," Evie says breezily, before I can respond. "It's a charming old place, you'll come to see. I hope with all my heart that my future husband agrees to move here—I would suffer a complete bereavement if I were forced to leave. Could you imagine me anywhere else? Has my brother given you much work to do?"

I shake my head at the last question, then eye him. "Not yet."

At first, I think he hasn't heard a thing. But then he lifts his head and stares piercingly at me. "After you deliver my breakfast, your duties are complete."

Complete?

I sit straight, shocked. "But at the very least I'm supposed to clean your suite—"

"The butler can do it. I certainly don't need you wasting everyone's time when your help isn't needed in the first place."

"Brother!" Evie scoffs. "Even for you, that's rude."

"And while I'm on the subject," he continues, completely unperturbed by Evie's scolding. "Never again dress as a servant. I suppose I should have said something this afternoon when you were lurking around the offices."

So, he did notice. I really need to be careful with him. Even when he seems preoccupied, he's paying very close attention. "But I was told—"

"And *I* am telling you now."

At that moment a drove of servants descends on the room, clearing away dinner plates and positioning a tea service on each table. Rebecca fills three teacups with steaming hot tea.

I stare at the viscount. My duties are complete after the delivery of breakfast? The thought excites me, but it also fills me with dread. No polishing his shoes, no vacuuming up his crumbs...and yet, what to do with all that time? I'm not an idle personality, and my aunt and friends will be busy with jobs of their own—

Hot liquid soaks through the gray crimped dress, scalding my legs and prompting me to jump to my feet. I pull the fabric from scorched skin, swearing, as those from the nearest tables stare.

"Oops," says Rebecca dryly, scooping up the dropped teacup. "My deepest apologies, aye, miss."

"What terrible luck," Evie laments.

She has no idea.

ten

. . .

TIMOTHEE ALLEN. *Jill Nightingale. Timothee Allen. Jill Nightingale. Timothee Allen. Jill Nightingale.*
—*Glitch.*

That's what I think about as I search through the overflowing closet of my guest room. Not Aunt Jo, who had sent a very sweet message that morning wishing me the best. Not Rebecca, who had greeted me cheerily in the basement as I fetched the viscount's heavy breakfast tray. And definitely not Wolfe himself, who had seemingly vanished by the time I dragged his meal into the entrance hall of his chambers—the door to his private quarters partially open and the sound of a vacuum whirring from inside.

Instead of all that, it's that mysterious scroll that's on my mind...

Who's Timothee? Who's Jill? And most importantly... Glitch. It can't be a coincidence that I used that exact term following my Selection...can it? There has to be a connection. Maybe the sender of the scroll knows a glitch really did occur! Maybe Jill and Timothee are all that's needed to prove my case, to overturn my results—

False hopes, likely. I shake my head. I really shouldn't let myself get so excited.

I drop another cardigan, then rip the bandages off my hand and study knuckles stained a dark purple. Sore when pressed on, but moving my hand and clenching the fingers is nearly painless. No broken bones, then, but if I give King reason to lift that walking stick again, I might not be so lucky. Even the servants I need to be careful of—my injured legs are proof of that. And yet it's my back that gives me the most grief, and all from dragging Wolfe's heavy breakfast up three flights of stairs.

How the other servants do it on the regular, I don't know.

Suddenly I smile. Because at the very back corner of the closet, shielded by lace and taffeta, I spot clothes that actually suit me. The riding gear. Maybe it isn't the herringbone that I wore back in Quire, but the navy blazer is well cut, and the pants look a lot more comfortable than any silk gown. Even riding boots are included in the ensemble, ones that are supposed to fit small, and therefore fit me almost perfectly.

I change quickly, setting aside the chiffon dress and ivory cardigan I pulled on that morning, then stand in front of the full-length mirror hanging on the back of the closet door. The well-dressed girl staring back at me lifts an eyebrow, impressed. I may be out of place here at Strath Glen, but at least now I'll feel more like myself.

Next, I pull on a thick black cloak made of heavy wool. Floor-length and with a large hood, it'll be warmer than my uncle's stained coat. Because today I don't intend on staying palace bound. Instead, I plan on stretching my legs a little, exploring the grounds, especially the stables where Rebecca came across that strange scroll.

And with a bit of luck, I won't come across a single royal in the process.

But as soon as I step into the House of Mirrors, a silver walking stick taps me on the behind. I turn to see King standing there in the skin of a wolf, smiling so broadly I can make out each gleaming tooth. "My dear little Alex! Don't you look sharp all dressed for the cold. Might I ask where your duties whisk you?"

"I-I wished to explore the grounds of your beautiful palace, sir." Even though I don't perceive danger right now, I'm cautious...and for good reason. "Your nephew was kind enough not to saddle me with work, at least for today," I continue, trying my best to make a better impression than before, "so I thought I'd use the time to familiarize myself with my new, um...residence."

"A wise endeavor," he gushes. Then his gaze drops to the floor, lingering for a moment on my bruised hand. "I take it you're growing accustomed to your newfound position?"

"By the minute," I assure him.

"Such an agreeable little soul, you are. I wish I could pick you up by your cloak and stick you right here, in my pocket!" He slaps his breastbone. "I don't think it will take you very long to charm your way into everyone's graces, girl from Quire. Now, there's a record I'm in search of with a voice on it sent from the heavens. Ta!"

"Ta, King." I lean against the wall and exhale once I see his backside, even if the exchange was much friendlier than our first. Finally, I turn for the servants' stairs.

I pass no fewer than four servants on them, but none of them glance at me, and even my greetings go unreturned. I wonder if I've offended them, too, by trying to get my results switched.

Great. Not only will I never know love in these old walls, not only will I be without work...but I'll also be without friends.

"Wherever are you going, sister?" demands Evie. She wears her usual uniform and carries a stack of books in her arms. Next to her stands a woman with round eyeglasses and a severe look made worse by a well-fastened bun.

"For a walk, since your brother hasn't given me much work to do."

"In this frigid cold?"

"I'm well-dressed for it," I say, shifting the cloak to show her the riding pants and boots. "Besides, I'd like to look around the stables, and I'm sure it'll be warmer in there."

"Do you ride? It's far too cold for me to take a turn, but in the warmer months I care for it, absolutely! Do you fancy this weather, then?"

Do I *ride*? Dressed up in riding gear and off to the stables, it sure looks that way.

"Uh, well—no," I admit. "But I received a letter yesterday that came from the stables—have you ever heard of that happening before?"

"A letter from the stables, my! You really are a funny bird."

I take that as a no. With another thought, I ask, "Have you ever heard of Jill Nightingale or Timothee Allen?"

"Who?"

"Never mind. Please, what's the best way to reach the back yard?"

"The rear exit down that corridor there, through the golden arch, past the second statue on your right, but I presume it's locked. Probably my dearest big brother hasn't bothered to give you a key?"

James traipses by just then, whistling loudly. A trio of acrobats follow behind him doing cartwheels, forcing me to the edge of the hall where the smell of wood polish lingers. I look at Evie and shake my head.

"Your best bet, then, if you wish to step outside, are the front doors," she continues, not looking twice at the performers. "They're kept unlocked since they're guarded. Does that excite you? How are your legs? Are they badly burned? You missed quite a dessert last night. Pots de crème and palmier—my *favorite!* And the party that took place afterward must have been splendid—Aubrey and Morocco and a few of the others are still fast asleep, can you handle it? And here I am in the midst of a geometry lesson! How boorish and unfair," she pouts.

"You didn't stay for it?"

"Do you mean the party? Brother won't allow it," she laments with a scowl. "Every evening he sends me away just as things get interesting. He really is a terrible bore. All work and no play—I think it's dreadful."

The woman with the bun makes a show of checking her watch.

Evie exhales like a train whistle. "Oh, yes, Roberta, I'm coming, I'm coming. Can't I have a moment to myself? Well, sister, I suppose I must be off. Enjoy your freedom, you lucky rascal!"

Feeling not terribly lucky or free, I wave goodbye to Evie, then set off for the towering front doors. But when I'm close to the imperial stairs my ears pick up the sound of muffled thuds. For a second I think it's King's walking stick, and I'm about to turn in the opposite direction. But as a leg flies through the air, I realize it's the acrobats, tumbling down the staircase. I pause to watch them and immediately am caught around the waist.

I gasp as James pushes yellow hair from his face and flashes me a smile. "The escape attempt, the wardrobe malfunction, the scalding—so much drama surrounding such a minuscule girl. And here I thought you'd turn out to be a plain old Jane. Dare I ask what's in stock for us next?"

"With a bit of luck, nothing out of the ordinary," I admit as I pull myself free.

He scrutinizes me for a moment, then says without inflection, "You don't shy away from me."

My breath catches ever so slightly in my throat, and I feel uneasy, like when I'm talking to his father. "Should I?"

"Most do, girl from Quire. Do you know who I am?"

"The prince," I whisper.

"No. Not the *prince*." He says it dejectedly, then throws out his chest. "The Prince! At the very least you should curtsy."

I fumble my feet into position.

"No, don't. I think I find myself liking your lack of deference and decorum. It smells of spring. Don't tell a bird I said that." He starts up the stairs without another word and the acrobats fall into line behind him.

As I push through the palace doors, air catches in my chest and makes me cough like I have a lungful of icicles. Once I catch my breath, I stare down with wonder at Airo-Aurora, no longer worrying about James or King in the slightest.

Newly fallen snow blankets every turret and spire, every winding roadway and cobbled alley. It cascades down the side of the Bavarian Alp segment with grace. Even the chords of smoke that trill from the chimneys look like they're added by paintbrush. Its beauty is so overwhelming that for a moment I think maybe, just maybe, I can make peace with the results of my Selection; I can put my faith in the artificial intelligence that lays claim to all this.

A moment later I head down the steps. I take the roadway around the palace, past the underground parking garage and up a sharp slope to the rear. There I spot the stables and, on the far side of the property, the guest house where friends and relatives stay. Given last night's rumored debauchery, I wouldn't be surprised if most still slept soundly inside.

Horses bray softly to one another in the stables, completely uninterested in me nosing around them and through their quarters. I sigh. No scrolls. No clues. Nothing out of the ordinary. Empty-handed, I head outside and begin scouring the perimeter. Why would the scroll writer, the so-called *Glitch*, leave the note here, anyhow?

Maybe it was a servant. Access to the stables wouldn't be an issue. Poor penmanship might be expected since there doesn't seem to be much writing involved with our duties. And they would've heard about me running around the Mainframe blaming my results on a glitch. But why go to the trouble to hide such a harmless message in the first place?

Just who *are* Timothee Allen and Jill Nightingale?

Maybe Counterdown Abbey holds the answer. Maybe these individuals are well-known for something, something that could, somehow, prove helpful.

I think about how good it would feel to free myself from a future here, and all at once the palace shutters begin to rattle in the wind, and an assortment of weathervanes adorning the roofline screech like nails on a chalkboard. Shielding my eyes from a wave of blowing snow, I run toward the woods—

White birch crisscross like a shield around me as soon as I'm inside. *Pliable limbs,* I hear in the back of my head, *to survive the weight of snow.* A fact taught to me by my mother, a gardener for the city, years ago. Trying to ignore the rush of sadness that the thought brings, I pick up a fallen branch and snap off the twigs to make a walking stick.

I smile. Because here the wind whistles loudly through the trees, but it barely ruffles my hair. And with the palace out of sight, I feel cocooned in a world all my own. One of my choosing, this time.

Enjoying myself, I walk down a slope, and eventually the birch begins to thin, dense evergreen brush spring up to fill the space. Distantly I hear the sharp call of a crow, I even feel its watchful gaze.

It'll be okay, Alex, I tell myself—more determined than before to look on the bright side. After all, if I was working as a pianist, or pilot, or librarian right now, I wouldn't be able to enjoy such a beautiful walk through the woods.

A minute later I tighten my cloak as the cold becomes biting. It's darker now, too. Looking skyward, I see why: branches criss cross overhead, blocking out the sunlight.

Returning my gaze to the forest floor, I almost step on something—a pile of innards—and I let out a shriek. For a while I just stare at that neat arrangement of intestines, and a kidney, and God knows what else, and then I keep walking, more unsure than before.

Vaguely, the sensation I'm being watched by more than just the crow washes over me.

All of a sudden, twigs snap with a vengeance; the ground shudders.

A horse steps into view, and I jump so hard that I trip on a root and fall to the frozen ground. But the horse isn't nearly as startling as the man sitting on top of it.

The viscount.

He steers the beast close, so close that I have to draw in my legs to stop them from being stomped on. In one fluid motion he dismounts, and I notice the glint of a knife tucked into his waistband and the gun slung around his back. I see a collection of slaughtered rabbits hanging from the saddle, blood fresh and dripping. What I *don't* see is the look on his face until he stands directly over me.

His eyes are made alive by something unrecognizable.

"You stupid child," he seethes. "You stupid, idiotic *child*. Who was it? Who sent you in here?"

Any relief I felt at seeing a familiar face deep inside the woods, even one as contemptible as his, vanishes. "Nobody sent me," I say, then I lift my chin. "I wanted a walk, that's all."

He grabs a fistful of cloth from under my chin and hauls me to my feet, but he must spot the look that cuts across my face, because he lets go and his voice loses a bit of its edge. "Get on." He motions to the horse.

I let out a short laugh.

"Get on," he instructs again. The even and detached tone I've already come to associate with him has returned. That sliver of emotion, raw and menacing, has been pushed cleanly behind a curtain.

"No."

The viscount glares at me, then mounts the horse and does something unusual. He fits his fingers to his neck as though taking his pulse. Then he says through his teeth, "Fine. I'll follow behind you."

"Follow behind me?"

"Back to the palace."

"I don't need an escort."

"Yet you are getting one. Now."

Sighing, I pick up my stick and begin the return journey with the viscount on my heels, careful to avoid the pile of organs sitting nearby. "Let me guess," I begin, lifting my voice over the crunching of ice underfoot. "I'm not allowed to ask questions at Strath Glen, and I'm not allowed to leave it, either."

He scowls. "What you do during your free time is of no interest to me. As for these woods, only those with a death wish would venture in as you did."

I don't say so, but I'm surprised by his words. They're completely out of place with everything I know about the man, even the way he stares at me now, with nothing but disdain. "Because of beasts?"

"Of course, because of beasts," he snaps. "And with the current rate of crossbreeding they grow deadlier by the day. Even *Evie* knows better."

"And I'm supposed to believe that you care about my wellbeing?"

"I couldn't care less what you believe," he replies coolly.

"And I couldn't care less about you. I do, however, require that you never again step foot into these woods without an armed escort."

I snort. "Do you have any idea how ridiculous that sounds?"

He pulls at the reins. Eyes flash like metal, but for some reason I'm not as uneasy around him as I am with King, or James. "You have been warned before to hold your tongue. Your questions, too."

"But because of our different stations, it's fine for you to insult me. It's fine for you to suggest that I'm a mere *child*."

"I am not *suggesting* anything," he says pointedly.

Carefully I push the hood of my cloak down so that my words are crystal clear. "If you have an avenue, Viscount, to stop this marriage from happening, I beg you to use it swiftly."

Eyes narrow. "What makes you think I have an avenue?"

"Were you married before? Because it seems to me you might have been. You definitely don't look my age, and according to the paper you only underwent Selection for a spouse. Who was that girl I saw you with yesterday, before dinner? And don't tell me again to hold my questions—it won't work, no matter how many terrible punishments you and your uncle have in store for me."

From a distance hawks call to one another. Wolfe, meanwhile, appears to study me. "The girl with whom I spoke goes by the name Claudia Patel. She is the daughter of a well-established businessman in Airo-Aurora and someone who shared my company from time to time prior to the Selection. I refuse to answer any more questions on the topic."

"Then permit me from now on to ask questions on others."

He exhales noisily, then urges the horse forward. "What is it you wish to know?"

"Well, for starters," I say, as I hurry to keep up, "are you a hunter by trade?"

"I hunt mainly for sport," he replies dryly. "As I am not wasteful, I see to it that the kitchen staff make good use of the meat."

"So, what is it you do for a career?"

"Tend to Airo-Aurora's international economic concerns."

I lift an eyebrow. "You're familiar with the world at large?"

"Indeed."

"And what do your parents do?"

"My father's role is also international in focus, dealing with matters outside my own portfolio. My mother travels with him."

"And King?"

"He oversees the Mainframe, and the general security of our state."

"What about the others? The prince and princess?"

"James takes care of procedural matters affecting Airo-Aurora. He delegates responsibilities outside of the palace."

"And Aubrey?"

"One day, presumably, she will carry on the lineage, but for now she is content to send away her husband and engage in endless acts of triviality."

Carry on the lineage.

The phrase strikes so much fear into me that it distracts me from the news that the princess is married. Because it's without question that one day *I'll* be expected to fulfill that role. I will be expected to *carry on the lineage.* I glance at the viscount's stern profile and quickly he looks in the opposite direction. He, too, must be thinking about that dreaded expectation.

Perfect. We both find the idea detestable; ours will be a marriage by contract alone.

"And what do you expect me to do," I continue, "if you have no work to give me in my role as handmaid?"

"As I've already said, it doesn't concern me."

"You realize, I hope, that it wasn't my desire to serve in that capacity in the first place."

"Of course."

"And you realize I don't have any traits that would make me a decent servant or, for that matter, an ideal spouse to an aristocrat such as yourself?"

He glances coldly at me. Dappled light that streams through the treetops throws his antiquated features into relief. "Those are dangerous words. I have warned you before."

"Beasts I can understand being warned against. But words?" I eye him, but he's firm in his silence.

Once clear of the trees, he dismounts the horse and turns it in the direction of the stables. "And to respond to an earlier comment of yours," he calls over the wind. "I cannot stop this union any more than you can."

A stone sinks to the bottom of my stomach.

If that hope is gone, my only remaining one is that strange scroll, the one signed Glitch. Not great odds, and so outside the stables I grab him by the sleeve. "Sir, we're *completely* ill-suited to one another. You're not an idiot. Surely you don't believe this *union* was chosen by a properly functioning Mainframe."

He removes the slaughtered rabbits from the horse and lays them at my feet in the snow, as if he dares me to gaze at them. Next, he removes the saddle and tosses it to the ground. The movements make his face flush so that he looks ever so slightly alive and ever so slightly less the heartless aristocrat I recognize him to be. Finally, when there's nothing else for him to do but respond, he says, "My ancestors began the Selection. It is the sole reason for the success—"

"I know," I interrupt. I lift my chin so I can stare him straight in the eye. Treading lightly around him and the others is essential for my survival. But bowing to their every whim is not something I'll do. "I know all that. The success of Airo-Aurora. The errors that come with human choice. The same algorithm for every Selection. I know it all, but—"

"Then you know it unwise to question the Mainframe." He steps over the rabbits so we stand with only a foot of space between us and grabs my hand. He lifts it close to his face and examines my bruised knuckles. "You *should* know, that is," he says, as he drops it.

I shift my weight into my heels. Questioning the Mainframe resulted in my punishment, true. But who's Wolfe warning me from right now? Himself?

"Maybe it's unwise," I say, lifting my voice over the wind. "Maybe I should know better. But...I don't care. Whatever the price is for saying it, so be it, because I know that a properly functioning Mainframe wouldn't have placed me here. And if I'm wrong, then the system is more flawed than I ever imagined, so flawed that many others in Airo-Aurora probably feel like I do—duped out of a future to call my own. Now, as you so kindly alluded to in your chambers, I don't hold any sway. Being nothing more than a girl from Quire, my words will fall on deaf ears. You, Viscount, are in a different position. A future with me doesn't hold any appeal to you, I know that, and so please...*please* use your influence to intervene, not for my sake, but for your own."

"That was quite a speech," he indulges, with a tip of his head. "But alas, you are imbuing in me more significance than I have."

"False," I push. "Your father spends most of his time abroad. King's son has an empty portfolio, all work delegated to others who are more competent. Women in the palace are relegated to the making of babies. You are King's right-hand man; I'd stake my life on it."

Wolfe stares at me with more interest than any occasion before, and this fact alone speaks volumes. I'm right—I know it now without a doubt.

In a restrained voice barely audible over the wind, he murmurs, "To challenge the Mainframe would be to risk my position, and that is something I do not intend to do. I would sooner wed the likes of you, girl from Quire."

"Yet even with a position of power, you won't find happiness with a partner you hate by your side. Please reconsider."

"You have spoken your piece, Alex, and I have lent you my ear. The time has come for you to accept your Selection results and silence your grievances. If we must have this conversation again, you will have forced my hand."

Forced his hand? Before I can question him, a servant appears by his side to tend to the horse, and he turns for the rear of the palace. He shouts to me over the blowing wind: "Be mindful to stay far from the woods and take care not to bother me again—you've already prolonged my hunt longer than necessary."

———

MY LEGS BURN as I climb the front steps of Strath Glen. By the time I reach the top, my entire body groans from the effort needed to stay upright against the unimpeded wind.

The words of the viscount ring in my ears. He cannot—or will not—stop our union. He would rather wed the likes of me than see his position of power erode. It isn't, to say the least, the most romantic of tidings. And yet barring a miracle from that curious scroll, this is my future...whether I like it or not.

Usually, two greencoats flank the front doors of Strath Glen, but today, three stare at me. I greet the closest, a woman with a shaved head.

"Identification?"

"Identification?"

"Identification." She holds out a hand expectantly.

"But I don't have any, not on me. I-I live in there. Surely you saw me leave this morning?"

"What'd you say?" the woman hollers over the wind.

"I said, surely you saw me leave this morning!"

"Didn't see anything. I'm tied up training a new hire," she explains, nodding at the girl beside her who's roughly three times as wide as I am and at least a foot taller.

"I remember the cloak!" yells the other uniform, a man. "But can't say for certain—didn't catch her face."

"Not enough to grant entry, right there," the woman explains to the new hire. She turns to me. "What's your name, anyhow?"

"Alex. Alex of Quire. I'm...a new servant."

Eyebrows lift, then cinch. "Servants don't come and go out the main entrance. Don't wear clothes like that, either."

"Well, I'm going to marry one of the members of the royal family," I explain.

Now all three greencoats glare at me with suspicion, and I can't really blame them.

"Jill, I'm going to call Gerard—that's the head butler, see if he can confirm this girl's identity. You stay here with Stanley, man the entrance, and keep your eye on *Alex* here."

She disappears inside and I stare at Jill, suddenly with interest.

"What?" she asks.

"Did she say *Jill*?"

Thick red eyebrows narrow over a nose that looks as though it's been broken a few times before. "So?"

"Your last name isn't by any chance Nightingale, is it?"

More silence. Telling silence, and I can hardly believe my luck. The very person I was looking for in what promised to be a fruitless search, right here, in front of me! And yet there appears to be nothing out of the ordinary about this young woman, aside from her size. No telling claim to fame, nothing to explain why her name was sloppily scratched inside that scroll.

Instead of clearing up the mystery, it only seems to deepen it.

"How'd you know?" Jill asks. She spits, then shoves a large fist toward her nose. Otherwise she's still, like a block of stone.

"It's a long story—"

"This," interrupts the woman with the shaved head, as she returns to the landing with the butler trailing behind her, "is the one claiming to live on in. Does she ring a bell?"

Gerard nods, somewhat begrudgingly, then ushers me inside the palace. I wave goodbye to Jill and am immediately struck in the stomach by a series of hat boxes. They're carried by a band of haughty-looking and dazzlingly dressed women in violet.

"Watch your step! Don't crumple the peacock feathers on that girl! Matilda, did you remember the swatches?" The commentary comes from a woman standing head and shoulders above the others, one wearing a sky-blue fascinator adorned with electric pink feathers. "Open the doors! Lift my skirts! Block the wind—"

The rest of her sentence is lost to a shrill cry. I see her fascinator fly skyward.

"Who was that, sir?" I ask Gerard as the palace doors seal themselves shut.

"The princess's personal milliner and her team of assistants, of course."

"A personal milliner?"

"Have you no work to do, Miss Alex?"

I shake my head. "I think the viscount wants to keep me out of his hair completely."

Gerard goes still. "Perhaps," he says, after a while.

"Perhaps?"

The question earns me a disapproving look. "I get the sense you are digging for something, Miss Alex. The help doesn't gossip about the family it serves, by obvious necessity. Take care to remember that. With Sir Viscount Wolfe of Airo-Aurora, even more so."

Even more so? "Will you at least indulge me why that would be?"

"You do know the rank of your fiancé, do you not? He is an important man, through and through."

I nod, although I don't really believe him. Those here with power have cultivated it from the ground up, no matter their station—Monsieur Sawyer had said so himself. If the viscount's given special treatment by the servants, it's either because he's earned it, or because he frightens them. I have a feeling I know which one it is.

"I trust you've been finding your stay at Strath Glen satisfactory?" he asks as he shines the nearest Ming vase with a handkerchief pulled from his sleeve.

"Uh, yes," I say. "Although…"

"Yes, Miss Alex?"

"It's just that I don't seem to be too well-received by the other servants."

"Oh?"

"Would you know anything about that?"

He shakes his head.

"I take it you know what happened last night during dinner?"

"Nothing out of the ordinary, from what I heard," he mutters as he puts away the handkerchief and straightens his coattails.

A show of allegiance?

Just then, a clatter sounds from the far end of the hall. The breaking of porcelain, followed by several expletives. A small group of servants bend over something that has shattered across the floor.

I start toward them, but Gerard swishes his wrist. "Unnecessary," he calls.

"Excuse me?"

"Your portfolio extends only to the viscount, Miss Alex. You won't earn friends by stepping on the toes of others." With that he strides past me and disappears inside Devonshire Commons.

So I stand there, my snow-covered riding boots creating puddles on the glittering black floor. Sounds whisper from all corners of the palace—drilling from upstairs, chatter from Devonshire Commons, cackles of laughter from beneath my feet, the mutterings of servants and tinkling of porcelain pieces from up ahead—but it only makes me feel more alone, more alone.

Unwanted by everyone within these old walls, royals and servants alike. There's no sense in staying here. And I might not be able to spend my nights in Quire any longer, but there's nothing, I realize with a surge of excitement, stopping me from spending my days there. I turn happily on my heel.

eleven

. . .

IT HAD BEEN BEYOND COMPARE.

An afternoon passed in Quire, walking the snow-capped streets and visiting the shops and patisseries with my aunt, then sitting in front of the woodstove sampling an assortment of hand-baked pies whipped up for the occasion. I hadn't realized I was so ravenous until handed a fork, how deeply I missed what had become my home, and my aunt, for that matter, who had in the past three years become so much more.

But eventually it had come to an end. I hugged my aunt tight, thanked her for taking the afternoon off work, and took the bus back to Strath Glen with only just enough time to slip into my seat in Carnegie Reserve, hair disheveled, cheeks burnt pink from the persistent north wind.

Now I blink up at the staggering collection of chandeliers as Evie, dressed in a short black dress instead of her usual school uniform, pulls at my ponytail. Across from me sits Wolfe, crisply dressed in storm-gray, his elbows resting on the edge of the table, his gaze on the wall somewhere over my shoulder. His fingers once again wrap around a glass of amber-colored liquor; they rock it ever so slightly back and forth so that the ice chimes. He appears completely impervious to the party surrounding him.

Since dinner has yet to be served, aristocrats and the affluent mingle. They laugh loudly; they clink glasses before depositing goblets of wine down their throats. Groups swell as others vanish, and all against the backdrop of a melancholy melody performed by choir. The joviality of the room stands in contrast to their tune, an effect I find strange, and unsettling.

"Sister, may I attempt a French braid?"

I make myself comfortable by tucking one leg under the other before agreeing.

"See that boy over there?" Evie asks as she removes the elastic from my hair and busies herself at the crown. "Blond hair, blue eyes, fit—*very* fit."

Across the table, Wolfe's steely eyes narrow into slits. I twist my neck as best as I can with my hair being pulled at until I find a young man matching Evie's description. "Yes, I see him."

"Unbearably attractive, don't you find?"

"I suppose there's nothing about him that's offensive."

Evie's laugh sounds like the tinkling of china. "You strange bird! Tell me straight away if he looks at me, won't you? His name is Theodore from East Barrymore Estates and I really do find him dashing."

"But he seems interested in that redheaded girl he speaks to, don't you find?"

"It's a ruse, I'm sure of it. I caught him staring at me just as you entered. Tell me, won't you?"

I agree, even with my neck forced out of position. Because at least it's something to distract me from the viscount, someone who hasn't bothered to acknowledge me since I swept into the hall a few minutes ago. I'd hoped after our encounter in the woods this morning he'd be a little more familiar. After all, just because a life of intimacy isn't in the cards doesn't mean we can't be polite.

Just then the blond boy grabs a handful of chestnuts from a bowl and begins juggling them, causing the redheaded girl to clap. He grins, then out of the corner of his eye shoots a glance straight at Evie.

"He's looking!" I shout, genuinely surprised. "You were right," I add, glancing up at Evie. "It really is a ruse."

She sniggers into my hair, then shushes me. "You'll expose me! Have you no experience in the game of romance?"

I shake my head. "I didn't realize there was any game involved in the first place," I admit.

Evie gives me a sad little smile.

With nothing else to do but hold still, I straighten my silverware, wipe my jacket of pie crumbs, and peer around the room. The boy Theodore glances twice more in Evie's direction, something Wolfe no doubt notices by the way he glowers at him. King, meanwhile, stands next to his bust at the front of the hall. He uses his walking stick to spear a pastry passing by on a silver platter and his wife claps mindlessly at the stunt. On the other side of the room, Aubrey, in a gown of white feathers, does shots with an attractive young man whose hair is pulled back in a bun. She stares at him the way I imagine a cat stares at a mouse.

Several minutes later, James and a voluptuous woman approach our table. I recognize her as the one donning the dress of chains the day before, the one who found the sight of me in the tartan nightgown so amusing.

The prince's stomach grazes the viscount's shoulder and immediately Wolfe's features harden. His eyebrows arch with distaste, though James doesn't seem to notice. He merely motions to a servant for a refill of his aperitif and says loudly, "Father mentioned you've managed to tidy up that trade rift before the tariffs rolled in. Close one, that."

Wolfe leans back in his seat and crosses his arms over his chest. "Next time I won't be able to clean up such a mess. Take care not to play such games with foreign nation-states again."

James nudges the voluptuous woman, who strokes his arm. "Can't have a smidge of fun if his life depended on it, didn't I tell you? How was I to know that a game of strip poker would devolve into such an apoplectic mess?"

The look on Wolfe's face answers the question.

"Dearest," coos the woman. Her gown is cut unapologetically low, almost to her navel. "You must forgive the viscount for his morose ways. Think of the shock all of us endured when we learned his newly betrothed was such a far cry from the shiny new object we were all hoping for, and from such a sordid neighborhood to boot. He must be devastated beyond repair."

The words make my face flush. Above me Evie's hands pause, but quickly they resume their busywork. Wolfe, meanwhile, acknowledges me for the first time that evening with his gaze, one that is unnervingly stern. I blink, but already his gaze has returned to the far wall, looking bored.

Well, whatever it meant, I'd be stupid to think it came from a place of kindness. No, it wasn't intended to assure me...it was to warn me to keep my silence.

"Morocco," murmurs James as he places a hand over hers. "Your heart is too generous. My cousin has been this sullen for all of eternity, so much so that I'm afraid a shiny little plaything would have been altogether lost on him. It's the *rest* of us who must suffer."

Morocco considers his words as she fans herself. She inhales deeply from a vial clenched in her hand then turns to me with a crystalline sigh. "My name is Morocco Moody, of the great Moody clan, house of weaponry production for domestic use and exports. And you...you are the girl from Quire."

I stare at a black diamond affixed to the woman's incisor and bow my head. "From the house of mere mortals," I add.

Wolfe examines me darkly.

Morocco, meanwhile, looks put out by my little joke. "My prediction?" she begins, drawing herself upright. "You'll be picked to pieces before the marriage itself. Gobbled up and spit back out. Eaten alive and—ah, I see the bouillabaisse is being served."

"Let us dine!" exclaims James. He steers Morocco away from the table, but he watches me over his shoulder.

A shiny little plaything—is that what was said? What exactly *is* that? And if the viscount doesn't care for one, why should they? Then there's the dirty business of me being picked to pieces—

I shake my head. It's as though the entire palace lacks in morals, royals and servants alike. Backstabbing and betrayal are as commonplace as tiaras and bowties—not a lifestyle I'll ever get used to.

"Done!" shouts Evie. She takes a step back to admire her work, adjusting her own hair as she does. The choir chants softly in the background. "Braids suit you, did you know that? Has anyone ever told you that you have a bohemian look?"

I shake my head as thousands of bulbs overhead dim. A team of servants sweep through the room, leaving steaming soup bowls in their wake, and the choir files out of the hall as a string quartet takes their place. "Not that I can recall."

"Is it typically your style of dress, sister? You know, back in your hometown."

"If I'm being honest, I don't even know what a *bohemian* is," I admit.

Evie picks up her spoon and touches it to her nose. "Sister, might I ask what you wore back in Quire, when you were, er, playing piano, flying a helicopter, and—what was your third pursuit?"

"Reading."

"Ah, yes. *That*. Reading for pleasure—can't say it's my cup of tea." She checks on Theodore, who now sits beside the redhead, then returns her attention to me. "Go on. Tell me everything about your personal style—your manner of dress, your favorite shoes...it would help in the planning of your wedding, really it would."

"You don't have to put so much time into the planning. I know you have your studies—"

"You sound just like my brother! Cease and desist at once, sister. It's my pleasure. Besides, once my studies are finished and adulthood begins in earnest, this is exactly the type of pursuit I wish to have occupy my time. And there's no better place for a party than Strath Glen." She speaks this last sentence with absolute gravity.

"Okay, then," I agree. "I've never cared for dresses or skirts. Well-cut blazers and herringbone trousers are my favorite. But a fine wool vest—"

Evie snorts so loudly into her bouillabaisse that Wolfe sighs. Or maybe it's me that he finds so tiring. Yes, that'd make more sense. *Devastated beyond repair* was how Morocco of the great Moody clan had put it.

"And so the riding gear," continues Evie, gesturing to my outfit once she composes herself, "might I assume that was a deliberate decision?"

I shrug. "I'm more comfortable in this type of thing than in a gown."

"Will you at least wear a dress for your wedding, sister?"

I glance at Wolfe, disarmed to find him staring openly at me. "I—I don't expect to have much say in the matter," I finally admit. After all, I wasn't allowed a say in the groom.

Evie bows her head. "You really are accommodating. Because I don't see how menswear would work for a wedding, to be honest, not on the bride. And certainly, my family would never approve. But..." She clasps her hands together. "*But*—wouldn't a bohemian-themed wedding hit the proverbial nail on the head? Wouldn't it dazzle the eye? Wouldn't it suit that tiny figure and virtuous face?"

Wolfe lifts a spoonful of soup to his mouth and carries on as if he hadn't heard a thing.

"Flowers, lace, braids," Evie continues, counting each item on her fingertip. "Check, check, check. Sister—quick. What is your favorite color?"

"Brown."

For a moment Evie just stares at me. Next, she bursts into laughter. "Why, you must be absolutely ravenous for my brother, then, given his complexion!"

I blush, and Wolfe, usually immune to his sister's antics, glares at her with such intensity that her laughter is swallowed in one breath.

"My mother was a gardener for Quire," I explain. "Her fingers were always stained with earth. Even her fingernails were wedged with it. The color brown reminds me of her."

Evie glances down at her own perfectly manicured nails, painted rose-pink and affixed with crystals, and does her best under Wolfe's watchful gaze not to recoil. "She'll be at the wedding, I presume—"

"Her parents are dead," he interrupts. His voice is so crisp and detached he may as well be discussing trade disputes.

"More bouillabaisse, m'lady?" Rebecca stands next to me with a soup tureen, smiling sweetly.

"A gardener, a gardener," Evie murmurs, as she drums her fingers on the table. "Yes! It fits splendidly into a bohemian-style wedding, if you think about it. Do you see it, sister? Can you imagine the flowers? We'll even weave them through your hair, how's that? And what a way to honor your mother. Can you think of anything better? Tell me, is there a flower that the two of you particularly favored?"

After declining Rebecca's offer, I rub my head. These are

intimate details, not to be shared with just anyone. But Evie's intentions seem true, and Wolfe doesn't appear to be listening, anyhow. "Baby's breath."

"Baby's breath?"

I nod. Too often to count, my mother would bring a bouquet of the delicate white blooms home for me, having planted a little extra all over Quire for that very purpose.

"But that's perfect!" Evie gushes. "A timeless classic, and easy to incorporate into all manner of things, from the head-dress to the centerpieces. Any others?"

"Uh, well...tulips, especially the parrot variety. Actually, we had a plot of land devoted to them, to deliver to the hospital every spring."

"But whatever for?" Evie asks, puzzled. Wolfe, too, considers me from across the table.

"To pass out bouquets to the sick and injured," I explain, feeling the point really should be obvious. And yet both members of the Rocksavage clan look dumbstruck by the small act of goodwill.

"Your virtue knows no bounds," Evie finally gushes. "And your father, was he a gardener as well?"

"He was an engineer at the parts factory, down fifth."

"An engineer, *oh*. But did you have any hobbies in common? Did you like any of the same things?"

"He's the one who taught me to fly," I tell her, and then I push away my soup bowl. All this talk of my parents...

It's been one week since I last visited the memory bank at the Mainframe. One week and counting. Because going back doesn't hold much appeal, not now. Not since the Selection. Even thinking about them has been made more painful. Because surely if they were alive, they'd wonder what it is about their piano-playing, helicopter-flying, book-loving daughter that makes her a perfect fit at the unconscionable and Machiavellian palace, betrothed to the perennially icy viscount who she's expected to serve both personally and professionally.

Surely, *surely*, they'd wonder if they'd ever even known me at all.

I wonder it about myself from time to time.

"...don't think we can fit an engineering angle into a wedding," Evie is saying with that well-plucked brow scrunched together in thought. "Even the helicopter connection, fascinating as it may be, might be a stretch."

Across the table Wolfe drains his glass, then waves away a servant approaching from the shadows with a refill. Tonight, instead of reading the paper, his eyes carefully dissect the occupants of the room, and I wouldn't be surprised if despite his apparent disinterest he could rhyme off the name of every guest right down to their seat. The one place his gaze rarely extends to, is me.

"Are you wearing mascara right now, sister?"

I blink at her. "Mascara? Uh, no."

"Are you wearing any makeup whatsoever?"

I shake my head.

"You have very thick eyelashes, did you know that about yourself? I bet you didn't. I think you're going to be the most breathtaking bride in all of Airo-Aurora—I really do." She reaches her hand across the table and squeezes mine.

The touch catches me off-guard. The kind words, too. Because without me realizing it, Evie has quickly become the closest thing to a friend that I have around here.

Before I can reply, there's a commotion at the far table, the Queen having knocked over a bottle of wine. Servants rush to sop up the liquid as the lady of the palace smiles placidly. Out of the corner of his eye King watches her. Then, quick as an arrow, those beady eyes slide onto mine.

I return unsteadily to my barely touched bouillabaisse.

"Aunty really is clumsy lately, isn't she?" Evie says from behind her silver spoon.

Wolfe says nothing.

"She never used to be such a scatterbrain—"

"Evie," he begins quietly, but there's no need. Already she's distracted by Theodore offering his assistance.

Promptly she stands. "I'm going to make sure Aunty is unscathed. You two. Discuss your wedding, won't you?"

Wolfe stares after her, frowning.

As for the wedding, we don't say a word about it. It's much more palatable for me to pretend that it simply won't happen, and he must feel the same way, because when Evie returns a few minutes later he hisses, "Can't you give the wedding talk a rest?" Then he eyes her outfit. "And what is it that you're wearing? It's rather short, isn't it?"

I smile behind my napkin. I wouldn't have pegged the viscount as such a protective older brother, but there you go.

Evie, meanwhile, snorts. "You know how *dashing* I find Theodore, and it isn't every day he dines at Strath Glen. My Selection is now less than a year out so it's only prudent I start banking options."

"Banking options?"

"For the Mainframe to sift through, of course."

Wolfe glances coolly at me. "You will be paired with whomever the Mainframe sees fit, banked option or not."

I can't help it—I think of Patrick. A banked option of my own, I guess, although it never felt forced like that. It felt easy, and comfortable—everything I was looking for in life. Vaguely I wonder if Wolfe had any *banked options* before landing with me, an unmemorable girl from Quire.

"True," Evie's conceding, "but it doesn't hurt a fly to try. And often it does shake out that way, you know that as well as I. Think of Betty and John, Beatrice and Timothy, Bernadette and Elon! And for the record, big brother, in regard to my dress, I didn't see you complaining about Claudia's hemlines over the past year."

The statement is met with deafening silence. Then Wolfe

sets down his napkin. "Evie," he says in a level pitch. "That will be all for you this evening." His voice may not betray his anger, but I can sense it in the way he holds himself. "Off to your quarters, at once."

"Oh, no. I didn't mean to, brother."

Her reaction is more startling than her reference to Claudia, a woman that Wolfe obviously shared a romance with, and probably still does. The thought doesn't bother me at all. What *does* bother me is that if Wolfe can strike so much fear into his own sister, what will he be capable of with his unwanted fiancée?

"Right now, Evie."

"Please, brother. The main course hasn't even been served, and I really would like a chance to speak with Theodore—"

Wolfe pushes his chair back and prepares to stand, prompting Evie to jump to her feet. "You really are ghastly," she spits at him. "I *pity* your poor bride."

twelve

. . .

I CAN BARELY OPEN my eyes the next morning. I'm so groggy that moving is almost impossible, and a pounding headache quickly sets in. From someplace in the palace comes the sound of a broken violin, like nails on a chalkboard, and I pinch the bridge of my nose, wondering what's wrong with me.

I'm not sick...and last night after I returned to my room following dinner, Gerard had delivered tea around nine o'clock, the same as every evening. So, what caused such a deep sleep? What caused such a rough wakeup?

Then I groan, remembering Wolfe's breakfast tray that needs to be delivered. I swing my legs over the side of the bed, lost in a daze until my foot lands on something that doesn't belong. I bend over, more awake than before, and spot the discarded core of an apple.

I stare at it. I didn't eat an apple...I haven't brought a single food item into this room since I arrived.

A minute later I unlock my door, step into the corridor, one that feels even draftier than usual, and set the core on the tea service still positioned outside my room. With the sound of the violin screeching in my ears, I close the door firmly, deciding it must be a mix-up, a harmless one, and push the matter out of my head.

thirteen

. . .

"SPILL, GIRL. THE GOOD STUFF."

"I did," I say, over the screaming of a young child from the next room. I pull off my cloak and unbutton my blazer, then fold those items across my lap. Neither's necessary with the recent turn in the weather, one that's bronzed my complexion all the way to a healthy glow.

Agnes washes her hands of peanut butter and starts making a series of small buns through her hair, fastening each in place with a pin. "The kids pull it otherwise," she offers, by way of explanation. Then she sighs. "That creepy scroll is interesting, sure. But come on, Alex—I want to hear about your fiancé!"

"My fiancé?" I scratch my chin. "I barely know him."

"You've met him, though, haven't you?"

"I've *met* him. But only on a few—"

"Then dish. This is royalty we're talking about, and it's not every day somebody from Quire chats that up."

"Yes, sure...but first, Patrick. Have you heard anything?"

"Like?"

"Like who he wound up with?"

She shakes her head. "Haven't seen him, sorry."

I fan myself with a napkin and stare around the lunch-room. Red bins are stacked in every nook and cranny, with labels marking them as property of the Quire Nursery. A dozen baby bottles sit on a drying rack left in the sun, and boxes of diapers take up most of the legroom under the table. I tap my toe against one and fix my gaze on my friend. "You really want to hear about the *fiancé*? Fine. His name is Wolfe, he's impossibly tall, rude, and uncaring, he thinks I'm an idiotic child from a lowly neighborhood, and we can barely stand the sight of one another. That about sums him up."

She leans back in her chair and whistles. "You paint one hell of a picture," she says eventually. "Come on, it can't be that bad. And if he's not making you clean his shoes, he must *sort* of dig you, right?"

I shake my head. "He doesn't want me near him. *That's* the reason."

A new round of crying erupts from the other side of the wall and Agnes glances over her shoulder. "At least you don't have any work to do." She lowers her voice. "I'd trade with you in a second. This place is a grind."

"But it keeps you busy. And there's probably some satis-faction involved, isn't there?"

"We were talking about your viscount. Any jewels to show me?"

I roll my eyes. "Surely you're joking."

"Is he hot, at least?"

"Hot? You're not understanding. We *detest* one another. There'll never be any romance in our marriage, and so *hotness,* there or not, doesn't matter."

"Come off it."

"The palace doesn't seem to take marriage very seriously, anyway. Oh, and I think he already has a girlfriend—a woman named Claudia."

"He's two-timing you?"

I nod.

"Wow, girl. Bummer."

I just yawn in reply, the grogginess from the morning still lingering.

"I'll make coffee for both of us. These kids are cute, but man, they're exhausting. Loud, too. You still take cream?"

I have to lift my voice to be heard over the hammering of a toy. "Sugar, too, if you have any. How are things with Miller?"

Agnes goes still, but only for a second. Quickly she fills a dusty machine with beans. "He's picking me up from work this afternoon so we can go stationery shopping. Expect your invitation in the mail within the month."

Stationery shopping? I can't imagine Wolfe having the slightest interest in our wedding, not even in the larger details let alone *stationery*. Not that I can say anything. If it weren't for Evie planning the whole thing, there'd be nothing more than two people plainly dressed exchanging the sparest of vows sealed with a handshake.

"Yesterday," continues Agnes, as the machine sputters to life, "he made me a spaghetti dinner. The day before that he brought me roses."

"A true gentleman. And a smitten one."

Agnes presses her lips together and nods. She takes a sudden interest in a stain on her tank, one that looks a lot like sour milk.

"What is it?"

"What is what?"

"Miller. You don't care for him?"

"Are you crazy? He's who I wanted all along. Besides, I wouldn't be matched up with him if he wasn't perfect for me, *obviously*." She grins, then looks me up and down. "That's a fancy-ass outfit you have on, by the way. Is that compliments of the palace?"

"It's what aristocrats wear when they go horseback riding, apparently."

"So you've taken up a new hobby?"

"Very funny. It's either this or a gown."

The coffee maker announces itself over the shouts from the next room, and Agnes prepares our drinks. "You know, I bet you could melt your viscount's heart if you threw on something flirty."

"His heart is cut from stone, not ice."

"He can't be *that* bad."

"Worse. I'm telling you, we were put together because of a glitch at the Mainframe—not because we're suited for one another."

Agnes considers me for a moment from behind her mug of coffee. She taps her fingertips against the sides, and I notice the nails are bitten back to the quick. "Message received. So, back to this Jill chick from the scroll. What makes her so special?"

"I don't have a clue—we don't even have anything in common. She's a greencoat, she has the build of a fighter, and, well, the friendliness of the same."

"As opposed to your social prowess?"

"Very funny," I say again.

"Have you asked her about it?"

"Not yet. Whenever I see her, she's working."

"So ask her to lunch!"

"Maybe."

"And the other guy—Tony?"

"Timothee. I still haven't tracked him down. That was my goal this morning but, clearly, I wound up tracking you down instead."

"Always a good choice," and she winks. "Did you check the Selection Announcements in the paper? We've got the whole week over there if you want to take a look." She points at an overflowing recycling bin stuffed with newspapers and milk cartons. "You sure you don't want a biscuit?"

I wave away the offer. "Do you think Timothee's our age?"

She shrugs. "Why not? That's pretty much the only thing you and Jill have in common."

So setting my coffee aside, I grab the stack of newspapers, flipping each one open to the Announcements section, one usually dominated by birth proclamations and death notices. The past few days, however, it's swollen to accommodate three full pages, as beaming parents post bulletins about their children's shiny new careers and exciting engagements. Some even announce weddings, I notice, with dates and locations already decided on.

The whole thing causes a heaviness to sink over me. My name is nowhere to be found. My parents aren't around to share the news, and even if they were, I doubt my engagement to royalty could be officially announced, given the reclusive nature of the family. And besides, my *career* amounts to the barest of breakfast duties—not exactly something to brag about.

A minute later I choke on my own laughter. "Look at the happy couple!" I shout, waving the paper under my friend's nose.

Agnes rolls her eyes. "Miller's family put it in there, not mine." She snatches the paper out of my hand and studies the small snapshot of her and her fiancé against a backdrop of icicles. She scrunches the whole thing into a tight ball and throws it into the receptacle. "Timothee wasn't in there," she adds, as I stare at her.

The paper that I grab next goes into the receptacle as well, but the one after holds promise. "What'd you say his last name was?" Agnes asks.

"Allen. Timothee Allen."

She grins. "Am I a genius, or am I a genius? It's right

here—two announcements, back-to-back." She drains her coffee mug, then clears her throat. "'We are thrilled to announce that Timothee Jeremiah Allen has been assigned work at Hallah International as a Computer Programmer—a childhood dream come true. Go Timothee, Go!'" She pretends to gag. "Don't worry, the next one's less vomit-inducing: 'We are excited to announce the upcoming nuptials between our son Timothee Jeremiah Allen and his beautiful bride-to-be Alexis Erin Egelton, on the third Saturday of September. We wish a lifetime of love and happiness to the wonderful couple!'"

I take the paper. "I can't believe you found him," I say, eyeing her. "You might just be a genius after all."

"Was there ever any question?" She stretches her hands over her head and yawns. "And I thought Miller's family was bad."

"I'd take enthusiasm over what's waiting for me back at Strath Glen," I say with a sigh. "All of them hate me, even the servants."

Just then the door to the lunchroom flies open and a harried woman with a screaming baby in hand yells, "Break's over!"

Agnes places her head down on the table. "Coming," she whimpers. Then she pushes herself slowly upright as if resigned to her fate. "Come back when you can, if you don't mind the noise," she adds.

A moment later I see myself out, onto the Quire sidewalk, the sky overhead azure blue, the blinding sun forcing me to squint. I walk toward the bus stop feeling unsettled.

———————

BY THE TIME I make it across town, sweat curls the hairs framing my face. The cloak and blazer are still tucked under my arm, and the white shirt I wear sticks to me like skin.

Climbing the steps to the palace only makes it worse. "A nice break from the snow and wind," I say between breaths, once I make it to the top. "If not a bit too warm."

"Least you can take your jacket off," Jill grunts, and I notice that she looks just as bothered by the heat as me. The sleeves of her olive-green jacket are pushed back to the elbows and she's red all over.

"Do they let you have water, at least?"

"One of the servants brings us some snacks and stuff."

"Speaking of...refreshments," I begin carefully, clearing my throat. "I'd like to steal you at your next lunch break. Please."

"For what?"

"Uh—well, to explain to you how I came to know your name, for starters."

She crushes a fly against her forearm, then spits out of the corner of her mouth. "Yeah? You supplying lunch?"

I hesitate. Supplying lunch means stealing a few things from the kitchen, and I'm already unpopular enough with the servants. But with no other choice, I agree.

"Where're we headed?"

"Hallah. It's not a far walk. I promise to explain it all once we track down Timothee."

"Who?"

"Timothee Allen. I take it you don't know him?"

She shakes her head.

And then, before I can say anything more, goose bumps slip over my sunburnt skin. My throat goes dry.

It's the distinct sensation that I'm being watched...

Yet the other greencoat on duty picks his thumbnail. Looking down the steps and over the grounds, I see they're empty—only a stray cat weaving in and out of the well-manicured bushes. And the roaring avenues of Airo-Aurora are too far removed to attract a single eye.

Then I notice it. Far balcony, top floor. A crown glinting

fiercely under the afternoon sun. Slowly the scent of cigar smoke reaches me, and despite the sweat clinging to my back and the burn on my neck, I shiver.

Jill claps her hands together an inch from my nose. "Hell-o?"

I force the saliva building in my mouth down to my stomach and stand up straighter. "Yes—hi. So? Will you accompany me during your next lunch break? I promise I won't bite."

"*Fine.* I have the weekend off. Let's say Monday."

Resisting the urge to hug her, I thank her, then head inside. After the bright sunlight and its pulsating warmth, the corridors of Strath Glen feel cold and exceptionally dark. I step quickly along the black polished floor, but I pause at a burst of laughter from Devonshire Commons. Peering inside, I see Aubrey dancing to a violin concerto with smelling salts in one hand and a drink in the other. A well-dressed man watches from his knees with a tie wedged between his teeth.

"Miss Alex." The old butler speaks straight into my ear.

I almost knock over a vase.

"Do I frighten you?"

"Of course not," I whisper.

"His Majesty wishes to see you."

I go still. "His Majesty?"

"Indeed. The King."

"But...why?"

"It isn't my job to know." Then he sets off along the corridor, completely unperturbed by the princess and the man she holds hostage in the Commons. "One mustn't keep his Majesty waiting," he reminds me over his shoulder.

I set off behind him feeling unwell.

What does King want with me now?

As we reach the imperial staircase, I see the Queen descending with a candelabra in hand, her movements as smooth as silk, her smile unwavering. But despite my raised hand, she doesn't seem to notice me or the butler.

Up and up, we climb, and I feel more nervous with every step. Then a group of young women wearing matching midnight-black corsets and fishnet stockings spill onto the staircase, and I need to press myself against the wall to let them pass. At the same time a gust of wind whips through the stairs, whistling so loudly it drowns out their chatter. I stare after them, but Gerard registers no reaction whatsoever. Silently he pushes on, leading me through a dead-empty Bishop's Aisle, past floating head after floating head, all the way to King's office.

For a moment I think about running, but then, with a rush of relief, I see that he isn't alone: James and Wolfe sit across from him with files spread along the desk. So, I've been beckoned during a work meeting. The question of why lingers loudly in my mind.

Only after I'm shuffled forward and around several coffee tables does Wolfe lift his head. I see then the truth—that he wasn't aware of my summons. "What's this?" he demands. His gaze shifts to his uncle.

"Is that my dearest little Alex gracing us?" booms King, and I notice that both of his eyes are sealed shut. James looks faintly amused, Wolfe scowls.

After a moment of silence, the butler nudges me in the ribs.

"Uh, yes. King."

"Good, good. Do come, child. Come now, right on over—my eyesight has failed me today, I'm afraid."

I walk past the prince who plays tic tac toe in the margins of his notebook. Wolfe, meanwhile, seems to refocus himself on his work. He passes James a sheet with numbers scrawled across it. "Is this the current health of the treasury float?" he asks.

James glances at the figures and shrugs. "Haven't got the foggiest. Ask my assistant."

"You're right here," Wolfe replies tersely. "Have you not a clue as to the state of the city's finances?"

I inch around the mammoth desk, carefully discarding onto the floor the blazer and cloak from under my arm, finally coming to a standstill with three feet separating me from the King of Airo-Aurora. "Yes?" I say, in a voice so quiet my own ears can barely decipher it.

King smiles broadly. He places his cigar down and swivels his chair around with his eyes still shut. He beckons me closer, and I can feel Wolfe watching out of the corner of his eye as I inch forward. James pulls from his pocket a box of candy.

Finally, when I'm within reach, King opens his eyes, grabs me around the waist and forces me onto his lap.

"We have pressing financial matters to discuss, Uncle," Wolfe says in a low undertone. "Plus a decision concerning beef imports from Egeltonia. Are these constant interruptions necessary?"

Vaguely I think of the corseted women on the stairs.

"Since when is a fiancée an interruption? You should be rejoicing having your little vixen drop in on your day!"

At the word *vixen* James chokes on a gumball.

"Alex, my dearest," King says, snuggling me like I'm a doll, "I couldn't help but notice just now your arrival at Strath Glen, and in the middle of the day to boot. Was it official palace business that occupied you?"

"I told her to take the day for herself," Wolfe interjects as he flips through a thick file on the desk. I stare at him. He doesn't bother to lift his gaze; instead he studies what appears to be a series of graphs. Like always, he shows me no interest whatsoever. Yet he just lied on my behalf.

"Don't you worry what your little one might get up to without your supervision, my boy?"

Wolfe lifts his dark eyes briefly to his uncle. "No."

Softly King clicks his tongue. "Nephew, you are invaluable to this beautiful nation-state of ours, beyond compare, and yet you can't neglect what will soon be your loving wife. Turn your back just once and already she'll be cocooned in another man's arms."

Growing more uncomfortable by the second, I struggle to free myself from King's lap.

"Be still, my dearest," he coos. "King is kind, King is kind. Now, since my nephew here won't say it, I will. No more are you to wander off on your own into the city—a man must watch out for his woman, do you see? And your noble viscount can only do that if you are safe within the confines of Strath Glen and its beautiful grounds."

I'd been writing against King's shackles, but now I go slack. Because I see, alright. He'll keep me prisoner of the palace just as fiercely as he keeps me tethered to his lap right now, and fight as I might there's nothing I can do about it.

I'd prefer the clap of the walking stick.

Wolfe buries himself deeper into his work, now seemingly determined to ignore the entire situation. James, on the other hand, applauds his father. "Well said, Papa. I wouldn't dare let Morocco get too far out of sight. But of course—with a body like hers I've far more to fear than my dear cousin has."

"It is rather frightful," Wolfe says placidly from behind his papers. "As for restricting this girl's activities, Uncle—do as you will. Keep in mind, however, that she is nothing more than a stupid child, unworthy, I would think, of your brother."

I stare at him. The words are biting. And yet...were they said with the intention to help? Before I can sort it out, King propels me from his lap. He grabs me by the hips and whirls me around, then stares up at me from beneath his crown of jewels. "I don't find her stupid in the slightest." For once I don't find him play-acting or pretending. Those words are spoken in earnest.

Wolfe merely returns to his notes.

"Did you insult my Morocco, just now?" James insists.

"I don't recall," Wolfe replies lazily. "Did I?"

"My new cigars," King commands to the butler.

"I should hope not," James continues, "as I've rather bit my tongue about your bad luck up until now."

"Bite it or don't, it makes no difference to me."

Over their bickering, I look at the door. Nobody looks my way. So I shuffle sideways, doing my best to fade into the shadows, because what I need right now—is to leave. Get away from King. Figure out a way from under these new restrictions.

But just then James turns, he stares at me, assessing me from top to bottom as though I'm a statue constructed for his gaze. "Too slight for a proper dress, aren't you?"

I say nothing. Each conversation with the prince feels like a one-eighty from the last. Every encounter is a new one. No evolution, no way to predict what might come next.

"Cat got your tongue?"

"Maybe I am too slight, sir," I agree, stepping out of Gerard's path as he passes a wooden box to King.

"Splendid!" King cheers, as he slides a cigar under his nose.

"You've nothing to fear from me," James continues, and he reaches out and squeezes my little finger. "That said, I'd sooner die if my wife presented herself to the world as you do."

"You're wasting your energy," Wolfe mumbles from beside him. He pulls a red pen from inside his jacket and circles various figures on the page in front of him.

"I detect a note of citrus," King exclaims. He passes the cigar back and forth under his nose like a saw. "And could that be cocoa?"

"I really should be going." I bend down and scoop up my blazer and cloak.

"Do you even ride?" he asks, as he eyes my outfit. "I can't imagine many from whichever derelict district you're from do, no offense."

"What's that, now?" calls King. He places the cigar back inside its box and retrieves the one at the edge of the desk that sends an endless cord of smoke to the ceiling. The air in the large office grows thick and more unbearable by the second.

"Her riding outfit," James says. "She fancies herself an equestrian."

That Cheshire grin spreads across King's face, it puckers his eyes. "Might I suggest, my dearest Alex, that you try one of the paths through the birch forest out back? It really is beautiful out there."

Two reactions play out to these words, both of which spare me from replying. The first is that Wolfe goes rigid; the color drains quickly from his face. The second is James's sharp howl of laughter.

"How silly of me, how silly of me," King wheezes, as Wolfe draws his long body to standing. "It was thoughtless, my boy."

Slowly Wolfe rounds on his cousin, who continues to snicker. "You think it funny?" His voice is detached and even, but something in his tone gives me pause. It must give James pause, too, because his laughter turns into a poorly disguised cough.

The atmosphere in the large office grows strained.

I edge closer to the door, more desperate than ever to escape. But there's one thing I'm certain of as I take my exit: I've never seen Wolfe so furious.

fourteen

. . .

I LEAD Jill through busy streets. A paper bag weighed
down with food snuck from the kitchen is tucked under my
arm, and the rest of my body is held against gusts of wind
that try to toss me into the path of oncoming traffic. The
balmy weather of the weekend is already a distant memory.

Not that I was able to enjoy much of it. Twice I walked
the perimeter of the grounds of Strath Glen, but that quickly
lost its appeal, especially after coming across paw prints
near the woods the size of my head, along with a severed leg
once belonging to a fox, and a duck still clinging to life
despite a large piece of its belly missing.

And wandering farther into Airo-Aurora would be
idiotic after King's warning. The only reason I decided to
risk today's outing is my own curiosity concerning that
scroll, and King's absence from the palace.

As far as I know, he's currently at a billiard tournament
at the estate of a wealthy pharma-tycoon, a detail I'd learned
when a pool table was brought into Carnegie Reserve so
King could practice between bites of steak tartare.

Of course, if James notices I'm gone, I'll be in trouble,
because no doubt he'll pass along the message. Good thing

he seems to notice little of the comings and goings around him. Wolfe, on the other hand, is a different matter. In fact, I'm confident that he could easily keep on top of my whereabouts if he desired. Whether or not he'd pass along the message to King, I don't know.

I tried to speak with him about the whole predicament over the weekend, but he hadn't been at dinner, and his mood seemed stormier than usual when I'd spotted him in the House of Mirrors. Once, when I found a piano in what appeared to be a sunroom and with nothing else to do, I'd begun to play a piece by Chopin only to have Wolfe himself walk in halfway through. Despite calling his name, he had quickly removed himself from the room.

"Oi! How much farther?" Jill shouts.

"Not very," I reply, and a block later our footsteps slow. For a minute we just stare at the brown cube with a small sign identifying it as Hallah, then I pull open the door. Inside are a sea of cubicles, along with a ping-pong table stacked with boxes, a modern eatery, and a series of low-slung leather couches. None of the employees lift their gaze.

"I'm not actually sure what Timothee looks like," I whisper to Jill.

She rolls her eyes, then hollers Timothee's name.

A thin boy with jet-black hair and milky skin sits straighter. He stares at us from behind a computer screen. A few other techs glance up with interest but return almost immediately to their work. Finally, Timothee Allen rises from his chair, serenaded by clicking keys.

"Who're you?" he asks. The question doesn't seem to be spoken with hostility or friendliness.

"This is Jill, and I'm Alex. I was, well…I was hoping to steal you for a few minutes."

"Steal me?"

"Just for a word. It shouldn't take long. Do you have a lunch break?"

He checks his watch and nods.

"Maybe we could sit on the front step? I brought food," I add, lifting the bag.

"Too windy," he says, shaking his head. "Right here." He points to the couches.

"Are you sure?" I ask, staring around at the others.

"They won't mind. Programming requires intelligence. Intelligence requires focus."

So Jill and I follow him to the nearest couch. I spread the contents of the paper bag on the coffee table positioned in front of it, then sit back as my guests help themselves.

"You're a greencoat," Timothee says as he and Jill butter croissants. He drops his knife to the floor and knocks over his juice box with his elbow as he grabs it.

"What's your first clue?" She glances down at her olive uniform, then nods at me. "You going to dish what all this is about? 'Cause my break doesn't last all day, and Strath Glen's not next door."

"Is that what you're guarding?" he asks, sounding impressed. He picks up a pear and uses his black and white striped T-shirt to clean it.

"Sometimes I'll do rotations at the Mainframe or the Sky Center. Most of the time you can find me at the front doors of the palace."

"Cool. You meet any royals yet?"

"Just this one," she says from the corner of her mouth.

Timothee fumbles the pear. "*You're* royalty?"

"Not by blood," I admit. "And not until the engagement period is over."

"So you just underwent Selection, I take it."

"And even though we have *nothing* in common, I've been betrothed to a viscount. I work for him, too," I add. "As his handmaid."

"He can't give you much work," Jill says. "You come and go more than anyone, at least through the front doors."

"Not any longer," I say, sighing. "According to the King of Airo-Aurora himself, I'm not allowed to leave palace grounds."

"You're off palace grounds right now," Timothee points out.

"The King's away for the day," Jill says. "That's why, right?"

I nod. Around us the incessant clicking of keys ramps up enough that I need to lift my voice: "Do you know his calendar?"

"All the guards do. For security reasons. I can let you know next time he takes off, if you want."

"You'd do that?"

She shrugs. "I'm always for helping people break the rules, especially stupid ones like that. What'd you do, anyway?"

"I made the mistake of visiting the Mainframe the day after the Selection. A really short-sighted, misguided attempt to have my results switched. King took it to heart, and he's hated me ever since." I drum my fingers against my knee. "All of them hate me, actually. As you can see, royal material I'm not."

Jill snorts with laughter, and soon Timothee and I join in.

"Hold up," he says, eventually. "You still haven't explained what you're both doing here, with me."

I wait for a girl with a pixie cut to get a bottle of soda from the fridge. Then I pull the scroll out of my pocket. I pass it around and watch their expressions as they see their own names scratched in near-indecipherable cursive. Both of them frown, looking as confused by it as me.

"Someone left it in the stables behind the palace," I explain. "A servant found it and passed it along. I don't know what it means, but I'd like to, and I figured at the very least I should track down the two of you."

"Sounds like a logical first step. So, how'd you find me?"

His face flushes. "Not my parents' bloody Selection Announcement."

"Yes, that," I say, smiling.

He groans. "They are such dorks. Lexie is so embarrassed."

"Your bride-to-be? I'm curious, does she seem like a good match?"

"I was skeptical going in, especially after what happened to my brother, but she seems like a nice girl. Works just down the road doing human resources for Richler's. Likes video games and that sort of thing, same as me."

"So clearly we're not linked by dissatisfaction with our spousal selections."

"Meaning what? You don't like your viscount?"

"It's not a match made in heaven," I admit. "And your fiancé," I continue, turning to Jill. "Is he a good match?"

"He's just like me, but a dude. So yeah, I'd say so."

Timothee kicks Jill's steel-toed boot with his sneaker. "You're succinct. I like it."

"Cheers. So, what happened to your brother?" She helps herself to another croissant and leans back on the couch.

I open a packet of saltines and watch as Timothee's mouth tightens. For a moment I think he'll sidestep the question completely. But after running a hand through his hair, he says, "He was matched up with a nasty girl. Quite a shock to him and his longtime girlfriend. The pair of them were heartbroken. A year later he offed himself."

I almost choke on my cracker.

"No wonder you were skeptical about the whole thing," Jill says. "Sorry."

"That's the official version, anyhow. Suicide. I know he was miserable, but you won't convince me of it."

"Did the blackcoats investigate?"

"They took over from the bluecoats, who must've had a

file on him as thick as my fist. Suicide was their theory from the get-go. Confirmed it to us the day after. Not sure how hard they worked, but tough to blame them. Shitty job, that. Best you got slotted into the guard division." He taps the rolled-up scroll against Jill's leg, then hands it back to me. "Can't help you with it," he adds.

"Any theories?" Jill asks.

I shake my head. "Especially not after learning the two of you've been matched up with perfect spouses and jobs."

"So you think it's related to the Selection, I take it?"

"Well, afterward, at the Mainframe, I kept saying there was a glitch in the system, using that exact term—"

"The same as on the scroll."

"Sorry to dash your hopes of said *glitch*," interrupts Timothee, "but the same algorithm is used for every Selection. It doesn't make sense that yours would be a mistake."

"So I've been told."

Jill places her combat boots on the coffee table and stares at him. "You're a computer nerd. Hack into the Mainframe and change her results."

"If only it were that easy."

"Is it possible?" I ask. My body straightens, and the racket from around the room disappears like it's been sucked into a black hole.

Quickly he crushes my excitement: "The techs at the Mainframe know their stuff. And since a virus introduced to the system could dismantle the whole thing, they've got more firewalls up and anti-malware programs running right this instant than Hallah will have during its entire life cycle as a business."

"So I'm stuck with my viscount."

"You're stuck with your viscount."

The sound of the clicking keys returns like a freight train. I rub my head. These aren't the words I'd like to hear. Worse yet is the fact that the three of us were brought together for a reason that appears unrelated to the Selection. And if the scroll has no bearing on that, my last hope for escaping a future at Strath Glen is gone.

Jill checks her watch. "I need to head back," she says, angling its face toward me. "Weird place," she adds to Timothee, nodding at the sea of workers who don't bother us with a single glance. "You programmers half-robots or something?"

He grins. "We're not, but we're probably the closest thing there is. Trust me, once you get into the coding zone you're hooked."

Jill coughs into her fist, and it sounds suspiciously like *nerd*.

"If you figure out that scroll," says Timothee, kicking my riding boot, "you know where to find me. Count me enthralled."

"Same," admits Jill.

And despite my disappointment, I smile. Because maybe in finding Jill and Timothee I've gained something just as valuable as the answer to that strange scroll...

Friends.

fifteen

. . .

I STAND IN THE WOODS, trees bent at odd angles around me, raindrops falling on my cheek. They taste salty like tears. But that isn't what causes the furious ticking of my pulse. No. It's the beast that does it.

It circles me, just beyond the shadows. I can feel it, I can sense the danger, but I cannot run. The Duchess of Airo-Aurora speaks in my ear. "He will worry over you." The words echo through the woods like thunder. When I turn my head, there is nothing but a cool breeze that caresses my neck.

Now Wolfe stands in front of me. He doesn't move that sullen mouth, yet I can hear his icy voice with precision. "You gave me your word." His face is impassive, but he strikes me with enough force that I land on the forest floor. Scrolls fan out from under me like a bed of leaves.

The beast, meanwhile, draws closer, its circle tightening with every step. I spot it through the trees—towering and vicious. I scream for Wolfe, but his retreating back doesn't slow. He is completely engrossed with the petite young woman on his arm.

I blink and the beast is on top of me. It has me by the

throat, and the blood that drips from between its fangs matches the crown of rubies on its head—

My eyes snap open, my breathing shallow and quick, and despite the way the temperature plunges in the palace every night I push off the covers. *Just a dream.* It was just a dream. No need to analyze it. No need to concern myself over those fangs, that crown.

I turn on the lamp and check the time. Not even midnight. Below, from Carnegie Reserve, comes sounds of revelry: laughter and the clinking of glasses, and it drowns out the noisy thumping of my heart.

It's because I've been stuck inside, going crazy from being so confined. That's what caused the dream, probably.

After all, several days have passed since my lunch with Jill and Timothee, an outing I escaped without consequence, and almost a week since King imposed the restrictions on my ability to come and go.

Too long, way too long.

And yet I've seen very little of the viscount. Normally it wouldn't bother me, but seeing as how King hasn't budged from the top floor since the billiard's tournament, my need to speak with him about the predicament has grown more urgent.

I tap a finger against my lip. Now might be just the time to do it. Too bothered by my dream to return to sleep, I need something to do. And it's unlikely, knowing what little I know of him, that he'd still be downstairs with the revelers. I doubt too, given his work habits, that he's already asleep.

I sigh. Going to his private quarters doesn't hold much appeal...but maybe it's the only way to finally corner him on the subject.

I slip out of bed and into the House of Mirrors. The checkerboard tiles are so cold underfoot that it pushes all thoughts of that dream from mind—perfect. I walk faster. My fingers drag along the wall, forever attempting to uncover the source of that relentless draft. Down the hall and near to his quarters, my footsteps slow.

There's a girl inside. A very upset one. Her words are indecipherable to me, but Wolfe must make sense of them, because I hear his deep voice mutter something between her muffled cries. Suddenly the doors swing open, and two figures push into the black and white hall. The girl throws her arms around Wolfe's waist.

Claudia.

He allows the embrace, but only for a moment. Swiftly he frees himself, and the look on his face is more startling than anything else. Completely impassive, just like the face in my dreams. He doesn't care about Claudia—he cares about nobody aside from himself.

She's the first to notice me.

Mascara-stained eyes narrow. They take in every detail of my cotton nightgown several times too big, my thick hair rumpled from sleep, my skin flushed from a nightmare. A look of anger pushes away turmoil and her mouth contorts.

Wolfe's mouth, meanwhile, presses into a hard line.

She draws herself to her full height, somewhere above my head, smooths her sequined dress, and tosses glossy locks behind her shoulder. "*You*," she hurls at me. "You're the girl from Quire, aren't you? The *fiancée*." Then without warning she shoves me to the checkerboard floor.

The impact is stunning. And it definitely doesn't help my sore back.

"Claudia," comes Wolfe's voice, muttered as a warning.

She rounds on him. "Fix this, Viscount," she says, and there're claws in her voice, though they don't seem to have any impact on the man before her. "Use your influence. Speak with the King. *Fix* this." A moment later she disappears through the House of Mirrors, the scent of perfume lingering behind her. Sharp, almost spicy, and I wrinkle my nose.

"You do have a knack for impeccably bad timing," Wolfe says. He stares down at me with arms crossed, and his stern profile is echoed throughout the corridor in its many reflective surfaces.

"I'm sorry," I say, as I stand. "I didn't realize I had to plan my visits around your *girlfriend*."

We stare at each other, and he's the first to look away. After a long hesitation, he ushers me through the open door, into the entrance hall where I prepare to make my case. But he walks past me and pushes open the door to his private chambers, standing aside for me to enter.

I go still. It isn't that I fear for my safety, tucked out of sight. It's that the invitation into this private portion of his life marks a subtle yet definitive shift in our frosty relationship...

Doesn't it?

I edge by him and through the door.

The room's vast size is the first thing that strikes me. Every surface is lacquered with a glossy navy blue, and a giant hearth framed in stone houses a roaring fire, the only light source. The effect is both sinister and strangely alluring. The bed, tucked along the far wall and enveloped mostly in darkness, is twice as wide as my own and outfitted in crisp linens, impeccably dressed.

So, whatever Claudia was doing in here, they weren't, well...

He walks past me, removing his jacket so that he wears only a white button-up shirt, one as crisp as the bed linens, then sits in a chair set far from the fire. He leans forward so his elbows rest on his knees, his profile cut from steel. Just as quickly he stands, shoves his hands into his pockets, and says hurriedly, "Claudia is not, as you say, my girlfriend."

"Oh?"

"She is an opportunist who for the past year has made herself a fixture in my life, most likely an attempt to trick the Mainframe, just as my sister is attempting to do in her endless and senseless pursuit of male suitors. There is nothing untoward happening behind your back, I can assure you."

For a moment I'm speechless. *Nothing untoward happening behind my back.* The phrase makes it sound like he and I...when, of course, we aren't...

I clear my throat. "So—she wished to marry you?"

"Yes."

"And by spending time with you, by making you fall for her, the more likely you'd be matched with each other," I finish, more to myself than to him. It makes sense, this ploy, it even echoes of things between Patrick and me, and yet both him and I and Wolfe and Claudia ended up matched with others.

"I never said that I had *fallen* for her," Wolfe mutters in an even tone.

I turn to the fire and stare at the dancing blue flames. No, I suppose he never did, given the little care he'd shown her just now in the corridor. "And yet you never put a stop to her company, either..."

"That is correct."

So. Either he wished to marry her, though not for love, or he simply enjoyed the company she offered. I frown thinking about what form that company may have taken.

"I gather," he says, a little while later, "that you came to my quarters tonight because you wished to speak to me about something." His tone's all business. "Sit, make yourself comfortable, but do get on with it. I have a long list of things needing doing in the morning."

I take a seat on the navy-blue couch placed in front of the fire. "Things needing doing, you say." My voice is full of tact.

"Ah, you're here to complain about your inability to come and go from Strath Glen freely," he says, jumping several steps ahead as though he can read my mind. "I wondered when that would present itself."

My eyes widen. But before I can open my mouth, he takes a step closer and opens his own: "I'm of the understanding, however, that you ventured out with one of the guards a few days prior, conveniently when my uncle was otherwise occupied. No doubt by befriending a guard you've assured yourself access to his schedule. So. Since you have already found a solution to your problem, I'm rather confused by your need to bother me with it now."

I stare at him with a mixture of embarrassment, fear, and intrigue. "How did you—?"

"It isn't important."

"The policing of my movements qualifies as important to me," I insist. "Did you call the Mainframe?"

"If you must know, another of the guards alerted me to it. You are not the only one with allies around here." He sighs noisily. "And I wouldn't qualify that as *policing*."

I concede the point with a small nod of my head.

"Had I contacted the Mainframe," he continues, as he stokes the fire with his back to me, "which scenario would they have described?"

"A scenario where I was having lunch with the guard I left with, Jill, and another." I say nothing of the scroll, the reason for the lunch.

"And the other day, when my uncle beckoned you to his office?"

"I'd been visiting an old friend by the name of Agnes. She works at the Quire Nursery. Why do you ask?"

He glances coolly at me over his shoulder. "Prudence."

"*Prudence*? You said yourself that you couldn't care less what I get up to during my spare time."

He moves away from the fire and though his face is cast in shadows, he looks annoyed. "It is only prudent that I have some idea of your whereabouts," he says curtly, as he takes a seat across from me. "You are, after all, to be my...wife."

I dig my fingernails into my palm. *Wife*. Hearing him say it makes it seem too real.

"My outing the other day with Jill," I say, changing the subject. "Will you...turn me in?"

He laces his fingers together. The muscles along his jawline twitch. "No."

No. So, whoever this man is sitting across from me, he may not be an ally, but he isn't an enemy, either. The revelation's relieving, but it still doesn't solve the problem of long days languishing in and around the palace with King close by.

"Out with it," he commands.

I stare at him. He may be harsh to the point of rude, but without question he's astute. "Well," I begin. "It would be nice to come and go from the palace without resorting to such tactics. Besides, King could go weeks without leaving..."

"Yes."

"Maybe if you speak with him—"

"My hands are tied. Be content instead with my willful ignorance of your defiance."

His words leave a heavy silence, and even though I want to press the point, I know instinctively that he won't budge. I bow my head. "Very well."

"You must be exceedingly discreet, do you realize?"

I study the hand now healed from King's silver walking stick. "I know that."

"How is it?"

Instead of responding, I eye him. "I had a dream about you, just now."

He lifts his chin. "Yes?"

"I was in the woods. You were cross with me for going."

For a moment he stares at me, surprised. Then he brushes it aside. "Be grateful it was nothing but a dream."

"What is it about the woods that holds such significance to you, Wolfe?"

"It is of no consequence to you." He glances at the clock. "The night is getting late. Alex."

I stand, our conversation obviously complete.

And so I'm surprised when he speaks again: "You know, the fewer feathers you ruffle around here—with the others, I mean—the better."

"Better for who?"

"Have I done something to betray your trust?" he demands.

"No," I say, thinking, "although I suppose you've done nothing to earn it." Then I add, "Besides, I think my presence here as a girl from Quire ruffles plenty of feathers as it is."

"And yet you are not completely blameless."

It's as close to a scolding as he's come for me trying to get my results changed. "No," I agree. "No, I'm not."

The rigidness in his body seems to deflate, somewhat, and he walks me to the door. "Bite your tongue when they attack you," he advises. "I'm not saying it is fair, what you must endure here. But there is only so much of it I can shield you from. The rest you'll have to navigate on your own, and I can assure you that keeping a low profile is the best way to deal with these people."

These people? These are *his* people. I turn to question him but already the door has clicked shut in my face.

sixteen

. . .

DAYS PASS. Slowly they give way to weeks, each longer than the last.

But not once does King depart from Strath Glen, and so neither do I. No visits to my aunt, to Agnes, to the memory bank at the Mainframe. No strolling through Quire, or along Central Boulevard enjoying the unseasonably warm weather. Nothing. The only fresh air I get is when darting around the palace, fruitlessly scouring the stables for another clue from the scroll writer. News from Airo-Aurora I hear only in snippets—a group of hunters killed by beasts to the east, a fire off Central Boulevard that left a family home-less, an arts festival in full swing at City Square—otherwise I'm completely cut off from the rest of the world.

As for Wolfe, I see little of him, preoccupied by work as he seems to be, and instead I pass the time with Evie when she's not busy with her studies, or with Jill on the front stoop. But mostly I keep to myself. Monotonous hours are passed playing the piano in the sunroom, or spent curled up in the library window, book in hand. My back continues to ache from lugging the viscount's enormous breakfast tray up three flights of stairs from the basement every day, but at the very least the other servants have lost the intense hatred for me that marked my early days at Strath Glen. Even Rebecca's now quick to slip me a piece of fruit or bun from the kitchen at lunchtime.

Still, the boredom is almost too much to bear. The only thing I dread more than an empty day stretched out before me is a run-in with King himself. It isn't often; he spends most of his time in his office, but every so often he'll traipse the corridors in search of Wolfe, whose importance to Airo-Aurora, I've come to realize, is unparalleled. Even James would have to be willfully blind not to see it.

When King and I do cross paths, he isn't abusive, or even particularly nasty. In fact, he appears more like the man I remember from the television screen, the one revered by the people of Airo-Aurora, and less like the sociopathic version I've glimpsed. Still, I don't trust him. There's something about each of our interactions that leaves me feeling distinctly uncomfortable. As though I'm coated in petroleum, one spark away from going up in flames.

It's a feeling so potent that it leads me to another conclusion—that I'd been wrong, that night, speaking with Wolfe in his private quarters. It isn't because he hasn't earned my trust that I can't put my faith in him. It's because of his allegiance to King that I must be cautious.

One Thursday evening, after a long day of languishing almost behind me, I slip into Carnegie Reserve, by now such old routine that the other royals don't bother to bat their false eyelashes in my direction. An orchestra plays in the corner, horns shimmying from one octave to the next, while servants pass around drinks garnished with candy.

I take one, pinching the head of a gummy bear between forefinger and thumb glumly.

Because even the evenings are nothing but the same

endless cycle of entertainment, dinner, and drink. Debauchery, excess, and inebriation. The same powdered faces pass through my vision, the same cackling laughter rises from the shadows, the same game of seduction and betrayal dogs the residents and guests alike.

"It's nearly impossible to believe the Rose Ceremony is only two days away!" a voice trills in my ear.

I smile at Evie, happy to have someone to chat with. Light from a hundred chandeliers reflects off her hair. "Rose Ceremony?"

"I'm excited, sister! Have you thought about your look? Shall we try a bohemian one on you? I'm going straight-up princess-style," she adds, her gaze flickering to Aubrey, who dances to the horns like it's club music.

"Rose Ceremony?" I repeat, louder.

She clicks her tongue. "Don't tell me. You're hopeless, dear sister! Or perhaps it is my brother to blame. Did he really truly not tell you?" She snatches up a passing glass of wine and holds it up to the light, as if admiring it.

"He didn't tell me a thing." I turn my attention to the room and scan the crowd for a tall figure.

"He isn't here," Evie interjects. "He's abroad for a couple days with a work issue. Don't worry yourself, he'll be back in time for the ceremony. Mother and Father would be absolutely beside themselves if he were to miss it."

So. Wolfe had left the palace without bothering to tell me. Meanwhile, I'm kept virtually under lock and key, ready to pull my own hair out from the boredom. "Please, Evie. Which ceremony are you referring to? Wolfe barely bothers with me, I'm afraid."

She tilts her head to the side and pouts. "Try not to take it too personally, sister. He really is very busy with work, and then there's all that is behind him. It still occupies him, you know."

"What does?"

Something passes across Evie's eyes. She coughs lightly into her fist. "Nothing. What I mean to say is that he's a busy man, that's all. As for the Rose Ceremony, brace yourself, sister, for what a festive time at Strath Glen. The last one I attended went on for days!" She laughs gaily at the thought. "And, lucky me, I expect Theodore will be in attendance," she adds with a sly smile.

"But aside from it being a party," I continue, as servants deposit escargot around the room and seats begin to fill, "what does it involve? Why does Wolfe need to be back for it? Do I have to go?"

"But of course you do."

"But why does it concern *me* in the slightest?"

"Why, it's a chance for you to honor my parents, of course! You know, in advance of the nuptials, which reminds me—we really must set a date. Is there a particular month that catches your fancy?"

"But a chance to honor them, for what, please?"

"For all the love they bestow upon you, or something along those lines." She tips the drink down her throat, then drops into her seat. "It is terribly nice not to have big brother around depriving me of the finer things," she adds, tapping her nails against the empty glass.

I sit next to her, stare down at the snails, and feel faintly sick. "And what am I supposed to wear to such an event?"

"A beautiful gown, of course! No trousers allowed," she adds with a pout. But seeing the look on my face, she pats my arm. "Fear not, sister. I have several gowns left over from last season's balls. Probably they're too small for me now, but they should fit you like an absolute glove. I'll be sure to bring along some proper shoes for you, as well."

I thank her, relieved, then stare at Wolfe's empty seat. It would've been helpful if he'd bothered to inform me of the ceremony himself, and with more than two days to spare.

Yet that'd involve talking to me, something he clearly has no interest in doing.

I lean toward Evie. "Am I supposed to do anything at this ceremony?"

"Besides drive my bore of a brother mad with your beauty?" she teases. "Nothing too arduous, no. Talk up your in-laws, I suppose. Oh, and present to them their roses, of course. It isn't called the Rose Ceremony for nothing!"

"And where do I get these roses?" I ask, chewing my nail.

Just as always, I seem to amuse Evie to no end. After first piercing a snail, she explains, "The servants take care of the whole thing, don't fret. They'll have the box sorted, now, learn to enjoy yourself. I fear you are too much like my brother in some regards."

Too much like her brother?

That *can't* be true. Because our union's the result of a glitch—I'm sure of it. Absolutely *nothing* more.

———

THE NEXT MORNING, around ten o'clock, my sullenness gives way to excitement. My headache fades; my fatigue is forgotten about. Barely able to contain my smile, I race up the steps of Strath Glen, and with a quick greeting shouted to Jill, I slip through the palace doors. I take the stairs two at a time and run along the House of Mirrors, one that reflects a face made suddenly alive.

Another scroll.

What perfect timing—my brain needs something to fixate on instead of the Rose Ceremony. Besides, I reached a dead end with my investigation into the first scroll; maybe with this one I'll have better luck.

I toss my cloak onto a nearby chair, then go still.

It's another half-eaten apple, mostly hidden under the

bed. I bend over and pick it up, once again thinking back to the previous day, the evening, the night...

Nothing had been out of the ordinary. No visitors, no reason for this apple core to wind up here. And my sleep last night? Solid, but considering the way I toss and turn most nights, wasn't it due?

I throw the apple into the waste bin. Between the Rose Ceremony and the scroll—I don't have time to worry about a discarded apple. Probably it's just a servant, anyway, having a bit of fun.

I take a seat on the velvet sofa and smooth the scroll open.

There, written in sloppy cursive, are two names—a man by the name of Reginald Worthers, and none other than the Queen of Airo-Aurora herself. It isn't signed this time; there are no extra markings whatsoever, not even my name.

I frown. Because what bearing could these names possibly have on my Selection results? On my contention that a *glitch* placed me here? To make matters worse, there's even less to go on this time.

Of course, this time I know the scroll's for me, don't I? And I know the sender is the mysterious Glitch. I know who the Queen is, too, although Reginald Worthers is anybody's guess.

Reginald Worthers. The name's familiar, that much I know.

Well, whoever he is, he can wait. The Queen of Airo-Aurora is someone I have relatively easy access to, don't I? Someone I can *investigate*...

But...to what end? Why does the scroll writer want to draw my attention to her in the first place?

I bite my lip—I can't answer the question without first finding the woman.

Without any official duties, though, without a desk she's tethered to, without an office to call her own, finding her might be difficult. Typically, I've spotted her roaming the palace almost at random, usually in the middle of some small task, such as fetching candlesticks or tending to the plants in the sunroom. Her existence must be sinfully boring, and yet she always looks perfectly content, never flustered, never upset. It's not a future I can stand the thought of.

All the more reason to find her, then. I pull myself off the sofa, then set out for the top floor, the least likely option, so the quickest to cross from my list. Besides, to leave it to the end would risk King coming out of his office in search of lunch.

But Bishop's Aisle boasts more activity than I anticipated. Scantily clad women take up the whole corridor, so many that I have to flatten myself against the wall to allow them to pass. With a door handle pressed into my back belonging to the Department of Food & Agriculture, I turn the knob and find it unlocked. I step inside. Best to wait out the women, none of which are the Queen, in here.

I freeze. It's nothing more than a broom closet, four feet deep by six feet wide. I reopen the door, get hit in the face by a passing boa, and check again the placard hanging out front. Department of Food & Agriculture, just as I saw the first time. Mystified, I wait for the last of the women to pass, then pull the door shut and continue my search.

Almost immediately I'm distracted by a growling sound, coming from the prince's office.

I hesitate outside the door, then push it open, just enough to peek inside. One of the corseted women sits on James's lap with her breasts exposed. She feeds him grapes that he snatches up like a dog, and my eyes widen with surprise.

Well, then. Definitely his mother, the Queen, won't be found in there.

I walk on, more disenchanted by the minute—so disenchanted, in fact, that I barely even notice all those disembodied faces staring at me as I pass.

Farther along comes another distraction. Music, this time, and it grows louder and more pronounced as I near King's office. It's his voice, caught up in the singing of an operatic number. Every few minutes it's interrupted by the sound of tapping, and, pressing my ear against the door, I hear the voice of another man offering advice. A singing lesson.

Sinful pleasures and adolescent whims; that's all to be found up here. It's no wonder Wolfe is saddled with so much work.

I return to the comparatively docile House of Mirrors and set out for the west wing, where the Queen lives. It's identical to the east wing, except for a hint of body odor that lingers in the air. The men in overalls, the ones usually drilling upstairs, are working down here, this time on ladders and examining a hole carved into the wall near the ceiling. As I get closer, my ears pick up the sound of buzzing, and I take a moment to examine the hole myself.

My jaw drops at the sight. Thousands of honeybees, crawling on top of one another, their sap shimmering in the artificial light.

Resisting the urge to run back to my room, I stumble forward, nodding to the men as I pass, wondering if after all that I have enough nerve to knock on the Queen's private residence.

Morocco propels herself through a door just then, into the hallway, only barely avoiding running headfirst into me. She vomits across the floor and turns the black and white tile electric green, then cackles, revealing teeth sparkling with diamonds and smeared in lipstick. "That's what you get for doing jelly shots before noon!" she shouts, and at first, I think she's addressing me. "The green apple tastes like asses!" she adds over her shoulder, before disappearing back inside her quarters. Before the door can shut, I spot a totally nude man inside holding a white dog and looking bored.

Deciding I don't have enough nerve for the west wing after all, I retreat quickly, past the massive beehive hiding behind the walls, down the stairs to the main floor, now so bewildered that I can barely remember the point of the walkabout in the first place. From above comes the sound of drilling, thunderous inside my brain, and over that...the sound of footsteps. A man's voice erupts in the practice of scales.

I curse, then duck out of sight. Because running into King is something I'd like to avoid, especially after the past half hour.

Peering around the banister, I see him walk toward Devonshire Commons, clapping his hands together like an excited child.

At that moment, and before I can escape, Monsieur Sawyer emerges from the Commons and bows deeply. He steps aside for an older gentleman donning a white coat, with hair and beard of the same color. He and King embrace like old friends.

Who is this man? He looks nothing like the well-dressed, well-manicured guests that the palace typically hosts. And why's King so excited to see him?

"I shall await Dr. Lebwitski's departure," Monsieur says graciously before disappearing back inside the sitting room. The drilling from way up high ceases, and the silence it leaves is tomb-like.

"Always a killer," I hear the parrot chirp.

King and Dr. Lebwitski turn for the stairs, and I flatten myself against the wall, crouching as low as I can, even as my back screams in protest. My heart feels like it could explode, it hammers so quickly.

"Quite kind, having your chauffeur fetch me like that," says the man in white.

"A small courtesy for a dear friend. It's been far too long since we've enjoyed one another's company, since before my insurance plan began, I declare. I'm anxious as a scarecrow to know how the chips are working without the benefit of data."

"Just as we thought, my Lord. Your plan has been a perfect success. I tip my hat to you."

"Would the override be evident to the untrained eye?" asks King as they reach the second floor.

"Terribly so," echoes the doctor's voice.

Insurance plan? Override? *What are they talking about?*

"Whatever are you doing, Miss Alex?" comes a voice over my shoulder. Gerard stands there, peering down his nose at me.

Thinking quickly, I blurt out the first thing that comes to mind: "Looking for a dropped earring, sir."

The butler draws away, sighing.

And then— "A strange place to lurk, dearest Alex," calls a voice from overhead, and slowly—dreading every second of it—I lift my gaze to meet King's.

He leers down at me from over the second-floor railing, eyes sparkling darkly. They drill into mine for a minute more, and then he's gone.

I groan. Caught *eavesdropping*...why did Gerard have to come along at that moment? What punishment will be in store *now*?

Then again, maybe it was worth it. Whatever they'd been discussing had a color of conspiracy to it, that's for sure. Which plan were they referring to? And what about the other things—the untrained eye and the chips?

"Miss."

I bang my head against the wood paneling as Rebecca drops into a curtsy. "Aye, I hope I didn't startle yeh."

"Not at all," I tell her. "I was just headed to...Counter-down. In search of a book."

"Very good, miss. I wanted to say how excited we are for tomorrow's Rose Ceremony, aye. It's such an honor and all, to share in your special day. Are you properly excited?"

"My special day? I-I thought the whole thing had more to do with the duke and duchess than with me."

"Of course, miss. Suppose I misspoke, miss." With another curtsy, she rounds the stairs and disappears, and I head for the library, now more worried about tomorrow's ceremony than before.

The library will cheer me up—it's my favorite room in the entire palace. The plain wooden tables, the dusty books that reach to the ceiling, the cozy chairs surrounding the hearth—compared with the rest of Strath Glen it's less exaggerated, less polished, less overblown. To make it even more appealing, it's almost always deserted, the perfect place to stop and think.

Not today.

A wing chair near the fireplace is occupied by a perfectly groomed woman sitting placidly, a book held gracefully in hand.

The Queen, and I smile at the much-needed, well-deserved stroke of luck.

But as I watch her quietly from the shadows, I can't begin to guess why she was named in that scroll. She's *Queen* of our nation-state, a title that sets her apart from the citizenry, and not by a small amount. There's nothing she holds in common with the others listed, not the Reginald character, or Jill, or Timothee—how could there be? And surely, she can't have anything to do with the glitch at the Mainframe.

I sigh, finally emerging from the shadows, still staring intently at the woman with the impeccably set curls, watching her eyes tick back and forth over the text, admiring that mouth set in its ever-pleasant expression.

She seems totally unaware of the figure slowly approaching.

And then I shiver. My boots go still, they begin their silent retreat. It's the book held in the Queen's hands, the one she reads so calmly.

It's upside down.

seventeen

. . .

THE NEXT DAY, Strath Glen is a bustling hub of activity leading up to the evening's festivities. Half the servants run from one end of the palace to the other carrying large boxes, while the rest polish the silverware and scrub the baseboards—they even line the hallways with twinkling fairy lights and scatter rose petals across the black polished floors. A group of designers decorate the ballroom known as Birkland Grand with lush rose vines and tea candles.

The royals, too, I notice, are caught up in preparations: a team of hairstylists and makeup artists move from one suite to the next, followed closely by a small army of tailors for last-minute fittings. Since all of Airo-Aurora's finest will be in attendance tonight, no expense is spared, no extravagance considered surplus.

I sit by, watching all of this from under the rotunda, wondering if Wolfe will return from his mission abroad in time for the ceremony. I wonder too—do I care? For some reason, I think that I do, I just can't figure out why.

Down the hall, a servant named Joel hauls boxes of spirits from the basement to Carnegie Reserve, now outfitted as a staging area. Sweat glistens along his hairline, and it makes my sore back ache just watching him. "Can I help?" I offer.

"Miss!"

Rebecca and Simon, another of the younger servants, walk toward me with a heavy white box several feet long held between them. I head down the remaining stairs to meet them after Joel refuses my offer to assist.

"We've just taken delivery," Rebecca continues, nodding at the oblong parcel. Her eyes sparkle with excitement. "Care to steal a look?"

Carefully I lift a corner. From rim to rim the box is stuffed with long-stemmed roses, all a soft blushing pink, their heady aroma filling the entire rotunda with their sweet scent. "Wow. How many are there?"

"Aye, at least one hundred, miss. Can you smell 'em?"

I nod. "They're stunning. Thank you for getting them, really."

"A servant's duty, tis," Rebecca says with a curtsy. "We'll place them up in Carnegie," she adds, as she leads Simon in that direction. "The presentation isn't 'til after dinner, miss, just so you know."

I shout my thanks after them, feeling a bit more at home than usual, then check my watch. Evie offered to make me ball-worthy once her own transformation is complete, but that won't be for another hour or so. Maybe a visit with Jill will fill some time, and I smile a little. It feels good to have more friends around here, and fewer enemies.

After being shoved aside by several men carrying a series of whole-cooked pigs, I go outside, onto the front landing. The sun shines from low in the sky, purple along the horizon.

"Shouldn't you be wearing a dress and tiara?" Jill glances at me from head to foot.

"My help is having something called a blowout done

first," I say with a smile. "I think it has something to do with the hair, although I never did ask."

"Can't throw on a gown by yourself?"

"Very funny."

"You were in a hurry yesterday," she continues, as the other guard checks the identification of a new round of caterers, this batch carrying mounds of fruit arranged into bouquets. "Looked excited about something, too."

"Another scroll, found in the stables."

"And? Did yours truly get another shout-out?"

"Not this time," I say, nudging her. "Two more names were listed, though—the Queen, and a man called Reginald Worthers. Do you recognize the name?"

"Nope. Guess you've got someone else to track down. Least you're well-practiced, by now."

"It'll be difficult to do, stuck here like I am. I really wish King was a bit more adventurous."

"I'll catch up with Timothee, see if he knows the guy. I wouldn't mind knowing why my name's wrapped up in all this." Down below, yet another white van screeches to a halt in front of the palace. A series of men and women in bakers' hats pour from inside, balancing an assortment of trays of colorful mochi. Jill gestures to the other guard. "Looks like Lacy could use a hand. I better get back to work. Enjoy yourself tonight, princess," she adds with a wink.

Ten minutes later I stand alone, inside my room, staring out the window at the birch trees, thinking about the evening ahead. Soon I'll pay tribute to Wolfe's parents, who —despite living with them for weeks—are still strangers. My own parents, on the other hand, will never have a chance to meet their son-in-law, and if they could, what would they say?

I roll my eyes. *Make the most of it,* that would be my mother's advice. Enough sulking, enough feeling sorry for myself. It's time to stop grieving for that easy life in Quire I *so* wanted—it's time to embrace my new future here, with *him*. Life's too short to do otherwise—words I know from experience are true. And really, things here haven't been so bad, have they?

I think about it for a while and decide that they haven't. I'm still hopeful that the scrolls will offer me a path out, sure, but I think with the right attitude I can make peace with the present. I lift my chin at the thought.

Then I trace a finger along the windowpane, thinking again about the Queen's reading habits. I wonder if her strange behavior could have anything to do with the scroll—

There's a commotion at the door, loud voices and knocking—then Evie bursts through in a swirl of ruby tones and gaiety. Three servants follow behind and deposit on my bed a series of gowns, a duffel bag overflowing with high-heeled shoes, and what looks like a steel suitcase. Once the entourage files out, Evie steps to the center of the room and spins.

I have to hand it to her. The red dress flecked with gold is magnificent. The rouge makes her look older than her teenage years, and her hair is wound into such an elaborate up-do it's worthy of the likes of Aubrey. "Theodore doesn't stand a chance," I say.

She beams, kisses me on the cheek, then gushes, "And now, sister, it's *your* turn." She pushes me to the assortment of gowns fanned out on the bed. "Which one do you fancy? Does one catch your eye? Take your pick, although I really think I have the perfect one already selected for you." Without waiting she picks up a delicate strapless number— gauzy white, with an attached skirt of silver that fans gently out. "It's you, isn't it? Not too revealing, not too bold, and— most important—I think my brother will adore it best. He doesn't care for loud colors, the bore."

Silently I size up my other options. One's blue satin, encrusted with jewels, another features a dramatic train of black silk, and the last is the shade of strawberry syrup. I finger the one that Evie holds, liking its simple design. "It might show too much skin," I finally say.

"Only your shoulders!" she exclaims. "That will be tame, by tonight's standards, I promise you. Here are some shoes that match. Quick. Strip this instant and let me be the judge."

I do as asked, changing in the corner while covering myself as much as possible in the process.

"You don't need to be so shy in front of me, sister," she says, shaking her head. "Has my lovely brother gotten a glimpse of you yet?"

"Of course not!" I shout, blushing. I turn my back so she can zip me up.

"I didn't think as much. You'll give him a taste of what he's missing tonight. There you go—have a look at yourself. What do you think? Is it to die for? Do you love it?"

Standing in front of the closet mirror, I'm surprised by the girl staring back. For once, the garment fits like a sleeve, and I have to admit that despite my love for pleated pants and blazers, the dress is exquisite. I remember my first meal here, at Strath Glen, looking like I was dressing up in my grandmother's finest. I was so nervous, I felt so out of place —so alone.

Somehow, without me even noticing, those feelings have changed. *I've* changed.

"Well, sister?"

I clear my throat. "On close inspection, my shoulders do look a little bony—"

"Nonsense," she interrupts as she begins lifting and twisting sections of my hair. "Your small stature is endearing. Now, what are you thinking for an up-do?"

"I hadn't really thought about it. A ponytail, maybe?"

"A *ponytail*?" Her laughter chimes like bells. "Let's enhance your curl, then experiment with a loose braid right here, to the side. Consider it a dress rehearsal before the wedding." She drags me to the washroom, then begins curling carefully selected sections of my hair.

With my mind wandering back to those scrolls, I ask, "Are you close with your aunt?"

"She's *delightful*, isn't she?"

I nod. "You mentioned one evening that you find her clumsier than before, do you recall?"

"Oh yes—*then*. Theodore was in attendance," and she sighs as if enjoying the memory. "As for Auntie, who knows, don't you think? People are always changing. Why, when I was a little girl, I never shut up—can you imagine? My!"

"That *is* hard to believe," I say tactfully.

"Certainly she's far calmer than she used to be," she adds.

"Oh?"

"Yes, she used to have *quite* a temper. But Uncle said she started meditating and—*bam*—an overnight transformation!"

"What sort of things would upset her?"

"I don't really remember, sister. Oh—but one time, Uncle bought her all these supplies for needlework—absolutely gorgeous ones. He even brought in a tutor from California, can you imagine? Auntie mustn't have had any interest in the pursuit because she burned up the whole lot of fabric and wool right in the middle of the dinner table. What a commotion!"

For a while I'm silent. So, the Queen didn't appreciate King choosing a hobby for her. And yet...the Queen I've glimpsed would never do such a thing. The Queen I know would take up needle and thread without a second thought, with that tranquil expression stitched to her face.

"What about your uncle?" I try next. "Are you, er, close with him?"

"You're such a curious dove! My uncle is a *very* busy

man," she says, and I think of the music lessons. I have to work hard not to roll my eyes. "But," she continues, "he's such a treat when I do get to see him, don't you find?"

I don't say anything, which is just as well, because Evie finishes weaving my hair into a braid that's both intentionally messy and casually elegant, and trills, "Ta-da!"

"I like it," I admit.

Evie frowns. "I'm not convinced. It's much too similar to what I was picturing for your wedding, and I want to keep the big reveal for the special day."

I laugh. "Any big reveal will be wasted on your brother, I'm afraid."

"Meaning what, sister?"

"Meaning that I don't interest him, of course."

Evie looks at me out of the corner of her eye. "I'm not so sure I agree. But if you wish to keep with the same hair and dress, fine. It is rather getting down to the wire."

"What time does the Rose Ceremony begin?"

"As soon as night falls," she replies, "and I don't want to miss even a minute." We glance out the near-dark bathroom window; the orange sun must lie flush against the horizon. "Don't move, sister. I'll be back in a twinkle." A moment later she reappears with the silver suitcase in hand. She props it open on the vanity, and I stare at an impressive array of makeup.

"Not very much," I say nervously.

"Don't fret."

"Why do you not agree with me?" I ask, as my eyelids and lashes are prodded. "Concerning my, um, assessment of your brother's interest in me, I mean."

"So you *do* like him, then!" she exclaims. "I was rather beginning to wonder if his feelings were reciprocated. You've proven to be even more difficult to read than he is."

My eyes open wide. "What? No. I never said *that*. I'm just curious why you think he—"

"Because a sister always knows," she says with a wink. "Besides, he's considerably less sullen as of late, haven't you noticed?"

"I haven't," I admit. "He seems just as detached as ever. And since I've hardly seen him lately, any change in his mood can't have anything to do with me, can it?"

"Doubtless he has been nothing short of a terrible fiancé to you. Even as a brother, he can be trying. But he will be a faithful husband to you, sister, and he is far from wicked, despite appearances. More aloof than anything, I'd say, particularly after what happened with—well. You'll have to decide for yourself, won't you? There. A star is born." She turns me in the direction of the mirror. "What do you think?"

I turn my face from side to side, transfixed by the transformation. My cheeks are rosier than usual, my lips with more color, and my eyes...they pop with assertiveness. I glance at Evie and lift an eyebrow.

She glows with self-satisfaction. "I take it you quite like it?"

"I'm speechless."

"What are sisters for?" Without waiting for a response, she marches me from the bathroom and gestures theatrically to the windows. Velvety blackness pushes against the panes. "And now," she exclaims, as she tucks her fingers through mine, "we party."

———

AT THE BOTTOM of the stairs, we join a throng of people being ushered forward by servants in their finest ensembles. A symphony erupts from Birkland Grand and echoes to all corners of the palace. Rose petals crush underfoot and fill the hallway with their aroma, and tiny white lights twinkle with so much festivity that it becomes tactile in the air.

Goose bumps slip over my skin as I step into the ballroom.

At the front, the melody of a chorus fifty-strong swells into a crescendo, a full orchestra supporting every note, so loud and overpowering that it reverberates against the bottom of my ribcage. Overhead, rose vines clamber across the ceiling and arch around doorways, while beneath, clustered along every available surface, glow thousands of tea candles.

It's impossible not to be swept up by the beauty of it, and for the first time since leaving Quire, I'm grateful to be here, to experience something so surreal.

I smooth my gown and begin scanning the sea of people. There're all sorts: young to ancient, portly to skeletal, provocatively dressed to the outrageous. All have the same haughty look about them that I guess comes from a life of excess. None of them are the viscount.

Maybe he hasn't returned from his trip abroad, after all.

I step aside to avoid being speared by a woman's feathered fascinator, and then backward, as a purple-powdered face drops just inches from mine.

"Well, ho-hum. Looks like you aren't quite so unbecoming after all," Aubrey purrs. "All eye, thick lashes, a well-carved mouth? Div-*ine*." She positions herself so we're cheek to cheek, then stands upright with a shudder. "Yet you still stink of Quire," she concludes. "Cousin deserved better—you'll never please him."

"Maybe not."

"*Definitely* not," she corrects me. "Soon enough he'll learn to laugh again, and at your expense." She winks, then catches Evie around the wrist. "Was it you, dearest cousin, who took such pity on this precious little ditch piggy of ours?"

Evie nods, reverence crystal clear in her brown eyes.

"You've a grand old heart. Now, want to see a trick, cousins?" Without waiting for a reply Aubrey plucks a rose from overhead, pulls off all the petals and drops them into her flute of champagne. She drains its contents and winks. "Now it's true what they say about a princess shitting roses!"

"God help you," comes a voice in my ear, and a man with a shaved head pushes by, then loops his arm through Aubrey's. He drags her in the direction of an hors d'oeuvres platter as she continues to cackle.

"Who was that man?" I ask, staring after him.

"Aubrey's husband. Matthew."

Her *husband*. I'd forgotten that little detail. "And why doesn't he live here, at the palace?"

"If only I knew. Nobody tells me a thing, can you believe it? But I know it drives Uncle mad. Frankly, I think Aubrey would rather enjoy herself than have a husband around her all the time. She really has the most fun of anyone I've ever met. Isn't that grand?"

Without waiting for an answer, she pulls me forward, to James and Morocco.

Morocco, who is naked aside from some well-placed jewels seemingly glued to her skin, hugs Evie tightly. She gushes over every aspect of the young girl's hair, makeup and dress. "Really, really, really," she finally concludes, "you live up to the family name in every inch." She sighs, then casts a sidelong look at me. "But you're wasting your efforts on this little one. Dearest husband, don't you find her incredibly small and plain, even dressed up in something pretty?"

It's funny—all the snarky comments from her and Aubrey...they don't bother me that much. I don't even dislike these women, not really. There's something almost sad about them, something I can't put my finger on.

James, meanwhile, seems to consider Morocco's question. He stares at me with one eyebrow raised. When he says nothing, she gasps.

"Dearest," he chides, "we must make an effort, for cousin's sake. I think she looks almost passable as a young lady, frankly. And there's nothing wrong with her face, once properly powdered."

"You have a heart of gold, my prince." She pulls him in for a kiss, but his eyes don't close as hers do. They stay locked on mine, like they're hungry, and out of the blue I'm reminded of those apple cores under my bed.

"Let us look for my Theodore, sister!" Evie shouts, pulling me away. Happy to go, I use the opportunity to search for Wolfe; tall as he is, he should stand out with ease.

But what about Aubrey's prediction? That he, Wolfe, would learn to laugh again at my expense. What exactly had she meant by that? Had something happened to stop Wolfe's laughter?

And then there's Matthew's warning: *God help you.* All of it leaves me unsettled, including the look in James's eye, and I search with more urgency through the shrieking faces for the viscount.

Eventually, I give up and turn to the orchestra instead, as Evie chats with girls from a south-side estate. How *different* life would be if I'd been given a career of musician, like the people seated here. Free of King, free of all of them. Free to have my own home, my own movement...

Maybe that's all I really want in life—freedom. And if I could somehow secure that here, maybe a future at Strath Glen wouldn't be so bad. One thing I'm sure of, though: whether I secure myself that freedom or not, I need to get to the bottom of those scrolls.

A few minutes later, I turn from the orchestra just as the crowd parts. I smile politely at nearby guests, and then, halfway across the room, I spot a towering outline through the glow of a thousand candles.

"A toast!" exclaims Evie, the girls now gone, and she pushes a glass of champagne into my hand. A group of men in tuxedos storm by and block the towering figure from view. "To sisters and friends!"

"To sisters and friends," I echo. Dry bubbles sting my tongue, but I take a gulp, and then another. I smile at my soon-to-be sister-in-law under the flickering light, enjoying myself.

"You're too young to be drinking," chides a cold voice from up high.

"Splendid to see you too, brother!" Evie replies gaily. "Do you like my dress? Mother had it imported specially for the occasion—bet you didn't even know about it! It's glorious, isn't it? Have you seen Theodore? Does he look unbearably handsome?"

Wolfe, dressed crisply in navy, scowls, and I can't help but wonder if she says those things just to get a rise from him.

"What about your darling fiancée? I saw you admiring her just now from across the room. Isn't she fetching? I promised you a beautiful bride, and didn't I deliver?"

With that disinterested look of his, he looks me over. Only when our eyes meet does he seem to lose his composure. The steeliness in his gaze wavers, so that he's left looking almost human. It passes quickly, though—so quick, in fact, that I wonder if it was nothing more than a trick of the light. Turning his attention back to his sister, he merely shrugs. "I had rather gotten used to the riding ensemble."

"That's despicable, brother! And what would Mother and Father say if your little bride-to-be turned up tonight in trousers, hmm?"

He concedes the point with a nod. "In that case, you did well."

Evie pretends to fan herself.

Meanwhile, I stare at him. That's *it*? The gown, the hair,

the makeup—and all he can say is, "you did well." The compliment isn't even directed at *me*!

"There's Theodore!" Evie squeals. "He looks tremendous, doesn't he? Have you ever seen such biceps? A strange color for a suit, that lime green, but still, I really must say hello. I'll be back shortly, sister!"

I finish my champagne, place the empty glass on a tray passing by, and take up another as Wolfe raises an eyebrow.

I'm not sure why, but I feel embarrassed all of a sudden. Foolish. Foolish that I cared what I looked like in the first place, maybe. Foolish that I cared at all! Well, I decide, from behind a cloud of champagne, I won't make that mistake again.

I start to walk away but a hand wraps around my arm, and he squares himself to me. "My sister, I take it, has filled you in on the details of the evening."

"That I have to deliver a box of roses to your parents?"

"Yes, that."

"She was surprised that you didn't bother to mention the whole thing to me yourself. And, well, I was too, for the little it's worth."

A servant with long coattails bows deeply to Wolfe and delivers a glass of amber liquid. "I believe Evie is quite taken with you. I felt she would be better suited to prepare you for the evening."

I nod, staring into my glass.

"Is there something else?"

"Well, I was *also* surprised," I tell him. "That you'd leave, to another nation no less, without telling me." Immediately after I say it, I feel myself go red. I really hope the lighting is dim enough that he doesn't notice.

He furrows his brow. "I didn't take you one for goodbyes. Besides, my portfolio in trade limits my travels to neighboring countries. Rarely am I gone for long."

"Viscount, my Lord, greatest apologies," says a man

whose elbow strikes Wolfe in the arm. He bows deeply but Wolfe merely dismisses him with a curt nod.

"Rarely are you gone for long?" I repeat. "That's not really the point."

Slowly Wolfe tips the contents of his glass back and forth, studying the ice, tracing the movements with his eyes. It looks to me that he is suppressing a smile. "And what is the point?"

"Forget it."

"No, tell me. I'm now curious."

"For starters," I say, vaguely aware that the champagne is making me more forthcoming than normal, "you know where I am at all times. And the past few weeks I've been trapped at the palace—"

"Through no fault of my own," he interrupts. With a grimace over his shoulder at the flock of girls twirling to the music, he steps closer to me to avoid their skirts.

"Well then, how about this. You ask me to put my trust in you, but how am I supposed to do that when I don't even know which country you're in?"

I expect a quick rebuttal, even a reprimand, but instead all he does is nod thoughtfully.

The response is so out of character that it's startling. And yet, my words were pretty out of character, too. Really, what's it to me if he's gone?

"Have you reviewed the latest peace treaty I placed on your desk, Viscount?" barks a voice. I step to the side to make room for Wolfe's father, red in the face and with a drink in either hand. The duchess joins him, dressed head to toe in jewel tones of yellow and orange.

"Don't bother him with work right now," she scolds. Her gaze moves back and forth between Wolfe and me, as if she's trying to understand some unknowable detail between us. Whatever that detail may be, I suddenly realize, I wouldn't mind understanding it myself.

"I have reviewed it, yes," Wolfe speaks curtly, like he converses with a business associate instead of his own father.

It's definitely an odd family dynamic these royals maintain.

"As we already abide by the terms of the treaty," Wolfe continues, "I see no reason not to become a signatory. It will boost international confidence and therefore our bottom line."

"Very well," says his father, while girls dressed as fawns toss confetti around the room. "I'll issue orders first thing Monday morning."

Silence settles over our group, and I think of the last time I spoke with the duchess. It was after the fiasco at the Mainframe, and I don't think it's likely her opinion of me has changed much since.

"I hear from my daughter that wedding planning is going inordinately well," she says eventually.

I clear my throat, pleasantly surprised that she's speaking to me at all. "We've settled on a theme, madam, which seems to be making all other decisions much easier."

"Evie assures me you are most accommodating. Is that her old dress that you wear?"

"She was kind enough to lend it to me for the evening," I agree. "I'm afraid the gowns delivered to my room are all a little big."

"You are terribly delicate," she agrees, and her gaze tips down, assessing me from head to toe. "Has your life at Strath Glen been so miserable that it has robbed you of an appetite?" The question is delivered mildly, yet it slices me with its claws. Just like her son, she's completely unpredictable.

"Mother," Wolfe says in a low voice.

The woman smiles brightly. She lifts well-plucked eyebrows at him.

"I-I'm not miserable, madam. I've always been on the small side."

"A shame. It does make you easy to pick on. Has my son been protecting you from barbs?"

"Don't answer that," Wolfe says tersely. "It's a loaded question; she is needlessly digging into our relationship."

The woman laughs. "If you were more forthcoming, my son, I wouldn't need to resort to such tricks."

"Mother!" interrupts Evie, reappearing with a flushed face. "Stop *hogging* sister. I need her help with a pressing matter." She drags me through a crowd and onto the dance floor, then wraps her arms around my waist and orders me to do the same. "We *must* capture his attention."

"Who?"

She looks shocked. "Theodore, of course!" Her gaze darts in the direction of a lime green tuxedo dancing the foxtrot with a girl in turquoise.

He shoots a look in our direction, and I duck my head, laughing. "But he's already watching you!" I shout, grabbing Evie by the fingers.

"Sister," she says with a shake of her head. "Of *course* he is. This is a game of seduction, don't you know?"

I sigh as we begin dancing rhythmically to a slow waltz. "I'm afraid that's an art that will always elude me."

"Really?"

"Oh, I'm pretty sure."

"And yet, my brother can't take his eyes off you."

I go silent, then focus my attention on my feet. Eventually, though, when I'm sure Evie isn't looking, I scan the crowd, just to see...

He speaks with James, nodding now and then in a show of listening, but—just as his sister had said—his gaze doesn't waver from me for even a second.

———

IT'S MUCH LATER in the evening when dinner is served, steaming bowls of pork belly on rice, surrounded by delicate greens dressed in peanut sauce. Wolfe dines with King, the Queen, and his parents, as is custom, and I sit with Evie and several other young faces who spend the entire meal brainstorming ways to influence their Selection results.

"Jumping jacks while staring at your most desired ought to do it!" one boy shouts.

"Train yourself in only one skill and remain willfully dumb to all others!"

"Or resort to tantrums and violence while performing tasks you loathe!"

"And when speaking to mates you don't fancy!"

By the time the desserts are served, I'm ready to call it a night. The champagne has left me dazed, and between it and the heavy meal the urge to sleep is almost overwhelming. Just as I think about sneaking upstairs, the orchestra ceases its music and Gerard's voice lifts over the crowd: "Would Miss Alex of Quire please do the honors!"

I sit upright, fatigue instantly forgotten. All eyes in Birkland Grand turn to me. Some laugh under their breath. Morocco mouths the word *Quire* with exaggeration. Wolfe, meanwhile, stares at his watch with a stern face. All four of his tablemates rise from their seats and move to the head of the ballroom, smiling breezily at guests as they go.

The presentation of the roses. In all the excitement of the evening—and all that champagne—I had completely forgotten.

"Good luck," Evie whispers, as I stand on unsteady legs.

Rebecca places in my arms the heavy box full of roses, and then I start along the winding path to the head of the ballroom. My stomach pinches with nerves, and the silence of the room doesn't help—after an evening full of thundering music, it seems to carry with it a weight of its own.

I give myself a shake. In another minute, my duties will

be complete, and I'll slip upstairs unnoticed by the rest. There's nothing to worry about.

Finally, after what seems like an eternity, I approach the four most senior figures in all of Airo-Aurora. I smile, and curtsy, then lift the box to Wolfe's mother.

The Duchess of Airo-Aurora bows her head with her son's rigidity. Her husband doesn't seem to notice me at all, and instead speaks under his breath to the Queen, who smiles blithely. King, on the other hand, watches me with such grave attention that I shiver.

Then a smattering of applause wells up from around the room, and I feel my muscles unclench. Roses delivered, and, apparently, accepted. I turn toward the exit, smiling easily now.

I only make it a couple of steps when a hush blankets the ballroom.

It's the look on the duchess's face, I soon see—brow digging together, lips pursed. Slowly she lifts the cover the rest of the way off the box and dumps the contents to the floor.

One hundred long-stemmed roses, massacred into a million pieces.

eighteen

. . .

BIRKLAND GRAND ERUPTS. The anger is visceral; outrage radiates from all corners of the room. A devastating act of disrespect, and this from a girl from Quire.

People lift to their feet, they holler obscenities. A man in a bowler hat shoves me to my knees, Morocco slices my arm with her nails. Fawns whip confetti at my face. Then three loud thumps sound through the racket; they restore a semblance of order to the maddened ballroom. King's silver walking stick.

A feeling of foreboding ripples along my spine. A feeling of *dread*. "Please!" I shout. "It wasn't me who butch—"

"An act of betrayal," he interrupts, eyes glinting red in the light.

I shake my head. "I swear to you—"

"An act of defiance!"

"I didn't have a clue, I promise—"

He lifts a finger to quiet me, then points it at my face. "A punishable offense." In the blink of an eye his walking stick arcs through the air, this time landing with a sharp explosion of pain across my exposed shoulder. Two more blasts find me before I lie prone along the polished floor, blood trickling across my collarbone.

Hazily, I see two things. The first is the viscount pushing through the crowd not in my direction but in the direction of the door. The second is the look of triumph pulsating in Rebecca's eye.

"Punishment complete!" calls the duchess. "Please, do return to the party!" As voices once again fill the ballroom, as the orchestra begins a lively waltz, she runs a hand over King's face. "How kind you are, jumping to my defense like that," she says as he kisses her on the nose. "I do fear, however, that the punishment was misplaced."

"You believe our darling little Alex's pleas of innocence?" His eyes round at the novelty of the suggestion, but even I can see it's a farce. The punishment had everything to do with yesterday's eavesdropping, I'm sure of it.

Then Evie's beside me, helping me to my feet. "Mother, I know she didn't do this," she's insisting. "I know her well, I promise—"

The duchess wraps an arm around my waist. "I know, child. Go, enjoy your evening." Without another word, she propels me through the room, out the door and into a hallway still twinkling with fairy lights.

I can't put thoughts into words. Everything's a blur. My shoulder aches, though the full brunt of pain is masked by alcohol, and soon I'm clambering up steps, moving like a bullet through a world of black and white. Finally, we stop in front of a set of familiar doors.

When I spot the viscount standing over me, I see eyes that are snake-like, distorted with rage. He thinks *I'm* responsible, he thinks *I* mutilated the roses. The realization makes my stomach hurt in an unexpected way.

But after a while, as he and his mother speak, it becomes obvious that I was wrong. "Find out who was responsible," he finally hisses.

"It's impossible. The servants will blame the florists, the florists will blame the servants. Here. She's been badly stunned. Show her compassion." A moment of silence passes between them, replaced by the clicking of the duchess's heels.

I blink, then a hand grips my back and I'm guided forward, through the entrance hall and into Wolfe's private quarters. A fire crackles in the hearth that I'm positioned in front of, and I sit on my heels. There's confusion over the past ten minutes, sure. But there's also something else. Like a profound sadness laced with defeat.

Wolfe positions a washcloth over my shoulder, cold and soothing, then retreats into the shadows. For a long time, I merely stare into the fire, contemplating nothing but the dancing flames and the slow decay of wood to ash. But eventually I stir, pull the pink-stained cloth away and examine my wounds. Three stripes of red, one considerably worse than the others. It's this one that has split open.

I remember my aunt's parting words, I remember my own conviction to be strong, and I sit up straighter. Lift my chin. It's nothing more than a small injury, these stripes—they'll heal, just as my knuckles did, and the scalding along my legs.

But staying here, making the best of it, letting go of that dream of an easy life—it's more difficult to do now. I'm not allowed to come and go from the grounds of Strath Glen, I'm subjected to physical abuse from King and to insults from the rest.

I need to find a way out. Maybe if the scrolls are of no help, I'll run away—across the border. If I'm somewhere unrecognizable, they won't be able to track me down, will they? But then...Evie had mentioned those fences surrounding Airo-Aurora. Something tells me they won't be easily breached. Besides, do I really want to leave my friends? My aunt?

Wolfe watches from a far chair, enveloped in darkness. Then his chest rises; he pulls himself to his full height and approaches me with a face carved from stone. "If it helps," he says, distantly, "it gives me no pleasure to see you like this."

A burning sensation floods my chest without warning. The daze that had gripped me breaks like shattering ice. "It was your *mother* who defended me," I hurl with as much conviction as I can from my spot on the floor. It isn't much, but still, I can see that my words reach him.

He turns away. "Yes, well...my hands were tied, I'm afraid."

"Your hands are always tied when it comes to my wellbeing."

"Trust that I am acting in your best interest. I know it doesn't seem—"

I laugh loudly. "The only thing I *trust* is that you prioritize your position within the palace head and shoulders over the welfare of your fiancée!"

"Aside from the sting of pain you must endure in the short term, this turn of events isn't worrisome—not in regard to your overall welfare. Word will spread that this wasn't your doing, I'll see to it."

I begin to protest but he waves me aside.

"Had I stayed to defend you," he continues, "something I knew others would do, I would have a much larger mess on my hands. At any rate, you've been unhappy with me all evening and I don't expect to turn your mind now."

I return my attention to the fire. "I never said I was unhappy with you," I mutter.

"Nonetheless, I have been giving that matter some thought, and I believe I have a solution that would appease both of us."

"Which matter's that?"

"My absence from the palace. Now, sit on a chair, please.

I find speaking to your back disconcerting."

"I need help to stand."

After a long hesitation, he rounds in front of me and extends a hand. I just glance at it. Frowning deeply, he bends lower, grips me around the waist, and lifts me to my feet.

I sit on a chair closest to the heat of the fire, and he pulls a chair around so that he faces me, more accommodating than normal. Next, he removes his jacket and hands it over. "If you're cold," he mutters, staring at the arm of the chair.

"It'll ruin," I say flatly.

"It's all right."

So I pull it around myself, letting the satin lining settle over my shoulders. Faintly I pick up the smell of something masculine, and I clear my throat. "As you were saying, Viscount."

His gaze tightens. "Since when do you address me as such?"

I say nothing, just fiddle with one of the buttons on his jacket.

"You say you can fly a helicopter."

My fingers go still. Whatever I was expecting him to say, it isn't that.

"Well?"

"Yes. I can."

"So act as my personal pilot, then. That way, you will always know where I am."

The words are shocking. Astonishing—so astonishing that I almost forget the anger in my chest. *Almost.* "I knew where you were tonight, and it wasn't any help at all."

He leans forward, clearly agitated by my words. He swipes at his mouth. "Consider it a new job, one more befitting, perhaps, than handmaid."

I have to bite my smile away. "Does that mean I don't have to drag your breakfast up three flights of stairs anymore?"

He looks momentarily puzzled. "There is a dumbwaiter just past my room."

"Sadly," I sigh, "receiving that information sooner would've spared me a lot of pain."

"Bring me my breakfast or not, it makes no difference. What say you?"

"I say that I like that idea, sir," and even though I'm angry at him, I can't hide my smile any longer. A pilot. A pilot!

Relief seems to wash over him. No matter how distant he likes to keep himself, no matter how detached he might be, he cares in some respect about my opinion—he must. "I'll have the chauffeur take you to the Sky Center in the morning to sort out the paperwork."

"I look forward to it," I tell him. "Thank you."

He leans back in his chair and links long fingers together. "When you are my wife, it is my belief that the others will be gentler with you. My uncle included."

Gentler? King? I shift in my seat—never before has our ever-approaching status as husband and wife seemed so real. "That would be a relief," I murmur eventually. And it's true. If King and the others were kinder, a future here might not be so bad, especially with my shiny new job. It might even be better than *not bad*.

So, what about my contention that I was placed here by mistake? Could the Mainframe have been right all along?

I dismiss the thought immediately. It was a glitch that put me here, nothing more.

From downstairs come filtered sounds of revelry—swells of laughter, bursts of music, and after a while, it underlines the silence between us. Then he stirs: "I can't give you a love story, Alex, if that is what you are after."

I turn my gaze to him, genuinely surprised. "Do you really take me for that type of girl?"

"I don't," he concedes. "And yet you wanted me to like

your dress this evening, and I didn't take you for that type of girl either." His eyes are completely impenetrable now, just like the windows of the palace in which we sit. They look only out. The slit of vulnerability I glimpsed earlier has gone.

Yes. I had wanted him to like it. All of it—the hair and makeup, too, and for a reason I can't really pinpoint. "I suppose," I say, "I was swept away by it all. The music, the décor..." Blushing deeply at what amounts to an admission, I search for something else to throw between us. Anything. This talk of love stories and dresses—it won't do. I need to change the subject, quick. Words tumble from my mouth: "Are you familiar with a Dr. Lebwitski?"

He lifts his head. Hawk-like eyes narrow. "Why do you ask?"

"He was here at the palace yesterday, meeting with King. I'm wondering who he is."

He stares into the fire, and the shadow it creates across his face makes it look hollow and unkind. "I didn't realize a meeting had been arranged," he mutters, then shrugs. "He's my uncle's doctor, that's all."

I rest my head against the side of the chair. He's lying, I know he is. But why?

"The Queen," I try next. "Are you close with her?"

"These are strange questions to be asking."

"I'm curious."

"Too curious, is my thinking."

"Well?"

"Well, she's my aunt."

"I found her in Counterdown Abbey yesterday, reading a book. It was upside down."

A coolness washes over him. He doesn't move a muscle, but I can feel his razor-like focus sharpening. "Oh?"

"Why would that be?"

"She's peculiar." He comes close to whispering it, so

restrained is his pitch. It's like his stillness extends to his lungs.

"How about Reginald Worthers? Does the name mean anything to you?"

He stands so swiftly that he knocks the chair over with a loud bang.

I withdraw to the farthest corner of my chair and my hand moves protectively to my wounded shoulder.

"Tell me this instant why you ask such questions. Do not leave *anything* out."

With him standing over me, with the fire so close, with the back of the chair not giving an inch, I feel like I'm suffocating. So I say nothing. A few seconds pass, then Wolfe moves to the far side of the room where he paces back and forth.

Why did those questions make him so upset? Just who are Dr. Lebwitski and Reginald Worthers? *What's wrong with the Queen?*

Eventually, he goes still. He lifts his head and stares at me, eyes flashing even through the darkness. "Tell me now, or I will personally go to the Mainframe in the morning and review your feed until I have my answer."

The words stun me. They settle over the room like acid. Surely he's bluffing—the invasion of privacy is unimaginable. Criminal. And yet he's the second most powerful man in all of Airo-Aurora—I would be foolish to doubt him. I would be foolish, too, to try to talk him down, to make him reconsider when I can see plainly across his face that he won't budge.

So without any other option, I stand and with extreme carefulness, slip the jacket from my shoulders. "Then we should go to my room," I say.

Wordlessly he gestures to the door.

———

SERVANTS HAVE COME AND GONE. My room's tidy, Evie's items returned to their owner. Perfect—I don't want any reminders of the evening. Just my luck, then, that the music and liveliness from Birkland Grand are louder here than in Wolfe's suite.

Another thing that's different is the temperature—without a fireplace, I can see my own breath. "I'm going to get changed," I tell him.

His body stiffens with impatience, but he says nothing.

Once inside the closet, I take a moment to examine my shoulder—frowning at cuts that don't belong—then, shivering, kick off my shoes and begin to unzip myself. The zipper won't budge. Not on the first pass, and not on the second. After trying from several different angles, I swear, then kick open the closet door: "Uh—I'm afraid the zipper on my dress is stuck. Maybe you could call for a maid?"

There's a beat of silence, followed by a loud sigh. The next thing I know, Wolfe's hand lands on the closet door, and he pushes it all the way open. "Turn," he instructs. He wrenches the zipper down several inches, then stalks out.

Well, I think without amusement—that's one way about it.

I pull on the ugliest nightgown I can find, the plaid flannel one I wore on my very first night, plus a housecoat, and emerge from the closet. Carefully I remove the scrolls from the desk drawer, acutely aware that his gaze follows my every move. Walking as close to him as I dare, I tilt my gaze up at him, holding the scrolls behind my back and out of his reach.

For a while, he simply matches my stare with his own. Then he opens his palm. "The letters."

"You're forcing my hand." It isn't that I care about keeping the scrolls from him, not really. It's the circumstance that I don't like.

He shoves his hand closer.

Frowning, I pass him the scrolls, then sit on the sofa. A mixture of relief and hurt, peace and anger sits inside my chest as I watch Wolfe's face. Aside from a brow drawn in on itself, it gives nothing away, and finally he places the scrolls back into the desk drawer. His body is brassbound, his movements forced.

For several minutes he gazes out the window at the full moon that illuminates the forest of birch with its silvery glow. He touches the glass lightly with his fingers as if recalling something, then marches to the couch. "When did you receive them?"

"Since arriving here, at Strath Glen."

"Be more specific, please." His voice is calm. Too calm.

"The one signed Glitch on my very first morning. You spotted it yourself when I delivered your breakfast. The other one just yesterday."

"And how were they delivered?"

"A servant found them on the grounds and brought them to me."

"But only one bears your name. How would a servant know to deliver the other one to you?"

"Oh—that's right. The other one I stumbled across myself."

His eyes narrow, but he continues with his line of questioning. "Where, precisely?"

"I can't remember exactly where," I lie. "Outside, somewhere."

Stony silence. Then, "Do you know who the letters are from?"

"I don't."

"Do you know why you should be targeted with them?"

"Not in the slightest."

"Do you know the meaning of them?"

"No."

"I take it Jill Nightingale is the guard out front?"

"Yes."

"Who is Timothee Allen, please?"

"A computer programmer at Hallah."

"Were you familiar with these people prior to receiving the letters?"

"No."

"And what do your three have in common?"

"Seemingly nothing."

"Were you ever planning on telling me?"

At this last question I lift my head. I wish I hadn't. Those eyes of his have once again become unfriendly slits.

"There seem to be plenty of things you don't share with me," I say in an undertone.

"If I choose not to share it, there is good reason. Listen, and carefully. If another of these scrolls manages to make its way to you, I expect you to come to me at once. Do I have your word?"

"Only if you tell me your thoughts on them."

His brow lowers. "This isn't a negotiation, *Alex*."

"They're *my* letters," I insist. "I don't have an obligation to share them with you, or anyone else." I pause for a moment, then add with an assertiveness I didn't know I had: "But I'll oblige if you meet my terms."

He drops heavily onto the couch next to me. Between gritted teeth, he says in a low voice difficult to decipher: "Fine. You are curious about them? The writer is attempting to avoid a stain on his or her feed. That is why the cursive is so poor."

"Meaning?"

"Meaning they were written in the dark so that the Mainframe has no record of them."

I turn to him, bewildered.

"This is not a game," he snaps, reading my expression. "It is not a puzzle. The purpose of these letters, whatever it may be, is clearly a devious one. You must not, under any circumstance, fall under this person's spell. Do not search him or her out, do not search out the people listed more than you undoubtedly already have, do not start poking your nose into things that do not concern you. Do you understand?"

If anything, I'm more intrigued than ever, but I simply look at him and nod. "I take it you don't care to tell me who Reginald Worthers is?"

"You take it correct."

"And the use of the term Glitch? Do you have any thoughts on that?"

He shakes his head, eyes suddenly unfocused. "Probably a ruse to capture your attention," he murmurs.

I stare at his profile and frown. "I think you know a lot more than you're telling me, Viscount. If you want me to trust you, maybe you should try doing the same of me."

He angles his body to me and lifts his hand.

Immediately I draw back.

After a long hesitation, he folds his hand away. "Those marks," he says, eyeing my shoulder, "they are nothing if you do not heed my warnings. As for the rest of it, you are right. There is much that I am not telling you. There are forces at work larger than you, and as knowledge can prove deadly, I intend to shield you from it whether you like it or not."

———

ONLY WHEN I'M ALONE, tucked between my sheets much later in the night, shoulder throbbing, teeth chattering from the cold, do I wonder how much of what Wolfe says is true. To shield me from information to protect me is one thing, sure. Something touching, and kind. Just like making me his pilot. But what if there's another reason? What if the only person he wants to shield is himself?

nineteen

. . .

AS THE SUN begins to warm the lithe limbs of the birch, as it fills in the shadows cast by the old palace, as it slips between gray satin curtains, I wake.

It had been a late night, one with far too little sleep. The Rose Ceremony had been a disaster by all accounts, Wolfe had forced me to share with him those strange scrolls, and my shoulder still throbs. But for the first time since arriving at Strath Glen, I wake with a smile on my face.

Pianist, pilot, or librarian.

How many times did I chant that under my breath, leading up to the Selection?

And now I'll hold one as my own—all thanks to Wolfe. I'll serve as *pilot* to royalty! To make matters even better, I'll have an excuse to leave the palace, one King can't take from me, *and* I'll have the pleasure of once again flying a helicopter.

Things here might not be easy or simple—not even close. But they could definitely be worse.

I get out of bed and go to the closet to get ready. The least I can do is take Wolfe his breakfast—hardly a chore with the help of a dumbwaiter. And besides, the feelings of mistrust and anger that I had toward him last night, well... they've dimmed with the light of the morning.

A few minutes later, I stand in the House of Mirrors, surprised to find it completely void of life. No bustle of expensive gowns, no overworked servants running from one room to the next, not a sound emanating from even a far off corner.

Well, the festivities *had* lasted well into the night. In fact, I had been lulled to sleep by the tireless choir, their chants finally pushing me into a restless slumber. No doubt the royals still sleep soundly, and most of the servants, too.

In the basement, though, the kitchen staff are fast at work, even behind bleary eyes. "Heard you got an ouchie on your shoulder!" shouts a middle-aged cook named Bryson. He winks as he rushes past me with a ladle in one hand and a bag of flour in the other. With his elbows, he catches a bag of frozen blueberries tossed his way by a servant named Sue.

"One could say that," I agree.

Then a familiar voice adds, "A little change-up from her usual pampering, aye."

I turn to see Rebecca standing there, smirking. I want to scream at her for doing what she did to me, but all I do is scowl. "And what pampering is that?"

"The kind that comes from a handmaid living on Floor Two, how 'bout!"

"I didn't ask to be put there!" I retort. "It was King who ordered it." And then a lightbulb goes off in my head. My placement on the second floor with the royals was to make sure I was hated by *all* inhabitants of Strath Glen. To make sure I found no allies even among the other servants. *That's* why I was given such generous accommodations...and that's why most of the servants won't even look at me. I lift an eyebrow—clearly, I've underestimated King.

Rebecca, meanwhile, makes a show of brushing off her

shoulders. "He said, she said, none of it gone matters. Point is, you haven't got a friend in us."

I roll my eyes. "So I've noticed."

"I'd say you got off easy last night with the duchess leaping to your defense. Did you notice how fast the viscount cleared out? Can't imagine you've been invited on many dates with 'im."

"You're right. He doesn't really care for me."

"Poor little fiancée!" Rebecca cries. It draws sniggers from the servants within earshot, who carry out their duties without making a single sound. If it weren't for the sizzling of sausage, the basement would be as tomb-like as the rest of the palace.

"He doesn't care for me," I continue, "but he does believe me. He knows it wasn't me that hacked up those roses. The same with his mother."

"Aye. Too bad King thinks it you, then."

"Maybe he did at the time, but not anymore. Actually, the duchess will be investigating whether it's the servants or the florists to blame. I still need to tell her that you and Simon presented the box to me yesterday afternoon, with all the roses in perfect condition."

"She won't believe the likes of you."

"Of course she will. Why do you think she came to my defense in the first place? Obviously she's going to hold allegiance to me—I'm marrying her *son*!"

"A second marriage," Rebecca snaps. "Nothing sacred in that."

Immediately after the words are spoken, she draws into herself. The other servants gape at her; they glance uneasily at each other. And when there's nothing else to do, they carry on preparing breakfast with stern expressions.

I feel the color drain from my face. My anger vanishes. "The viscount," I whisper. "He was *married*?"

Rebecca presses her mouth together and stares over my shoulder at the stone wall.

"What happened? How did the marriage end? Who was he wedded to?"

The girl shakes her head.

"Viscount's breakfast is ready!" shouts a line cook. He nods in the direction of a heavy tray.

I simply shift my gaze back to Rebecca. "Tell me," I say.

"Can't. Won't."

"But—"

"Can't. Won't."

I pinch the bridge of my nose and wait for the sudden aching in my head to subside. Finally, I lift my chin. "A second marriage, you say. I guess the viscount himself ordered the palace not to mention it." I watch her closely for any indication that I'm correct. "And now you've gone and blathered it. Do you think you'd be out of a job for an offense like that? Worse? Add to it the fact that I saw for myself the roses yesterday—"

"Okay, you've got my back against the wall, yeah?" Rebecca snaps. "Out with it. Out with whatever it is you want."

"I want you to leave me alone—*that's* what I want. No more snarkiness. No more tricks. The uniform, the tea, the roses. You even hid the existence of the dumbwaiter from me! Nothing like that again, or I'll go straight to Wolfe and lay it bare. All of it."

Reluctantly she nods.

I hold out a hand. "Deal?"

"Deal."

As we shake on it, I add, "Were you the one leaving the apple cores in my room in the middle of the night?"

Her eyebrows lift at my words. "Apple cores? No," she says heavily, with no trace of amusement. "I like me sleep."

Sighing, I carry the heavy breakfast tray to the dumbwaiter, load it, then press the button for the second floor. As I head to the staircase, I find myself overcome with emotion. Partly I'm happy. I'm happy with myself—with how I handled that just now. I'm happy that Rebecca won't be bothering me anymore.

But there's something darker there, too.

Previously married. *Married.*

I shouldn't be so surprised, I remind myself, as the torches begin to flicker, and my shadow elongates against the wall. The possibility had been there in the newspaper, right at the very beginning. And then there was that day in the woods with him. He hadn't denied a previous wife. He had refused to respond, had told me about Claudia instead.

Just how many serious lovers has he had? And how did he come by a second wife when divorce isn't even allowed?

I grab the breakfast tray from the dumbwaiter with my head still spinning. A moment later, I ram the tray into Wolfe's side, knocking over a bone china pitcher of orange juice and causing a carafe of syrup to turn over onto my blazer. Sighing, Wolfe turns the pitcher upright and lifts his ruined breakfast to its usual spot in the entrance hall.

"I'm sorry," I say in a rush of embarrassment. "I didn't notice your door opening." I take off my blazer and wipe my hands.

"I'm leaving anyhow," he says gruffly. I must look up at him with a strange expression because he pauses, and some of his displeasure at having a breakfast tray thrust into his hip dissipates. "What is it?"

Previously married. So. What kind of life has he known? What kind of *love* has he known? It's bad enough that he hides information about those scrolls, but this too? The man is nothing but secrets.

"Is something the matter?" he continues, a hint of concern in his voice. "You've gone pale. Your shoulder, is it worse?"

"Pardon me? Oh, no. My shoulder's fine."

"Right, then," he mumbles. He motions to the ruined breakfast. "Help yourself to whatever is still edible. Monsieur Sawyer awaits your arrival in Devonshire Commons." With another curious glance, he strides out the door.

———

THE CHAUFFEUR STANDS by the window, watching with interest the black clouds that roll in from the west. "Ah, yes," he murmurs as I join him. "So our paths cross yet again."

"Looks rather like rain."

He digs a finger into his chin and stares at me. "Aren't you as self-assured as a honey badger. And here I was, thinking you'd never settle into life at Strath Glen."

"And what makes you think I've settled in?" I ask, surprised. "On the contrary, I'm as much an outsider now as on my very first day."

"Nonsense, Miss Alex. I can practically smell palace life upon you, just as the others could smell Quire radiating from your pores when you first stumbled into this room over a month prior. How quickly things change."

"You overestimate me," I say as I lean on the window frame and shift my gaze from the darkening sky to the sparkling city beneath it. "I take it you didn't hear about the fiasco last night at the Rose Ceremony?"

"Indeed, I did. Word travels fast around here, didn't I warn you? From what I heard, however, you have allies left and right, not to mention next to no work handed to you in your role as handmaid. And now comes a request from the viscount himself to trot you off to the Sky Center so that you may become, dare I say, his pilot?"

I nod.

"Once a killer, always a killer," shouts the parrot from the corner.

"What an honor, Miss Alex. Your powers of seduction surpass all expectation!"

I roll my eyes. "My *powers* in that arena are as lacking as ever. I can assure you that my promotion had nothing to do with it, though I should warn you the implication could definitely cause offense."

"Take none of it, Miss Alex, but do spill the details."

"The details," I repeat, now laughing. "Let me think. Okay—here you go. It was nothing more than a tacit agreement to smooth over a source of friction and best serve two competing interests."

"How romantic," he replies wryly.

"Sister! I've been looking all over for you." Evie bustles into the room, holding a raspberry scone. "How is your shoulder? Does it hurt something terrible? Uncle shouldn't have been so quick to cast blame. Tell me, are you okay?"

"There she is!" hollers a new voice. The Prince of Airo-Aurora strides past Evie and right up to me, chewing a crumpet. "The girl of the hour! You do know how to liven up a party, though all that is nothing compared to this morning's turn."

"This morning?" I repeat, doing my best not to stare at his satin pajamas. "What happened this morning?"

"Only a memo sent out by your once-dull fiancé. He's quite earnest in proclaiming your innocence concerning those silly roses. It gets a man to thinking." He pauses for dramatic effect.

"Yes?"

"Why, he cares about his fiancée! So. What is it exactly that he finds so alluring?" He walks slowly around me, examining me from top to bottom. "I can think of several things, personally—"

"Cut it out," scolds Evie. "Don't go sniffing about, or I'll go straight to brother."

The prince's face lights up at her words. "But do, dearest cousin! Tell him I've got my paw prints all over—"

"Time to go, Miss Alex!" shouts the chauffeur. He angles me toward the door. "We must get you to the Sky Center without delay," he adds, and after I give a quick wave to Evie, we slip down the stone steps and into the sprawling underground garage. Rows of closely spaced yellow bulbs shine brightly overhead, and the sight stops me in my tracks, pushing away thoughts of roses, and memos, and marriages, and even Wolfe.

"Miss?" asks the chauffeur when he notices I've fallen behind.

"There was a man in a white coat down here when I first arrived. He was working alongside those bluecoats taking away the servant."

"What about it?"

"Dr. Lebwitski. That's who it was, wasn't it?"

The chauffeur shrugs. "I don't have a clue who was involved in the sacking of Mr. Worthers, and I don't care a trifle either. Come now, or the viscount will have my head for dicking about."

I don't budge. "Mr. *Worthers*, you say? Reginald Worthers? Is that the name of the sacked servant? And don't chide me," I add quickly, spotting the look on his face. "Wolfe and I have a special arrangement allowing me to ask questions."

"On a first-name basis, are we? *My*." He folds his arms across his chest and walks straight up to me, studying me with unabashed interest even as the lightbulb overhead bursts and scatters glass at our feet.

"I don't follow. With Mr. Worthers, you mea—?"

"No, not with that shady old bastard. The sacked servant Reginald Worthers, indeed, though I don't know why you'd give a toss. I'm talking of the great Lord Viscount."

I frown. Reginald Worthers, *the sacked servant.* No wonder the name sounded familiar, and yet...why would he be listed in that scroll alongside the Queen?

"I'm growing old here." Monsieur Sawyer jingles the keys to the limousine in front of my face.

"I'm afraid I still don't follow."

"You called the viscount *Wolfe* just now. Plain as day. Not even his own family calls him by his first name."

Now he has my attention. "Are you sure?"

"I'm surprised he hasn't whipped you for your insolence, child."

I have to admit that I share his surprise. After all, I have called him *Wolfe* from almost the get-go, so why hasn't he bothered to correct me? Sure, our relationship over the past several weeks had developed into something approaching cordial, but early on? I really am lucky I escaped a whipping.

"Unless, that is," he continues with a wink, "you've led me astray on your skills as a seductress."

I grin as I walk around the broken glass to the behemoth. "I haven't led you astray, I promise." Then I swing open the door and eye him. "Maybe," I begin tactfully, "Wolfe's used to his betrothed being informal because of his previous marriage. Did you know the woman?"

The words have an immediate impact. Monsieur Sawyer's eyes widen, then without a word, he shoves me inside the limousine and slams the door.

"Sir?" I ask as we pull free from the parking garage and roar into the quickly darkening city.

"Hush."

"Why? I know Wolfe was married." Then I add, "He told me as much."

Eyes glint in the rearview mirror. "Well, Miss Alex. I see you are just as intractable as when I first fetched you from your aunt. If you think I'm about to fall for that cock and bull story, you've risen far too late from bed. Already all the servants know that the cat's sprung from the bag, but just, and it surely wasn't from the viscount's mouth as you claim. You'd take care not to mention it to him either, unless you want to lose that pretty little head of yours." With one last knowing look, he lays his foot upon the accelerator. We speed along a sapling-lined avenue headed west.

"It was worth a shot," I say with a sigh. "Usually I don't play games, but I guess curiosity got the best of me. My apologies."

"Curiosity has been known to kill the cat."

"I guess that means you don't want to discuss the woman? Or their marriage?"

"For once, you are correct."

"What about Mr. Reginald Worthers, then? A sacked servant...what'd he do?"

"What did I tell you about curiosity? Your fiancé might indulge you in your questions, but I certainly shall not." A minute of silence passes, then he exhales. "Earning a pretty penny for offering up a bit of information here and there about royal life to the papers, that was his main offense. Of course, once the mole is known, a succinct sacking is without question. Quite happy?"

So, that was the royal source mentioned in the *Morning Herald*, all that time ago. Strange it wasn't the blackcoats taking him to the prisons for something like that. "What business, Monsieur, did the Mainframe's *bluecoats* have with him?"

"Don't have all the answers. What do I look like? Word is, though, that none other than your fiancé kept him from the gallows."

"Oh? Why would he interfere?"

"A simple act of kindness to a man who spent decades serving the palace, Miss Alex. The great Lord Viscount of Airo-Aurora, indeed."

I tip my head, surprised. I'd assumed the servants catered

to him out of fear, but it appears I misjudged him. "Thank you, Monsieur, for all that."

"Sometimes it pays to have friends in high places."

Normally I'd ask if he considered me a friend. Right now I ask, "You think I'm in a high place?"

"Though from what's been whispered in my ear, no date has been set, the wedding draws ever nearer with each passing day. That bestows upon you high rank. The real power that you claim, however, comes from the fact that *Wolfe* appears to be sweetening for his little fiancée from Quire, after all."

"*Sweetening*?" I repeat, coughing and tripping over the word. "You're mistaken on that front."

"Why, then, am I taking you to the Sky Center so that you may act as his own personal pilot? It's no matter to charter out a pilot and with short notice to boot, especially for a man of his stature. So *why*, Miss Alex?"

"I already explained—"

"Oh, tacit agreement, my arse!"

"I promise you it wasn't a bleeding heart that did it." More like business negotiations.

"If you say so."

"Oh, I do," I say as we turn into a private drive lined with ornamental pear trees. *Sky Center* is written in metal on a nearby sign, rusted purposefully to orange for effect. "He won't even share the major details of his life with me," I mutter, mostly to myself, "let alone the small ones."

"Such as having been married previously?"

I give him a halfhearted smile. "That's the one."

"His reasons for doing so have more to do with his own needs rather than yours. Anyhow, we've arrived, so no more chatter. I'll be eagerly awaiting your return," he adds wryly over his shoulder.

A minute later, I stand on the curb and stare at a building constructed entirely of blue-tinted glass. Off in the distance are runways, and pylons, and little tractor-like machines used for carting people and luggage from place to place. None of the machines are in motion, no planes or helicopters come or go, no passengers await. Most days, I guess, are equally static. Because most people in Airo-Aurora, particularly from areas like Quire, never step foot outside the nation-state. International travel is as uncommon as news from other countries, a direct result of nations turning inward generations before, a once interdependent and well-connected world pulled of cables. Still, a lucky few come and go—like Wolfe. Like *me*, soon.

But I hesitate. I learned to fly at a young age; the Hobby Hangar became my second home. This place is nothing like home. There's no rusted half-cylinder housing the aircrafts, no stretch of pavement with weeds growing through the cracks serving as a tarmac. Besides, their air travel was restricted to the airspace directly above Airo-Aurora— venturing far from the city and across international borders will be a new experience entirely. So will transporting an important figure such as Wolfe. Yes, this is definitely different. *Too* different.

Minutes pass until suddenly, the silence is interrupted by the unfriendly blast of the behemoth's horn. With a frown at its driver, I head inside.

I speak to a man with a faux hawk at the front desk, who passes me a clipboard and a mountain of paperwork. He points me in the direction of an empty bank of chairs, and when I finally finish, he instructs me to wait. Twenty minutes later, he returns with a woman named Ruth, who wears a blue jumpsuit zipped to her chin.

"Let's go, little lady," Ruth says. "By the time we do a quick twirl, it'll be nearly lunch. Besides, not sure how much longer the rain'll hold off."

My jaw drops. "A *twirl*?"

The woman's eyes turn skyward.

"I-I'm expected to fly?"

"Not going to get your commercial license otherwise, do you think? All you've got right now is personal class—not enough to fly in and out of the Sky Center with. And not with a member of the royal family aboard. Come on, let's get you suited up."

Lost in a daze, I'm led into what looks like a locker room. Because when Wolfe said I'd have some paperwork to sort through, well—it never occurred to me I'd be expected to *fly*. That I'd undergo a *test*.

"Any time you take out your sweetie, come here first—"

"My who?"

"Your sweetie. He called first thing this morning, telling us to expect you. He said you were his fiancé?"

"Oh." I swallow. "Yes, technically, that's true."

"Not another way to make it true, little lady. Now, as I was saying. Flight suits are kept in here, goggles right over there. Hurry up, I told you about lunch."

Five minutes later, we walk onto a pristine tarmac in matching jumpsuits. At the Hobby Hangar, me and the owner, Al, have to hoist the beat-up chopper onto a trolley and pull it into position; here, someone else has done the heavy lifting. We head for the lawn-green helicopter that sparkles even under the overcast skies, and I smile. Maybe I could get used to this.

Once buckled into the cockpit, however, with Ruth watching my every move, nerves rob me of my steadiness. For a moment, I just sit there, staring at the controls like they're completely foreign.

What's that knob for? And that switch?

Then I give myself a shake—I didn't come this far for nothing. I remember the contentedness that had filled my chest that morning and sit straighter. I have the chance to serve as a commercial pilot, and a commercial pilot needs a commercial license.

I open the throttle and pull up the collective stick with my left hand. My right hand grabs the cyclic stick in an attempt to keep the green beast even, but it's more sensitive than what I'm used to, and I only just manage to correct it in time.

A tense minute follows as I take us higher, as I transition from vertical motion to forward motion. It causes the sprightly machine to shudder, but finally we're off, and I make several adjustments to reduce engine noise and smooth a bumpy ride, both of which Ruth seems to appreciate. Only then do I allow myself to breathe.

But the sight of Airo-Aurora below catches me off-guard. The last time I looked down on it from under the hammering of rotor blades, my Selection was hovering on the horizon. My future promised to be the straightforward, easy one I was so desperate to have. Airo-Aurora and its Mainframe shone with glory.

And now...?

"Take her south to the city limit," Ruth shouts. "You flying out the King in the morning?"

I aim the sparkling beast toward the far end of Airo-Aurora. Gray clouds evaporate into small beads of moisture, and off in the distance, the sun pokes its nose from its hiding spot. I glance at Ruth. "The King's going away, is he?"

"That's what the schedule says," she shrugs. "I take it that's a no, then."

I shake my head. "I'll only be flying the viscount around, as far as I know." My voice may be level, but inwardly I couldn't be happier. A sanctioned outing today and freedom tomorrow. I'll use the opportunity to visit Agnes and my aunt. Maybe Timothee and Jill as well, to update them on all the latest developments.

The next half hour is spent carefully criss crossing over Airo-Aurora, the Alps, and the forest to the west, the one closest to the Sky Center. I do all I'm asked: hovering, flying at varying altitudes and speeds, and finally positioning the beast gently back to earth.

"Two points lost for a shaky start, but otherwise you passed with flying colors, little lady," shouts Ruth as I cut the engine. "Who taught you to fly, anyhow?"

"My father. It was a hobby of his."

"A useful one at that. Cheers to you both. Come on inside, and I'll finish up your papers. Congratulations— you're now a commercial pilot."

I smile, and the question mark obscuring Airo-Aurora and its Mainframe gets a little smaller.

twenty

"ONION IN THE POT. Give it three, then stir in the garlic and thyme. Pinch of salt, too."

"Do you really think I've forgotten already?"

Aunt Jo winks. "But I'd think the art of cooking is lost completely when you have a small army preparing your every meal."

"It's only dinner I'm served," I explain, as I use a knife to scrape onion into the sizzling oil. Immediately the kitchen fills with its aroma. "Besides, it was only a month or so ago that I was helping you prepare ours."

"Only dinner you're served? The cheapskates! If your prince isn't keeping your belly full, my refrigerator is always stocked. You know you're welcome anytime, whether I'm walking post or not. Still got your key?"

"Viscount, not prince. And thank you, but I already come as often as I can. King doesn't think it's...proper that I make a habit of leaving Strath Glen," I say tactfully.

Immediately her face contorts. "Well, if that isn't the stupidest thing—"

"That's enough," I say, suppressing a smile. I add the minced garlic and thyme to the pot and pick up a wooden spoon. "Was it a problem finding someone to cover your shift this morning?"

"Joan's always quick to pick up extra work, you know that. Now, hurry up and get the meat cooking—we still need to peel the peaches for dessert."

It'd been Timothee's idea to meet for lunch at the palace. It had been my aunt's idea to prepare the pies. Carefully I add a pound of ground lamb to the pot.

"Salt one dough and sugar the other," she instructs next as she rolls up her sleeves and begins peeling the peaches herself. "And tell me some good news about your life up there on the hill. I've grown an ulcer since your last visit— all that talk about your miserable fiancé and how much the whole lot hate you..." She shakes her head.

"What sort of news did you have in mind?"

"That the viscount's shown you a kinder side. That you've made friends with all those lunatics up there. That you've been kept busy with an interesting project."

Hands immersed in dough, I half-turn to look at my aunt. I lift my voice over the sizzling from the stovetop. "Actually, I have wonderful news."

She looks up at me, stunned. "You do?"

"Wolfe asked me to be his personal pilot for international travel; I got my commercial license yesterday!"

She inhales. "Just like you've always wanted! Why didn't you tell me straight away?"

"I was too worried about feeding my lunch guests, I guess. It's not often I throw a party."

She hugs me. "Your father would be so proud. Remember your first time in the sky? You were simply vibrating after, telling me and your mom all about it, eyes on fire, hair a complete mess. I remember it like it was yesterday."

I begin to knead the dough. "So do I."

"Visited their memories lately?"

"I haven't, no," I admit quietly.

"No shame in that."

She watches me, but I don't say anything.

"It's about time you gave it a rest, you know."

I lift my head. "Visiting their memories?"

"It's hard to move on when you're doing that. Sometimes closure is the real medicine. You know, they say the memory bank is a great gift of the Mainframe, but you won't convince me of it. After your uncle passed, I went there every day for months and months, walking home weeping each time. Then one day, I woke up and realized that was it. He was gone, and watching our life together in the past wasn't going to get me moving into the future.

"And you," she continues, "I still remember seeing you weeping your eyes out singing Christmas songs in the middle of July! I know exactly which memories you were visiting that day, and what good did it do you?"

"Maybe they were happy tears," I try.

"They weren't." She laughs.

I return to my work, trying to imagine a world without a memory bank, where loved ones are reduced to a few static photographs and nothing more. Maybe closure *would* come quicker, but the loss—it'd be even more pronounced. Wouldn't it?

"It's nice to have the *choice*," I finally say. "To go visit their memories, or not."

"Choice? Is it ever really a choice? When a parent or spouse or, god forbid, a child goes, seems to me it's almost impossible to resist. At least until you give your head a shake, as I eventually did."

"So what're you saying—that choice…is an illusion?"

She shrugs. "We humans aren't exactly well-equipped to make good ones. Why do you think the Selection system was introduced in the first place?"

"Sometimes computers can choose badly, too," I remind her.

She smacks the countertop. "A job promotion, and only a month in! Maybe this viscount of yours isn't all bad, is it possible? Maybe the computers knew something all along!"

I roll my eyes, kneading the dough with more focus than before.

"You can try to hide that smile all you want, but you can't fool me. You're softening on him! I can see it a mile away. And this new job of yours tells me he's softening just the same."

"I don't know about that."

"Well?"

"Well. It's more complicated than that."

"But maybe it doesn't need to be. Roll out that dough now and let it rest."

We keep chatting as we finish the pies, as they fill the house with their enticing aromas, and when the oven timer beeps, Aunt Jo carefully positions them in carrying bags made of canvas. "Mind not to let them tip," she instructs over a commotion from outside.

I nod, then pull back the lace curtains and peer through the window. Nothing out of the ordinary, aside from the sound of a man shouting close by.

Suddenly the voice grows louder, followed by the slamming of a door. To the side of the property, a young man moves into view, gesturing with his hands.

"Is that Mary Beth's son?"

Aunt Jo peers around the curtain. "He's been around lately more than he hasn't," she says. "Getting on in years, she is, and he's a help, or so she says. Even building a deck for her round back. Don't find him all that pleasant myself, as if you couldn't guess. Flying off the handle and disrupting the whole neighborhood while he's at it. It's no wonder his wife doesn't want him at home."

I raise an eyebrow. "So I guess I'm not the only one wronged by the Mainframe when it comes to romance?"

"Well, all that glitters isn't gold, or so the saying goes. Even the shiniest of unions are bound to hit a rough patch."

"I'm beginning to see."

The man grabs a shovel and begins digging it needlessly into the patch of frozen earth at the front of Mary Beth's house, muttering under his breath as he mutilates the wintering perennials.

"It won't be long before the bluecoats pay another visit," Aunt Jo adds as she watches him. "They've been earning their keep with that lad."

I look sharply at her. "Because his temperament sets off alarms at the Mainframe?"

"The measurable pieces of it," she says with a shrug.

"Meaning?"

"Meaning the ones the chips can pick up on. Heart rate, blood pressure, and the like."

I shiver. Though Aunt Jo looks no more bothered by it than by the weather, the thought of the constant surveillance that'll kick in when I turn eighteen leaves me feeling uneasy. Uneasy and exposed. Will the bluecoats be kept busy by me, too? Considering my near-constant state of dissatisfaction since the Selection, I suppose so.

"I think I'll head off before the officers arrive," I tell her.

So after a quick hug, I take my pies and head in the direction of the Quire Nursery. A few minutes later, I'm joined by a harried-looking Agnes, and together we catch a bus to the Mainframe where Timothee and Jill agreed to wait.

As the three of them shake hands, I place the pies on the sidewalk and stretch out my sore back. The walk ahead is short but almost completely uphill, and my body aches just thinking about it. My mind still lingers on Mary Beth's son, and the bluecoats.

"Hey," Jill says, elbowing me in the ribs as we start moving. "I heard the Rose Ceremony didn't go so well. You have a temper I don't know about?"

I grin. "I promise it wasn't me."

"Wasn't you who did what?" Timothee asks.

"I presented the duchess with a box of mutilated roses. One of the servants did the mutilating, unbeknownst to me. Oh, and in case you didn't know, the duchess is my soon-to-be mother-in-law."

Agnes winces. "I guess that didn't score you any brownie points."

"Thankfully, she didn't think it was me...not that I escaped without punishment."

"Punishment?"

"A sore shoulder," I explain.

"She *hit* you?" Agnes's mouth hangs open. Even Timothee lifts an eyebrow. Across the street, blackcoats tend to a traffic mishap, but the group's too transfixed by my news to pay any attention.

Part of me wants to laugh—if only they knew—but all I do is shrug. "Not the duchess. The King, on the other hand, doesn't object to corporal punishment."

"Damn, girl. That's rough. I get hit all the time at work but it's a little different coming from a two-year-old."

"On the bright side," I say, lifting my voice over the sound of a truck idling nearby, "I have a couple of developments to share on those scrolls."

"Scrolls, plural?" Agnes asks.

I nod, then explain the contents of the most recent scroll, my investigation into the Queen and Mr. Worthers, and last, the reason for the poor penmanship. "The scroll writer's been writing under the cover of darkness so his or her feed will never capture it," I finish as we start up the front steps. "If the authorities ever conduct a review—"

"It'll turn up nothing," concludes Timothee, looking impressed. "Brilliant. Why didn't I think of that?"

"Doesn't that mean that whatever this dude's up to is borderline illegal?" Agnes asks, frowning.

Struggling under the weight of the pies, I just shrug.

"Here's what I'm wondering about," Timothee continues. "How could a few names, especially mine and Jill's, be so incriminating this person needs to *doctor* their feed?"

"I don't know," I admit.

"And how'd you figure out the bit about writing in the dark?"

"Wolfe told me."

"Your fiancé?"

I nod. Between breaths, I add, "I showed him the scrolls after he twisted my arm. He wasn't too happy about it."

"Because?"

"Because there're forces at work bigger than myself," I say as we reach the landing. "Whatever that means."

Jill greets her colleagues flanking the front doors, and I nod politely as well, all the rotating greencoats now familiar faces. A moment later, we step inside.

A hush falls over my visitors. The scrolls are clearly forgotten about as they stare at the glittering black floor underfoot, the towering Ming vases lining the walls, the frescoes alighting the ceiling. Strange, I realize as I watch them that I never had the opportunity to see Strath Glen this way. I arrived with one thought, and that was to leave. For me, it was nothing but a mistake at best, a prison at worst. And now? I can't really be sure.

"I thought I heard pitter-patter," interrupts a voice, and James emerges into the corridor from a study. He raises an eyebrow at Agnes, then those beady eyes narrow in gleefully on me. He strings his thumbs through his belt loops. "Now. What's cousin's little fiancée doing out and about? My father, the King, made his wishes well-known, didn't he?"

I swallow, and my friends glance uneasily at me. But before I can reply, Wolfe emerges from the study with a stack of file folders in hand. "What's this?" he asks, his voice as crisp as his freshly pressed suit.

"Just stumbled upon them myself. Seems your little love muffin didn't heed Father's words."

Cold eyes sweep over our group. Just like the man himself, they're impossible to read. And then, "She isn't to invite friends over? I don't recall such talk."

James rolls his eyes. "That she isn't to leave Strath Glen, of course. Look at her—wearing a cloak and everything, and just out shopping!"

Wolfe clears his throat and turns to me. "Is the accusation true?" This time the hardness in his eyes is completely decipherable. I must lie, and lie well.

"I didn't leave the grounds," I say, thinking quickly. "I met my friends out front to help them past the greencoats. And to help them with the lunch they were kind enough to bring," I add, lifting the heavy bags an inch.

"I can vouch for her," Jill says, and the prince's eyes meander over her work clothes that add a touch of legitimacy.

"Lunch, you claim?" James eyes the bags.

I set them down and lift out a pie.

"There you have it," Wolfe says icily. "In the future, mind yourself with your own spouse rather than mine."

For a moment, James stares disbelievingly at me. I even think he'll march outside and quiz the guards on duty. Instead, his face breaks into a grin and he turns to Wolfe. "I daresay you shall dine with your fiancée, then, dear cousin, once you unload those files. My Morocco would skin my backside should I snub her visitors." He shoves me into Devonshire Commons, then disappears.

"That was close," Timothee whispers. "Was that—?"

"The Prince of Airo-Aurora," I confirm, and even though

my voice sounds level, I'm rattled. It *was* close. Too close. Because if Wolfe hadn't been there, I'd probably be facing yet another punishment from King.

I place the food near the window, on the tea service. Agnes helps unwrap the still-warm pies as Timothee and Jill examine the tapestries and the slumbering parrot.

"Crazy-nice digs you have, girl," she says, looking around.

I follow her gaze and then sigh. "Yes, it is pretty."

"But?"

"I still miss Quire, that's all. Speaking of which, have you and Miller sorted out all the details for your wedding? Last time we spoke, you were picking out stationery."

She stares at the curtains. "Oh, yeah. That."

"Well?"

"Let's see. We had a big fight over the stationery, which led to an even bigger fight about...everything else."

"Everything else?"

"Miller and his parents want a traditional wedding," she explains, looking glum. "And I want something low-key—" She pauses as a servant delivers a stack of plates to us. "Long story short, I put my foot down, and now we're having a super chill afternoon in the park. All of Quire's invited. And you, obviously. Food truck and done."

I smile. "Sounds very much up your alley."

"Yeah, well, I wish my in-laws were so understanding. Miller's pretty pissed about it, too." She sighs. "So, tell me all about the fancy-ass wedding you're sure to have."

"Well, I don't know when it'll be, but—"

She turns to me. "You don't have a date set?"

"No," I say, surprised. "And I don't think it'll be anytime soon, either. Maybe a year out, at least. As for the rest of it, Wolfe's sister is taking care of all the details."

"You don't want a say in your big day?"

"I suppose not."

"Your fiancé doesn't either?"

"Oh," I say with a laugh. "I don't think so. It's not something we've really discussed, now that I think about it."

Agnes stares at me, plates drooping from each hand. "Why?"

"I guess we'd both rather pretend it won't be happening."

"Damn, girl. Tough break. So that was him in the hall, then?"

I nod as I slice and plate the meat pie. "The one with the file folders."

"He's tall."

"That he is."

"And not really one for words, I'm guessing?"

Just then, the far door opens, and lo and behold, Wolfe stands there. His attention remains fixed on James, who stands in the corridor. Whatever pleasantries they exchange appear far from pleasant, and a minute later, Wolfe steps into Devonshire with his normally stern face downright stormy.

"Not friendly ones," I agree, as Jill and Timothee join us around the tea service.

"Looks great," Jill grunts. She picks up a plate. "You make these yourself?"

"With my aunt."

Timothee drops his fork, and Jill, rolling her eyes, picks up his plate and carries it for him to the couch. Neither of them notice the long and glowering figure of Wolfe walk by.

Out of the corner of my eye, I see Agnes nab him. "So, you're the lucky man marrying my best friend," she says.

Wolfe nods his head curtly.

"This is Agnes. From Quire," I explain. "Here," and I place in his hands two plates, one with meat pie and the other with peach. "You don't need to join us—I know you're working."

Wolfe raises one eyebrow as he watches me. "I have time."

"Yes—well, okay." All of a sudden, I become aware of the way I stand, the way I hold my arms. I distract myself by picking up a plate of my own.

"Who are your other guests, please?"

"Uh, yes. Right there—that's Jill, the greencoat. And that's Timothee, the computer programmer."

For a moment, he stares in their direction, silently dissecting them with his bellicose gaze. "You've made friends with them?" he asks, obviously recognizing their names from the scroll.

"Yes."

Next, he looks down at the pies. "Where did you acquire these?"

"I made them with my aunt this morning."

"In Quire?"

"I knew King was away," I explain. "I guess I should've been more careful of James."

"You did well to extricate yourself from the situation, though typically, I don't consider fabricating the truth to be a point of honor."

"Typically, I don't either," I admit as the door to Devonshire swings open once again. This time Evie streams inside, drawing more interest from the others than Wolfe did. "Cousin told me you were having a party in here, sister!" she exclaims good-naturedly. She breezes around the room shaking hands with everyone, much more at ease among strangers than her brother.

Wolfe, meanwhile, focuses only on me. "I didn't get a chance to speak with Monsieur Sawyer yesterday, and I missed you at dinner. I take it things went smoothly at the Sky Center?"

"I now have a commercial license," I agree, with a tip of my head.

Slowly he contemplates me from his spot up high. "Then I suppose that settles it."

"I suppose it does."

We exchange a look but say nothing more. A moment later, he takes a slice of pie to his sister and joins her on the couch. Agnes slides into his place and whistles.

"What?"

"I knew you were full of crap, that's what! He doesn't *hate* you. Did you really think I wasn't watching you guys just now, whispering away like schoolchildren?"

I laugh into my arm, causing Wolfe and the others to glance my way. "I admit," I say, once I regain my composure, "that since we last spoke, things between us have gone from glacial to merely cool. Happy?"

"Terribly happy," she replies, deadpan. "A *merely cool* relationship is pretty much hot and heavy for you, Alex. It won't be long before things get hot and heavy in another way."

"There'll be none of *that*."

"Oh, please. Soon enough, you'll be married—"

I shake my head and glance at him, making sure he's deep in conversation. I lower my voice. "That reminds me— I need to tell you something, but you have to promise not to tell anyone."

"Consider it done."

"Okay," I whisper, and I take a breath. "He was married before. I don't know to who or what happened. I'm not supposed to even know about the marriage in the first place. But there you go. I'm going to be his second wife."

Agnes's eyes pop. Then she turns away from the group and places her plate on the windowsill. "Wow," she says.

I lean onto my elbows next to her. "I know."

Both of us glance over our shoulders at Wolfe, and I squint, trying to picture him with a wife on his arm. Impossible. He exudes nothing but coldness. The thought of him showing someone tenderness or affection? Out of the question.

"How old do you think he is?"

I shrug. "A few years older than myself? Maybe more."

"Have you asked him about it? The wife, I mean."

"I can't. Like I said, I'm not supposed to know."

"Oh, you have to ask him. I mean, you *have* to. The suspense must be killing you."

"In more ways than one," I admit.

At that moment, Wolfe lifts his head and stares directly at me. His gaze is so piercing it feels like lightning, and I turn back to the window with my face flushed. Agnes stabs a piece of pie with her fork and points it at me, giggling. "There's energy there, girl, between the two of you. I'm calling it."

"Energy?"

"Yeah. You know—*energy*."

I shake my head. "Is it something that a marriage typically entails?"

She rolls her eyes. "It definitely helps, don't you think?"

"Is that what you and Miller have?"

For a while, she eats in silence. "No," she finally admits. "There's none of that."

I look at her out of the corner of my eye. "You don't like him, do you? Just admi—"

"Of course I do! There's more to marriage than just *energy*. Anyway, let's not talk about my boring old life back in Quire. Tell me more about palace life."

"Have I told you that Wolfe asked me to be his pilot?"

Agnes stares at me. "But that's amazing news!"

"I got my commercial license yesterday."

"That's more valuable than jewels, in your book."

I smile. "It is."

"So alas, your Prince Charming has gifted you with diamonds." Her eyes glint with satisfaction.

I'm spared from answering by Timothee, who shouts from the couch, "Pie here's top drawer. Whip me up a spare next time you have the urge."

"You made this, sister?" Evie chimes. "Your talents know no bounds!"

I thank her, grinning, then the peach pie is passed around, places are shifted, and Wolfe ends up taking Agnes's spot in front of the window while Agnes sits next to Evie and begins describing to her in great detail her role at the Quire nursery.

"Is James upset that I have company?" I ask, and I use the opportunity to glance at his dessert plate. His pie disappears quickly, an observation that fills me with relief and the hint of something else. Like a shiver, but not quite. Could it be the elusive energy that Agnes had mentioned? I really am hopeless in the department of romance. Fortunately for me, Wolfe doesn't seem all that interested in the concept himself.

He leans against the window frame, his long body looking somewhat relaxed, at least in comparison to his usual rigidness. "I don't know," he says eventually. "I think probably the presence of Evie and myself have added some legitimacy to your gang of misfits. His words," he adds, seeing my expression. "I don't consider it a matter of concern, at any rate." He begins to run a hand through his hair but quickly folds it away. He seems suddenly unsure of himself. "Your shoulder. How is it today?"

"Better than yesterday," I say before sighing. "I really dug my own grave where King is concerned, questioning my Mainframe results like that."

"Dissidence isn't tolerated in Airo-Aurora," he agrees.

The words ring true. In fact, Monsieur Sawyer had said the same thing when I first arrived, a time that now seems forever ago. *Dissidence isn't taken lightly at Strath Glen, and now you can't say that you haven't been warned.* I stand straighter. Because his warning had been slightly different.

"It isn't tolerated in all of Airo-Aurora? Or just at Strath Glen?"

"Does it matter?"

I guess it doesn't. Because King is ruler of Strath Glen *and* Airo-Aurora. "King doesn't like dissidence, does he?" I ask, thinking about the Queen dissenting on those needle-point lessons.

Wolfe shifts his weight forward. "You're very curious, tiringly so."

"I know you don't care about me or my life," I say, as I roll my eyes, "but it's pretty important to me. Obviously I'd like to know as much as I can about the one I've been stuck with."

"I never said I didn't care about you," he says, then a boyish grin breaks across his face, and my anger is cut with shock. Never before, I realize, have I seen him smile.

It's disarming and unnerving...

"Perhaps I did say as much," he continues, "but I didn't know you very well back then. Keep in mind the Selection results were as surprising for me as they were for you."

I set down my pie plate. "You still don't know me, Viscount. Excuse me," I add, then I push off from the wall and across Devonshire as the parrot screams.

Out in the corridor, I take a deep breath and wait for the knot in my chest to loosen. What I said to my aunt was spot-on—things with Wolfe are complicated. *Impossibly* complicated.

And all I've ever wanted was something simple.

I think of Patrick, and Quire, and then turn my thoughts back to Wolfe. Why did that interaction bother me so much? He's said far ruder things to me in the past, so what's changed?

Eventually, I'm distracted by the sound of the opening and closing of a door. Wolfe says tersely, "Come, Alex. To the library."

I follow him inside, toward the empty hearth.

He takes a seat and leans forward so his elbows rest on his knees, then fixes me with a thunderous stare. "You state that I don't know you," he says loudly, "and yet I am entrusting you with my life by having you act as my pilot."

Carefully I sit across from him. "It's a gesture that hasn't gone unnoticed—and it's one I'm very grateful for. But you don't say two words to me at dinner, and I hardly see you otherwise. Your indifference I can accept. Your suggestion that you know me? I can't."

"Viscount, sir, my bill needs settling." A man with a bow tie pushes inside the library, holding a leaf of paper. "My hourly rate here, matters I attended to down here, all dates noted over—"

Wolfe scribbles out a check for the man who, after pocketing it, disappears with the same speed in which he arrived. Then Wolfe leans back in his seat so that shadows obscure his face. "Whether you accept it or not, I know you as well as I know anyone else. Not that well, perhaps—but rest assured, you are in good company."

"Which is to say, sir, that you aren't very close with anyone?"

For a few minutes, he's completely silent. He examines me with inscrutable eyes. "I am a private person," he eventually concedes.

"Your immediate family—?"

"Are kept at a cordial and arm's length distance."

Your prior wife? I can't let myself say the words, no matter how badly I want to. "I take it, then," I say instead, "that you have no desire to know more of me. That you will keep me locked here forever, a cordial and arm's length space away." The thought both pleases me and fills me with dread.

Complicated—*definitely* complicated.

Dark brown eyes harden. The ticking of a nearby clock

grows louder as it marks out each passing second. The empty hearth rattles with the wind. Finally, he breathes. "I don't object to your company, if that is what you are getting at. Now. Your opinion of me, please."

I stare at him, bewildered by his response, and his demand, and the way it lays things between us so bare.

"Well?"

"My opinion of you? Is that—is that what you said?"

"My sister assures me of some degree of fondness for me that you harbor, however slight. But I have yet to see evidence of it with my own eyes."

I shift in my seat. I pull my heavy ponytail forward and begin sectioning it, just to keep my hands busy, and the scent of vanilla shampoo lifts into the air. "I suppose that I don't object to your company either."

Ever so slightly, he nods. It's a small admission we've made to each other, but an admission all the same. *We don't object to one another's company.* I feel almost naked by it, and I can only imagine how he feels. Then suddenly and without warning, he leans forward in his chair, agitated. "Your use of language that you are *stuck* in this life…"

"Yes?"

He takes an interest in his shoes, even taking a moment to shine a dull spot. "I don't care for it."

To remind him of how accurate it is would be too harsh, so I say instead, "Maybe I spoke in haste."

The faint assurance must be enough because he stands, stuffs his hands into his pockets, and strides in the direction of the door. "You should return to your friends," he commands over his shoulder, back to his usual brusque self. But at the threshold, he pauses. "The pies…" he begins, as he examines the grain of the wood, "they were very good."

Before I can respond, he disappears from view, and I'm left staring at the empty doorframe with a smile forming on my lips.

twenty-one

. . .

A FRESH SHEET of icy snow dresses Airo-Aurora. It mounds over shrubs and cradles the windowpanes of Strath Glen. And just as I was getting used to the milder weather, even if it brought with it long bouts of gray skies and sheets of rain that flood the cobblestone streets in the city below.

I brush snow from my eyes and sigh. In my mittened hand, I hold a scroll, one found tucked behind the saddles. Then, with a north wind making my teeth chatter and Wolfe's warnings ringing through my mind, I shove the latest message into my cloak pocket and hurry around the palace, up the towering front steps, and into the relative warmth of Strath Glen.

A few minutes later, I spread myself out on my bed and smooth the paper open. Inside are only two words, both of them, as always, just barely legible:

Seek Mavericks

Seek Mavericks? Who, or what, are Mavericks?

I prop myself up on my elbows and frown. Whoever's

going to the trouble of sending me these messages could make my life easier by being a bit more specific. This is the third scroll, and I still can't make sense of them.

I slide off the bed and stare at the clock. Mid-morning. Wolfe will be busy with work, but waiting until dinnertime to speak with him isn't an option, at least not a good one. Besides, he had ordered me to report any new scrolls to him at once, hadn't he?

Not that I intend to share it with him right away. No, I have to play my hand carefully, or I won't glean a thing.

I step into the House of Mirrors and almost run headfirst into the Duchess.

"Madam." I drop into a deep curtsy and feel myself blush. "I was just headed to find your son. I mean, of course I know he's hard at work, and I won't bother him for long, it's just a small matter—"

"Alex."

"Madam?"

"You weren't so skittish in our previous interactions. Is all well with you?"

"Yes—of course."

"Then I take it as a good sign," she concludes.

"I'm sorry?"

"I believe my son is pleased with you. And if you are nervous around me, you must care, somewhat, of my opinion. That suggests that you, in return, are pleased with him."

How am I supposed to respond to *that*? And, more pressing, *am* I pleased with Wolfe? Is it really possible *he's* pleased with me? "I think maybe, madam," I say cautiously, "we're getting used to one another."

"And yet he appears to be under considerably more stress as of late, and I can't help but suspect you're the cause. Why would that be, girl from Quire?"

There's no need to be secretive; why Wolfe would be under more strain, I really don't know. Yet the question makes me uncomfortable—like there's something lurking between the lines. "Maybe the stress of the wedding?" I suggest. "Because if the Rose Ceremony was any indication of how the wedding will go, well...on that note, I'm sorry for all the drama. It wasn't my intention—or my desire—to ruin your evening."

"Yet a jealous servant intended to ruin the evening for you. All for being the fiancée to royalty, a title that seems completely lost on you."

I nod. "I have nothing but respect for you and your family, but tiaras and ball gowns have never been for me."

"No, my son has said as much. A shame; I suspect it would be easier for everyone and particularly for him if you could allow yourself to be taken by such things."

"To love him for the status he gives me, you mean? Wouldn't you rather I love him for the man he is?"

She smiles in a sad way. "My son is many things. Highly intelligent, ambitious, hard-working, and honor bound. He is not, however, a man whom a woman can love."

"I'm not sure why you say that, madam," I breathe, and for once, I hold her gaze.

"You will in time, my dear. Even he knows it to be true." She takes a step forward and lifts a hand to my face, stroking my cheek. "The flying of helicopters, the playing of pianos, the baking of pies—it shall be interesting to see what effect you will have on the monarchy, being the fresh shot of blood in the arm that you are."

"To speak again of intention, it was never mine to disrupt your way of life." I bow my head, which also has the effect of freeing myself of her grasp.

"And yet here you stand."

I gently correct her, "And yet here I was placed."

With half a smile, the woman tilts her head, eyes dissecting mine as though they wield a scalpel until finally, she draws wordlessly away. Her gown cascades behind her.

Only when she's completely out of sight, do my muscles unclench. Slowly I turn in the direction of the third floor. What I need right now is to focus on the mystery of the scrolls—not the mystery of the man I'm supposed to wed.

I place my ear against his office door a few minutes later. Voices echo from inside, and I hesitate. Then I stand straighter, lift my hand, and knock.

The murmuring stops, and a few seconds later, the door opens with a tall, shadowy figure standing inside. When Wolfe sees me, his eyes narrow. He steps into the hallway and pulls the door shut with an impatient click.

"What is it." His words are a statement, a far cry from the man complimenting my pies the day before. And definitely, he doesn't seem *pleased*, as his mother had said.

"I won't waste your time," I begin. "I'm interested in something called Mavericks, and since you know so much about our nation-state, I figure you're the best person to ask."

Angrily he swipes a finger over his mouth, his impatience palpable. "*That's* what you wish to discuss? Do you realize that I am in the middle of—"

"A quick description is all I'm looking for," I say innocently.

He squints down at me. "Why do you wish to know?"

"I came across the term recently and it left me wondering," I say, which is half true. "I'd check Counterdown, but since it lacks any sort of catalog system, I figured I'd save myself time and simply ask you."

"Fine," he grunts. "The Mavericks are a group of people born outside the Mainframe system. Through what I can assume are sustained and intentional efforts to evade authorities, the Mavericks are impossible to monitor, given the complete lack of recording devices implanted inside their brains. They are, quite succinctly, outsiders."

I stare at him, dumbfounded. All thoughts of the scroll go out the window.

Because the thought of living without the Mainframe making my most important decisions is almost too much to comprehend. Free to choose my own spouse, my own job, my own path, my own life? And without it monitoring all I see and hear and feel? I would be untraceable. *Free.*

The thought is thrilling. And if the Mavericks can survive on their own without the Mainframe determining their lives, why can't I? Why couldn't *all* of Airo-Aurora?

I've never thought of the Mainframe as the enemy before, but now it's glaring. And who oversees the Mainframe? King, of course. So, maybe to escape a future here, I should have *him* in my crosshairs. I almost laugh at the thought. The ruler of Airo-Aurora versus a girl from Quire?

"Is that it?" Wolfe asks.

Is that it? Hardly. Millions of questions now fly through my head, and I choose one at random: "Do they live among us, these Mavericks?"

"On occasion, they enter Airo-Aurora to gather supplies, but mostly they live in the woods. I believe, from my own time spent there, that their numbers have dwindled significantly in recent years."

"Oh." I can barely hide my disappointment. "And you think their dwindling numbers is because of poor choice?"

He crosses his arms over his chest. "I don't believe so, no."

"So you think people can thrive without a computer dictating their lives?"

He leans toward me and speaks in a hushed tone. "Careful, Alex."

"So then why have their numbers dwindled? Please."

"I don't have any idea."

"Have you met any of them before?"

With stern features, he says quietly, "I know one well

enough due to circumstances I am not about to recount. That fact should not and will not be repeated by you."

I glance up at those dark eyes of his, then let my gaze rest on the buttons of his dress shirt, the part of him that meets my eye line. "I take it the Mavericks aren't looked kindly on around here."

"They are outlaws. From time to time, they are caught within the city and prosecuted to the fullest extent of the law by the blackcoats. Efforts in the past have been made to rid the forests of them, but I believe, given their unparalleled survival instincts, those efforts were long ago abandoned."

"They are dangerous?"

"They survive in the woods among an array of loathsome creatures, do they not? They have weapons, and muscle, and a familiarity with a tortuous landscape unknown to most in Airo-Aurora. I would say that makes them fairly dangerous, yes."

"And yet you're friends with one of them."

"I am familiar with one," he corrects me.

I use my thumb to pull at my bottom lip, thinking, remembering the reason I'm here—the scroll. "I'd appreciate it if you could help me find the Mavericks." No reaction registers on his face. Instead, he continues to stare placidly down at me without comment. "I'd really like to have a word," I add.

Slowly and as if it pains him to move into position, he lowers his face right down to mine. "That is the most foolish thing I have heard you say. Do not mention it again."

With that, he returns to his towering height and turns for the door. Before he can make headway, I grab hold of his arm. He looks down at my fingers, clasping his jacket and pauses, finally tilting his steely gaze to mine.

I lift the scroll from my pocket, now at a dead end in my fact-finding mission. "I found it this morning on the grounds at the rear of the palace," I tell him.

Immediately Wolfe devours the contents. Once finished, he plays idly with it, snapping it back and forth between his fingers and saying nothing at all.

"Now will you take me?" I ask. "I know you're not keen on me investigating these messages, but surely you're now curious yourself?"

Like the weather in Airo-Aurora, his mood changes in an instant. His words shoot at me like lightning: "You are not to set foot in the woods. I don't care what this or any other note says! How many times must I warn you—"

"Viscount!" comes a woman's voice, and I see over Wolfe's shoulder Claudia emerging through his office door. "Whatever is the matter?"

Her expression of concern sours on seeing me, and Wolfe uses the interruption to regain hold of his temperament.

Meanwhile, I lean back on my heels. So...*that's* who the other voice belonged to.

"Go inside," he snaps at her. "We will conclude our meeting in a few minutes."

She half-turns, seemingly heeding his words, but then she pauses, and her chameleon eyes slide to mine. "It certainly is tragic, this Selection result you're forced to endure, Viscount. No wonder your nerves are fraying."

"*Go,*" he directs her.

When we're alone again, I clear my throat. Now I'm the one trying to regain my composure. "I thought," I begin hoarsely, "that you were working. Not tending to personal affairs."

"Claudia's father owns one of the largest manufacturing companies in Airo-Aurora, where Claudia herself now works." He speaks dismissively, attention still on the scroll.

"And what does that have to do with you?"

"What is it you think I do?" he barks, sounding fed up. "All international trade deals go through me."

I'm silent. Wolfe and Claudia would've been ideally matched together—the Selection let them down as much as it did me and Patrick.

"For the record," I say, as I tug the scroll from his hand, "I don't plan on going into the woods alone, but only because I don't want to be attacked by a beast—not because you've ordered me not to." I stare him straight in the eye and lift my chin. "You've warned me against pursuing the mystery of these scrolls, it's true, but considering all you hide from me, and the fact that it's truth I'm after, pursue it, I will. Maybe with your help, we can get to the bottom of it and place the whole thing behind us. In the meantime," I say as I turn to go, "enjoy your *meeting*."

———

THE NEXT DAY a dark cloud hangs over my head, dampening my spirits and ruining my mood.

Maybe Wolfe's right about the whole thing. Maybe I should forget about the mystery of the scrolls. I'm no closer to understanding whatever message they're trying to communicate, if there even is one, and it only seems to be causing a rift between the two of us. Not that I should care about *that*. Clearly *he* doesn't care, given the amount of time he spends with his ex-girlfriend. So, maybe she isn't an *ex*-girlfriend at all.

And then there's the apple core I found, another one, on the floor near the foot of my bed. It isn't Rebecca doing it, of that I'm sure, so who is it? Someone with a key, obviously. But that could be anyone. Yet who would want to slip inside my room in the middle of the night while I'm in a deep sleep? To what end?

I could ask Wolfe about it, and yet quizzing him about the Mavericks had gone so poorly...

I give myself a shake. The mystery of the scrolls. *That's*

what I should focus on. Not so long ago, I had clung to these scrolls as my best chance to escape a future at Strath Glen. My best chance to return to an easy life in Quire.

Maybe that's still true.

Glitch...the Mavericks. A glitch in the Mainframe...a group of people living outside of Mainframe rule. Yes, there's a connection there, a loose one. And then there's the recipient: me. Slotted into a life that doesn't suit me, publicly blaming my results on a glitch.

It's senseless. The more I circle through it, the murkier it becomes. And what could Reginald, Timothee, Jill, and the Queen possibly have to do with any of it?

Then there's Wolfe, and his role in the whole matter. His insistence that I leave it alone is so intense, so unrelenting, it's almost...suspicious. So, what if the message trying to be communicated incriminates *him*? Is that the reason the scrolls make him so mad? Is that why he's so emphatic that I abandon my search for the truth?

I know very little about him, that's for sure. Cold and distant and ill-mannered, he could be sitting on a mountain of secrets. Sinister ones. So, maybe he's the key to the whole thing. I lean forward. Yes, maybe he is.

Once again, I head for the third floor.

But as soon as I enter Bishop's Aisle, a hand smooths itself over my shoulders. James's beady eyes shine down on mine. Beside him is a well-dressed dignitary with a bowler's hat and a sly grin, and he tips the hat to me.

"This fine jewel," begins James, "needs no sparkling gems to set her apart. Alex of Quire, meet Sir Carthy Gold."

"You've the face of an angel," the man declares.

The prince squeezes me tighter. "She does, doesn't she? Now run along, old boy, and I'll join you in a minute." The man promptly disappears into an office, and I see what James holds in his hand.

An apple.

He draws it to his mouth and takes a sharp-sounding bite. "See?" he says as I try to escape his vise-like grip on my shoulder. "Now I've met your friends and you've met mine. Perhaps it is me who will be slipping a ring over this little finger," and he bends down and kisses it. The smell of apple lifts into the air, and I gag.

"Too bad a ring already rests on your own," interrupts a leaden voice. Wolfe.

I use the opportunity to disappear halfway down the servants' stairs. Then, with a candle flickering on the wall beside me, I try to listen to Wolfe's exchange with James, but his voice is too low and knife-like to decipher. Once their rumbling dissolves into silence, I try my luck in Bishop's Aisle for a second time.

It's empty, aside from the far end of the corridor where three men once again hunch over that hole in the wall, the one full of honeybees. I inch toward Wolfe's office.

His door, which is usually sealed shut, is ajar, and I feel a surge of excitement. Up ahead at the very end of the hall is King's office, his door wide open, and, inside, one of the servants lifts his chin to watch as I push forward on tiptoe.

Wolfe's office is empty, so I step inside and freeze—gaze locked onto the beast anchored to the wall behind his towering desk. The head of a grizzly, one much larger than any creature I've ever seen, its mouth open with fury, its dagger-like teeth glinting white.

I shake my head. Because if I was looking for reassurance concerning the man I'm supposed to marry, I don't think I'll find it in here.

"Lost, dovey?"

I whirl around, expecting to see the Queen. Instead, her daughter stands there in lace. She shoves me backward until I'm deep inside Wolfe's office, then snaps shut the door.

"A-Aubrey, Princess," I say, surprised, "I was just looking for the viscount—"

She lays a finger on my lips, then moves to the window and throws it open. At once, the north wind pushes inside. It lifts sheets of paper from the orderly desk and tosses them around the room.

Aubrey sniggers as I try to catch them. "You and me, girl from Quire, need to have a chat."

"Concerning?"

"Concerning the way I hear your name uttered from every corner of every room, as though you're the most fascinating being in all of Airo-Aurora. I declared you unmemorable and you've proven me wrong in every possible interpretation." The joviality that typically alights her face falls away like a mask. "Do you think I enjoy being wrong?"

"I—"

"Do you think I like to be upstaged at every turn by a pleasant little nobody such as yourself? With your plain old locks and your too-big, sweet old eyes? Just what sort of ditch-pig black-magic charm do you possess?"

To this, I have no answer. Upstaging the princess? Hardly, unless she considers me making a fool of myself charming. Quietly I fit the papers I've collected under a paperweight and step toward the door. Getting away from Aubrey feels almost as urgent as leaving Wolfe's office before he discovers me here, among the mess.

She stomps her foot. "You defy me an answer?"

Not wishing to provoke her anymore and angling for the conversation to come to an end, I keep my gaze down and say, "I'm sorry, madam. I don't know why you'd have that perception. Certainly I haven't been looking for attention, and, frankly, I don't consider myself charming in the first place."

"There," she hollers, pointing at me. "Right there. That downturned gaze and those pouty, self-deprecating lips. You're playing the kitten!"

"No, madam."

"You're asking for it, aren't you? *Whore.*"

I stumble backward, shocked. I lift my palms.

She mirrors my motions, mocking me. "I knew if I could just corner you, I'd piece it together. That's all your charm is: acting the shrinking violet, the bashful damsel, the timid little loner because you know—"

"I know *nothing*," I interrupt fiercely. "I know nothing about palace life or how to go about it without causing offense or upset—"

"Are you talking back to me?" she asks plainly.

Wolfe's warning about keeping a low profile echoes through my mind, and, with effort, I bite my tongue. I need to be clever—not impulsive, not emotional. A second later, I walk out the door. Glassy eyes scream through my peripheral until, once again, I take refuge in the servants' stairs, heart thumping loudly in my ears.

That wasn't something I'd been prepared for...

I sit down on the step and listen to the bustle of Aubrey's skirts as she passes by overhead. Between her and her brother, it's difficult to stay focused. It's difficult to stay positive, too.

I think about returning to my room, but I really want to know whether I can trust Wolfe or not, so after a few more minutes, I decide to try my luck in Bishop's Aisle one final time.

Tomb-like, thankfully—even the men doing the drilling have disappeared.

Up ahead, the servants in King's office have vanished from view, and there comes from inside the clattering of china. As I walk closer, I hear the reverberation of low voices. *Men's* voices.

Could it be...?

King and Wolfe.

Perfect. I flatten myself along the wall next to the doorframe, heart thumping even harder than before. They must occupy one of the seating areas instead of King's desk, given the closeness of the rattling china.

Right now, it's the servants who speak, asking how their subjects wish to take their tea. I can hear the pouring of liquid and King requesting several helpings of biscuits. A moment later, two servants file out of the room, their empty tea service in hand. Neither one notices the statue-like figure pressed against the wall.

"To return to the surplus, Uncle," Wolfe begins, and his voice is so orderly I feel guilty to think of the mess waiting in his office. "The projected GDP at year-end will account for—"

"Enough, my boy. Have some orange crisps, won't you? No? The peppermint? Well, then. A man such as myself doesn't enjoy his tea and talk business at the same time. Really, you should know that about me by now. So come, come! Tell me something interesting."

I hear Wolfe sigh. "What is it you wish to discuss?"

"I heard through the grapevine that Morocco skinned James's backside the night before last. Is it true? Have they sorted out their matrimonial woes? Tell King every juicy detail."

"I believe the purchase of some rare rubies from the southern hemisphere has reduced the friction."

"Ah, so the rumors *were* true. Fascinating."

"I'm not sure I'd call James's insatiable thirst for women fascinating, but to each his own."

"He's right about you, you know. Such a prude." He slurps his tea. "So, they've resolved their differences, you say?"

"Rubies," Wolfe reminds him.

"Excellent. It doesn't do the palace any favors to have them fighting, I know you can understand."

"Surely even a perfect match by the Mainframe doesn't make for endless marital bliss," Wolfe murmurs. He must thumb through papers because their rustling obscures his words ever so slightly.

"Your aunt and me, my boy—you won't catch us in a tiff. Dare I query as to your own match?"

There's a heavy, prolonged beat of silence from inside the room, and I shove my hand over my mouth to quiet my breathing. This is *it*. The moment I've been waiting for. My ears strain, they bend around walls—I even dart across the open archway so I can better hear his response.

"Clearly," Wolfe says placidly, "the Mainframe is aware of data from both our lives that make us well-suited for one another. That being said, she really is terribly stupid."

My jaw drops.

"Is that a fact?"

"It is."

"And yet you were awfully quick to proclaim her innocence following the Rose Ceremony, hmm? You even had the audacity to go against your King—unusual for you, my boy."

"They would have eaten her alive, otherwise," Wolfe replies swiftly. "As for the rest of it, she has other traits I find almost comely, but her mind? As thick as a brick. Practically primitive, in fact."

King laughs languidly. He munches noisily on biscuits. I edge closer and closer to the doorframe. Ever so slightly, I push my face into the open space so that I can peer inside—

Wolfe sits in a cushiony armchair *staring straight at me*.

I drop from view and swear. Caught eavesdropping, by Wolfe this time. *That* should go over well.

But why should *I* feel ashamed after what *he* said? I decide that I don't and keep listening.

"...and the Mainframe knows its way around romance," comes King's voice.

"Of course it does. I haven't doubted my results for even a second."

"I'd expect nothing less from you. Now, what I'm really curious about is what a Quire girl is like in the sack. I'm willing to bet she makes for a decent romp. On the nose?"

A chill washes over me.

Inside the room, there's nothing but silence.

King draws in his breath with a helping of theater. "You quite mean that you haven't yet taken it to the little lady? What are you waiting for, my dear boy! I hope it isn't for consent. Given your position—"

I don't waste any time leaving my spot on the wall. I shoot along Bishop's Aisle, because that's enough. *Enough.* Of all the horrible things to say—I'm not wasting another second listening to it. Not waiting for consent? Thick as a brick? The entire conversation is enough to make me sick.

At the very last moment, I notice the sound of heavy footsteps drawing up behind me, then a hand wraps itself tightly around my arm. It forces me to a stop. I see the menacing face of the viscount bearing down on me, and his inexplicable fury shatters mine.

It should be *me* who's mad, shouldn't it?

He jabs his finger silently in the direction of his office. Not once does the anger stitching together his brow ease. For a minute, I just stare up at him with some mixture of hurt and confusion, then I walk wordlessly into his destroyed office as he slams the door. He freezes when he sees the mess. But he wastes no time considering it, just shuts the window that Aubrey had left open, which causes the last of the floating papers to fall. "Sit," he instructs in a short, terse voice. He walks around the desk, sweeps loose-leaf out of his way, and drops into his chair.

I sit and stare at the grizzly. His words twist so quickly through my head they make me nauseous. One thing I'm sure of, though, even through all that: I'd rather the beast be my mate instead of the arrogant, insufferable brute sitting beneath.

He rubs his hands together as he watches me. Then he exhales and rests his forehead on them. It's out of character, this action. It's so unexpected that I lower my gaze and study him. He looks more bent than I can remember, his cheekbones more angular. But when he lifts his knife-like eyes to mine, I see the same fierceness that I've come to expect.

"Explain why you were spying on me. Or was it my uncle who was your target? Make it quick, my patience is thinning." The words come out as a whisper, sharp and raspy at the same time, demonstrative of their meaning.

"I believe it's my patience that's been tried," I reply. My hands shake. "Or is someone thick as a brick incapable of that sentiment?"

He stands menacingly. Fingertips dig into his desk as he leans forward. "If you believed my words to be true back there, then you really are as stupid as I said."

"You knew I was there all along?"

"Of course I did. I was alerted to something out of the ordinary by the way that servant was staring in the first place, not to mention the fact that I saw you dart across the hall. Now, to my questions."

"But what about King's words?"

Carefully he sits himself back into his chair, movements forced and unnatural. "What of them?" he replies tersely.

"So you agree with him, then?" A lump forms in my throat, but my voice doesn't waiver: "That given our difference in status you may act upon your...your *urges* at any instant?"

"You really are stupid." He spits the words at me.

I glare at him. "And what's *that* supposed to mean, Viscount?"

"I shouldn't need to explain myself."

"Yet you do!"

Disdain contorts his dark features. "Don't you think that

if I agreed with my uncle, I would have acted upon such urges by now?"

"Not necessarily."

"Clarify."

"I don't exactly look like the women you're used to around here."

Instead of responding, he seizes the moment to tidy his office. Only when all the papers are stacked on his desk does he glance at me. "Rest assured I am not an animal." He sighs loudly. "Tell me now who you were spying on and why, please."

"I was passing by and decided to take the opportunity to listen in, that's all."

"You were passing by. You expect me to believe that? Have you received another scroll since yesterday?"

"No." I lift my gaze to the grizzly. "Did you kill that beast?"

"With immeasurable pleasure," he says through gritted teeth.

His words are chilling, and yet—I still feel better than before. He *doesn't* think I'm stupid, he *doesn't* think he's above consent...

"Tell me why you were on the third floor," he continues, "both before and after I removed you from my cousin's clutches."

I can't blurt out the real reason for coming up here: to investigate *him*. So instead I say, "Sometimes I come up here to look around."

"Did you speak with anyone? Aside from James, I mean."

"His sister."

"Aubrey?" For a moment, he looks puzzled. Then his eyes sweep the room. He fingers the unorganized pile of papers on his desk. "Is she responsible for all this?"

"She wanted a word with me," I explain. "Maybe she

thought she'd make more of an impact with wind at her back."

Eyes narrow. "What did she want with you?"

"It seems she's unhappy with the amount of attention I've been receiving."

He rubs his temple. "That would make two of us," he mutters. "So. In regard to the third floor, there's very little of interest up here, for you."

"I'm not allowed to go into town, so my options are limited," I remind him. "Nonetheless, I wouldn't say the third floor is completely without interest."

"Why is that?"

"For starters, I've noticed that some of these offices are nothing more than broom closets, though their nameplates say otherwise. Why's that?"

He stares at me, then shakes his head. "Nothing but queries."

"It's a simple one."

"It's for the benefit of foreign dignitaries visiting the palace, happy? The various divisions and departments give the appearance of what the outside world considers normal governance, as opposed to our reality of consolidating power within the family. It was James's idea," he adds.

"So these dignitaries think others from Airo-Aurora work here at Strath Glen?"

"I didn't say it was a good idea, keep in mind."

I consider him. He's different from the rest of his family, especially King's side. But his allegiance to this man is manifest.

As if he can hear my thoughts, he stands and motions to the door. "I must return to my meeting."

I don't waste any time pushing back my chair, but before I can go, that hand of his once again wraps around my arm. "I understand how little you wish to be here," he says. "I understand you are bored and that perhaps you think solving the mystery of those accursed scrolls will be your ticket out. But you must heed my warnings." He releases me and swings open the door. "Please," he adds before I can go.

The slip of vulnerability I hear in his voice is what lingers in my mind all throughout the day.

twenty-two

I UNDERSTAND YOU ARE BORED, *and that perhaps you think solving the mystery of those accursed scrolls will be your ticket out.*

Why had Wolfe said that? I never mentioned to him that that's my very hope. Does he know something about those scrolls, or the names listed in them, that suggests they really could be my ticket out of here? They have something to do with the Selection, or the Mainframe—I'm sure about that. So will solving them, as he says, reveal something that could completely discredit the very bedrock of Airo-Aurora?

I need to track down Reginald Worthers. And I can't do that from inside palace walls, which means I need an excuse to leave them.

With that in mind, I set down the viscount's breakfast tray in its usual spot, then eye the door to his private quarters.

It swings open just then, and Wolfe stands there, lifting an eyebrow. "Another attempt to spy on me?"

I shake my head. "I was just thinking. And trying to figure out whether you were in."

"What is it?" he asks, curt as always and straight to business.

"Well, I need to return my aunt's pie plates," I say, bending the truth, "and I thought maybe Monsieur Sawyer could take me…"

"Sir, sir!" shouts a servant from the House of Mirrors. "Were the new terry washcloths to your liking?"

Wolfe shuts his eyes for a second as though willing the young man away. Really, the constant interruptions he endures would wear on anyone. Is that all *I* am to him, then? Just another annoyance?

"They're fine," he finally responds.

"He likes them!" the servant shouts up the corridor. The message is echoed from one to the next, like dominos.

"The request seems reasonable," he grumbles once the corridor is silent. "I'll place the orders and have him meet you in the Commons." Without another word, he disappears out the door.

Yes. A step in the right direction.

Twenty minutes later, I enter Devonshire with the pie plates and tote bags in hand, happy to be escaping the palace for the morning without having to worry about King, excited about the prospect of tracking down Mr. Worthers. Now, how to go about doing so without making Monsieur suspicious…

Maybe I could have him drop me at the national archives. There might be some record of him there. Or maybe I throw caution to the wind and just ask the chauffeur where Mr. Worthers is. He knew the man well so he might know where he lives—he might even take me there if I'm nice enough.

"There's the wee bold one," chirps the chauffeur, a remark echoed several times by the parrot. He rests on the daybed with his loafers kicked off. "At this rate, you're proving to be more demanding than the princess."

"Surely not," I insist, smiling. "Did Wolfe tell you our destination?"

"The beloved district of Quire, my lady." He pulls on his shoes, and a few minutes later, the behemoth lurches into the elements with us buckled inside. "I hope your fiancé hasn't taken to the hunt this morning," he says, as wind hammers us from side to side and snow encases the hood of the car.

"Are the woods particularly dangerous in this weather?"

"Are you concerned for him?" He watches me through the rearview mirror.

"I wouldn't want to see anyone hurt, Monsieur. But I guess if anyone is well-acquainted with the woods, it's him. Have you seen the beast that he keeps inside his office?"

"Indeed."

"He's a skilled hunter."

"Yes."

"Is there a story behind it?"

"One worth more than my job," Monsieur confirms. "Stifle your questions on the matter."

"Did you tell him that I know about his prior marriage?"

Monsieur Sawyer twists his neck around to look at me. "Good God, little woman. The man has a temper, haven't you noticed?"

"I take that as a no."

Another icy blast hits the behemoth, and with each block, visibility gets worse. My hopes of finding Mr. Worthers dwindle. The chauffeur mutters to himself as we inch along Central Boulevard, but by the time we pull up to Aunt Jo's house, the snow has stopped, and the roar of snowplows promises easier driving. Through the window, I spot my aunt dressed in her postal uniform shoveling snow from the front stoop.

"I won't be long," I tell Monsieur as I swing open the door.

Once outside, I stare longingly at my old street. The thick layer of cottony snow only adds to the sense of melancholy. The quiet, too, although I know from experience it won't last long. By the time dinner hour rolls around, the neighborhood children will be busy with the making of snowmen while their parents chat to one another as they clear their stoops. The normalcy is something I miss about Quire. Strath Glen is full of small commotions—servants arguing over silverware, royals in a drunken tussle—but rarely does the palace play host to the little moments.

"There was no real rush on those plates," my aunt calls as I start up the drive. "You know I don't run short on my essentials." She pulls me into a tight hug. "How did your friends enjoy your handiwork?"

"They were impressed," I say, smiling. "Just as you predicted."

"And did your fiancé manage a taste?"

I nod.

She pokes me in the ribs. "Fastest way to a man's heart, that."

"I'm not sure he has a heart to begin with," I reply. I don't bother to add that both the man and his mother had said as much. And if he's *pleased* with me, if he doesn't object to my company—well. One would never know it to look at us.

"We all have hearts. It's what makes us human!"

But before I can reply, a noise comes from next door. Whistling, and a moment later, the young man I saw at my last visit strolls around the corner with a shovel slung over one shoulder. "Can I give you a hand with your stoop, ma'am?" he calls.

Aunt Jo shakes her head. "I've almost finished up, thanks anyway."

With an amiable wave to us both, he turns to Mary

Beth's stoop and begins to calmly clear it of snow. He whistles a tune that I recognize from my early years—a lullaby.

"That's a turnaround from the last I saw of him," I say.

"His mother's over the moon," she agrees.

"I'm guessing his wife is, too."

"Oh, for sure."

"Did the bluecoats pay him a visit after I left, like you thought?"

"They did more than that, from what I could tell," she says as she brushes snow from the wrought iron railing. "They took him! Don't know for how long, but whatever they said must have scared him straight because things have been coming up roses ever since."

I stare at her, then at the man. "*Took* him, you say?"

She nods.

"Did you see any more than that?"

"More than that?" she asks, taking a break from shoveling and lifting her head. "Like what?"

"Oh, you know—small details, like whether all the bluecoats were dressed in blue, for instance. It's just...casual curiosity."

She frowns. "Sounds like a bit more than that, but go on. Let me see, let me see. Yes, they were all wearing blue uniforms, from what I can recall." She must notice the look on my face, because she nudges my arm. "Why?"

"I'm sure it's nothing, but I saw something similar happen on my first day at Strath Glen, that's all. Except at the palace there was a man dressed distinctly in white so—"

"Oh, yes—him."

I blink at her. "Was he here, then? With Mary Beth's son?"

"Clear as day." She blows her nose, then explains, "You asked if all the bluecoats were in blue, and yes, they were. This gentleman in white, there's no way he was a bluecoat."

"What, then?"

"A doctor, maybe?"

Dr. Lebwitski—it *must* be.

I search my memory for any other similarities between the case of Mary Beth's son and the sacking of Reginald Worthers. "Aunt Jo," I finally say, "did something happen when they were taking him that made him go...still?"

"Can't say for certain. I was cleaning my carpets at the time, not paying much attention."

I nod, disappointed. "Well, if you won't accept my help with the drive, I'd better be going. Thanks again for helping me with those pies."

A minute later, I'm back in the limousine with my head spinning. Why did the bluecoats take Mr. Worthers and Mary Beth's son? Is there a connection? Just who is this Dr. Lebwitski?

"Pull over here," I blurt out as we near the edge of Quire. There's no sense in beating around the bush any longer. The need to speak to Mr. Worthers feels far more urgent than before—and I decide to ask for Monsieur's help point-blank.

But once the behemoth comes to a standstill next to the curb, he turns straight around in his seat and points in my face. "Is this what you've become? Barking orders like a blue-blooded aristocrat? Because it wasn't that long ago, Miss Alex, that I fetched you—"

I hold up my hand. "Monsieur, I didn't mean to bark at you. And I promise you there's nothing blue about my blood, and no matter how long I live at Strath Glen, it'll never turn even a hint of purple. I'm sorry for speaking to you like that—really, I wasn't thinking."

He lowers his finger. "Now that we have that settled, then, what's your purpose here?" His gaze darts across the windows as though the vehicle might be attacked at any moment. A woman walking by with a baby strapped to her chest waves at him.

"It's a friendly community," I say, rolling my eyes. "Just as all communities in Airo-Aurora are."

"Doesn't mean they resemble palace life, now does it. Quick—be done with your mission, Miss Alex."

"My mission is farther afield, I'm afraid."

"Meaning?"

"Meaning it's wherever Reginald Worthers may be. Do you know where he lives? Would you take me there?"

For a moment, he looks at me like I've grown a second head. Then he bursts into laughter. "If you think I care to see that snake-nosed crook again, you're quite mistaken. Besides, the viscount didn't place me at your disposal for the whole bloody day, now did he?"

The viscount. He'll get wind of all of this, of course. And he'd been crystal clear that he doesn't want me investigating those scrolls. But I have the feeling I'm on to something, and I can't turn away from that feeling now, especially after so many weeks of making such little progress. Besides, I had told him I was going to continue my investigation, hadn't I? He can't be *that* angry, then.

"No, sir, of course not. But it's only a few minutes I need with him."

"What do you want with him, anyhow?"

I hesitate. "Well...it isn't important."

"Well then, your mission can't be either. Let's get back to the palace."

"I was bothered by his sacking!" I shout before he can drive away. "I wouldn't mind checking in on him."

"He was a miserable coot, and he doesn't deserve a check-in."

"Consider it a personal favor, then. For a friend in a high place, just as you said."

He clicks his tongue. Then, grumbling, he shifts around in his seat. The limousine lurches away from the curb and turns south.

I cover my smile with the sleeve of my cloak, and twenty minutes later, we pull in front of a well-landscaped apartment building. *Restful Manor*, reads the sign.

"What is this place, Monsieur?"

"A residence for seniors. Those who lack a home, as Reginald obviously would after decades at Strath Glen, or for those unable to care for themselves. Do you know nothing about the basic workings of society?"

"Evidently not." I tap my fingers against the leather upholstery. "Can I ask why you hate Mr. Worthers so much?"

"Everyone at Strath Glen hated him. In all my years, I've never met someone so down in the mouth as he. Bemoaning this and that, dejected and desolate and a pain in the arse to be around. And did he ever stop his ranting and raving? Oh, hardly ever did he. Not one to share, either, oh no. But stab you in the eye when you glance away? You can bet your bottom dollar on—"

I lift my hand. "I think I get the picture, thank you."

"Right, well, you're about to *see* the picture, so best to get you primed. Mind the door yourself, Miss Alex, you've quite put me out enough for one day."

I hurry after him, my stomach flipping with anticipation, across a parking lot not yet cleared of snow, through revolving glass doors and into a well-kept lobby. We speak with the woman behind the front desk, then a man in candy stripes leads us to Mr. Worthers's flat.

Monsieur Sawyer glares at me as I knock on his door. "You'll regret coming the moment you meet him, I promise you that."

"You don't need to stay. You can wait in the car, just like you did at my aunt's."

"I think not," he replies satirically. "If you thought old Reginald could give you the inside scoop on the viscount's prior marriage or that blasted beast on his wall, you've sprung from bed far too late. I'm not moving a foot."

I raise an eyebrow. The thought to question Mr. Worthers on those topics hadn't occurred to me, but now that he'd mentioned it...I grin. "You don't trust me, Monsieur!"

"Only as far as I can throw you, how's that? Well now. It seems the delightful man of the hour isn't even home, a crying shame. Let's be going, then, and take care not to forget this kindness in the future."

"Wait, I can hear something." A second later, the door swings open, and I brace myself for vitriol.

"Sawyer!" the old man shouts gaily, and he wraps the chauffeur in a hug. The chauffeur, for his part, looks shell-shocked. "It's been too long," Mr. Worthers wheezes, smiling serenely. "And who's this young beauty?"

"Her name's Alex. She works at Strath Glen. And for reasons I don't understand, she wants a word with you."

"Me?" The old man looks momentarily puzzled. His eyes are unfocused as they set on mine.

"Y-yes, I just wanted to see how—you're doing." I don't feel well all of a sudden. Maybe I've grown used to the dizzying world of Strath Glen. Maybe that's why I feel so faint here, in the quiet and ordinary hall.

"How I'm doing? I don't have a complaint in the world, dear! Why should I?"

"It's just that I saw you being...fired. Last month."

"What, me? Fired? Heavens, no. Do you see the years on this face? I was ready to hang up my shoes!"

Monsieur Sawyer makes a show of rolling his eyes, but Mr. Worthers doesn't notice. He simply stares placidly at me.

"I saw the bluecoats take you away," I insist. "Do you remember?"

"The bluecoats? Why would they bother with a little old man like me?"

"That's what I was wondering," I mumble. Either he's a

skilled liar, or he has no recollection of it. Either way, it's yet another dead end.

Then with another thought, I add: "Since I have your ear, can I ask, were you and the Queen close?"

Monsieur gives me a reproachful look.

Mr. Worthers, meanwhile, seems to relish the attention. "Such stories, dear! If only those old palace walls could talk. She's quite a minx, that lady."

"A minx?"

"And a real lively one!"

"I don't find her all that lively." I glance at the chauffeur. "Do you, Monsieur Sawyer?"

He places a finger alongside his nose. "A servant doesn't gossip about his mistress."

"I heard Evie say she's far clumsier now than she used to be. Calmer, too. Do you agree?"

"Are you deaf?"

I turn back to Mr. Worthers. "And what about the viscount?"

"Ah-ha!" shouts Monsieur. "I knew you were fishing, Miss Alex. Warming him up with questions of the Queen, isn't that right? Come now. It's time to depart."

"An uncommonly sharp brain, too sharp for his own good," begins Mr. Worthers, mindlessly. "But he always showed me kindness. Oh sure, I questioned his motives, but when the horror—"

"That'll do, old man!" Monsieur Sawyer hollers. "You," he adds, pointing at me, "shame on you. Quick—off we go."

"So soon, my friend?"

"Friend? What in hell are you puffing, Worthers? You think you sent in your retirement letters, do you? And your time at Strath Glen was peachy, is that right? Seems to me you're full of—"

"Monsieur," I warn him, pulling at his sleeve.

Mr. Worthers shifts his gaze between us, but there's no

shift in his features, no sharpening in his eye. He merely smiles tranquilly. "You were always my favorite, you." He pokes the chauffeur in the stomach. "Not a day goes by when I don't miss the whole gang. Thank you for the visit, dear friend." A moment later, his door clicks quietly shut, and I lead a stunned Monsieur in the direction of the behemoth.

I ONLY JUST MANAGE TO SLIP INTO my dinner seat before a plate of linguini is set in front of me. A glass of red wine is poured by another servant while a third wordlessly tucks a napkin across my lap. I thank all three, mind still reeling from the morning. From all it could mean.

And so I almost miss the look on Wolfe's face from across the table. Normally he pays me little attention, rarely caring to glance up from his thoughts or his notes, not bothering to engage me in conversation. Right now, his attention is all mine.

"Yes?"

"Monsieur Sawyer tells me you went on a little adventure today after returning the plates to your aunt." His voice is sonorous.

My eyes widen. I had been expecting him to be annoyed, but not like *this*.

So, in a breezy voice, I say, "Simple curiosity," then I pick up my fork and start on my meal.

Even without lifting my head, I can sense his thunderous gaze. I pretend not to notice. Instead, I chew thoughtfully on a mussel and smile at a young girl sitting at a nearby table, hoping my nonchalance will rub off on him.

He leans forward in his chair. "You've gone and made me rather angry," he says in a low voice.

I almost drop my fork.

Evie, meanwhile, stares between us with interest. "What is all this about?" she finally demands.

"It doesn't concern you," Wolfe says severely, without bothering to look at her.

"Viscount, sir—" comes the voice of a man with a goatee.

"Not now," he snaps.

"Maybe we should discuss something else." I turn to Evie. "Theodore, for instance. Have there been any developments on that front?"

She brightens at the question, then begins telling me about the close of the Rose Ceremony. A kiss, apparently, had been shared, an interesting turn as their social calendars are scheduled to overlap time and again in the coming weeks. I nod in a show of attention and Wolfe ultimately returns to his meal.

But I don't think he's finished with the topic, not even close.

Not that I have any regret. Because now, *finally*, I've made headway on the mystery of the scrolls. The lives of my aunt's neighbor and Reginald Worthers are strangely similar: both unhappy, both taken away by Dr. Lebwitski and some bluecoats from the Mainframe, both mysteriously content following their visits. Eerily content. And who else do I know with remarkable contentedness? With eyes ever so slightly out of focus? Why, the Queen of Airo-Aurora, of course. The very woman named alongside Mr. Worthers.

By the time the dessert plates are cleared away and the string quartet packs away their instruments, I decide it's time to go. I slip out the door when Wolfe isn't looking and head to the servants' stairs.

"You and I are going for a walk," his voice echoes.

With a sinking feeling in my stomach, I turn. "I guess if you'd like to walk me to my room—"

"We're going for a walk outside."

"But I'm without my—"

"I don't care if you lose all of your extremities to frost-bite," he hisses as he points me toward the rear exit. Next to the door hang several spare cloaks, and wordlessly he hands me one. He positions a brick along the door jamb to prevent the lock from latching, then urges me out.

A sharp blast of icy air takes my breath away, but still, I lift my face from the confines of the cloak and point it to the skies. Because not once since moving into Strath Glen have I been outside after dark, and the sensation of being under the far-reaching velvety sky is so liberating that I forget about my eventful morning, the scrolls, and even about Wolfe who currently mutters to himself under his breath.

As he leads me in the direction of the stables, I stare at the birch forest, one I usually gaze at from my room. It looks sinister from here—the unearthly twists of white branches cast shadows deep into the heart of the overgrowth. The sight makes me shiver even more than the cold.

By the time we reach the stables, my teeth chatter so loudly I can hear them over the hissing wind that pushes through the old barn board.

"Explain yourself," he demands.

When my eyes adjust to the darkness, I spot him nearby, staring down his long nose at me. "Explain myself?"

"Yes, *explain yourself*." I can feel his mounting frustration like pinpricks against my skin. "Explain at once your actions this morning with Monsieur Sawyer. You had him take you to Reginald Worthers. You went against my orders. And after I was kind enough to supply the chauffeur to you in the first place, I might add. Which warning that I issued was not properly heard by you?"

"I didn't see the harm in it, I guess." My voice is lost to the whistling wind.

"Pardon?"

"I didn't see the harm in it," I say again, louder. "Really, it was just a quick visit."

"And?"

"And?" I repeat.

"Tell me what you found."

"I found an old man...unable to recall any of the events in question."

"In question? Which events are *in question*?"

"Nothing, really. It's just that when I arrived at the palace, I saw some bluecoats and a man in white taking him away. It made me wonder, that's all." Then I bite my lip. Because according to Monsieur, Wolfe had helped spare Mr. Worthers from the prisons. Is it possible, then, that *he* knows what happened during Mr. Worthers's sacking? I ask him.

"It strikes me," he says in a stentorian voice, "that you fail to read the magnitude of the situation properly. Does it seem like the time or place for questions of your own?"

"I suppose," I say, pulling at the fasteners of my cloak, "that it doesn't."

He's silent, and I can see his eyes glinting in the moonlight that fights its way inside the stable. I can see every muscle and tendon along his exposed neck, rigid and taut. I can feel his displeasure with me loud against my ears.

"No," he finally agrees. "Despite my warnings, you not only managed to discover who Reginald Worthers is, but you also managed to track him down and query him. Can you guess how I feel about all that?"

"You've already said."

"What's that?"

"You've already said that I've made you angry. There's no need to repeat yourself."

"Evidently there is. Do you now have a theory as to why Reginald's name was put to you in the first place?"

"Do you?"

He steps closer, his anger contained by only the thinnest veneer.

"I don't see why any of it has been put to me," I say quickly. Only once his chest deflates somewhat do I add, "I told you that I planned to continue investigating the scrolls."

He squints down at me. "Well, Alex, I have given you plenty of warnings. Now you have forced my hand."

"What do you mean?"

"I mean that your in and out privileges at Strath Glen have been officially rescinded."

I scrunch up my face. "Weren't they already?"

"You are not to step a single foot outside of the palace without my accompanying you, not even onto the front stoop. I will see to it that a guard is tasked with keeping his eye on you, and I will ensure that Monsieur Sawyer won't take you from the palace again without my written permission. Guests will not be allowed without my express consent. All correspondence mailed to you will go through me. I believe these restrictions, while admittedly harsh, are warranted given your tireless history of defiance."

"You're *kidding*. You're punishing me with all that—"

"Not punishing," he interrupts. His eyes glint like molten metal. "That isn't my aim. I am trying to protect you. And since you have failed to heed all my warnings, I have no choice but to take drastic measures. Do not try to protest; the matter is settled."

A tingling sensation creeps along my scalp, then down my spine. Hands ball into fists. "Maybe the only person you're looking to protect is *yourself*," I shout. "As for being held captive in this palace by you, *Viscount*, and subjected to abuse by your uncle, it's not a future I'll just lie down and accept."

My words have an impact—and for a moment, he can say nothing at all. By the time he regains his senses, I've already turned for the door, and so only out of my peripheral vision do I see him crouch on the dusty floor of the stables and drag unsteady fingers through his hair. As if from a great distance, I hear him swear sharply into the night—and, as I push into the icy air, I hear the clatter of the pail that he must kick against the wall. All I can really hear, though, are the loud accusations coursing through my mind, shouting at myself for being so stupid.

For I know now, I feel it deep within my stomach. Somewhere along the way and without even realizing it, I had started to like *and trust* the loathsome Viscount of Airo-Aurora.

twenty-three

FUNNY.

On waking just a few days ago, contentedness had filled my chest. Now the air in my lungs feels acidic, eating away at tissue and trachea and bronchi so that it's difficult to breathe. Thunder rumbles far off in the distance, but there's no ticking of rain against my windowpane—I'm cocooned in silence.

Hopefully soon the rains will come. It'll be easier to be stuck inside the palace if it's miserable out.

I'd been up until the early hours of the morning thinking the whole mess through, and already I have a plan to ask Jill to check the stables for scrolls—an easy solution. What will be difficult, if not impossible, will be exposing King and his beloved Mainframe from inside palace walls. Because not long ago, I was fixated only on relieving myself from an unwanted future. Now I know I'm not the only one with a future needing fixing. Far from it. How many others out there are discontented with their lives? How many more *were* discontented until the doctor and the bluecoats took them against their will?

It's the Mainframe at the epicenter of it all. It's the Mainframe responsible for slotting citizens into lives they don't want, for alerting its bluecoats to unhappiness, to unrest, to insubordination, even for dispatching Dr. Lebwitski to clean up its mess. It's the Mainframe that must go.

But there's the danger—it's the Mainframe that's always watching. And someone else seems to be watching me closely, too: King.

Something strange and sinister happened to Mary Beth's son and Mr. Worthers and even to the Queen—I'm sure of it. And if I'm not careful, it will happen to me. Part of me feels it may already be too late. I'm already caught inside this piece of machinery that I'm powerless to stop. But I need to try.

Growing hot under the covers, I push them down. I slide off the bed and land on the floor with a soft thud, then move to the windows, throw open the drapes, spot a sky filled with nothing but gloominess. Ominous clouds move in from the west, and faraway thunder continues to rumble. I gaze miserably at the birch that bend in the wind.

That's when I spot him.

Him, emerging from the woods on foot, leading a horse with a dead beast as white as snow strapped carefully to its back. The beast is nearly as large as the horse itself, and it leaves a trail of bright red droplets in the snow.

He's methodical and ruthless and fearless; that man I stare at. He's completely unknowable. He is, just as his mother had said, completely unlovable. Liking him and trusting him, however slightly, was a mistake I won't make twice.

And then, as if he can hear my thoughts, he turns his precision-cut face up to the window and stares straight at me.

I gasp.

When I chance a second look, he's busy issuing orders to the servants. They untie the ropes that fasten the beast to the saddle, and before long, he disappears to the palace without bothering to lift those dark eyes again.

—————

OUTSIDE MY DOOR, I stare at a man—a young one, with honey-hued skin, muscle, and eyes that match his olive-green uniform. Down the hall, a group of female servants giggle loudly.

"I'm guessing the viscount asked you to watch over me?" I finally ask.

"You take it correct."

I nod. Even though he'd warned me he was doing this, part of me didn't really believe him. It's so over the top. It's so outrageous and unfair—it's the *opposite* of the freedom that I crave. I push the hair from my face and ask, "What's your name?"

"Sedaris."

"When did you begin?"

"Yesterday."

Yesterday I hadn't left my room once, not even for dinner. "And what exactly are your orders, Sedaris?"

He shakes his head. "We've exchanged names. That's enough."

I blink at him. "Pardon?"

"The viscount thinks you have a persuasive way about you. I have orders not to engage in conversation, unless necessary."

"So you're to follow me around the palace without saying a word?"

"Looks that way," he says, slinging one boot over the other. "If you have any other questions, take it up with him."

I bite down on my lip, not sure if I should laugh or cry. I pull at the collar of my blazer, suddenly hot, then head for the servants' stairs, determined to pretend he doesn't exist.

But his footsteps echo loudly after me, and as soon as the servants in the kitchen notice him, they begin their catcalls.

"Care to explain your little friend?" shouts one of the older servants.

I take a bacon roll and shake my head. "I wouldn't."

"Come, now. There must be a reason your viscount has gifted you with such. And there's only a great few rumors running wild with it—care to straighten things?"

"Apparently, I lack deference."

"No wonder you've been assigned no work as handmaid then!"

"You taking your sweetie his breakfast this morning?" shouts another.

"I don't think so," I reply, ignoring the cackle of laughter that follows me to the main floor.

Morocco walks by, hand in hand with an old man, ignoring me and Sedaris. Firearms drape over the man like jewelry, no doubt a member of the Moody clan and its house of weaponry. I watch them as I take a bite of the bacon roll, wondering if Aunt Jo would ever be allowed to visit.

"Sister! You weren't at dinner last night, and now you have this rather handsome young man stationed outside your door all hours of the day. My curiosity has never been so aroused! The rumors this is sparking throughout the palace...you really wouldn't believe the chatter. It has something to do with that fight at dinner the other night, doesn't it? My brother said you'd been on an adventure. Oh, tell me, sister! What kind of adventure? Is it another man?"

"What?" I just about drop my bacon roll. "I stuck my nose into a matter that he asked me not to, that's all. Clearly, I angered him," I add, glancing at Sedaris, who stares at Evie.

"Poor, poor sister," she laments. "I warned you that my brother is a dreadful old bore, didn't I? I'm sure he will soften on you soon, but in the meantime, you really do have the most terrible luck." She brushes by, bumping Sedaris intentionally on the shoulder as she goes. With his attention fixed firmly on her backside, I head for the door.

"Oi!" he shouts as Airo-Aurora spreads out before me. "You can't go out there!"

"I'm not going to," I call over my shoulder. Then, standing with my toes pressed against the open threshold, I motion to Jill.

"New orders handed down from the viscount, I hear," she calls as she edges over. She spits over the banister. "Can't even step a foot outside. It's got me wondering."

"I tracked down Mr. Worthers," I tell her in a low voice. "I guess Wolfe wasn't impressed with my investigatory work."

"You better've found something good, at least."

"Theories, interesting ones," I admit. Then a thought strikes me: the theories, those shadowy suspicions...if I share them, could they endanger Jill?

With the Mainframe recording my every conversation, it definitely seems that way. I'll have to be very careful discussing it with her, Timothee and Agnes in the future, then. Good thing I never told Evie about it, or my aunt. And so what about Wolfe? All along, he's insisted that his refusal to divulge information was to protect me. What if he's been truthful all along?

Jill catches sight of Sedaris, and whistles. "A greencoat assigned to tail you?"

I nod.

"Your man is no-nonsense."

"On that note, I was wondering if you could do something for me—"

"The scrolls?"

"The scrolls."

"They're always in the stables, aren't they? I'll have a look before I start my shift."

"You're a lifesaver, thanks. And if you do find one, make sure the viscount doesn't see, or he'll take it."

"Good thing he'll be away soon. The whole lot, actually. Looks like you and your bodyguard there will have plenty of time to get to know each other," she adds with a wink.

"The *entire family's* going away? When? Where? For how long?"

"Don't know. Apparently they always go away around this time of year. A ski trip or something, planned by the princess. I'm guessing you won't be invited?"

I shake my head. "I hope it's a long trip."

"I'll keep my fingers crossed for you."

"Enough gabbing," Sedaris calls from over my shoulder.

"I'll be quick," I tell him, then turn back to Jill. "Have you ever heard of the Mavericks?"

"Yep. Why?"

I tell her about the most recent scroll.

"My dad used to run into a couple when he was hunting. And so, what?" she continues, looking me up and down and clearly finding the idea amusing. "You're supposed to pick up and go looking for them?"

I shrug. "Maybe."

"You know," she begins, "if you ever regain clearance to leave this place, we can take my guy's ATV out. Might be easier than looking for them on foot."

"That sounds like a great—"

"According to orders," Sedaris interrupts, "you're not to have friends over. I'm going to lose my job if I keep allowing it. Hi Jill," he adds heavily.

"But she's *outside.* I'm not having her over."

"This is what he warned me about. Semantics, just like that."

"It's not semantics—"

"Let's go ask him, shall we?"

"No need," I say, exhaling. "We're finished, anyhow."

Jill and I nod meaningfully to one another, then the lofty doors of Strath Glen swing shut in my face. Just like that, the outside world is completely cut off. I'm locked inside, a prisoner of the palace, a captive to the loathsome viscount I'm expected to wed.

———

DAYS DRAG BY, each one as monotonous as the last.

The mornings are the easiest to bear. First, I stare at the birch, my only company. Next, I go downstairs to the kitchen for a bite with Sedaris at my heels. After this, I go to the front doors, where Jill updates me on the scrolls, always a quick thumbs down. Next, I return to my room, my only respite from the greencoat, and there I sit for the rest of the day. This stretch is the hardest, one that breaks my spirits time and again.

Often I think of my parents, of how much I miss them, of how different my life turned out from what they'd envisioned for me. I think of my aunt, too, and sometimes Patrick—and I think of that simple life in Quire I was so determined to make mine. But mostly I lie immobile, staring at the ceiling and sleeping on and off.

I go to dinner only when I really need to. My weight has dropped enough that Evie spends most of her time prodding me to eat more. On the bright side, there's no longer any talk of the wedding. As for the viscount, I pretend that he doesn't exist. He, too, doesn't say a word to me, although often I can feel him peering at me from behind his newspaper.

I'd warned him of a war, hadn't I? But his restrictions so far have been surprisingly effective—I can't discuss the matter of the scrolls with my friends, I can't investigate Mary Beth's son or Mr. Worthers, who reside outside palace walls, and I've been robbed of the will needed to spy on King, or the Queen, or even Wolfe himself since it doesn't seem wise to risk any more punishments right now.

The most sensible thing to do is speak with Wolfe. Convince him to lift these restrictions and back off. I'm not completely powerless, he cares somewhat about my opinion, or at least I *think* he does. So I need to be smart. I need to play my cards just right, and I will. I just have to wait for some of my anger to subside before I broach the subject.

And then one morning as an icy blast of air hits me in the nose, Jill's flushed face pushes close to mine, and a scroll is shoved into my hand. I quickly conceal it under my blazer, my pulse ticking faster than it has in almost a week. "Did you read it?"

She nods. "Coordinates. Makes no sense to me."

"Nothing else?"

"Nope. But I did find out something." She grins widely from the other side of the threshold. Airo-Aurora sparkles behind her. "Footsteps, through the snow. Can't say for certain, but I'm pretty sure your mystery caller hails from the Mainframe."

My eyes widen, and I feel like I'm waking from a long slumber.

"Time's up," Sedaris interrupts. His fingers wrap around me.

"The Mainframe—are you sure?"

"Yep," she replies. "I—"

"Don't make me drag your boyfriend into this," Sedaris warns. He pulls me deeper inside.

"...followed them and everything!" Jill shouts before the door swings shut. Sedaris pushes me past the Ming vases, looking pleased with himself. Probably these past few days have been as boring for him as they've been for me.

"Naughty, naughty, bending the rules like that," he chides.

"The girl from Quire!" shouts a breezy voice just then,

and Aubrey appears from around the corner, three green-coats trailing behind her. "See? You aren't the only one to travel with an entourage." She gestures to the men proudly.

My eyes widen. "This wasn't my choice. Or my desire." *Obviously!* my brain screams.

She looks put out, but just as quickly, the crease between her brow disappears and she laughs gaily. "Word is your fiancé wasn't happy with you poking into things none your business. True?"

"That sounds about right."

She comes closer. "I've got an offer for you, one sweet as syrup. How's this: I'll indulge you your secrets, all the juicy ones you're after concerning his past. Splendid?"

Splendid? Wolfe's secrets, in exchange for what? A deal with the devil, *that's* what it'll amount to.

"If you don't mind me saying so, those weren't the secrets I was after." After a slight hesitation, I add, "And even if they were, it's from his mouth I'd want to hear them."

Aubrey laughs darkly. Then she pulls something from her dress—an apple. "You really are a dull old girl," she declares before biting into it. Juice dribbles down her chin, but she doesn't wipe it away. I stare at the trail of liquid and try not to shiver.

"Just an innocent little thing from what I can tell," Sedaris mutters once Aubrey disappears. He lifts my chin to the light and tilts my face back and forth.

I pull away, frowning. "An innocent little thing couldn't survive at Strath Glen," I tell him. And it's true. When I first arrived here, I didn't think I had what it takes to survive this madhouse. But I have. I've even made friends, managed a job promotion, and discovered secrets that very few in Airo-Aurora know. Just as my aunt had said, I'm stronger than I knew.

So maybe my parents would be proud of me, after all.

"Whether you are or you aren't, you've got the most important people in the nation running scared."

"Scared?"

He shrugs. "You got another interpretation? If you do, I don't want to hear it. Semantics, remember? Still, there's something about you..."

Footsteps echo from the imperial staircase, and I turn, catching sight of Evie and Wolfe.

"Sister!" Evie calls as I head at once for the servants' stairs. "Wait, won't you?"

I keep my gaze away from Wolfe as I do. Still, I can't help noticing out of my peripheral vision the way he scrutinizes my every move and the way his eyes dissect Sedaris from head to foot.

"I never see you anymore," Evie laments, "and you haven't been very chatty at dinner lately, when you even bother to join us. Did you know we're going away tomorrow?"

"Tomorrow? I remember hearing something, now that you mention it. A ski vacation, I believe?"

"With only about a hundred potential suitors," she gushes. "I may have to give Theodore a boot to the back burner, given all the lookers I've been noticing as of late." Her gaze shifts to Sedaris, while Wolfe's frown is so pronounced it must give him a headache. "In all seriousness, sister, we retreat to a lodge on the southern edge of the Alps for some skiing and comradery with the most prestigious of company. Doesn't it sound to die for? Will you miss me? I'll be sure to fill you in on all our adventures the *minute* we're back."

"It sounds lovely. Will you be gone very long?" I ask, my fingers crossed.

"Fear not, just a few days at most. But not everyone will be going away this year, I'm afraid. My bore of a brother here just informed me that he won't be able to attend, which means the two of you will have the run of the palace. What a perfect opportunity to fix up this dreadful little rift," she adds with an elbow thrown into his side. "Isn't that right, brother?"

"I've work to do," he says cuttingly before turning away.

"I think he's staying behind because of you," Evie says once he's gone. "Honestly. It was only after it was decided you wouldn't be included in the excursion that he pulled out. Besides, I don't think he is all too pleased with the silent treatment you've been giving him. That and the fact that you don't look very well—you're getting to be as thin as a pin! I bet he'd like to make amends."

I laugh. "I really doubt that."

"He truly is overworked, sister. I think it makes him a real grouch. Try not to take it too personally."

"I don't think it's his work that makes him grouchy."

"Oh? So what do you chalk it up to, then?"

"Me," I say bluntly. "My presence here. The fact that he has to marry me. I don't mean to doubt your sisterly instincts, but these restrictions show how little he cares about me. And he definitely wouldn't be doing it to Claudia if he'd been promised to her like they planned—"

"How do you know about Claudia? Did he tell you?"

"He told me they used to enjoy each other's company, which I think means they were intimate, at least on some level."

She laughs in an easy way. "Yes, I'd say they were intimate on all levels, not that he ever felt very deeply for her. She was more of a necessary distraction, or at least that's how Mother and I saw it."

"A distraction from what?"

She's spared from replying by the sudden clearing of a throat. Standing with half her body inside Counterdown, the severe-looking woman with the too-tight bun lifts a clock into the air and taps it noisily. Evie wraps me in a hug. "I want things all back to normal by the time we return, sister," she murmurs. "He really does care for you," she adds with an imploring look before disappearing inside the library.

For a while, I just stare after her. How's it possible he cares for me? And what did he require a distraction from? Then there's Aubrey and that apple...

Finally, accepting that I won't get the answers, I'm looking for, at least not right now, I head upstairs, retrieving the crumpled scroll from inside my blazer once I reach my room.

Same barely legible writing. Same indecipherable, far-too-cryptic message. Coordinates this time, just as Jill had said. Well. At least it'll be easy to investigate; all I need is a map, and the library must be full of them. Too bad Evie's taking her studies there.

Tomorrow, then. After the royals leave for their holiday, when I'll have the place to myself. Wolfe's decision to stay behind won't be an issue; he wishes to speak to me as much as I want to speak to him—not at all.

Spreading myself out on the bed, I remember the news brought by Jill: that the scroll writer comes from none other than the Mainframe itself. It makes sense, in a way. A short walk from there to here, making the stables accessible. And then that signature, *Glitch*, right after I ran around the Mainframe shouting that very word through the halls... unlikely, then, to be a coincidence.

Could it be that bespectacled woman who administered my Selection? Seems unlikely. She was an ardent supporter of the Mainframe. And yet all the other techs are nothing but faceless strangers. Except, maybe, the young man with the thick-framed glasses and black hair, the one unsurprised by my sudden appearance in the heart of the Mainframe. I haven't forgotten *his* face.

I shake my head. Regardless of who it is, the question remains the same: why's someone at the Mainframe sending me cryptic messages, ones that seem to implicate that very system in something scandalous? And why *me*? That, I realize, as I cast my gaze around the lavish room that became first my home, and then my prison, is a good question indeed.

twenty-four

. . .

THE NEXT MORNING, I expect to wake to a flurry of
activity, but instead the palace slumbers. After asking
several servants, I learn that the royals' departure across
town isn't scheduled until late afternoon, after the duke and
duchess have returned from an international mission. Such
is the sorry state of relations with my in-laws, I hadn't even
noticed them gone in the first place—not exactly the idyllic
family life I'd pictured in the days leading up to the
Selection.

I head back to my room with footsteps echoing close
behind. This time they don't come from Sedaris. He's been
replaced with a blonde woman who's refused to reveal to me
even her name. Why Sedaris has disappeared, or when,
aren't questions that interest me. The only thing that *does*
interest me is searching through atlases in the library for
those coordinates, something I now won't be able to do until
the evening.

It looks like I'm facing another long, difficult day stuck
inside my room. Funny, all I wanted was an easy existence
in Quire, but then I think of Agnes, who doesn't seem all
that happy with Miller or her job; I think of Mary Beth's son

and even my aunt who lost her husband years ago, and I wonder: just how many people have a truly *easy* life? Does it even exist?

Maybe not. So maybe I *haven't* been chasing after that so-called easy life, after all. Maybe what I've really been doing is running away from a difficult past.

Once the clatter of servants racing the halls with cart-loads of luggage echoes through the wall, I lift from bed. With my ear pressed to the door, I gather first that the duke and duchess have returned from abroad, then that Aubrey's lost a tiara, apparently a priceless antiquity. The palace is searched, turned on its head until finally, it's located in a hatbox, and the regular clatter of the servants resumes. As the afternoon dwindles to a close and the sun begins to sink toward the horizon, the bustle moves downstairs, and finally...*finally*, I leave my room. I stretch out my limbs, ignoring the blonde woman, then sit in the rotunda at the top of the steps where the others can't see me.

They bicker over sleeping arrangements. Monsieur Sawyer readies the limousine. Their journey is delayed once again, however, when James slices his finger on the well-sharpened edge of a ski. Morocco bursts into tears, and King hollers for his physician to be called.

I slip down a few steps so the front doors are within view.

As expected, it isn't Dr. Lebwitski who arrives fifteen minutes later. Wolfe, dressed crisply in navy, steps out of Devonshire to greet the woman. Then, spotting me, he makes a point to stare directly at me as he ushers her inside. I return to my room to wait out the departure, and when finally the palace settles into silence, I breathe.

Peace, or something close to it.

But when I step into Carnegie a short while later, I falter. Not a vulture to be seen, no royal visitors, no family or friends. Just him. *Him*, in his usual seat with a drink in one hand and a pad of paper in the other. The only other place setting is right across from him.

Perfect, Alex, I try to tell myself. A perfect opportunity to talk to Wolfe, to persuade him to drop the restrictions. I'll just have to lie convincingly—make him believe I've given up investigating those scrolls, then be far more careful when I do.

I stand there for a long time, but finally, with the gaze of the servants on me and my stomach growling, I drop into my spot.

He doesn't bother to look at me. Instead, he writes tirelessly on the notepad, breaking only to peruse the newspaper. Cellists play quietly in the corner, knowing, maybe, that their audience tonight is completely disinterested.

I study him from the corner of my eye, observing angles to his face more pronounced than I remember. The rest of the time, I study the silverware, twisting it between my fingers, willing the kitchen staff to be quick with their work, and trying to decide just how to broach the subject of those restrictions. When dinner is finally served, he drains his glass, then picks up his knife and fork. He slices his steak with disinterest; he pierces his potatoes with indifference. But he cleans his plate nonetheless and picks up his pen, all without bothering me with a single glance.

"I take it your sister was wrong," I finally say.

Slowly he lifts those near-black eyes to mine. "I don't know what it is you speak of."

"She thought you were ready to make amends."

"She was mistaken." He returns to his notes, but before I can respond, his falcon-like eyes snap back to mine. "Did she tell you that a date has been set? The last weekend in April. Best to mark your calendar."

"A date," I repeat, confused. "For what?"

"The wedding, of course."

Something hard drops to the bottom of my stomach.

Something dark and writhing. All thoughts of discussing those restrictions evaporate.

It can't be. That sort of thing happens only in marriages that come to fruition, and surely...*surely* this one won't.

And then there's the date itself—in just *two months'* time? There won't be enough time for planning. There won't be enough time to expose the Mainframe and avoid the whole thing in the first place!

I drop my fork, and its clatter echoes through my head all the way to my room.

It isn't often that I completely lose control of myself, not since my parents passed, but now there's no holding it back. It just feels like too much for one person to bear all of a sudden. Too much injustice, too much ill-treatment, too much loneliness. I cry until I can't cry any longer.

After that, I blow my nose, change into a nightgown, and pour myself a glass of water. *Things could be worse*, I remind myself. *Look on the bright side*, comes my mother's voice. And finally, my own: I'm strong. Capable. Everything will be fine. I throw open the windows as wide as they'll go, all three of them, and stand back as icy air floods my room. It swallows up the stagnant air of the past week, and with a bit of luck, it'll usher in a new beginning. I breathe deeply. Tomorrow. Tomorrow I'll go to Counterdown, I'll investigate the coordinates. I still have two months to change my future.

Shivering, I shut one of the windows and stare through it. Under the silvery moon, the limbs of the birch begin to swivel; they cause the darkness to come alive, to push unapologetic against the pane. And then comes a sharp scream, followed by the blast of a gun, one shot after another, sudden and deafening, undeniably close. I step back, spilling water on myself as I do.

A minute later, there comes a loud and impatient knock at my door.

It isn't often I'm called on. Hardly at all, actually.

Tonight, given the emptiness of the palace, it can only be a servant, or Wolfe. Much more likely that it's a servant, yet there'd been a distinctive quality to the rapping.

It comes again, louder this time.

I pull open the door, and even though I'd been half-expecting it, I'm shocked to see Wolfe standing there. His features are stern, his body rigid, and before I can ask what he wants, or even tell him to go away, he notices the way my hair blows and pushes inside my room.

He closes the remaining two windows with vociferous thuds, then rounds angrily on me. Just as quickly, he turns away. "You've been crying," he mutters from the side of his mouth. I can see the observation has touched him in a mysterious way. Something startled and exposed had lit his eyes.

"Of course I haven't," I lie. Then: "Why are you here?"

"To warn you to stay clear of the windows."

"The windows?"

"I assume you heard the gunshots, and as I don't yet know their source, it's only prudent."

I laugh. Worrying about my safety? *Now*? "I'm sure it's just hunters," I say as I gesture for him to go.

"At this time of night? I think not."

"The Mavericks, then."

"They don't often have guns."

I glance at him. Why he stands near the door instead of exiting through it, I'm not sure. The silence in the room grows uncomfortable. Finally, he takes a step in my direction. "Why were you crying?"

The question catches me off-guard. "It's...it isn't important."

"Then you won't mind sharing it with me. Was it the date of the wedding?"

"It was everything, including that—yes," I admit. "I've barely spoken to anyone in days. You might find that exceptionally normal, but I find it exceptionally lonely." Then a lump forms in my throat, and it's everything I can do, all of a sudden, to keep my composure. So I focus on breathing. I will myself to remain steady. *This is nothing*—my aunt's words replay over and over in my head. And then a tear comes dislodged, my body defying my brain; it tumbles down my cheek.

Wolfe stares at it as though he's never before seen such an oddity. "Don't," he orders, then he pulls from his pocket a fistful of change and begins to count it with his back to me. "Let me know when you've regained your composure," he barks.

I wipe my face with my nightgown. "I'm perfectly composed," I tell him. "In fact, since you're here, I'd like to discuss those restrictions."

He nods, returns the change to his pocket, closes the door, and, as though he's made up his mind about something, approaches me with his normal assuredness. "I have come to realize, by observing you over the past few days and just now—" He clears his throat. "I realize that by trying to protect you, I have unfairly caged you. Consider the restrictions lifted and know, please, that it was never my intention to hurt you like this."

It was never my intention to hurt you like this.

I can hardly believe my ears. A nicety, from *him*?

And the restrictions lifted, just like that? All from one little tear? A balloon swells inside my stomach as I savor the feeling of freedom, however modest, restored.

Then he says in a low voice, "As I know you will now resume your investigation into the scrolls, I am going to share something with you, and by necessity, I must be in close proximity. Do you understand?"

I stare at him.

"Why do you look at me like that?" he asks, scowling. "Think what you will of me, but I wouldn't harm you."

The words are disarming, but this time I don't let it show. I just sit on the couch and wait while he does the same. He lowers his mouth to my ear, careful not to touch me, and the smell of his shaving cream is what I notice first. It's a good smell, clean and familiar, but it's so out of place on him that I falter. Shaving cream is human, after all, and he's something else entirely.

"There are several things you can do to avoid getting yourself in trouble through the Mainframe," he begins quietly, and my jaw falls open. "First, you must always consider the permanent record that the Mainframe collects —all that you hear and see and, to some extent, feel. As you might know from visiting the memory bank, the audio chips suffer when conditions are less than ideal. The easiest way to deceive, then, is to whisper or, likewise, communicate with a backdrop of loud noise. To act in the dark is another way to deceive, though of course this proves more difficult as you, too, will be deprived of sight.

"The second thing you must consider," he continues, barely drawing in a breath, "is the monitoring system that will kick in when you turn eighteen—not long from now, if I am not mistaken? If your pulse is elevated for too long, along with other hallmarks of stress, the Mainframe will deem you either angry or fearful. In either case, a phone call and even a visit from the bluecoats may be warranted. Once this happens, and depending on the circumstances, it is likely your feed will be monitored more closely for deviance. You must learn to control yourself at first instance. Finally, if you are desperate to avoid detection, cover your ears and close your eyes, but keep in mind that your last known recognizable location may be visited." With that, he turns away.

For a while, I sit there silently. Then, after what feels like hours, I ask, "Why are you telling me all this?"

He sighs. "Let me put it this way. I didn't want a wife, let alone one that I cared about."

"I'm afraid I don't understand."

"If you won't allow me to keep you safe, you must keep yourself safe. Clear now?"

No. *Definitely* nothing is clear. Not his words, not the way he looks at me, not the ball of emotions housed in my chest.

I lift myself to my knees so we're eye to eye, then whisper, "What will happen to me if I have repeated offenses? What happened to Reg—"

He shakes his head. "The less you know, the better," he says into my ear. "On that point, I must be insistent. But my uncle must never again suspect that you are critical of the Mainframe. If he does, he will have your feed closely monitored, and given your insistence upon investigating the scrolls, your insatiable curiosity, and your unwavering disdain for me, I fear the worst will transpire."

So, I've been right. Reginald and Mary Beth's son—something happened to them beyond a mere talking-to. Same, it seems, with the Queen. With everyone in Airo-Aurora, maybe, who's critical of the system of governance, or who suffers a certain degree of discontent.

The danger's real; Wolfe had been truthful all along. Yet while he attempts to shield me from knowing too much, someone working at the Mainframe seems intent on leading me, albeit in a cryptic and roundabout fashion, right to it.

But *why*?

Slowly it dawns on me that Wolfe and I occupy the same corner of the same couch, and even though we take great pains to avoid contact, we sit so close I can hear his measured breaths. "I don't disdain you," I tell him.

"Good."

One word. Just one. Short and plain. But it's said with such gravity, such earnestness, that I find myself doubting every exchange we've ever had. That steely heart cut from stone, it *has* softened—it must've. And without me even noticing.

"I have an international mission in a few days' time. A neighboring country, reachable by helicopter."

My breath hitches with excitement. "I look forward to it."

"Well, then." He clears his throat. "I suppose I should be going."

"Don't."

He glances at me, surprised. "Don't?"

I shake my head. My mouth moves on its own—no craftiness, no agenda. "It's just that I haven't had very much companionship lately. Any companionship, actually."

"Companionship," he murmurs. "I'm afraid that is one thing I don't exactly excel at."

"We don't even need to speak. It would just be nice to have someone to share the silence with."

And so he does.

twenty-five

. . .

SLEEP HADN'T BEEN MANAGED, not really. Fitful dreams, a churning mind. Question after question piling up in my brain, and none with answers, at least none that had revealed themselves when the moon was high and the hours were early.

One thing that's clear, however, is the need to speak with Wolfe. To thank him for the evening, for his kindness and company. I had fallen asleep on the sofa before he'd gone, but it was only a light slumber, and so I'd been all too aware of the blanket he placed over me, the hand he rested briefly on my head.

The touch, in particular, alarmed me, especially since the man typically went to great lengths *not* to touch me. So why had he done it? And then there was my own pledge not to like or trust him ever again. Yet I can't loathe him quite the same way as before.

I place his breakfast tray in its usual spot, disappointed to find that someone else has his ear—Gerard, speaking to him from the other side of the door. Peering in, I spot Wolfe looping a belt through the loops of his well-pressed pants. He exhales wearily. "Right to the back stoop, you say?"

"Frightened the hell out of Mrs. Bellevue when she let the cat out," the butler agrees.

"Food must be difficult to come by," he grumbles, "for it to venture so close. Warnings will have to be issued throughout the palace, and particularly to my fiancée, who likes to lurk in the most unlikely of places." Through the ever so slightly ajar door, he looks straight at me.

"Ah, your breakfast awaits, my Lord. I shall issue the warnings as requested." After bowing deeply to the viscount, he walks by me and evaporates into the checkerboard hall.

Wolfe, with his belt now fastened, buttons up the cuffs of his dress shirt. "You don't need to bother with my breakfast," he says without looking at me.

"I don't mind," I reply.

"Did you hear the news brought by the butler?"

"Not really, no."

He pulls on his suit jacket, then joins me in the front hall. There's nothing in his tone or demeanor that alludes to the tenderness he'd shown last night. Once again, he exudes only coolness, and once again, I'm confused about how it makes me feel. Both relieved and disappointed, two opposite reactions. Will I ever learn to reconcile them?

"A bear paid a visit to the neighboring estate last night," he explains. "Shot dead by the widow of the house. Those were the gunshots that rang out after dinner. You'll be wise to keep that in mind when you wander the grounds. I would ask you to refrain altogether, but we both know how well you take orders." With that, he walks out the door.

For a while, I just stare after him. Then I grab the latest scroll from my room and go to the library.

Servants are scattered across Counterdown, scrubbing the floors, feeding wood to the fire, dusting the window ledges. They don't pay any attention to me as I slip between the rows of books, scanning the towering shelves for a collection of atlases. The books on the highest shelves look as if they haven't been touched in years, and even a diligent team of servants can't keep the thick layer of dust from settling over their sleeves.

Twenty minutes later, I spread the most up-to-date atlases on a nearby table with satisfaction. I switch on a lamp dressed in emerald-green, tuck stray pieces of hair behind my ears, and draw up a chair. I locate the coordinates easily, but understanding where those coordinates lie relative to Airo-Aurora takes several more minutes and the flipping between pages of differing scales.

There. Almost a hundred miles north of the city, and I frown at the news. Completely unreachable. But with another idea springing to mind, I draw out the topography atlas, pull up the coordinates, and gasp.

A valley with a floor of rock, surrounded by low mountains. *Ashville Range*, reads the caption. Aside from King's own Alps immediately east of the city, it's the only irregularity in the otherwise heavily wooded nation-state of Airo-Aurora. Maybe I don't need to visit the site to appreciate its significance...

But as minutes drag by, as fingers tap against the smooth wood of the desk, as the green-dressed lamp hums in front of me, I can think of nothing significant, nothing to relate Ashville Range to the Mainframe, or King, or even the Mavericks. I keep thinking, keep thinking...barely noticing the library doors opening and closing, or the small cluster of people gathering inside. But one of them must be staring at me because it catches my attention, and I lift my head.

Patrick.

I stand, maps forgotten about, and stare at the boy I thought I would marry. Behind him are men exchanging notes as they gesture to artwork hanging along the walls. Wolfe enters the library next, significantly taller than the rest and looking impatient.

He's the opposite of Patrick in every way—dark to

Patrick's light, narrow to Patrick's bulk, thunderous and intense to the good-natured and easygoing boy I grew up with. He nods curtly to the men, and together they move to the edge of the library where a large oil painting hangs. The shorter man pulls out a tape measurer from his pocket while Wolfe stands aside, tapping his fingers against his arm and looking impatient.

Patrick, meanwhile, pushes between tables until he stands right in front of me. Grinning, he pulls me into a hug, and he feels so familiar, so much like home, that for a moment, I let myself relax into his arms.

Wolfe sees me now. I can feel his gaze like sandpaper against my skin, and I stand upright.

"Alex," Patrick sighs. He touches me lightly on the cheek. "What are you doing here?"

My stomach squeezes at his voice, and I can't help but glimpse the life that could've been. Easy and comfortable, even if it did lack passion, or energy, or whatever it was that brought two people together in the absence of computer chips and Mainframes. Things with Wolfe, on the other hand, are strained and complicated, and every conversation between us leaves even more unsaid. I doubt we'll ever have the kind of friends-first, easy closeness I've known with Patrick, even if the companionship he offered last night had been settling after a week of solitude.

I give myself a shake. There's no such thing as an easy life. Hadn't I already come to that conclusion? There are, however, dull lives, and one thing I can say about my time at Strath Glen, even while kept under lock and key, is that it's not that.

"Alex?"

"You haven't heard? I would've thought by now—"

"I haven't seen Agnes, either," he says, and I nod, wishing that Wolfe would go back to the oil painting as the others have. Instead, he stands watching my every move, still as an arrow.

"Do you work here?" Patrick asks. His gaze lifts over the soaring shelves crammed full of titles. "You always wanted a librarian post."

"In a way. And you? You're here for work, I assume?"

"Airo-Aurora's National Gallery," he explains. "The palace is lending some pieces for an upcoming exhibit." He rubs at the stubble of his chin, then studies me with soft eyes. "You look different, Alex. Thinner than I remember. Are things okay?"

"Oi, Patrick!" shouts one of the men, and he motions to him with his clipboard. "On we go!"

He grabs my hand and squeezes it. "I'll come back," he says. "Next week. I'll come back for you."

He'll come back for me. What does that mean? What are the feelings pushing around in my chest *now*? I don't know —I never do anymore.

Only when he turns to the others do I look at Wolfe.

His eyes slice through Patrick like a freshly sharpened knife. Next, they shift to me, and there they linger with something unknowable flickering inside. They harden quickly into slits of rock. He leads the others through the library door, letting it swing loudly shut, leaving me alone among the books and the floating chords of dust that glimmer under the morning sun.

I sit down, then place my spinning head down on the nearest atlas. Patrick. Here. *Coming back.* I squeeze my eyes shut, and the next time there's a noise it startles me. A figure hovers overhead.

"You're lucky," Wolfe says coldly.

I tilt my head back to meet his gaze. "How's that?"

"You're lucky that it was only I who had to witness such a display between you and that boy. For others, such dishonor would result in far more than a sore shoulder." As if to underscore his point, he rests a hand over my shoulder, the one that King had struck, his thumb pressing lightly into the area beneath my collarbone, the rest of his fingers curved over and down half my back.

"I don't see how I caused you any dishonor."

A thin smile curls his mouth. "I suppose my uncle was right about your in and out privileges, after all."

I draw away to free myself of his grasp, but he doesn't let go. So I lift my chin. "If you're suggesting that I'm engaging in...in *romance* with him, you're sorely mistaken."

"Am I?"

"I haven't seen him since before the Selection, which is more than can be said about you and *Claudia*."

He releases my shoulder. "I told you already that nothing untoward was happening behind—" Mid-sentence, he stops. He picks up something from the table. I see the open scroll in his hands, see an eerie calm mask his face. "When did you receive this?"

"A couple days ago."

"A couple days ago, that hulking fool was monitoring your every move. Did he allow you to leave the palace in exchange for something?"

"In exchange for something," I repeat. "Like what?"

"You tell me."

Exasperated, I stare up at him. "There's nothing to tell, *Viscount*. He didn't allow me to leave the palace, and he wasn't particularly gentle when he thought that I might."

Eyes narrow. "I take it you suffered no ill effects?"

"None other than that inflicted to my dignity."

He must not think those injuries are very serious. "How, then," he continues, his voice rising, "did you get those little hands of yours on this scroll?"

"I won't say."

He pulls back and scrutinizes me. "I knew you were

difficult, but I didn't think you were deceitful. First that boy, now this—"

I stand at his words. Heat fills my chest. "*Deceitful*? The restrictions you imposed on me were completely unfair, and I have no obligation to tell you about any *break* I managed from them."

"Then why didn't you inform me of the scroll last night after said restrictions were lifted?"

"Because, *sir*, last night we were discussing other things, and I forgot. Is that allowed? Oh, and before I forget this point—there's nothing to hide with *that boy*, and I don't really care for the suggestion. We were expected to be Selected to one another if you really want to know, but clearly...*clearly* that didn't happen."

"So you were lovers." Everything in his voice and his features—even in his stance—is judgmental and harsh.

"Actually," I say, angry. "We were nothing more than friends, not that it's any of your business. And you shouldn't be throwing stones, given your *extensive* history with women."

His face hardens, slab-like, and immediately I know I've gone too far. I busy myself with tidying up my nook of the library, putting as much space as I can between the two of us. With luck, he won't notice how deeply my face has flushed.

"Tell me what you mean by that." He speaks in a hushed voice. His eyes bore into mine in a way that doesn't seem to be natural.

"Claudia. I know that the two of you were intimate. That you engaged in—Evie told me. That's what I meant."

"Is it?"

He moves toward me, and I lift both hands: "Wolfe..."

"*Tell* me."

"One of the servants let it slip and it's senseless to ask

who, since it was nothing but an accident and no more was said on the subject anyhow so please, *please* let it go."

"Let *what* slip?" He speaks through gritted teeth.

I let both arms drop to my sides. "That I'm to be your second wife."

For several minutes, he gazes right through me. Then he nods solemnly. It's the exact opposite reaction that I'd been bracing for. "So, you aren't very upset?"

"I am rather irritated," he admits.

"I thought your reaction would be worse, since you forbid all the servants from discussing it. Can I ask why you took such measures in the first place?"

"It is a matter I wish to have firmly behind me. Even having this conversation is something I wished to avoid."

"I'm guessing, then, that you don't want to tell me what happened between the two of you?"

He flicks a speck of dust from his suit. "I understand your natural curiosity on this subject, but I will not be forth-coming. I ask too that you respect my privacy and don't go searching for answers. Can you agree to that?"

Even with my compulsive curiosity, I have to admit the request is reasonable. I bow my head.

He sits on the edge of the table and a weariness seems to slip over his features; it softens the sternness and makes him look younger. "The whole thing will have no impact on our marriage, so let's consider the matter closed."

Our marriage. He mentions our fast-impending nuptials so easily, like he's *comfortable* with the whole idea, when I know that can't be true.

"Alex?"

"Yes, sir. Yes, consider the matter closed."

"Very well. Now, to the scroll. Tell me what meaning you imbue the stated coordinates with. It seems you've been doing your research." He gestures to the collection of atlases haphazardly tidied into a pile.

"They point to a valley within Ashville Range, a mountainous region far north of here. I think it must have something to do with the Mavericks, although I can't figure out what. Maybe they live there. Is it a spot you're familiar with?"

"No. I assume you don't harbor any disillusion about reaching it?"

"It's too far away, I'm afraid. But Jill and I were speaking a while ago, and—"

"Yes?"

I'm still not sure I can completely trust Wolfe, but I decide that after everything he shared with me last night, I, too, should be forthcoming. So, using the chair as leverage, I sit on the edge of the table next to him. "I made a promise to you not to enter the woods alone," I begin. "It's a promise I'll keep. What I plan to do instead is go with Jill, who's armed, by the way, using an all-terrain vehicle owned by her fiancé. Probably it'll be a fruitless attempt to locate these Mavericks, but there you go. It's something I plan to do, and I thought you'd like to hear it from me."

With that, I slip off the table and gather up the stack of atlases. I return them to the bookshelf, then place the magnifying glass I had borrowed back in its case. All the while Wolfe remains seated, a pensive look on his face.

Maybe I'm being foolhardy. Yet, while I can't put my finger on it, the solving of the scrolls feels important. Initially I'd thought, or maybe hoped, that it would be my ticket out of here. Now, it seems that whatever secret I'm being led toward—whatever secret I'm uncovering—has far-reaching implications, much vaster and more important than my own life.

Wolfe, meanwhile, rubs both hands along his face, peering at me from across the room. "Since their numbers have dwindled so drastically in recent years, the last of their kind have become a paranoid and nomadic group. Whatever your coordinates are to indicate, it isn't their location. As for finding them yourself, upon a noisy and bothersome machine, no less, you will fail without a shadow of a doubt. Nonetheless, given just how stubborn you have proven your-self to be, I have no doubt you will venture out with your friend in a hopeless effort to locate them." He grips the edge of the table with both hands and stares at me. "You are never to enter the woods without me. On that point, I must be firm. Your friend, armed or not, will not offer you the protection necessary. In exchange for your word on this matter, I will attempt to take you to the Mavericks this evening, after sundown."

I stare at him, shocked. Those words are the very last ones I expected from him. And yet, he doesn't look so sure of them himself—his face has drained of so much blood that he looks sickly.

"But how will you find them if they're nomadic?"

"As you know, I spend a fair amount of time in the woods. I am more privy to their whereabouts than anyone."

"And yet you don't turn them in to the authorities?"

Slowly his spine straightens to its full length as he stands. He takes a deep breath and contemplates Airo-Aurora from a shadowy segment behind the window. "The one that I told you about—he has shown me kindness in the past. So no, I do not interfere with their way of life. Do I have your word? The woods, Alex."

I stare at him from my spot along a row of dusty books. It's almost unimaginable why he feels so strongly about the forest and its small yet admittedly ferocious collection of beasts. Nevertheless, I bow my head. "I give you my word."

twenty-six

WE EAT dinner together in silence. Partly I'm afraid to speak, as though it'll somehow change his mind about the whole thing. But there are plenty of other reasons to hold my tongue: Patrick, and Wolfe's angry, seemingly jealous and therefore puzzling reaction to him, for starters. Then there's the fact of the viscount's previous marriage, a detail now in plain sight between us, even if all surrounding minutiae remain hidden from view. Many questions linger around the information he'd shared in my quarters—ways to deceive a system of governance in which he's second in command. Why does he have such information in the first place? And given his willingness to share it with a girl from Quire, where exactly does his true allegiance lie?

It's all a whirlwind of thoughts and emotions that's only worsened by Patrick's pledge to return to the palace. And it seems to me to lead nowhere productive. Yes, it's best to focus only on the journey ahead.

After dinner's finished, velvety darkness pushing in through the palace windows, we head to our respective rooms to begin the task of getting ready for what promises to be a long and frigid night. I draw on three cardigans, buttoning each one to my chin, then wrap my scarf around my neck and face so that only my eyes remain visible. With the addition of the heavy wool cloak placed over the layers, I can barely move by the time I step into the corridor.

Wolfe stands waiting for me in the same spot Sedaris occupied just two days ago, a marked improvement, in my opinion. Despite his wilderness attire fit for the cold and the shotgun slung around his back, he manages to somehow maintain his normal regal appearance. Still, there's something different about him this evening. Something clouding his normally astute gaze and pinching his mouth.

He leads me downstairs and out the back door, then, stomping purposefully through snow that glints under the moonlight, he says, "It is not my first choice to venture into the woods at this hour. However, if we were to come across the Mavericks during daylight, you would be obliged to avert your eyes, or worse, wear a blindfold. They will not tolerate being recorded. In fact, I think it unlikely they would agree to speak with you at all."

"Why don't they wish to be recorded?"

"From time to time, they must venture into Airo-Aurora for supplies. Obviously, they are less likely to be detected if they are completely unknown to the Mainframe."

I blink up at the twinkling stars and try to imagine having so much freedom. "I have to admit," I say eventually, "their way of life sounds fascinating."

"You have the strength of mind to maintain surprising composure at the worst of times, yet you are far too delicate to survive their way of life. Be content with the luxuries I can provide you with." He obliges me to wait where I am with a point of his finger, then disappears into the stables.

I stare after him, rolling my eyes but also smiling, then shift my gaze to the birch trees in front of me—ones that seem to stretch higher, and twist at more unnatural angles. I can't really tell whether they warn me away, or if they beckon me headlong into the night—

"The saddle will be tight-fitting for the two of us, even given your small stature," Wolfe says as he emerges from the stables, interrupting my thoughts and leading a skeletal black horse into the snow. Its swishing tail awakens the darkness and I stare at it, skittish. "Do remember," he adds tactfully, "that this was your idea and not my own."

I nod. Does he really think I'd forget?

A minute later, I sit on the horse wedged between the front of the saddle and Wolfe. The sensation of being so far from the ground on something so wild is more daunting than I'd expected.

"It looks ill-fed, this horse."

"It's the fastest rider," he explains indifferently. "And I don't expect this will be a quick journey."

"It's strong enough to hold us both?"

"Of course."

"And it's well-trained, you think?"

He doesn't bother to reply as he steers us in the direction of the woods. At its edge, he grumbles, "You're holding yourself stiffly. It will be a long evening for you if you can't relax."

I force my muscles to unclench, but that only pushes me tighter into the curve of space left by his body. A long evening it promises to be, but, as he said, it was my idea. Besides, this is by far the best shot I'll get of speaking with the Mavericks, and any trepidation I felt is replaced with excitement.

"Once into the woods, we'll pick up considerable speed," he adds. "It is of paramount importance that you don't make any sudden movements and you hold yourself upright, without taxing yourself unnecessarily, of course. Know also that I will not be good company once inside."

I look sharply over my shoulder at these words, but as my forehead bumps into his chin, I straighten myself out.

Then, with a kick of his boot—we're off, the skeletal creature bursting to life with shocking speed. The cold tears at my exposed skin like a blade. Now and then, the treetops block out the moonlight and we're thrown into darkness so murky that Wolfe must pull violently on the reins to slow us. Navigating steep slopes is another impediment, but for the most part, both Wolfe and the horse seem to know the forest with accuracy, and we dart forward unimpeded.

Eventually, at a stream bordered with ice, Wolfe draws the horse to a stop, then lowers himself to the ground, allowing the horse to drink. The cold's overwhelming, but I don't question him on how much longer it'll be to locate the mysterious nomads—I'm just happy to get out of the palace and have an adventure.

It's only then that I notice the change that's come over him.

Usually so rigidly upright, now he's stooped forward. He breathes heavily, and through the dark, I can see that his usually watchful eyes are turned in. I could flail my arms in front of him, I think, without him noticing. A beast could jump from the shadows and he wouldn't try to shoot it. After a while, he crouches beside the stream, and his long and unsteady fingers trace the edge of ice. His face is totally unreadable, and it's more startling than the quivering darkness, or the woods that inhale and exhale in rhythm, or the demonic-looking horse that paws at the ground. I didn't realize how deeply I appreciated his steeliness until deprived of it.

"Wolfe?"

He tilts his head as if he half-hears, then he surfaces from whatever gripped him. He stands, combing the trees around us with one hand on the strap of the shotgun. "What is it," he replies eventually.

"It's...is everything alright?"

Out of the corner of his eye, he peers at me. A moment later, he returns to the saddle.

"Well?" I press.

"Everything is fine. Don't ask such foolish questions."

"It's not foolish," I insist as he steers the horse away from the creek. "It's obvious that something—"

"I explained to you that I would not be easy company in here. And yet, with all your nosiness and your threats, you've forced us into this situation. So be it, but leave it at that."

I don't want to *leave it at that*, but before long, we move so quickly that speaking is impossible. So. What is it about the woods that causes him so much unease? I've been made to promise over and again not to enter them, and yet despite being deep inside for well over an hour, I haven't seen a single beast. And why does he care so much about my safety in the first place?

He will worry over you, his mother had predicted, that very first day. The royal family is anything but close-knit, and yet the Duchess of Airo-Aurora must know her son well to have foreseen something so at odds with the rest of his personality.

As time wears on, every bone in my body begins to ache from being forced into such an unnatural position, tucked into Wolfe, holding onto the horse for dear life. How he can bear it with reins in hand, I don't know.

And then in the blink of an eye, he pulls fiercely at the reins. The horse stomps on its hind legs in protest. I bite my tongue to stop myself from screaming.

"If you see a beast, even a small one," he whispers in my ear, "yell for me at once. Otherwise, say nothing and do not move." I nod into darkness, then feel him disembark rather than see it. I listen to his footsteps that disappear into the night.

Surrounding me is nothing but closely knit trees, one of which the horse is tethered to. I breathe deeply and catch the smell of something foreign. I breathe again. Yes, it's faint, but it's there—the smell of fire. *People* are close by.

I feel a surge of excitement; no citizen of Airo-Aurora would be so far from home on a night like tonight, cobbling together a bonfire...it's the Mavericks we're near.

Minutes pass, and still no sign of Wolfe. If something happens to him, well...I don't have a clue where I am, or which way's home. I don't know how to help him, either. And then come the sound of footsteps, and suddenly and without warning, I'm jerked roughly to the side, off the horse and to the ground.

"It's not any that I'm familiar with," comes his low voice, straight to business. "Campinos, the one I know best, has gone missing, as so many of the others have. These Mavericks have agreed to speak with you and you alone in exchange for this." He pushes into my hand a heavy gold watch.

"It's yours?"

"Yes."

"I don't want—"

"It is the only way. They'll trade it for necessities the next time they pass into Airo-Aurora."

I wipe at the face of the fine piece of machinery, thinking.

"It's only a watch, Alex."

"Why can't you come with me?" I blurt out.

For a moment, he just stares at me. "Are you fearful?"

"No..."

"I don't like it any better than you do," he admits. "But they are exceedingly suspicious of strangers right now, and for good reason. Your size makes you seem like much less of a threat."

"Okay," I agree. I tap the watch against my bottom lip. "I'll be back in a few minutes, then."

"You don't need to do this. Any of it. You can ignore the scrolls. What is the end game, anyhow? Fight it as you may, your future with me is already settled."

"It is settled, Viscount, and I've accepted that, just as you have. But I want the truth, something you refuse to give me. Where can I find them?"

He turns me around. "Walk straight. The smell of their extinguished campfire will grow stronger. They will grab you when you are close."

Grab me? I glance at him, but there's no hint of amusement across his face. He speaks hard facts, underscored by the line appearing between his brows.

"If you need help, if you detect danger, even in the slightest, make yourself known. I won't be far."

With his words echoing in my mind, I begin moving through the trees, doing my best to follow the line as directed. The brush is so dense that quickly I lose sight of Wolfe behind me, and even the horse. It's as if the woods have closed in around me—they've trapped me in a world all their own, a terrifying one where darkness scurries at my feet. Roots twist underfoot as my heart hammers in my ears.

Well, Wolfe was right: I'm far too delicate to survive a life in the woods. So, just what type of people *can* survive?

With every step, the smell of burned firewood grows stronger, until it's so pungent that it catches in my lungs, and I cough. Immediately a hand lands across my mouth, smothering my cry.

"Got her," I hear a voice say, and it has an oily quality to it that I don't like. "Easy to find and easier to snatch, this wee one."

I'm pushed forward, down a slope and behind the root system of an overturned tree. Waiting in this pocket of earth is a small group of people. It's too dark to guess at age, or even gender, but thanks to the muted glow of dying embers, I can make out the twigs and leaves that cover their clothes. They watch me silently as the oily-voiced man forces me to sit. He kneels in front of me and lights a match.

As he holds it close to my face, studying it from every angle, I glimpse more of him—cavernous eyes, gaunt cheeks, rotted teeth. "Just a child," he mutters, snuffing out the flame and plunging us back into darkness. "That man— that terribly nasty man you travel with, he says you bring gold."

Silently I place the watch into his outstretched hand. It causes the others of the clan to murmur with excitement.

Wolfe's been too generous. He's taken me through the woods against his will; he's divested himself of jewelry on my behalf. Now I gift it to a man who insults him. It seems to me in that instant to be a horrible injustice.

The man examines the watch, tilting it toward the embers, letting it fall from hand to hand, seemingly impressed with its weight. "What does the wee pretty girly wish to discuss?"

"She's just a child, you said so yourself," comes a voice from the shadows.

"She came with him," the man hisses. "He's royalty, I can smell it."

Murmuring rises once again, except this time, it isn't with excitement. I can sense their agitation. "Royalty? You never said nothin' 'bout *that*."

"Could be this whole thing's a trap."

"We should've—"

"Please," I say, speaking for the first time. "There's no trap. That man—the one who gave you his watch—he's doing me a favor, that's all. I wanted to speak with...you. Your kind."

"Our *kind*?" The man cackles. "But share why, wee one!"

Share why? I don't know where to begin. "Because. I was instructed to."

"Yeah? By whom."

"I don't know, but I think it's someone working at the Mainframe."

More murmuring.

"Someone at the Mainframe's tryin' to get a read on us, is my thinking," says a voice.

"If that's the case," says the man, "then evidence won't be far for the taking," and with deft fingers, he begins folding back the fabric of my cloak.

"What are you doing?"

"Looking for a tracking device, wee one."

"I promise you this isn't a trap," I tell him as I push his hands away. "The authorities or whoever you're worried about won't be finding you with my help."

"So why all the fuss?"

For a while, I'm silent, thinking. "The messenger is critical of the Mainframe and its Selection system, or at least that's my theory. Maybe he or she thought you Mavericks would share those feelings. I know I do."

More terse glances. Finally, one from their group speaks, a girl this time. "We don't give a toss about the Mainframe you people bow to, but we have good reason to be critical of your King."

The man swats her, then grabs me around the wrist. "Fast—out with your questions, then our deal is done." He jingles the watch in my face.

"Jill. Timothee. Reginald. The Queen," I rhyme out, quickly now. "Do the names mean anything to you?"

All around the circle, I see heads shaking through the darkness.

"Do you know anything about a possible glitch the Mainframe might suffer from?"

More heads shaking.

"I understand your people have been dwindling over the years—"

"Not *dwindling*. Not *over the years*," the man hurls at me. "Two years, tops, and hundreds gone like that." He snaps his fingers. "That nasty man—that friend of yours—well, his friend Campinos was the most recent to go. His family, too. There's hardly any of us left now."

Hardly any of them left.

Could their disappearance be why the scroll writer wanted us to speak?

"What do you think happened to them?"

The sound of hissing rises up from the shadows. "Moving on," the man says gruffly. He makes a show of checking Wolfe's watch for the time. "One more thing. That's all you've paid for. All you're allowed."

"Yes, alright. One more thing." I rack my brain for any remaining details from the scrolls and find only one: the coordinates. "I'm wondering if you're familiar with a valley far north of here, one floored in rock, right in the heart of Ashville Range—"

I'm not sure which happens first. Whether it's the gasps that echo, or if the blow to my forehead precedes it. Whichever it is, I land flat on my back as someone exclaims, "She knows!" All around me, the Mavericks are jumping to their feet, stuffing blankets into sacks.

"You and I, wee shyster," the man hisses as the others flee. "Need to have a talk."

I cry out or begin to, but he lays a hand tight over my nose and mouth. Whatever he says next is lost on me, because the only thing my brain can focus on is finding oxygen…except none comes. I pull at his fingers, my vision glows red—

And then I'm released.

I gasp for breath and notice movement around me. That

and the unmistakable sound of fists colliding. Squinting, I spot a tall figure through the darkness.

I yell at them to stop, but neither hear me. The next strike is devastating, and at first, I can't tell which of the two curls tightly in a ball on the forest floor. But when the other pulls himself to his full height, there's no question.

"Wolfe," I gasp. "Please! It was all a misunderstanding!"

"A misunderstanding? You're *bleeding*," he seethes.

Then, under the light of the moon, I notice the dagger.

"This whole thing is my fault—all of it. Please, don't!"

"He would've killed you!" He kicks the Maverick onto his back. In one fluid motion, he pulls the man's arms down so they're pinned to his chest and pushes the knife alongside his neck.

I scream the first thing that comes to mind: "If you kill him, I'll *never* love you!"

In any other scenario, in any other minute, I would never say such words. I'd never *think* them. Because to do so would be to presume two things. The first is that one day there's a possibility I'll fall in love with this man. Outlandish. The second is that my love is something he cares about. Outrageous.

Up until that exact moment, I didn't think either presumption could ever be true. And yet, against all odds, the words have fled my mouth, they hang between me and Wolfe like lead. His jaw tightens. Then those steely eyes cut with rage falter. My words, for as little as they're worth, reach him.

A half-second later, a guttural noise erupts from his chest, something between a growl and a groan and a shout. He throws the dagger to the ground and uses both hands to drag the man to his feet, then shoves him deep into the night. After he picks up his knife, he leads me wordlessly around the tree carcass, back in the direction from which we came.

I'm too stunned to speak.

Eventually, we reach the horse standing in the dappled moonlight, looking as emaciated as ever. He points to the saddle, a clear indication to climb on, then lifts a hand to his neck. He takes his pulse, something I've seen him do before, and now I know why. If it doesn't slow soon, if the other hallmarks of stress that he no doubt exhibits don't quickly dissipate, an alert will issue from the Mainframe.

And then?

A few minutes later, when his breathing has slowed, he indicates again for me to climb on. Still, I don't move. Instead, my eyes trace the swollen skin that encircles his. One question leads to another, to a thousand more. All the while, he peers down at me with stony features. There's no hint of kindness or concern. There's no warmth in his gaze, or in his features, or in the curve of his body.

So I ignore my throbbing head and ask, "Why are you so protective of me when you look at me like that? You barely care for me. The real me, I mean—not the mere fact of me being your fiancée."

He says nothing. Just continues to peer at me as he monitors his pulse.

Slowly a thought dawns on me. "Wolfe—did something bad happen to your wife here, in the woods?"

It would appear to anyone watching that he didn't hear my words. Because instead of reacting to them, he takes off his glove and bends to better examine my forehead. He lifts his hand as if to dab away blood, and I brace for his touch, but he pauses, his hand hovers in space, then carefully he retracts it. He replaces his glove with surgical precision, then places his mouth to my ear. "If the bluecoats are waiting, say nothing." He straightens himself and speaks plainly. "Now we go."

He hoists me onto the horse, and I see him glance skyward as he maneuvers the beast through the tight-fitting trees, reading the stars like a map. With every step, my forehead aches. My brain, too. When we pick up speed, the blinking white birch makes me dizzy, so I close my eyes and tuck myself deeper into Wolfe's cloaks.

So much between us left unsaid, now more than ever.

He had listened.

With every minute that ticks by, the more it seems like some distant dream, completely unreal. *If you kill him, I'll never love you.* And so he turned his hand. I'd seen it clear as day with my own two eyes. And yet...

Had he hesitated *before* I said those words? Was I imagining my influence where there was none? Is it even conceivable that this cold-hearted man who said himself he couldn't provide me with a love story, whose own mother labeled him unlovable—that *he* cares about *my* love? The love of a girl from Quire?

And then there's the business of his first wife. He'd revealed nothing, ignoring my questions entirely, and yet I can't help but feel I'm on to something. His natural urge to keep me safe, particularly in the woods, had extended back long ago, back to the days when his disdain for me was so pronounced it was glaring. Even now, tolerable to him as I seem to be, it wouldn't explain the dagger he'd drawn at my defense. There's something else at play, I'm sure of it.

Next, I think about those Mavericks, about how my meeting really couldn't have gone worse. They distrusted me from the get-go; one tried to kill me and nearly wound up dead in the process, and I had gleaned next to nothing. Aside from one point, that is: whatever's located at the coordinates in the scroll, the Mavericks know it well. There's a connection between the two, and a very sore one at that...

twenty-seven

...

IT'S the sound of the horses that I notice first. I pull myself upright, then throw a furtive glance at Wolfe over my shoulder. If his heart hammers as mine does, he doesn't show it. He looks just as disinterested at the sight of the awaiting bluecoats as he does during our evening dinners. Either he's very good at hiding himself, or he cares very little about a great deal of things.

But neither explanation completely captures him. The man in the woods cared very much, and in plain view.

"Say not a word unless called upon," he reminds me, then we emerge from the woods through an archway of bending birch. Four sturdy horses stomp their hooves in the midnight air, breath glowing white under the moonlight, just as with the four uniforms sitting on top of them. An approaching warm front rumbles in the distance.

"Viscount," says the largest bluecoat, and he bows his head as he works to keep his horse still.

"How can I help you?" Wolfe grumbles in reply.

"We were alerted by the Mainframe about your state. Live feed pulled up by the tech suggested you were in here."

"And you didn't think to venture inside to offer

assistance?" Wolfe's voice grows icy and its effect on the bluecoats is immediate. Discomfort pushes between them.

"My sincerest apologies, Viscount," says the eldest uniform. "But surely you can appreciate that given the darkness, finding your exact whereabouts would have been nigh impossible."

There's nothing but pregnant silence as Wolfe stares at them.

Meanwhile, I do my best not to draw attention to myself. It's futile. All four men chance look after look. Maybe it's the way my forehead bleeds. Or the words spoken among the trees, some presumably recited by the technician. Or maybe it's simply because I'm in the company of the Viscount of Airo-Aurora. Whatever it is, the longer we stand around in silence, eyes darting here and there, the more uncomfortable I become. Finally, Wolfe kicks the horse forward, tracing an arc around our visitors in the direction of the stables. He disembarks, then helps me off with slightly more tact than he'd shown in the woods.

As the men approach, a redheaded one clears his throat. "Viscount," he begins, and he bows deeply, though Wolfe takes no notice. Instead, he busies himself with the removal of the saddle. "We were assured, see, by the time we reached your property here that your heart rate had gone all the way back to normal. Otherwise, you know, we would've gone on in."

"You were assured my heart rate had returned to normal, and yet here you remain." He tosses the saddle to the ground. "I'm fine, and so is my fiancée. Be on your way."

"She doesn't look so fine, really."

"She is."

Eyes comb over me once again. "We just have a few standard questions, sir, then we'll be off."

"Make it quick."

"Start by telling us what happened inside the woods," orders the largest.

"Start by telling me what the technician told you. I don't make a habit of divulging personal details of my life without necessity."

The uniforms exchange uneasy glances. Wolfe's clearly proving to be more combative than what they're used to, and I wonder if these same men tended to Mr. Worthers, and Mary Beth's son. I wonder if they're wishing Dr. Lebwitski was here...

The eldest speaks. "Given the darkness, it was difficult to make out much, Viscount, but apparently, it sounded like you were involved in some sort of altercation. Does that sound right?"

"My fiancée was attacked, as you can plainly see."

"Do you mind, sir, if we ask her some questions?"

Wolfe's long body stiffens. "I don't see why that's necessary."

"Aye, we won't bite," assures the redhead. "What's your name, then?"

"Alexandra Stephens." I see Wolfe turn his head and stare at me. Even he, I realize, didn't know that—he didn't know my full name.

"So you got into a scrape in the woods, aye?"

"A small one," I agree.

"Why didn't you set off an alarm, then?"

"Because she's a child, obviously," Wolfe interrupts. "Do you not have eyes?"

"I'm far from a *child*," I say as I give Wolfe a look. True to form, he doesn't seem to notice, or care.

"But you're not yet eighteen?"

"That's right."

"Well, Miss Stephens," says the redhead, grinning. "Once the bell tolls, you can expect a watchful eye and a helping hand from us bluecoats, you know. I, for one, would be happy to come to your service." He bows.

Instead of replying, I think again of Mr. Worthers and Mary Beth's son. Come to my service *how?* I wonder. And even though I know he won't tell the truth, at least not the full truth, I use the opportunity to ask: "Do you serve only by making—"

"This is a waste of time," Wolfe snaps, and he jerks me away from them before I can finish. "All remaining questions go through me."

The youngest uniform coughs lightly into his fist. "Um, sir, may I ask who her attacker was?"

"A man of the woods. I don't know anything about him, nor do I know where he escaped to."

"Do you wish to file an official report? Do you wish medical treatment for Miss Stephens?"

"I wish for you to leave us alone so that I may go to bed. The hour is late."

A moment later, the bluecoats murmur their farewells. But I can't help thinking it's with reluctance that they go, and by the way Wolfe stares after them as they disappear into the night, he must feel the same.

Still gripping my arm, he says in a low voice, "I ask for silence, and instead you deign to ask questions of your own?"

I stare at him under the moonlight.

"Let me guess," he continues. "You didn't see the harm?"

"I still don't."

He squints at me as thunder rumbles closer. Then with an exasperated sigh, he leads the black stallion into the stables, leaving me alone in the darkness. Lightning illuminates the sky to the east, and a cool breeze distinct from the harsh north wind of earlier rustles the hair at the nape of my neck. His frustration with me is mounting, I'm sure of it, and

I have to admit it's for good reason. He had battled himself in the woods, he had battled another, he had received a black eye in the process. He had lost his watch, and he had even been interrogated by the bluecoats. All because of me. All because of a whim. That scroll—that *stupid* scroll, left for me by some unknown person from the Mainframe.

Is it possible I've been wrong about the scrolls all along?

A minute later, Wolfe strides out of the stables, and we head for the back door of the palace.

Even though the palace is normally glacial at this time of night, its inner chambers fill my veins with heat the moment we step inside, awakening my extremities and reddening my cheeks.

"Sir," comes a voice from the shadows, and Gerard, wearing pinstripe pajamas and a nightcap, steps forward. "Strath Glen was alerted by the bluecoats to a matter in the woods. I take it they found you in good health?"

"They did," replies the viscount tersely. He doesn't bother to slow down, let alone come to a stop. "The same cannot be said for her. Bring some ice to her room and some painkillers," he adds over his shoulder.

I hurry after Wolfe, ignoring the way Gerard stares at me. I need to apologize for the whole evening, and I can't do that while speaking to his backside. If anything, however, he picks up more speed, taking the stairs two at a time.

Only when he reaches my room does he stop. Something clenches in my stomach once I reach him, and I busy myself by unlocking the door. Maybe I'm nervous about having to apologize—maybe *that's* why I suddenly feel so hot.

But before I can speak, he pushes inside my room.

"Wolfe?"

"What is it?"

"It's nothing, just…I thought you were in a rush to go to bed."

"I'd like a word."

"Yes, okay. Uh, just give me one minute." I head to the closet, where I unwind my scarf, take off my cloak, along with the extra cardigans, then examine my forehead in the mirror hanging on the back of the door.

A purple bump, punctuated by the remnants of dried blood—not so different from the injury I sported when I first arrived at Strath Glen. The rest of my face looks strange, both flushed and pale at the same time. My windswept hair is full of tangles, and frizz circles my face like a halo. In every way, I look the opposite of the perfectly manicured, highly polished women of Wolfe's world.

When I emerge from the closet, my sock feet slow. The room is blanketed in darkness; the only light comes from the bedside lamp, and it casts only a dim yellow glow. Music plays, slow and melodic. "The darkness?"

"The lack of stimulus to one's visual feed suggests to the Mainframe that of sleep, prompting less automated surveillance."

I nod. If this were any other man, in any other circumstance, such a setting might have different connotations. What it means right now, however, from the dim lighting to the music, is the ability to have a full and frank conversation without detection. And every full and frank conversation with Wolfe is a step closer to the truth.

He sits in a wing chair with his elbows resting on his knees, staring at me with unreadable eyes. The anger that was there earlier has gone, that much I can tell. "Does it hurt?"

I lift a finger to my forehead, then busy myself arranging the books on my bedside table. "Not terribly. Does yours?"

His response is nothing but silence, and finally, I glance at him. Only then does he speak. "No."

With a steadying breath, I walk deeper into the room until I sit on the sofa straight across from him. "I believe,

Wolfe, for this evening, that apologies are in order. I never should—"

He waves a hand. "Don't bother."

"But really," I insist. "Between your eye and your watch and the bluecoats—"

"I told you already, don't bother with apologies. I'm not interested."

"Gratitude, then. For taking me to the Mavericks in the first place. And for sparing me from violence—"

"I'm not interested in that, either," he interrupts. "Besides, you weren't completely spared, now were you." His gaze lifts to my forehead.

I frown, a little annoyed. "If you aren't interested in that which needs to be said, Viscount, may I ask why you bothered to *barge* in here?"

He studies me, and for the first time since knowing him, I see something dancing across his eyes that's totally unfamiliar. It's foreign, almost like laughter. The rest of his face is impassive—only his eyes betray something different.

A knock comes at the door, spoiling the moment. I pull it open to Gerard, who presses a pack of ice and a bottle of pills into my hand. He almost retreats into the night, but he catches sight of Wolfe sitting inside, notices the darkened room, and hears the music. Intrigue sparks in his eyes.

Not wanting him to get the wrong impression, I freeze, then fumble the ice to the floor. Scooping it up, I find my face has gone red.

"Close the door," Wolfe says lazily from his chair. His eyes are on the window that flashes with lightning.

Bidding goodnight to the butler, I return to my spot with the ice pressed to my forehead. "Would you like it for your eye?" I ask.

We're immediately interrupted by another caller.

This time a trio of servants enter the room and head for

the windows. The previously silent House of Mirrors bustles with movement.

"What's this?"

"There's a storm brewing, sir," the nearest servant says. "That means us sealing the windows, battening down the hatches, you get the drift." A moment later, they disappear. Thunder rumbles closer, but this time we're truly alone.

"Your eye—"

"My eye is fine," he insists. "The reason for my company, for barging in, as you so gently put it, is to hear about your conversation with the Mavericks. I believe after a somewhat arduous evening, I am at least entitled to that."

I smile. For all I've put him through this evening, it's a small ask. "I take it, considering how quickly you intervened, that you weren't far away. You didn't hear any of our conversation?"

"I was not eavesdropping," he responds coolly, as though he takes offense to the suggestion. "I stood only close enough to listen for your cries."

"Alright," I say, tapping my finger against my lip. "They were suspicious of me from the start. Well, more so of you, I guess. That man had no difficulty recognizing you for what you are."

"Which is?"

"Someone...you know." He makes no reply, no effort to fill in the blank, and I stare at him. "Someone important. Someone of royal rank."

"Continue."

"They thought the whole thing was a trap. That man even went so far as to check me for tracking devices."

His brow binds. "He laid his hands on you?"

"Through my pockets. I assured them it was nothing like that and explained I had received a mysterious message from the Mainframe suggesting I speak with them."

His mouth presses into a line, but he lifts a hand to urge me forward. "I assume that was met with suspicion as well."

"It was," I agree. "At that point, they told me, more or less, to get on with it so the trade for your watch could be complete. I asked them if they knew the names in the scrolls, which they didn't, and they weren't aware of any glitch at the Mainframe, either. But when I mentioned to them the valley in Ashville Range, they went mad. I think they thought it was definitely a trap I was laying for them."

"That's why that man attacked you?"

"Yes."

"And that's it?"

"That's it."

Wolfe steeples his fingers, then exhales noisily. "Are there other scrolls? Ones that you haven't shared with me?"

I shake my head. "None."

"And no other clues you've discovered as to who your mystery writer may be?"

Again, I shake my head.

He nods, but this time I feel his anger as much as I see it. "I have asked for your trust," he says in such a low voice that I have to strain my ears to hear it.

"And for all intentions, I've given it to you—especially after tonight," I reply, partly to placate him, but part of me is earnest, too. Sure, I hadn't forgiven him for the threat to personally review my feed, or for imposing on me those terrible restrictions, but after this evening, wasn't the stock I placed in him self-evident?

Hail begins to tick noisily against the windowpanes and gusts of wind rattle the palace walls. His eyes flash through the dark; they mimic the lightning on the other side of the windowpane. Slowly his long body stretches to the ceiling, and a moment later, it lowers itself onto the velvet sofa next to mine.

I turn to him, my gaze open, no longer wary.

"That isn't true," he begins, in that detached way of his. "Just now in our conversation you referred to the message you received from the Mainframe. The *Mainframe*, in particular—something you told the Mavericks about, apparently, and yet you failed to mention it to me. I fear one of these days I am going to really lose my temper with you."

I wince. "Please don't. It was a small detail discovered by Jill, and it wasn't kept from you on purpose. Really, I'm sorry that I didn't think to tell you."

"Share it with me now."

"Jill was the one who found the last scroll and passed it to me, though I'm sure you've already pieced that together. She noticed footsteps in the snow that led to the Mainframe. Maybe a coincidence, maybe not."

"This is information you should have come to me with at first instance," he says between gritted teeth. Then he rests his head in his hands, looking tired. According to the clock, it's now early morning. "Where precisely did she find it?"

I say nothing.

"You're not going to tell me."

Off in the distance, from someplace else in the palace, comes the sound of shouting. The storm picks up intensity.

"I can't tell you, or you'll confiscate them before I can even see. I know it."

"Do you?"

"Am I wrong?"

"No," he admits.

"They're my scrolls, Viscount," I explain, "and even though I might rethink how much energy I sink into them after tonight's mess, I don't think it's right that you hide them from me."

"Call me Wolfe. Always, from now on."

I stare at him. "Alright. Wolfe."

"You know, just because someone at the Mainframe is trying to pass along information to you, it doesn't mean they have your best interests at heart. You may very well be nothing more to them than a pawn. Did you ever stop to think about that?"

"Maybe not, but—"

"Whoever this is, they have a motive, and whether or not you ruin yourself in the process is undoubtedly of no concern."

"You make a strong case," I admit. "One I'll consider..."

"Yes...*but*?"

"It's just...well. It's true that the scroll writer may not have my best interests at heart. But it's hard to believe, at times, that *you* have my best interests at heart, either."

"How is that?"

"You dismiss me as a child, first off."

"What, my words out there, to the bluecoats?" He scoffs. "I had an agenda, clearly. Besides, I think you are far from a child. You have persevered through great hardship, you are proficient in an assortment of professions and pastimes, and your character and composure exceed those of practically everyone I know."

I go still. So still I can hardly breathe. Is it really possible he said all that? Is it really possible he *believes* all that? "I wonder if the punch you took," I begin, after a long stretch of silence, "hasn't interfered with things upstairs."

He smiles, then edges forward on the sofa as if to go. "It's late, Alexandra," he murmurs, using my full name. Nobody calls me that, not for as long as I can remember. It sounds foreign. And yet said on his tongue, it also sounds strangely familiar. "Try to get some sleep."

Instead of bidding him goodnight, I examine his injured eye. A shock of red at the corner and mild swelling around that. His face is often twisted with scorn, exacting in its intensity. But always it's regal. The injury looks terribly out of place.

The more I stare at it, the more the facts surrounding its

placement sink to the bottom of my stomach. I was in trouble, and he came to my side. He withstood violence for my sake, this strange man I'm expected to wed, and he doesn't want thanks or apologies for it. There's something very honorable in all that. I lift my hand and, in breach of our unspoken policy to withhold all contact unless strictly necessary, touch the injury lightly with the tips of my fingers. Slowly they slip over the rest of his face.

His body goes still, every muscle cast in iron, but he doesn't brush me away. Instead he watches me from his shadowy spot on the sofa, his gaze made animalistic in the dim light.

The air surrounding us convulses and the sofa shifts, but still, it doesn't rock my hand away, doesn't move Wolfe's voracious gaze from mine.

Finally, when the room around us goes still, and the music stops, when the storm sweeps off into the distance, I let my hand drop into my lap, considerably more tired than before. Without a word, Wolfe rises from the sofa, collects his belongings, and walks out the door.

twenty-eight
. . . . .

WITH WOLFE'S restrictions lifted and King and the others not due back until early afternoon, I make good use of the morning by taking the bus to Quire and spending long overdue, much-needed time with Agnes and my aunt. I awkwardly tell them the date of the wedding and, with fanfare, news of my first international mission as Wolfe's pilot scheduled for the following day. All other details I keep to myself: the meeting of Mr. Worthers, the ensuing house arrest, the run-in with Patrick, the trek into the woods, and last but not least, that moment I shared with the viscount—one impossible to pin down let alone explain. No, it's much better to focus my attention on Aunt Jo's new mail route and Agnes's most recent fight with Miller.

Only on the bus ride home do I allow myself to think of him.

I hadn't seen him that morning—instead I dropped off his breakfast as quickly as possible before leaving the palace. Because no longer can I claim not to know him at all. Last night I saw sides of him unseen by others. We've been bonded together in violence, shared a saddle, along with that surprising moment afterward in my room. In some ways, too many ways, it unearthed only more questions. Yet still, I feel closer to him than before, like a seismic shift in our relationship's occurred.

But does *he* feel that way?

I sort of doubt he's capable of such profoundly human observations in the first place...

One thing I'm sure of, though—whether he notices or not, our future encounters will be marked by the same detached, businesslike manner that he maintains always, with everyone. Maybe he'll even go to lengths to push me away again. Maybe by avoiding him this morning, I'm the one doing it.

These thoughts consume me so much that I don't notice the commotion at the top of Strath Glen's front steps until I stumble right on it: a man holding Jill in a headlock.

I feel my breath shortening with panic, but not for long. Jill delivers an elbow to the man's ear, then drives a heel backward between his legs. Just as suddenly as I found my friend captive, I now find her fastening the man's hands in cuffs, looking bored.

"Are—are you okay?"

"'Course I am," she says. "He was demanding to speak to the princess. When I wouldn't let him through, he charged me."

I stare around the landing. "Where's the other greencoat?"

"Inside," she explains. She digs an elbow into the man's side to stop his movement, then spits on the concrete next to his nose. "Talking to Gerard about scheduling."

I step over the man's head, one that issues a commendable range of expletives, pull open the door, and motion to the other guard. Next, under the midday sun that promises warmer weather to come, I watch as the blackcoats are summoned to the palace, as they haul off the man. Jill poses reluctantly for a picture for the papers, then Gerard presents her with a medal of bravery that he clips to her uniform. Finally, when all the dust settles, she joins me along the railing with a slap on the back. "Thanks for the help."

"The *help*?" I laugh. "I don't think I realized the extent of your capabilities until now."

"What can I say?" she says, yawning. "I lift weights and like punching things."

"You were completely fearless, is what you were! Did he hit you?" I add, noticing a bruise on the side of her head.

She doesn't answer, instead inspecting the medal of bravery and stifling yet another yawn. "Word is, your bodyguard's been given the toss. How'd you manage that?"

"Let's just say that Wolfe happened to catch me in a rare fit of emotion and caved."

Jill leans against the railing and surveys me. "He doesn't like to see his missus cry? No shame in that. So, I suppose I'm off scroll-hunting duty. Speaking of, did you figure out those coordinates?"

"They point to a mountainous region far north of here—Ashville Range. Well, to be specific, to a valley within it. Do you know the area?"

She stares at the horizon. "Don't think so," she says after a while.

"No, I don't, either." I pause. "Is everything okay?"

"Tired, that's all. My old man was coming off a bender last night, so he wasn't in the best of moods. Long story short, I didn't get to bed 'til half-past three."

"Half-past three?" I echo, then watch her carefully out of the corner of my eye. "Has he always been like that?"

"I've been counting down to my eighteenth year for the past decade."

"Why?"

"Why do you think? I'll be off living with the fiancé soon."

"It's that bad?"

"Worse. I just about split a few years back. Had my bag packed and everything, before I talked myself out of it." She eyes me. "What about you? Your life here isn't exactly rosy. You ever think about running for it, princess?"

I let out a halfhearted laugh. As if it'd be that easy. That fence, in particular, would stand in my way. Literally. But then I remember something. My commercial pilot's license. I might not be able to *run* away, but I suppose if things became really desperate, I could *fly* away. "Don't give me any ideas," I finally say, elbowing her.

She laughs.

"I'm sorry to hear about last night," I add, glancing again at the bruise on her temple.

"Can't get all the luck. Anyway, looks like yours is about over," she says, nodding down at a limousine whose snout arcs slowly toward the palace.

My soon-to-be family, returning from their trip. My stomach sinks at the sight. I bid goodbye to a yawning Jill and push inside.

The door clicks shut behind me at the same moment Wolfe exits Counterdown. He tasks a nearby servant with carrying a stack of books to his office, then scrutinizes my windswept hair and flushed cheeks. "Where were you?" he asks. No greeting, just as usual, though at least his tone isn't full of its usual iciness.

"In Quire." I remove my cloak and lay it over my arm. "Visiting my aunt and Agnes."

"Agnes."

"You met her that day here with the pies."

"I remember," he says quickly. An uncomfortable silence settles between us. He clears his throat. "I hear a man tried to gain access to Strath Glen just now."

"I saw it myself. Turns out my friend Jill's more machine than mere mortal."

"A useful friend to have, then. Your forehead looks markedly better."

"Sore to the touch but nothing more. The same can be said of your eye, I presume?"

"Certainly no worse," he agrees.

Our forced politeness and tactile silences are broken by a high-pitched wailing that comes from a distant corner of the palace. We exchange a puzzled look. Next the wailing bursts to full pitch, clearly coming from Devonshire Commons.

Aubrey, clad in neon pink ski gear, collapses onto the daybed in tears as the rest of the family push through the door from the underground parking garage. An army of servants bogged down with luggage and skis follow close behind, and the parrot looks put out as its cage is walloped by the passing equipment.

"What's this?" Wolfe demands. His gaze is fixed on his uncle, whose face boasts none of its usual black humor. Instead, he looks shell-shocked, pale, and pallid, and that wide mouth usually twisting itself into a Cheshire grin now presses into a thin line.

"Your cousin made a most startling discovery this morning," he replies under his breath as he passes through Devonshire. The Queen, meanwhile, does her best to massage her daughter's kicking feet, smiling serenely as she takes a strike to the stomach. Morocco and James wave elaborate gold fans over Aubrey, who continues to wail. Evie stands off to the side, watching it all with rounded eyes.

"You were missed, my son," the duchess says to Wolfe through the mayhem. She grips his arm, and I watch the way his body hardens at her touch; this isn't a man accustomed to physical contact. "I take it you have mended your rift with your fiancée. Certainly it was the subject of much debate at the ski lodge."

Wolfe snorts.

"Well?"

"Yes," he grumbles.

"Excellent! And yet you both bear such unusual injuries."

"A long and unnecessary story," he says dismissively. He stares at his cousin still languishing on the daybed. "Tell me what is wrong with her."

She hesitates. And then: "It would seem, my boy, that she is expecting."

The news hits me with force. Aubrey, *pregnant*? It must hit Wolfe hard too, because for a while, he seems robbed of words. Slowly he exhales. "I suppose the father could be anyone."

"That would be a scandalous thing to say," she reminds him. "Her husband will no doubt be joining us permanently at the palace at his earliest convenience. For all intents and purposes, *he* is the father."

Wolfe rubs at invisible flecks of dust along his sleeve, then juts his chin in the direction of his sister. "She is too young and impressionable to be exposed to such revolting behavior. How many times have I warned you, she will end up just like the others if you aren't more careful."

I stare at him. The words are a public condemnation of... who? King's side of the family? The ritzy set that frequents the palace in the evenings as if it's their own? Whoever they are, they're *his* people. And yet his disgust for them is undeniable.

The duchess considers him for a moment, then wraps an arm around Evie's waist, ushering her out.

I watch Wolfe out of the corner of my eye. He stares at Aubrey, and once again, his face has hardened over into a slab of unyielding rock. Plenty of times I've been on the receiving end of a look of displeasure from him, but never before have I quite seen this.

Total loathing.

The princess doesn't notice at all. Instead she accepts a

glass of water brought by one of the servants, and I almost feel sorry for her in the moment. She's far less adorned than usual, her face free of its usual thick application of pastel-hued makeup. In fact, she appears ordinary, as though she too could hail from a place like Quire.

"I NEED ICE!" she screams, and the moment's lost.

James, meanwhile, leaves Morocco to do the fanning. He lifts his brow at me. "No more guard covering your tail? Lucky me."

"How's that?" Wolfe demands.

He shrugs, then says to him with apathy, "Another babe en route to Strath Glen. Hard to believe, isn't it? Sister doesn't strike me as the most matronly of the lot."

"Matronly? There isn't a maternal bone in her body," Wolfe seethes. "But given the means of creating a child, I don't find the news surprising in the least. I do, however, pity the infant."

"A team of nannies and a silver spoon, what could be better?"

Wolfe's expression sours at the words but he says nothing, watching instead with open disgust as Aubrey vomits into the ice canister brought to her side, one typically reserved for aperitifs.

―――――

LATER THAT EVENING, after a dinner passed with Evie recounting every detail of their trip, including but not limited to a kiss shared with a foreign dignitary and the moment Aubrey realized she was pregnant, I walk back to my room with my spirits high. I think of my visit to Quire, and the international flight scheduled for the following morning. I think of how, between the adventure in the woods and the news of Aubrey's pregnancy, the long days are, at least for now, behind me.

And then come the echo of small thuds. King and his walking stick, striding through the House of Mirrors, draped in the fur of an arctic fox. The promise to spoil my good mood whispers through the air.

"Good ev-en-ing!" he sings in an operatic melody.

I curtsy and murmur the same to him: "Good evening, King." His reflection peers at me from no less than eight mirrors. The silver walking stick catches the light.

"Did you hear the splendid news regarding our darling fairy princess and her little bundle of joy?"

I cough to hide my surprise at the change of heart. "Indeed. It's a most, er, exciting development."

"And Dear Matthew will be beside himself with excitement, just as you say. Have you met Dear Matthew?"

"At the Rose Ceremony, sir."

"With a babe on the way, there's no question about him coming to reside here within these old walls. Finally! It wasn't a good look, having them under separate roofs. Speaking of which, I couldn't help but notice a man following you around mine. Syphilis was his name?"

"Sedaris."

"Aces. Now, according to the rumors, there was trouble in the roost between you and my nephew." He rubs his hands together darkly. "Share with King all the juicy details."

"I…"

"…went where you shouldn't have?" he finishes. His eyes round in a show of innocence. "Did you go against King's orders and depart from Strath Glen?"

"I-I had the viscount's permission to go," I insist. "I had to take something to my aunt in Quire."

"So why the surveillance offered by young Syphilis, hmm? Is it because you coerced poor Monsieur Sawyer into taking you to see that wretched old man Worthers? Something you *didn't* have permission for?" In the blink of an eye,

King's smile contorts. I take a step back, and all his reflections fall from the mirrors. "No need to be so cagey; the chauffeur already told me everything once I forced him. What I wonder about is why you would want to chat with the old man in the first place."

"He was fired on my very first day—" I begin, the same line I gave Monsieur, but immediately I'm silenced by the swish of his wrist.

"I didn't ask you, though," he says simply. Then he positions the walking stick between his legs. He leans forward so his weight rests on it. "And so my nephew was made angry at your disobedience and took swift action against you. Daisies. Yet, my dear Alex, your Quire loins must be powerful indeed, because just like that, he's whisking you into the woods, defending your honor and getting himself into a tither to boot. Again, I wonder, *why*? Why did you wish to enter the cold old forest in the middle of the night, hmm? I know for a fact it wasn't he who desired it." He stamps the walking stick loudly on the floor and sighs. "It doesn't do to have my bluecoats pay a visit to Strath Glen— the optics, the optics—and yet you're smart enough to piece that together like a well-made quilt. What worries me, I suppose, what grates at my heart of hearts, what awakens me from time to time in the middle of the night when all my beautiful nation slumbers, is the influence you exert over him."

I take another step back and shake my head. With my heart hammering, I whisper, "He cares for me very little, actually. He bothers with me very rarely. You...you imagine my influence where there's none."

"*He cares for me very little, he bothers with me very rarely,*" King repeats, mocking me in a whisper of his own. He lifts his walking stick and pokes it into my sternum. "You hide behind that innocent little voice and those big cottontail eyes, don't you? And yet I see defiance glinting inside. You condemn me, you savage the King! What exactly is it you think when you flutter those eyelashes in my direction? What is it you suspect when you play the spy outside my office and underneath the stairs, hmm?"

And then my arm is grabbed; I'm wrenched backward. A tall figure pushes in front of me. "Have you not seen my memos?" Wolfe demands impatiently. "As you know, the paperwork will be signed in the morning. Your attention is urgently required."

I squint at the back of Wolfe's head and consider the fingers still clenched around my arm—ones that force me to remain where I am, blocked from view. Deadlines are discussed, and tariffs, and then he releases me and walks with King along the corridor without a backward glance.

I stare after them, thinking.

It would be foolish to believe he'd come to my aid on purpose. He had his own agenda; I'd been nothing more than an easily removable impediment. Hadn't I?

From under the rotunda, King stops, then turns and calls up the corridor: "I depend on this boy. Pilot that helicopter tomorrow with exceptional skill, little one!"

I nod, sensing that another sleepless night lies before me.

twenty-nine

WITH WOLFE SITTING NEXT to me in the behemoth, Monsieur Sawyer is the definition of courtly, moving from one compliment to the next in a show of amiableness. What a shame, then, that the drive to the Sky Center is so short.

"Bon voyage," he adds a few minutes later as he pulls open Wolfe's door. "No doubt, Viscount, sir, that your fiancée will have you to your meeting and back in record time, and in maximum comfort, too."

Wolfe, as he's done all morning, says nothing. His bad mood is so pronounced that even Evie had turned in the opposite direction before our departure. His father had pretended to take a phone call rather than speak with him, and Gerard had ducked into an adjoining room as we marched behind Monsieur in the direction of the garage. And so I don't waste my breath trying to talk; instead I focus on the fact that I have something meaningful to occupy my day for once. Something meaningful *and* exciting.

But there are nerves there, too. Nerves where there shouldn't be. I have plenty of experience piloting a helicopter, after all, and the machine I'll be flying is miles better than what I'm used to. The skies are clear, and the route we'll take is completely unobstructed. By all accounts, it promises to be a straightforward mission. And so it's simply the company of Wolfe that makes me nervous—it must be.

Too much happened that night in the woods. Too many questions, too many unfathomable emotions. And now his bad mood? It all makes me very uncomfortable, and last night's run-in with King isn't helping matters.

Swinging the door to the behemoth open myself, I round the limousine and notice for the first time a number of people congesting the front entranceway. Some even hold cameras, and all of them move in the viscount's direction. Flashes go off and several people call out his name.

"Is it true a new trade line could be opening up to the east?"

"What is Airo-Aurora's official position on the Peaceful Specimens Treaty? Will we become a signatory?"

"Was the report accurate about you taking a wife? From which of the neighboring estates does the lucky woman herald?"

True to fashion, Wolfe doesn't respond to any questions; he doesn't even lift his chin from its place deep inside his coat. He pushes straight inside the Sky Center, leaving me to find a path through the crowd that has closed up behind him.

He doesn't wait for me inside, either; he heads straight for the locker room that leads to the helipad without glancing over his shoulder.

Twenty minutes later, strapped into the cockpit, I lift us into the air in a burst of adrenaline, managing this time to keep the shuddering of the lawn-green beast to a minimum. Once we reach a cruising altitude, I direct us northeast, quiet the motor, remove my headset, and chance a look at my passenger. He stares out the window at the deep blue sky, at our city that quickly becomes a distant speck, at the treetops that litter the landscape. The one thing those dark eyes refuse to acknowledge is me.

Is it Aubrey's condition that causes his terrible mood? Or my conversation with King? Or something else entirely?

"So, this country we're headed to," I shout over the clamor of rotor blades, "does Airo-Aurora engage in a lot of trade with it?"

Wolfe glances sharply at me, almost as if he'd forgotten about my presence completely. "Myopia is our main trading partner by far, so yes." He turns away, gazing down at the forest below, but he must feel like his explanation requires more, because he adds, "Most countries have no interest in Airo-Aurora."

"Why is that?"

He rubs his temple and sighs. "Back when our nation-state was laying the groundwork for the Selection system, most ties with the outside world were severed. It became a nation turned in, allowing little news or products from elsewhere inside country borders. The world, in turn, wants little to do with us."

I stare at his profile, stunned. "Most countries don't operate as Airo-Aurora does?"

He shakes his head. "Not in the slightest. Our reliance on artificial intelligence, in particular, has turned us into something of a pariah state. So long as we don't pose a threat to other nations, however, we aren't technically in breach of any international treaties and so are left to our own devices."

The news leaves me speechless. A *pariah-state*? All my life, I've been led to believe that the Mainframe system, with its chips and its Selection and its infinite wisdom, is the status quo—because it works. Because it ensures peace and prosperity. *Happiness.* And yet, if all that's true, why doesn't the entire world operate the same way?

I'm right, then. It *is* a flawed system—it *must* be. Those dissatisfied with it, like myself, have good reason.

"And Myopia, why does it bother with us if the rest of the world doesn't? Do they have a chip system in place?"

"No. But they are a peace-loving nation and one that shares a great deal of our border, and so they accept our exports in exchange for a few carefully selected imports of their own. I advise you to remain in the helicopter as much as possible during my meeting, otherwise you will be subjected to a number of looks. People outside of Airo-Aurora have difficulty wrapping their brain around the notion of chips being implanted in our own. Your questions are finished, I presume?"

For a while I oblige, turning the news around in my head. Then I say plainly, "You weren't at dinner last night."

"I wasn't hungry." He spits out the words, then fixes his gaze on me. "My uncle, once he recovered from the shock of Aubrey's condition, was interested in why the bluecoats paid a visit to the property the night before last. Is that why he cornered you in the House of Mirrors?"

"It is."

"Your response?"

"I was spared from answering by...well, you."

"Anything else?"

"He mentioned my visit to Mr. Worthers—"

"Worthers? That man's been more trouble than he's worth—I should've allowed him to be thrown to the prisons," he mutters. "How did my uncle get wind of that?"

"I think through Monsieur Sawyer."

Wolfe stares at the side of my face. "All conversations," he says bitingly, "that might throw his trust of you into further doubt must be masked just as ours is, now."

"I'm beginning to see."

"You must not forget that everything you say or do can be reviewed at the Mainframe."

"So you've said."

"What's that?"

"So you've said," I repeat louder. "You threatened to do just that, do you remember?"

He grumbles something indecipherable.

"You've done it before, haven't you?"

He looks sharply at me. "Done what?"

"Reviewed someone's feed."

"Why do you say that?"

"Because you've heard audio enough to know that it suffers from quality issues. It's something I guess I picked up on myself, visiting my parents' memories, though I never put much thought into it." I make several adjustments to our route and then glance at him. "I'm right, aren't I?"

He rolls his eyes. "You're *wrong*, actually. I've not once reviewed someone's feed in a professional capacity."

"So in a personal one?"

"I have a meeting to prepare for." He drags a black brief-case onto his lap, then presses a piece of paper under his nose.

I return my attention to the flight, checking our altitude and our fuel supply—but it's impossible to stop myself from wondering. Because if he wasn't reviewing a feed for professional reasons, he was doing it to visit someone's memories. But who?

His parents are both alive, as is his sister. And he doesn't seem the type to have friends, certainly not close ones—

His *wife.*

That'd explain how his first marriage came to an end; it would explain why he can marry again. It would explain his unwillingness to discuss it, and his insistence that I let it alone. It would explain his sister's little comments, about how he's still consumed with all that's behind him, how Claudia was nothing more than a much-needed distraction.

And then there's the other night, in the woods. I had

wondered then if something bad had happened to that woman deep within the birch. But what if it's more than *something bad*. What if she *died* there?

There's still so little about this man that I know. So little I understand. The only thing I *can* understand is just how inconvenient and unwanted I really must be.

A minute later, I give myself a shake. Because if my theory's accurate, it's Wolfe I should be feeling sorry for. The woman's family and friends, too. Besides, from the very start, I've been nothing more to him than a girl from Quire, and a tiring one at that. I've always been inconvenient and unwanted.

I return my attention back to the flight. I'm piloting a helicopter—I'm entering the airspace of another country...! *That's* what I should focus on. *The bright side, Alex.* But when Wolfe finally steps out of the helicopter and into a waiting limousine without so much as a goodbye, I throw down my headset and groan. Even the allure of a new country and all its chip-less inhabitants has gone pale.

I'd allowed myself to think that maybe, *maybe* his desire to keep me safe was because he actually cared about me. And that moment we shared in my room, the one after the adventure through the trees, that had been nothing. It had *meant* nothing. I've once again misplaced my trust in him.

I hold my stomach and think again about that simple life I'd envisioned for myself, in Quire, with Patrick. It seems less real than it used to, a figment of my imagination, but still, I cling to it. Then I sit straighter. So much has happened since that day in the library that I've barely considered Patrick's words. *I'll come back for you.* What did he mean by that?

Then another thought strikes me—the coordinates, this time. The ones from the scroll, the ones I'd been investigating at the very moment Patrick had stumbled on me.

Reaching Ashville Range from Strath Glen is impossible. But reaching it by helicopter?

After scouring the cockpit, I find a spiral binder of maps under the seat. I begin leafing through them one by one. It doesn't take long to locate the mountainous region, and after performing several calculations in longhand, I determine that a fly-by would lengthen our journey home by roughly forty-five minutes.

I bite the end of the pen. Forty-five minutes. It's possible that Wolfe won't notice our detour at all. And when else will I get the opportunity to see the region? It must hold some interest, not simply because it's the subject of the scroll, but because of the reaction its very mention had earned from the Mavericks. Yes, it must hold quite a bit of interest. I drop the pen and smile: to Ashville Range we'll go.

I throw open the door and drop onto the helipad, where I flag down a truck for refueling. As for Myopia itself, it holds little intrigue compared with the prospect of visiting the mysterious valley. Besides, from the sky, the city had looked plain—none of the flashing screens or twinkling lights of Airo-Aurora. Boxy buildings with gray rooftops surrounded by roadways that spanned the city like a grid. And around its border, only fields, empty and uninteresting—nothing like the howling birch forests of back home. How strange to think that to the world, me and my shining Airo-Aurora are the oddities.

A truck screeches to a stop in front of the green beast. "Where're you flyin' in from, lady?" calls the man climbing down from its cab, wearing a neon yellow vest and a ball cap.

As Wolfe had predicted, he looks at me with more interest as soon as I tell him.

"That a fact." He unrolls the hose and connects it to the helicopter's fuel tank, and a minute later, it goes rigid with the passage of liquid. "You're not one of the usuals from down under," he says as he lights a cigarette, disregarding the no-smoking signs. "Not that your lot passes in too often, 'course."

"I'm a new pilot."

"Cheers. So. You like it down there?"

Do I like it? An answer doesn't immediately come to mind. There are aspects of it I like—aspects I love, even. But between the unwanted Selection results, King and his punishments, and the sinister secrets I've begun to uncover about my once-beloved nation-state, well...I don't like any of that. I glance at the smoking man and counter him with the same question.

"'Course I like it," he says at once. "I can pick a job and a missus and my clothes, and that's more than your lot can be sayin'. Least from what I've heard," he adds.

"We can pick our clothes," I clarify, as a large aircraft taxis in front of us, from one tarmac to another. A prop plane lands at the farthest runway, and three shuttles cart luggage to an awaiting jetliner. The airport boasts far more bustle than the empty Sky Center back home. "I take it you like working here, then?" I ask, not wanting to answer any more of his questions.

The man throws his cigarette down and crushes it with the heel of his boot. "Nah," he admits as the fuel tank switches off. Then he cackles. "Don't like my missus, either!" He unfastens the hose, still chuckling, and retracts it into the side of the truck.

I stare at him. Freedom to choose one's career and spouse, and yet still he ends up dissatisfied? But how?

I think of my conversation with Aunt Jo, about whether or not choice is an illusion. Maybe she was onto something. Maybe we're all restricted by the circumstances of our lives. Even the Mavericks, who operate completely free of Mainframe rule—they can't choose a normal life in Airo-Aurora's city, can they? They're confined to the woods, where they're now on the run from a mysterious force—another matter outside their choosing.

I watch the man and wonder what invisible strings nudged him into the life he has and which ones now tether him in place. I wonder if freedom, true freedom, is ever really possible.

Of course, what's happening in Airo-Aurora is the opposite of freedom. Not only are we forced into whichever life the Mainframe decides, we don't even have the autonomy to be dissatisfied with it. The problem is that I don't fully understand what's happening to Airo-Aurora's dissenters, or *how* it's happening. And I don't have any evidence, either. So, exposing King and his Mainframe isn't something I can do, not yet.

The man walks over to me just then and crouches so we're eye to eye. "Am I on camera?" His pupils dart back and forth as though he might spot a lens with enough effort.

I'm not sure whether to laugh or feel offended. "In a way," I say, and he lifts an eyebrow.

"What's this?" comes a new voice. Its unique combination of derision and agitation make it recognizable as Wolfe's. He circles around the helicopter staring at the man.

The man jumps at the sight of the tall, glowering aristocrat from the pariah state, then ducks into his truck as I shout my thanks after him. I turn to Wolfe. "Your meeting's finished with already? That was quicker than I was anticipating."

"I was fortunate to sit down with someone as efficient as myself," he grumbles as we climb into the helicopter. I start the engine and speak with the air traffic controller, a position that's non-existent in Airo-Aurora given the infrequency of travel. My voice shakes at the prospect of visiting Ashville Range.

"Were you made to feel uncomfortable by that man?"

Wolfe demands as we lift into the air. His gaze remains on the fueling truck below.

"No," I reply, surprised by the question. For a moment, I just stare at his profile, trying my best to read him, but the helicopter begins to tremble, and I need to grab the controls to steady it. I turn it west, then scan the gray buildings below, the residential streets lined with broken sheds and scrap metal.

"Are you quite certain your route is accurate?"

Inwardly I sigh at his sharpness. "We'll pick up a tailwind faster this way."

The answer seems to satisfy him, at least by his standards, and he pulls out a thick stack of papers. He leafs through them, using the margins to scribble note after note. I say nothing, happy to have his brain consumed with something other than our flight. At this pace, he won't notice the mountainous range at all.

But half an hour later, he stirs. "Have we traveled far enough south? Have you checked our coordinates?"

I nod, and he returns to his notes with a noisy sigh.

A while later, I rub my hands along my jumpsuit. Nerves push uncomfortably in my stomach. With every minute that ticks by, the sensation worsens until only a minute separates us from my destination.

Like an apparition, the rock of Ashville Range crests the horizon.

Less than a minute now.

It feels like I could explode from the pressure. To make matters worse, I can feel Wolfe's discomfort as he stares at his notes. He no longer flips between pages. Pen is still. His unease with our route is obvious, his suspicions mounting by the second...

I'm risking my position as pilot, I know that. If he realizes I took a detour for my own interest during his busy work hours, no less, I won't have the privilege of piloting him again. It's a risk I'm willing to take.

I breathe deeply.

Probably the valley in question is nothing but a rocky plain, one he won't even notice us pass over. My worrying will be for naught; my excitement will vanish. I'll steer immediately south and pick up a tailwind, just as I said.

Yes. That'll work.

Another deep breath. Any second now and the trees will open up; we'll fly directly over the Range and the rock-lined valley that's the subject of my curiosity.

Almost there.

Then Wolfe's gaze lifts from the pad of paper on his knee. "Where are we?" he demands, and he stares beneath us at the jagged rock that reaches to the underbelly of the machine.

It's no use. He knows what I'm doing. That or he'll know very soon.

So I ignore his question, drop our altitude and slow our speed. Every cell in my body focused on glimpsing the valley below.

And then I gasp.

thirty

. . .

THE COCKPIT VIBRATES WITH SILENCE. Wolfe
and I stare down at the shield of rock, one covered in
hundreds of people, all of them marching in devastating
unity.

Not one lifts their gaze to the helicopter that skims by
overhead.

I blink.

The fly-bys complete; spiked rock lunges upward at us
once again. Soon after, birch trees reclaim the land. The
morning sun dips behind a cloud and plunges us into a pool
of monotonous gray. I breathe in. Out. In. Out.

I can feel it in the pit of my stomach. That's what he was
talking about, that day at Strath Glen. King—*that's* his
insurance plan.

Beside me, Wolfe's voice rings out, cold as ice, a forced
calm that's so unfriendly I'd prefer outright anger. At the
very least, it would reassure me that *he's* real. That *he's*
human. "Well, Alex. Your defiance knows no bounds. You
have your answer to that scroll and forever imprinted on
your feed for all to see."

Suddenly I don't care about Wolfe, or my future as his

pilot, or even my *feed*. "You *knew*, didn't you?" I yell at him. "All along, you knew what was happening!"

He stares at me, taken aback. "That he was creating an army? No. I suspected long ago, however, that those disloyal to the program or dissatisfied with their lives are interfered with, undoubtedly the same conclusion you have drawn based on your own investigation."

I shake my head. "You're King's right-hand man, his *protégé*. You know everything he does, don't lie about it now, *Wolfe*. You've been helping him—and trying to shield both of you from my prying all along!"

He laughs coldly. "You couldn't be more wrong. I am not his protégé—his moronic son will inherit the throne, and I am not privy in the least to matters within his portfolio. I doubt very much anyone is. And in regard to your prying, the only person I have been trying to shield is you. How many times must I tell you that? Should my uncle discover what you have been up to, or the discoveries that you have made, you will be tampered with, just like the others."

"So you *knew* people were being tampered with, and you didn't try to stop it?"

"Stop it, how?" he snaps. "Besides, I had no proof, and I had no business knowing. So, I decided to keep my head down and bide my time. And then *you* came along."

"*Me*? What did I have to do with anything?"

"You," he scoffs. "You were as disloyal and dissatisfied as anyone, and right under my uncle's nose! My energy was spent trying to keep you safe, a job made significantly more difficult by those blasted scrolls."

I turn away. No. No, I won't listen, I won't believe him. He knew far more than he let on, far more than I imagined. He wasn't trying to protect me—not *ever*.

"Please—"

"You claim you've been trying to keep me safe," I interrupt, now thinking of the Queen, and Mr. Worthers, and Mary Beth's son—

"Yes."

"Safe from *what*, exactly?"

"Direct us back to Airo-Aurora." Then, as I shift our direction south, he sighs. "As I am not privy to the operation, I can only speculate."

"I'm listening," I say abruptly.

"Whether the override chip is implanted into the brain via the ear, the eye, or an incision into the scalp itself, I do not know. But I can think of no other way to change a person than through a microchip powered by very advanced artificial intelligence indeed."

"Dr. Lebwitski," I say. The man in white.

"Dr. Lebwitski," Wolfe confirms.

"But surely someone would notice. A friend, or a mother—"

"Think about it," he says dismissively. "The Mainframe has a lifetime of data to work with. Isn't it conceivable the mechanized version of yourself is almost an exact replica, tweaked only to eliminate the unsatisfactory behavior?"

I think again of those people—the Queen, Mr. Worthers, Mary Beth's son—and I shudder. Every like, every dislike, every decision—it would all be recorded in the Mainframe. All of it could be used to ensure a seamless transition. I smooth my index finger back and forth over my lip, lost in thought. "But the Queen, reading a book upside down—"

"It isn't a perfect system, granted. Artificial intelligence could never perfectly mimic the human soul, could it?"

I check our altitude and consider the question. The AI employed by King could be strengthened; it could protect against errors such as holding a book upside down. But it could never make glazed eyes sparkle. It could never capture the zest of real life. "The army, Wolfe," I say. "Back there, inside Ashville Range. They're the missing Mavericks, aren't they?"

"Almost certainly," he agrees. "Without any prior data, there is nothing to inform the mechanized versions of themselves. They are merely, well…"

There's no need for him to finish his sentence. I already know. They're mindless machines, controlled completely from afar. It's no wonder the Mavericks I spoke with were so touchy when I mentioned the valley. They must know what's become of their people. They must know what's in store for them if they're captured.

When I glance at Wolfe, I see his mouth is pressed firmly together and that a harsh line rides between his brow, but those are the only indicators he's upset. "Doesn't it make you angry?" I prod. "Your friend Campinos is back there, at the Range, and his fam—"

"I know that," he snaps, and there's a spark of fire in his eye. His calmness is a veneer, it must be.

"Well, then. What are we going to do about it?"

He snorts. "*We*? Nothing."

"I'm sorry?"

"Your involvement has reached its natural resting place. The mystery of the scrolls has been solved. Congratulations."

"*Solved*? So what about Timothee and Jill, then? Why *their* inclusion? Besides, there's a reason someone wanted me to know all this, and it wasn't so I could walk away *now*."

"Leave it to me to take care of."

"And what will you do? Continue to bide your time?"

"Careful, Alex," he warns.

I glare at him. "According to your own admission, *Wolfe*, you wouldn't even know about King's army without my—"

"You want a pat on the back, do you?" His voice rumbles —he's angrier than I realized.

"Whether you want to offer recognition or not, someone decided that *I* should be the one to receive the scrolls—"

"You were sent those scrolls because of your proximity to my uncle and nothing more!"

The words feel like a slap in the face. "Or maybe it's because I had the courage to question Selection results that didn't make sen—"

"You think you're the only one unhappy with the Selection system?" he demands, that veneer of calm now cracking dangerously.

I sit back in my seat. "I know very well that you don't want me," I say in a voice that's hoarse. "But—"

"*I'm not talking about you!*" he explodes. "I'm talking about that foolish drunk of a woman I was forced to marry, forced to *impregnate!*" He breathes deeply now, and his face is flushed. "Do you think I wanted her? *Her*," he hisses, "who in her drunken stupor took that child into the woods?" He leans forward and drags trembling fingers through his hair.

I stare at him with my mouth open. "You...you had a baby," I stammer. "You had a wife *and* a baby." I swallow so deeply that my throat burns. "What happened to them, Wolfe?"

For a moment, I think he'll refuse to answer. Then, so quietly that I need to strain my ears over the sound of the engine, he mutters, "I didn't realize they were gone until the next morning." Fingers drum with agitation against his knee. "Campinos helped me find their bodies half a mile in."

I draw in a sharp breath. "A beast—"

"The very one that hangs over my desk," he confirms darkly.

No—that can't be right. That's far too horrible for any one person to endure. To lose one's family is bad enough, I know that much from personal experience, but to lose them like *that*? To hold witness to it? To something so gruesome? No.

And yet...

It's no wonder he worried over me going unprotected into the woods. No wonder he didn't want talk of his past floating around the palace and reminding him of such an unthinkable tragedy. No wonder news of Aubrey's pregnancy had such a profound effect on him.

Too cruel, too *unjust*.

Same with the innocent Mavericks who've had their lives taken away and the rebels of Airo-Aurora who've suffered the same fate. Too much—it's all too much.

A moment later, I glance at the unknowable, unlovable stranger sitting next to me, one who's endured something most could not even speak of. His face may be like marble, but I can sense the anguish that threatens to overwhelm him. It's the way his hand jumps on his leg, the way his chest rises and falls, the angle of his spine. Slowly he leans back in the seat, then lays two fingers alongside his neck.

His pulse is dangerously high; I know it without asking. His long body is contorted with markers of stress. Probably it's too late—too much time has passed, and so it isn't because of the Mainframe and its alerts that I do what I do.

No, I'm not sure what causes me to reach for his hand, the one that twitches with anxiousness, or why I twist my fingers through his.

It startles him; I can see it peripherally. But he doesn't pull his hand away, and in time, as we hurtle toward an unknown future intertwined for now too many reasons to count, his breathing slows.

Only when Airo-Aurora lifts into sight do I slide my hand from his. I edge us toward a city far more sinister than I ever could've imagined, and as we circle closer to the Sky Center, miniature cubes become buildings, dots become people. And that's when I see them.

The bluecoats, standing on the tarmac.

An alert sounded, a call was placed. By now, King must know.

Know what? How much of Wolfe's feed would've been reviewed? How much would've been relayed?

And that's when I spot him, his ruby crown glinting under ever-darkening skies.

I bring the helicopter closer to the ground, barely able to control the way my hands shake, then glance at Wolfe. "What now?"

His face is filled with its usual disinterested disdain. In a terse voice, he replies, "Now, Alexandra, it is finally time for you to put your trust in me." His eyes meet mine. "All of it."

My trust. How am I supposed to trust this man, this unknown person, one I'm barely more familiar with today than the very first day we met? Every time I learn something new about him, he becomes even more unfathomable. And yet, I have to admit as I touch the machine back to earth and cut the engine, my options are few.

The bluecoats edge closer to the cockpit—then something hitches in my chest. "Wolfe!" I whisper, but he stops me.

"I see him," he says darkly.

The man in white. He stands with the others, alongside King himself.

When we step onto the tarmac, my entire body convulses. But I do as Wolfe asks—I place my trust in him. After all, he's handled every other dilemma with efficiency and ease; this time will be no different. He'll defuse the situation. He'll counter the bluecoats and dismiss their concerns; he'll placate King with reassuring assertions.

And so I'm surprised when he does none of that when instead all he does is drill his iron gaze into his uncle's and say in a biting voice, "We have a problem."

There's no opportunity to gauge King's reaction; I'm too

distracted by Wolfe's fingers wrapping around my arm and pulling me forward through the staring bluecoats. He shoves me in the direction of Dr. Lebwitski and adds, "Sedate her."

Shock hits me in the sternum. It knocks the wind out of me. But before I can say anything, there's a sharp pain at the base of my neck. Immediately my knees buckle, and my eyelids begin to sag, and the last thing I see before the world goes dark are King's ruby-encrusted crown and the cold, unfeeling eyes of the viscount staring sternly down at me.

terminus

. . .

The dynasty's leadership and its reliance on Artificial Intelligence are the eternal treasures of the nation and a fundamental guarantee of the contentedness and prosperity for all of Airo-Aurora. The nation and its people, in turn, will forever uphold these unshakable pillars of governance in their pledge of unfettered love and undying loyalty.

a look at book two:

King's Salacious Secrets

The Selection dealt Alex Egelton a rough hand...but she's not about to let that stop her from righting a few wrongs.

It's been months since the Mainframe placed Alex at the Strath Glen palace—a frenetic madhouse where every move is theater, and backstabbing is second nature—to both serve and marry the perennially icy viscount with a haunted past. And in those few months, a series of mysterious scrolls led her to discover the heinous truth about her country of Airo-Aurora and its maniacal ruler.

With thousands of innocent lives hanging in the balance, Alex must now find a way to dismantle the entire system and dethrone the king—an impossible task with him lurking over her shoulder and the Mainframe recording every move she makes.

But between managing wedding preparations with her inscrutable fiancé and navigating the unwanted life thrust upon her, Alex soon discovers that she may have more allies than she ever realized— and that perhaps change *is* possible...if only she can survive long enough to make it happen.

Will Alex find a way to bring down the system and its ruler without getting caught in the crosshairs?

AVAILABLE AUGUST 2023

about the author

Jerri Chisholm is a YA author, a distance runner, and a chocolate addict. Her childhood was spent largely in solitude with only her imagination and a pet parrot for company. Following that she completed a master's degree in public policy and then became a lawyer, but ultimately decided to leave the profession to focus exclusively on the more imaginative and avian-friendly pursuit of writing. She lives with her husband and three children, but, alas, no parrot.